PRAISE FOR *THEATER OF SPIES*

"Stirling's sequel to *Black Chamber* showcases a sexy and intelligent female spy couple who garner comparisons with James Bond and Jack Ryan. A masterly mashup of historical context and sf plausibility."
—*Library Journal*

"Stirling knows how to write thrillers, and Luz is a fascinating and compelling viewpoint character."
—*Locus*

"Mr. Stirling injects existential peril immediately. . . . There is constant awareness of sexuality, fine weaponry exposure, and a superb climax. This is well worth your time."
—Manhattan Book Review

"Readers will have fun seeing the game of espionage played on a very dangerous court."
—*Crimespree Magazine*

PRAISE FOR *BLACK CHAMBER*

"As always, [Stirling] comes up with inventive twists that keep your mind racing and the pages turning. Bravo!"
—Robert J. Sawyer, Hugo Award–winning author of *Quantum Night*

"The nice thing about getting a Steve Stirling book in the mail is that you know for a few hours you can fly on dreams of wonder, travelling to a world so much *more* than this angry reality."
—John Ringo, author of *Under a Graveyard Sky*

"It's a great feeling being in the hands of an alternate history master, who knows his material and crafts an utterly plausible world. Stirling gives us Teddy Roosevelt's USA and a Cuban-Irish-American secret agent who's more than a match for an airship full of James Bonds."
—Django Wexler, author of *The Infernal Battalion*

"Imagine that World War One began in Europe with the activist Teddy Roosevelt in the White House instead of the academic Woodrow Wilson. You've got a dandy steampunk setting for a slam-bang spy thriller with an engaging female protagonist."
—David Drake, author of *Death's Bright Day*

"One of the most intriguing and entertaining adventures to come along in years."   —Diana L. Paxson, author of *Sword of Avalon*

"Serves us a World War One America under a Theodore Roosevelt presidency, spiced with all the possibilities, good and bad, that Stirling's ever-ambitious imagination and meticulous approach to historical can cook up."   —A. M. Dellamonica, author of *The Nature of a Pirate*

"This is a sheer joy of an alternative history. . . . If you can put this book down once you've picked it up, I'll eat my bowler hat."
                         —Patricia Finney, author of *Gloriana's Torch*

"One mighty fine read—sexy, action-filled adventure in a thoughtful alternate history."
                         —Lawrence Watt-Evans, author of the Obsidian Chronicles

"This novel provides a desperately needed infusion of courage and originality. How appropriate that Penguin, publisher of the James Bond novels, launches a hard-edged new spy series with Stirling. How appropriate that Ace, famous for classic science fiction, is on board for the adventure."
                         —Brad Linaweaver, Prometheus Award–winning author of *Moon of Ice*

SHADOWS OF ANNIHILATION

S. M. STIRLING

ACE
New York

ACE
Published by Berkley
An imprint of Penguin Random House LLC
penguinrandomhouse.com

ACE is a registered trademark and the A colophon is a trademark of
Penguin Random House LLC.

Library of Congress Cataloging-in-Publication Data

Names: Stirling, S. M., author.
Title: Shadows of annihilation / S.M. Stirling.
Description: First edition. | New York: Ace, 2020. |
Series: A novel of an alternate World War I
Identifiers: LCCN 2019039123 (print) | LCCN 2019039124 (ebook) |
ISBN 9780399586279 (paperback) | ISBN 9780399586286 (ebook)
Subjects: LCSH: World War, 1914–1918—Fiction. |
GSAFD: Alternative histories (Fiction) | Spy stories.
Classification: LCC PS3569.T543 S53 2020 (print) |
LCC PS3569.T543 (ebook) | DDC 813/.54—dc23
LC record available at https://lccn.loc.gov/2019039123
LC ebook record available at https://lccn.loc.gov/2019039124

First Edition: March 2020

Printed in the United States of America
1   3   5   7   9   10   8   6   4   2

Cover art and design by Adam Auerbach
Book design by Laura K. Corless

To Jan, for thirty years of love, happiness, and comradeship

ACKNOWLEDGMENTS

To Kier Salmon, longtime close friend and valued advisor, whose help with things in Spanish and about Mexico, where most of this book is set—she lived there into adulthood—has been very, very helpful with this series, as well as her general advice to which I have always listened carefully. My mother grew up speaking Spanish too (in Lima, Peru), but, alas, she and my aunt used it as a secret code the children couldn't understand, and Kier has been invaluable filling in those lacunae, as well as being a fine editor (and promising writer) in her own right.

To Markus Baur, for help with the German language and as a first reader.

To Dave Drake, for help with the Latin bits and a deep knowledge of firearms acquired in several different ways. Also, collaborating with him taught me how to outline.

To Alyx Dellamonica, for advice, native-guide work, and just generally being cool. Her wife, Kelly Robson, is cool too and an extremely talented writer now winning implausible numbers of awards. An asteroid would have to strike Toronto to seriously dent the awesomeness of this pair. Soon Alyx will have another book out and it is great; I say this with smug certainty, since I got to read it in manuscript. Fortunately, writing is one of those fields where you have colleagues, not competitors.

To my first readers: Steve Brady, Pete Sartucci, Ara Ogle, Markus Baur, and Scott Palter.

To Patricia Finney (aka P. F. Chisholm), for friendship and her own wonderful books, starting with *A Shadow of Gulls* (which she wrote when she was in her teens, at which point I was still doing Edgar Rice Burroughs pastiche fanfic) and going on from there. One of the best historical novelists of our generation!

And to Walter Jon Williams, Emily Mah, John Miller, Vic Milán (still present in spirit), Jan Stirling, Matt Reiten, Lauren Teffeau, S. E. Burr, Sarena Ulibarri, and Rebecca Roanhorse of Critical Mass, our writers' group, for constant help and advice.

And to Joe's Dining (http://joesdining.com/) and Ecco Espresso and Gelato (http://www.eccogelato.com/) here in Santa Fe, for putting up with my interminable presence and my habit of making faces and muttering dialogue as I write.

Love of peace is common among weak, short-sighted, timid, and lazy persons; and on the other hand courage is found among many men of evil temper and bad character. Neither quality shall by itself avail. —THEODORE ROOSEVELT

PROLOGUE

Washington, D.C.
Oval Office
White House
JUNE 10TH, AD 1917, 1917(B)
Point of Departure plus 5 Years

No, Mr. President, the decision to withdraw from France was sound."

General Wood's voice with its soft Massachusetts accent was steady.

"It's a defeat, and nothing but," Theodore Roosevelt growled over his shoulder, the words like acid in his mouth and his hands bunched into fists in his jacket pockets.

This was the day the last of the American Expeditionary Force had withdrawn from Europe, leaving only the sacrificial French rearguards holding a shrinking semicircle around Marseilles and Toulon. He stared out the Oval Office windows at tree-lined Pennsylvania Avenue and the White House gardens, but his mind's eye was seeing grim, grimy men filing aboard rusty transports under an acrid smoke-pall of burning buildings and supply dumps, as artillery muttered and flickered to the north, like a distant thunderstorm that never ended, and the thunder-reply as battleships and cruisers in the harbors pounded out broadsides in reply toward the horizon.

The green and flowery smell of early summer on the Potomac floated through the windows. Its warmth and sweetness felt incongruous in a world gripped in an iron winter of the spirit, as the Great War spread its infinite malice around the globe and whole nations were burned and beaten into dust. His trained naturalist's ear and mind automatically cataloged the birdsong he heard—he could identify more than fifty species by their calls alone—but for once there was no joy in it.

The president turned away and sat once more behind the desk that had been made from the timbers of a Royal Navy ship long ago. The chair creaked under his solid weight, even now mostly muscle, and he forced himself not to snarl as he confronted his two closest advisors. General Leonard Wood was Chief of the Supreme General Staff, winner of the Medal of Honor in the Apache Wars, a very old friend from the Rough Riders and before, and co-creator of the modern American military. John Elbert Wilkie was Director of the Secret Service and, far more importantly, its child the Black Chamber, the shadowy network of spies and operatives and analysts that was sometimes as important as the Army.

Both were of his generation, born like him within two years of Lincoln's election, finally taking over from the Civil War veterans in the new century and showing they too could reach for greatness.

"Yes, it is a defeat, Mr. President. With several real *buts*, but still a defeat," General Wood said calmly. "It's still the sensible thing to do. We can . . . we must . . . ask men to die for their country, but trying to hold on longer would have been throwing lives away for our vanity's sake. This isn't a war that will be settled by a single battle, or a single campaign either. Any more than the British wars against France under the Revolution and then Napoleon were—*that* took twenty-five years, and it was a whale fighting an elephant that time too."

"*L'état, ce n'est pas moi,*" Roosevelt said ruefully, flipping Louis XIV's famous bit of . . .

Vanity, he thought.

. . . on its head. "I myself am *not* the nation. The Republic can survive this, even if it's ashes in my mouth."

"No man has done the Republic greater service, Mr. President," Director Wilkie said. "My God, can you imagine what we'd be facing if *Woodrow Wilson* was president and trying to deal with this?"

They all grimaced slightly at the thought. Roosevelt had made the decision to withdraw, on the advice of these two and against the prompting of his own deepest instincts, what he felt in his heart and belly . . .

Yet my brain *agrees with my advisors, alas, and I'm going to listen to reason—it goes with sitting in this chair. But does anyone ever* enjoy *hearing someone else tell him to "be realistic" and "take a steady strain"?*

Roosevelt's eyes flicked to the portrait of Lincoln on the wall, and the bust in its niche; he always kept one of each in a place he worked for any length of time.

The president's anger wasn't really directed at the general or the spymaster, but it said something about them that neither quailed in the slightest. Even amid his frustration and rage he felt a flash of satisfaction at that; he'd never hidden the fact that he liked power and relished command, the ability to make things *happen*, but he despised the useless flabbiness of yes-men and refused to tolerate them in his inner circle.

Power is a fine thing because it lets you do, *do work* worth *doing. And you can't do it alone, not the big jobs. A* truly *powerful man needs powerful support— which means strong subordinates with strong minds of their own.*

"Wise men don't try to argue with arithmetic," Wood went on. "We hit the Germans a few good licks, and kept them from the Mediterranean for longer than I expected. Our *tanks* . . ."

He used the name that had started as a code meant to conceal a little self-consciously, however widely and quickly it had spread. The official War Department designation was *Armored Fighting Vehicle, Turreted, Tracked, Mk. I*, and absolutely nobody used it, except in official documents.

". . . were a very nasty surprise for them, and not the only one we handed out. But we just couldn't supply a large enough force when they were only a day or two from their bases by rail and we were operating across an ocean. Not enough ships, not if we were to keep Britain going at the same time through the U-boat packs and get at least *some* food and supplies to the French. And not enough harbor capacity with Toulon and Marseilles our only real ports of entry, even if we *did* have the ships."

"*A few good licks* boils no potatoes," the president growled. "Bobby Lee hit the Army of the Potomac a *few good licks* too in our fathers' time, and where did it get him and the Confederate States? Appomattox Court House, that's where, thank God. When I hit a man, I want him to fall *down*, not just wince and stagger a bit. Fall down and *stay* down."

He meant that too, and he knew the truth of it in his knuckles and his bone and gut.

A flash of memory, and he was face-to-face again with that drunken killer in Nolan's Saloon, one of the things that had defined him to himself, within the privacy of his own soul.

The mean brown-stained grin and stinking breath and bloodshot eyes . . . and the trip-hammer feeling of power as he'd replied to the threat of the six-shooters with a left-right-left to the jaw. The *crack-crack* and twin jets of smoke from the .45s amid a smell of rotten egg and cheap whiskey and chewing tobacco spat into the sawdust on the floor, as the gunman crumpled and thumped his head against the rail. A fraction slower and he might have bled to death on that floor himself, one more set of young bones in the lawless Badlands frontier of the 1880s.

He'd been too late for the Indians—just—but the white frontiersmen had been every bit as wild, more numerous, and much better armed.

"They're still letting masses of civilians through their lines outside the ports," Wood observed; he knew what Roosevelt had just said was a statement of opinion, or possibly principle, not an argument. "They could take Toulon and Marseilles now if they were willing to pay a hefty butcher's bill for pushing their heavy artillery within range of the docks, even with the naval gunfire support we're giving the French, but instead they're inching in very slowly and cautiously."

"Because while it may not have been what they had in mind last October 6th, now they've decided they want France as an empty waste-land they can settle with their own people, General," Wilkie said. "Marseilles and Toulon are the spout of the funnel and they're *letting* us hold it open while they squeeze at the top. They'll take the ports when the bag's empty as it's going to get, later this year."

Somewhere Ludendorff was laughing the particular, nasty laugh of a man who'd given his enemy a set of choices that started with *very bad* and ran on through various degrees of *even worse than that.*

"It's the dilemma from hell," the president said ruefully. "Damned if you do *and* if you don't. There must be more Frenchmen . . . and French women and children . . . in North Africa now than there are left alive in France itself, what with the horror-gas and battlefield losses and now mass famine and epidemics in the occupied zone. *That's* worse than Ireland in '48."

Germany's losses had been savage since they rolled the iron dice in 1914, but they'd broken Russia with their armies, and then smashed London and Paris and the Western Front with their *Vernichtungsgas*— Annihilation Gas, V-gas for short—last October 6th, just before the United States could intervene in force. In fact, they'd probably done it then as a desperation measure *because* America was about to declare war; they'd watched him build the country's strength since 1912, and knew a stand-up fight with what were now coming to be called "conventional weapons" would grind their bones to dust in a year or two at most.

So they got their punch in first, with the horror-gas.

The rest of the world called it *that* for good reason. A couple of pounds of it, a bottle you could hold easily in one rubber-gloved hand, contained a hundred thousand lethal doses, and the amount they'd used had been measured in tons, not pounds—*hundreds* of tons.

Enough that if it had been perfectly distributed it would have killed the entire human race. Killed all one-point-seven billion of us . . . In fact, it could have killed us all approximately twenty-one times over.

The mind refused to grapple with that, or at least his did, but by an effort of will he'd made it real to himself.

If the Black Chamber's operatives hadn't detected and foiled Germany's plans for what their code had called the Breath of Loki, the American cities along the East Coast would have been destroyed by the filthy stuff on the same day, launched by rocket-mortars from U-boats hiding in the harbors.

"What about the reports of clashes a few days ago between German and Japanese forces around . . . Irkutsk, isn't it called? That city near Lake Baikal in Siberia," he said, less hopefully than he wished.

"Ah." Wilkie looked at a paper in one of his files. "What's that Japanese type of theater, Mr. President, no attempt at realism, very stylized, with masks and broad gestures?"

"Kabuki," Roosevelt snapped.

He'd been the first American to get a brown belt in jujitsu, besides being the man who'd mediated an end to the Russo-Japanese war back in '05. Their arts and customs had fascinated him since he'd met Japanese students at Harvard in his youth; he respected and admired the Japanese people for their self-sacrificial courage and hard work, patriotic unity and disciplined intelligence, all things he wanted more of for America.

Which is precisely the reason *they're dangerous rivals.*

"It was pure Kabuki, Mr. President. Both sides made faces at each other and shouted nasty names and fired shots in the air. Meanwhile they're trading; German industrial chemicals and machine tools for rubber and tin and so forth from the new Japanese possessions in what used to be French Indochina and the Dutch East Indies. It's all supposedly being put through Outer Mongolia, via that mad Russian . . . Baltic-German . . . warlord who's taken over there, Baron von Ungern-Sternberg. The Bloody Baron, they call him."

"The one who claims to be a reincarnation of Genghis Khan," Wood observed dryly. "They certainly share an enthusiasm for butchery."

"Just so," Wilkie said. "They're leaving the capering lunatic on his stolen throne to give them a buffer and a tissue-thin pretense. And I'm morally certain Berlin has slipped the Japanese the horror-gas formula and engineering drawings for the equipment. We can't do anything but protest, of course, and Tokyo will give Ambassador Longworth a free fool's prize of bland lies."

"The ambassador will have to eat crow and pretend to believe them, Mr. President," Wood said, a slight edge of warning in his tone. "And so will we, in public. The United States *absolutely* cannot fight them and Germany at the same time, and they know it."

Roosevelt gritted his teeth. After the United States and Germany, Japan was the only other Great Power left standing. He wasn't in the least surprised their leaders were taking what must look like a heaven-sent opportunity to establish a position of unassailable strength—in their place he'd have done exactly the same. But . . .

I can see a shadow emerging, the shape of a world divided into three—the Central Powers dominating western Eurasia, Japan doing the same in east Asia, and we and the British and Overseas France holding the World Ocean and the peripheries . . . call it the Oceanian Alliance . . . and all three armed to the teeth and snarling and skirmishing and dreaming of the Empire of the Earth, but none able to deal a death blow. Though the Japanese at least aren't an open enemy. Not quite. Not yet. Put that to the side for now.

"The Germans haven't *used* the horror-gas since the 6th," he said, his voice thoughtful.

October 6th, 1916, was what the bare numeral meant now, a date graven into human history like a sword across time's neck.

"Everything else," he went on. "But not that. Yet the gas *governs* everything, like an invisible skeleton hand at our throats. It's the dominant factor in the world today."

Wilkie nodded. "My clandestine contacts with their emissaries in Scandinavia and Switzerland all agree that the Germans—the highest circles in Germany—say—"

"Say!" Roosevelt said.

Wilkie made a balancing gesture. "They *say* they plan to keep the horror-gas in reserve from now on unless we use it first, or unless we land in Europe in force. Then they'd hit us with everything they've got, and the British cities and North Africa too, consequences be damned. I'm inclined to believe them, because maintaining a stalemate is in their interests."

Wood spread his hands. "There's no predicting how things would end if both sides threw everything they have at each other, Mr. President. Except that the slaughter would make what's happened so far look minor. *That* I can absolutely guarantee you."

"Which gives even the most reckless pause," Wilkie agreed. "We captured a fair amount of the gas from the U-boats and we'll have our own production going well before the end of the month with . . . the Dakota Project . . . ahead of schedule. Public Works and the War Department have done a crackerjack job there."

"We'd better, Director," Wood said grimly. "What we captured won't last forever. The stuff decays in storage—and decanting and moving it from the rocket-shells we took from the U-boats was a nightmare that cost us lives. The only efficient way to do it is to store the two precursor chemicals and then make it up just before deployment, and rotate the old material back for disposal, which is like juggling nitroglycerine on a galloping horse. And the Germans don't have much more stored than the amount we took from their submarines either, since your people managed to wreck their plant in Staaken, for which I offer my hearty congratulations again."

"That was *bully!*" Roosevelt said sincerely.

"Thank you, General, Mr. President, but that was also a strictly *temporary* victory. The Germans have their Berlin factory working again . . ." Wilkie consulted a note before he went on: ". . . as of last week. And they're building a new one, bigger and more efficient, near Rostov-on-Don, in their Government-General of the Ukraine . . ."

He smiled thinly. "Or *die Gotische Ostmark*, as I understand they intend to rename it."

All three men snorted at the preening neomedievalism of *the East Gothic Marchland*; parts of the Ukraine had indeed been an Ostrogothic—Germanic—kingdom . . . for a century or two, sixteen hundred years ago, which was before Attila led the Huns into Europe and while there was still a ruling emperor in Rome and before anyone had heard of the Slavs. Wilkie continued seriously:

"And they're going to transfer the Berlin equipment to Rostov once the works there are up and running."

"They may be telling the truth about their intentions right now, but they'll change their minds fast enough if they see an opening," Roosevelt said.

"Not even a *scrap of paper* stopping them," Wilkie agreed, quoting the German chancellor von Bethmann-Hollweg's famous words in 1914 about the treaty guaranteeing Belgian neutrality. "Just the threat of our retaliating in kind."

Wood nodded. "That's stopping them *for now*. But they have a history of taking reckless gambles for immediate advantage . . . *rolling the iron dice*, as they say . . . and more than enough of the gambles have paid off to encourage the habit. To keep them from using the gas, we have to have it ready ourselves."

Roosevelt sighed. "I don't like the thought of touching horror-gas even with a barge-pole, but I agree."

"That's the best . . . the only . . . guarantee," Wilkie said.

"And I hate the thought of conceding them Europe when we have enough divisions to take them on, and better weapons," Roosevelt said. "Our troops are fresh, too, not fought-out. The more time we give the enemy to rest and recover, the stronger they'll be."

"Mr. President, attacks with horror-gas bombs . . . or shells . . . on landing beachheads packed with men . . ." Wood said, and shrugged.

They were silent for a moment; all three were hard men, ruthless at need and long intimate with violent death, but their keen imaginations revolted at the images that produced . . . and all of them were also too honest with themselves to deny the truth of what their minds told them. The general went on:

"The horror-gas is just too damned deadly, and retaliating in kind won't help if we're attacking. It's like machine-guns and barbed wire, only worse, because it lingers invisibly. It favors the defense because it forces you to disperse and take cover and dig in . . . and do it in a rubber diving suit."

"Our new *tanks*—" Roosevelt began.

He felt a moment's flash of a twofold pride: that he'd backed and pushed the project, and a more personal and intense glory that his eldest son, now *Brigadier* Ted Roosevelt Jr., had been among the commanders who used them to deal the Germans several stinging defeats.

He continued aloud: "—the *tanks* seem to go a long way to solving machine-guns and barbed wire."

"They do, Mr. President. But for the horror-gas we *don't* have a solution yet and it's thrown off all our plans. Millions have died in this war because generals tried to deal with unsolved problems by throwing flesh and blood and bone against steel and fire and poison; I'd rather not have the name Leonard Wood on *that* particular list."

Roosevelt growled slightly. "Mexican standoff," he said. "They might be able to get more of those special U-boats near our coast . . . and they're certainly working hard to improve the range of the rocket-mortars they carry so they don't *have* to get quite so close."

"Keeping them out of harbors is hard enough for the Navy," Wood said. "If they could launch from miles away, or worse still, if they could launch from miles away while they were *underwater*..."

There was another uncomfortable silence. Wild imaginings had become the merely unlikely and the unlikely had turned up in cold hard reality far too often of late.

Progress has its price, Roosevelt thought, and went on aloud:

"And they can certainly reach Britain with aeroplane bombers from the Netherlands or Belgium; another unsolved problem. Which is why Lord Protector Milner wants more shipping to move English refugees out."

He used the old names though the Netherlands had joined—at gunpoint, more or less—the new *Großdeutsches Kaiserreich*. And Belgium no longer existed; the Flemish parts—and French Flanders—had been given to the new German Kingdom of the Netherlands, and the rest was now the puppet Grand Duchy of Wallonia, its people allowed to live because their factories and skilled workers were so useful to Berlin's war machine.

Wilkie held up a warning hand: "It's not just people he wants the tonnage to move, Mr. President. My reports are that lately he's transferring as much British industry as he can, too, to South Africa and India and Australia. Steel, engineering, shipyards, chemicals."

"Lord Protector Milner and his government badly want to be less dependent on us, then," Wood observed.

"Naturally so," Roosevelt said. "They're patriots, just as we are."

And Milner's rather more of a dictator than I am, he thought. *But needs must when the devil drives. The 6th hit them very hard.*

"I'm inclined to give it all my blessing," Roosevelt said. "We're going to need them as allies for the long term, strong allies and willing ones; Milner's National Efficiency movement is their equivalent of our New Nationalism, and he . . . and what happened to London . . . is putting the iron back into their spines and the fire in their bellies. Milner didn't object when the Canadians and Newfoundlanders asked to join the United States, and so in honor we can scarcely cavil at this. Most of that shipping was originally British, for that matter, and the crews. Now that our Expeditionary Force is out of Europe, we can spare it."

Wood looked unhappy—the General Staff hoarded transport and logistical capacity the way a miser did gold—but nodded. Wilkie did too, less reluctantly. He and Milner's new Imperial Secret Service were cooperating closely now.

Some American corporations who'd been slavering at the prospect of global monopolies would be upset, even though they were already making more money than ever before, but then Roosevelt had always been astonished at how utterly *stupid* the very wealthy could be outside their narrow areas of interest. There was no satisfying that blind insensate hunger, but at least these days they did what he told them to do without much back-talk, a deeply pleasing change.

He sighed and shook his head ruefully. "The horror-gas . . . I'd never imagined a weapon so powerful that it's impossible to *use*," he said. "Though H. G. Wells did . . . Impossible to use against someone who can reply in kind, at least. On the one hand, nobody sane would want more attacks like London and Paris—even if we could match atrocity with atrocity and massacre with massacre, in the end that could bring down civilization itself. Western civilization, at least. H. G. Wells predicted that too! On the other hand, that paralyzes us and shields the enemy. Germany wants to get up from the table while they're ahead, and you're both telling me we don't have a way to stop them."

Wood looked even unhappier. "Our study teams have been wargaming along the lines you suggested, Mr. President, and you're right: Armies trying to fight each other with horror-gas . . . it's like a duel fought with hand grenades inside a locked closet. Yet the gas *will* be used if one side is facing a decisive defeat, given the unlimited stakes in this war. So we can fight, but only indecisively! If you can't drive an offensive home, battle becomes like . . ."

"*Kabuki*, but with real blood," the president said with venom. "How I detest pulling a punch."

Then Roosevelt grinned, his famous tooth-baring fighting grin. "If we can't hit them directly, we'll use stealth and undercover operations to keep them sitting uneasily on their ill-gotten gains—from the shadows, steel, eh?"

The others chuckled. *Ex umbris, acies* was the Black Chamber's motto, and that was a direct translation.

"We've won more of *those* battles than the Germans have, so far," he said.

Wilkie gestured agreement, but his expression had gone grim. "They're not going to stop trying on *that* battlefield either, Mr. President."

"Bring it on!" the president said. "But in any case we absolutely *must* have our own horror-gas production, and as quickly as possible, simply to make them fear using theirs."

His head turned to Wilkie like the turret of a battle-cruiser.

"I like your outline of the security measures for the Dakota Project, but in addition, now that we're getting so close to starting production, I want you to assign some good field operatives, including one with a technical background and someone with local experience, to hold a watching brief there."

He smiled again. "Watching *from the shadows*, and ready to use the *steel*. Someone young and energetic, but senior enough to have direct access to you . . . and me, for that matter . . . and one you can trust with override authority with the garrison commander and the FBS. Someone who won't use it just to show they're important."

"I'll make sure of smooth relations between Major-General Young and whoever the agents are, Mr. President," Wood agreed. "He's very sound, a real fighting man but a thinker who did good work in Military Intelligence when he was an embassy attaché, too, and the 32nd are a first-rank division, though they're new to the area."

"And I know the operatives you have in mind, Mr. President," Wilkie said, making a note. "I'll see to it. They're in San Francisco now, and I'll have them briefed and moving before next Friday."

"We'll need them," Roosevelt said grimly. "Somehow or other, something tells me we will. Because if *we* know how important this is . . . the enemy will too."

ONE

Horst von Dückler listened to the hollow clop of mule-hooves coming closer up the rocky slope where he lay, and the clatter of stones knocked free and bouncing downward. He picked up the ugly slab-sided Yankee CBSLR-13—Colt-Browning self-loading rifle, model of 1913, R-13 for short—with a slow minimal motion, winding a loop of the sling around his left biceps as he did. The guerillas had all concealed themselves with the same skill, or nearly.

He'd fitted a scavenged x3 telescopic sight to the helpfully provided standard mounts machined into the left side of the receiver, and wrapped a length of rough burlap around the barrel and stuck small bits of vegetation into it to break up the eye-catching outline. He brought it to his shoulder now and began carefully scanning, squinting against the bright sun. Nothing would show from below but another bit of mountainside. The Americans patrolled these mountains ... and sometimes their Rangers, or even worse, their *Filipino* Ranger mercenaries, would infiltrate in small parties and lie up for weeks to catch ... or just shoot ... or otherwise kill ... anyone unauthorized.

It was officially a national park around here now, Roosevelt's regime loved those, but he thought they also used it as a training ground with a chance of live targets that could shoot back to keep their troops on their toes. He had a good position, with a view through a narrow crack in the rock, several alternative firing points if there was a fight, and a covered path of retreat up a steep ravine that cut the bare pillars of the cliffs behind him.

And none of those verdammten *cactus spines digging into me, for once,* he thought.

It was a little hot in this afternoon of a summer's day, but the dryness of the high thin air made it easy to bear now that he'd adjusted to the altitude and learned how important it was to keep drinking water even when not thirsty; the heavy scent of baking pine sap and sweet yellow-flowered *huizache* trees and nameless spicy herbs hid his own sweat. Insects clicked and buzzed, much louder than in a European forest.

This was *much* easier to bear than August 1914 had been, in the endless thick brazen heat of the forced marches west and south that ended at the Marne.

Horst had been an *Oberleutnant* of twenty-six and in superb hard condition in that year, and sometimes his legs and feet still ached at the memory when he awoke from dreams of it. Dreams where he once more saw and smelled blood leaking from boots that marched and marched and marched, men staggering and falling in their tracks or moving with unnoticed tears cutting muddy tracks down their faces, tens of thousands of foundered horses stinking in clouds of flies by the roadsides, their blind eyes still seeming to beg. That even before they met the deadly stutter of the French Hotchkiss machine-guns. And the still-worse *fauchage* the 75 mm guns spat out, sweeping acres of ground at a time with shrapnel that cast up dust in a boiling cloud.

Racing toward you as if it were sudden hammering raindrops in a thunderstorm, sweeping across the stubble of the harvested wheat fields while the shells cracked like black flowers in the air above . . .

This was pleasant by comparison. And his recent and not-so-recent wounds had finally stopped hurting much, after a spell in which he'd kept going on drink and determination and awed the locals by the amount of *mezcal* he could consume with no visible effects. Hiding in these Mexican mountains like a field-mouse dodging owls and ferrets helped, climbing and running and carrying everything he needed on his back, because it sweated the poisons out and left him tired enough to sleep even through discomfort. And the process he'd noted since he'd lost his left eye to a Black Chamber agent's bullet in Boston last year had about finished, so that he could estimate distances fairly well again. Not *as* well yet, the world still looked flatter and he had to be more conscious and deliberate about it, but well enough.

The mules came into view around a switchback far below; beyond them through a gap in the twisted thorny trees he could see the plowed fields and pastures of the plain around Jerez in the distance, and the whitewash and colored stucco of buildings in the town, tiny around the dollhouse towers of the church. *Cuitlacoches* flew up out of the bush as the mules disturbed it, little red long-tailed birds he'd come to like for their sweet song.

There were a dozen of the pack-animals, plodding along with careful steps and big canvas-covered bundles in pairs wobbling on either side of their backs. Six men accompanied them, all in *campesino* garb of loose dirty-white cotton pants and blouselike shirts and straw sombreros and striped, fringed serapes flung back to lie down from their shoulders, different from ordinary peasants mostly in the way they also bristled with knives and machetes and bandoliers of cartridges and assorted weaponry. Three also wore boots instead of the ubiquitous huaraches . . . sandals. One of those halted and raised the brim of his hat, looking upward with narrow-eyed suspicion . . .

Ernst Röhm! Horst thought as the face leapt clear in the reticle of the sight.

He smothered a gasp and a galvanic start by an effort of will and felt his mind gibber and slip; he'd have been more surprised to see General Ludendorff here in Mexico, but not *much* more.

The Stoßtruppen *have come to Mexico, by Almighty Lord God!*

The square brutal Bavarian-peasant face with the distinctive scars on the cheeks and nose was unmistakable, despite the way he'd taken the sun and was as dark as a local. The stocky muscular body wasn't too out of place here either; much less so than Horst, whose six feet of narrow-waisted, long-limbed, broad-shouldered white-blond Nordic good looks and pale gray single eye were about as *un*typical as possible.

Neither man's scars were in the least unusual, in a country just coming off a vicious civil war and a massive foreign invasion.

Not far away one of the guerillas he was working with came to a knee and waved to the newcomers, calling:

"¡Hola, compadres! ¿Cómo estás?" Then he turned to the German.

"It is those we awaited, with our supplies," he said to Horst; his name was Miguel, and he was as much of a leader as this group of quasi-bandits had. "And … ah … Sehhh … eh … Ordo … Pablo is with them."

It had taken effort to get them to stop calling him "Señor" and adopt the shortened form of Ordoño for his name. Mexicans had respect for their social superiors beaten into them from birth, rather like peasants in Silesia, but even more so. These *revolucionarios* were careful about never using surnames, and often substituted nicknames or fakes instead of their real Christian ones too. Long before this the careless among them had ended up dead in battle, or in Black Chamber interrogation rooms squealing and babbling out everything they knew, or in the chain gangs of FBS labor camps building motor roads to remote villages for the next twenty-five years to expiate their membership in a terrorist organization.

Unfortunately, that means most of them are *dead or breaking rocks by now.*

"I must warn you, Pablo does not like gringos," Miguel said.

"But I am not a gringo," Horst pointed out in his excellent but occasionally slightly staccato Spanish.

Technically *gringo* could mean any foreigner; it had probably referred to Greeks, originally, back in Spain. In Mexico's variety of the Spanish language in the twentieth century's second decade it almost always referred to Americans, and it was not meant as a compliment.

"Yes, yes, of course . . . and you brave *alemanes* are our allies, allies of Mexico's sacred cause of freedom . . . but pardon me, Ordo, you do *look* a *little* like a gringo and Pablo is . . . *¡Ay! ¡Sacate, que!* Pablo is a *hasty* man. And the gringos burned his village, everyone died . . . He is a *busca sangre; un despiadado."*

Which meant *a seeker of blood; a man without pity.*

"That is Pablo's problem," Horst said, and forced down the flush of eagerness, a feeling at once hot and cold in gut and groin. "Not mine."

It was unwise and he knew it; he wasn't in a position to go looking for quarrels with his local helpers. And while he'd long been a fighting man, and a ruthless one at that, who could kill with his own hands without hesitation or remorse when it was necessary, unlike the description of Pablo he'd never been the sort who went looking for blood . . .

Not before . . . her.

Not until the Black Chamber spy who was posing as Elisa Carmody de Soto-Dominguez deceived him last year, the one actually called *Luz*. Even through the pain of his wounds and the blurring of a brain rattled by a steel-toed kick to the head he'd heard that and confirmed it later: *Luz O'Malley Aróstegui*, which meant she was Irish-Spanish by blood in truth.

Oh, that was a clever touch.

That smooth deception had led to one disaster after another. She was the one who'd shot him in the face and cost him the eye back last October in Boston when she ruined the American part of the Breath of Loki. And later she'd been crucial to wrecking Projekt Heimdall.

Not to mention Horst being led by the nose through northwestern Berlin, nearly blown up by a bomb she'd left behind for her pursuers— a man had gotten his head chopped off by flying debris six feet away, within blood-spatter range—barely escaping exposure to V-gas, actually being shot in the shoulder, pounded on with a large rock by a fourteen-year-old girl, and that kick in the head by Luz had been hard enough that he still had headaches sometimes . . . though it must have been very cleverly gauged despite stress and haste.

And ending up in the dusty, oven-hot U.S. Army POW camp in El Paso, a name that in his opinion translated into plain German as *the Godforsaken* Arschloch *of Texas*, from which he'd escaped seven months ago after killing two guards.

I am free of the camp but I have become too much a prisoner of my anger, he thought, forcing his teeth to stop grinding; Miguel was looking at him oddly. *Drinking doesn't seem to help enough; maybe I need a woman. Though* mezcal *is much easier to get here.*

There were some *soldaderas* with the little band of guerillas, but all of them had commitments of their own.

And it was *still* all going to be Pablo's problem, if he chose to make it one. Horst had looked like a handsome, dashing, athletic young German nobleman before he met Luz, with no distinguishing marks except a dueling scar on one cheek. Now he looked like a man much battered by life and very, very dangerous, which was as the Yankee saying went *truth in advertising.*

"One of the men with him is a German too, a German I know," he said, to change the subject from hasty Pablo's possibly hasty prejudices.

"Ah!" Miguel said eagerly; Germany was the guerillas' last hope. "An intelligence agent?"

"Perhaps now," Horst said.

Colonel Nicolai getting my message . . . messages . . . and sending him is the only explanation I can think of for him being here now. Assuming Nicolai is still head of Abteilung IIIb. How I hate this isolation! The world is being broken and remade, and I know nothing of it except rumors and Yankee propaganda!

"He was a soldier, when I knew him—a leader of *Stoßtruppen*, of special assault troops. A very dangerous man, fierce and cunning and fearless."

Miguel nodded respectfully. The war in Europe was legendary here . . . and even the American newspapers admitted that the German military had forced the U.S. Army out of France, which gave them major credit with the *revolucionario* remnants hiding in the wilderness. It was proof the gringos were not invincible, which was something these people very much wanted to believe.

Having been with these last sad holdouts for months, it was now Horst's considered opinion that Mexicans had joined Poles and Serbs among the irredeemably defunct ghost-nations of the world and that the remaining *revolucionarios* had about as much chance of driving the Yankees north across the border as Horst did of bedding the Kaiser's daughter Princess Viktoria Luise.

And doing it in the middle of the Unter den Linden *at high noon on Sedan Day*, he qualified. *Mind you, it's always easier to think objectively about someone else's problem.*

German help would get more of them killed and make things worse for their country as a whole . . . but he was here, instead of sitting out the war in a dusty camp, to do what he could for Germany, not for Mexico. The guerillas didn't need that depressing conclusion spelled out for them, since their wishful thinking would make them useful tools for the Fatherland. Whereas realism—despair—would just send them home . . . or somewhere they could assume a new identity . . . to make the best of things.

A man at the head of the mule-train waved, and a dozen guerillas rose from hiding and began sliding down the slope toward them. Horst came along a little behind, leaping from rock to rock with casual grace and landing with the battered and much-repaired pair of German Army *Marschstiefel* on his feet raising a puff of dust. He gave Röhm a nod and got an equally cool and expressionless one in reply. They respected each other's abilities and had fought together and each knew the other was a good patriot, but there was no warmth to it for reasons ranging from the regional to the personal.

Horst didn't share the common Prussian prejudice against Bavarians in general, partly because he was Catholic himself; oddly, like something seen in a mirror, Röhm was a member of heavily Catholic Bavaria's Lutheran minority. And a little because while Silesia had been part of the Kingdom of Prussia long enough to be reconciled to and even proud of the fact, Silesians were *Musspreußen*—Prussians-by-conscription, as the joke went—due to Frederick the Great's conquests, not Brandenburgers proper.

But he thought this Bavarian in particular was a vicious sadistic thug with the personality of a cannibal troll from the old legends . . .

. . . *not to mention the fact that he's a buggering arse-bandit. Not the poofy type of* Schwul, *granted—he's the mean, tough variety of warm boy.* And as far as he could tell, Röhm hated him; but then again, Röhm hated nearly everyone, possibly . . . probably . . . including himself. He loathed Prussians, in which category he put Silesians like the von Dückler family, about half as much as he hated Jews . . . and he *really* hated Jews. He didn't like the *edelgeborene* aristocracy either, and Horst's father was a baron with an estate near Breslau, which the von Dücklers had held since the *Drang nach Osten* in Henry the Lion's time, eight hundred years ago. *Röhm's* father was a minor railway official, a petite-bourgeois background that was a severe disadvantage even in the slightly less socially snobbish Bavarian part of the German Army. It was to the man's credit that he'd risen to captain's rank despite his lowly birth, but he had, as the Americans said—

A big chip *on his* shoulder *about it.*

The guerillas and the Mexican newcomers were exchanging the odd-looking Latin hugs they called *un abrazo.* Then the one named Pablo turned toward Horst, who'd let his sombrero fall down his back on the neck string. Pablo had a long black mustache drooping down on either side of a snaggle-toothed mouth, a nose that ended in a little blob of scar tissue where the tip had been once, and hot black hatred in his eyes. Those eyes scanned up and down Horst's body, and his full lips curled as he hitched his thumbs into his pistol belt.

"Hey, Miguel, who's the *güerito?*" he said loudly.

Horst carefully set the rifle down, leaning it against a boulder, and walked over to Pablo, who at close range smelled strongly of tobacco and marijuana and mule sweat. *Güero*'s literal meaning in Spanish was *yolkless egg*; it was a mildly unflattering term for the pale-skinned, especially blonds. Tacking on the diminutive turned it into *little blondie*, with an overtone of *pretty boy*.

It was a bit absurd for a Silesian soldier a hundred and eighty-three centimeters tall in his bare feet, with shoulders like a light-heavyweight boxer, fists like oak mauls, an eye patch, and a fine collection of scars here and there, but he couldn't ignore it if he wanted to be effective here.

Not that he would have anyway.

"I bet he thinks he's a real man because his country's big enough to fight the gringos," Pablo went on. "What do we need with a rich sissy from the city out here in the Sierra?"

Silence fell as Horst moved, and eyes followed him; these were mostly experienced fighting men, and they knew what the *way* he walked meant.

He halted close to the other man; the distance Mexicans preferred to speak at was closer than Yankees liked and much closer than German custom, but he went well inside that, forcing Pablo to look up at him and emphasize the six-inch difference in their heights, not to mention Horst's extra forty or so pounds of solid muscle and bone. He stared down at him for about the count of ten, his face coldly unmoved, waiting for an apology he didn't expect to get.

Pablo was obviously regretting what he'd said, and equally obviously unwilling to be seen to back down. Horst had learned that Mexicans didn't intimidate easily, and that the ones he was with now attached enormous importance to a public show of toughness. They called it *machismo*, and it meant an overwhelming pride in manliness. If an Italian had acted the way they did he'd have assumed it was a bluff hiding under a shell of blowhard bravado, but despite the theatrical gestures these people really meant it and would back it up with their very lives.

When Horst spoke his tone was casual and conversational: "This *güerito* is certainly not one of the two dozen who used your mother in the Zocalo, *morenito*. You are too dark for that. And as I recall, she liked dark meat, not light."

Pablo had been expecting a snarled curse or a blow. The flat tone disguised the content of the words from him for a moment, and then his eyes went wide as it sank in. His right hand flashed to the machete hanging at his hip and he started to step backward to get room for a swing as he drew. Horst let him, and waited until the heavy length of honed steel rose glittering in the sun and came down in a straight hack at his shoulder.

Then his left hand snapped forward.

There was no subtlety to it, just raw speed . . . and after the *smack* of wrist meeting palm, raw strength. Horst's hands were big even for a man his size. The Mexican had a working peasant's wiry build and strength, but the German noble had trained to the saber since he was six, among other things, and he hadn't been raised on a diet of corn and beans and not enough of those combined with illness and overwork from childhood.

Horst's long fingers closed almost all the way around the other's wrist in an iron bracelet, and muscle stood out like moving steel cables under the bronzed skin of his forearm as the loose sleeve fell back past his elbow, making the sun-bleached hairs bristle. The nearly healed wound in his left shoulder twinged, but he could feel the small bones of the other man's wrist begin to creak and bend under that grip, and the machete fell clattering and sparking to the rocky ground.

Pablo's left hand went for a knife, scrabbling blindly as he came up on his toes under the relentless twisting pressure. Horst had expected that. His right hand clamped the same merciless grip on the Mexican's left wrist, and began the same grim struggle. Pablo rose higher and higher as his elbows locked, his mouth opening in a sudden gust of bad breath as he wheezed in agony. Then Horst whipped his head forward, smashing the top of his forehead into Pablo's nose with vicious force.

It hurt, but he was prepared for it . . . and his forehead was much stronger than the smaller man's nose. That organ cracked as it flattened, and Horst struck again a split second later.

He dropped the now-limp body, extending one booted foot so the Mexican's head bounced off it and didn't fall full force on the rock beneath, which might well have killed him. Pablo lay moaning and stirring feebly with bubbles of blood swelling and bursting on his mouth and nostrils. Horst carefully, neatly blotted his own forehead with the loose cotton sleeve of his long tunic-like shirt; most of the blood there was Pablo's, though a little had leaked out through a pressure cut in his own skin. He opened his canteen, drank a little of the *mezcal*-cut water, and poured some into a palm that he rubbed across the minor wound as a stinging antiseptic.

"Well?" he said after he'd taken another swig and capped the canteen, with the same flat lack of affect, his pale eye meeting each man's in turn. "Does anyone else have anything to say about my looks?"

Suddenly he grinned. "And I'm a country boy, not from a city."

Someone murmured: *"¡Qué chingón!"*

Which meant *what a fucker* literally, and *very manly* in effect, and was about the impression he'd wanted. As much as he'd wanted anything but the pleasure of beating someone bloody and letting free some of the rage that roiled in his mind like acid in a sour stomach.

Ernst Röhm chuckled from where he leaned against a near-vertical face of rock with a stubby, ugly-looking automatic rifle cradled in his arms, one with a curved detachable magazine and a wooden handgrip on the forestock. Now that the diamond-point concentration of the brief fight was fading, Horst more or less recalled hearing the *click-clack* of the weapon being cocked. Which might have been just a precaution, or might have turned Pablo's hypothetical friends into pure spectators.

"I am belief we should all making these mules under cover to be, so we can the Yankees be fighting, not with each other the dance doing," Röhm said, in barbarously bad but comprehensible . . . mostly comprehensible . . . Spanish. "And the first of the presents you can see Germany has for your good fighting-ness to you sent."

I am back in the game, Horst thought, and smiled. *And who will the opposition be, this time?*

TWO

El Paso–Mexico City Express
American National Railways
Approaching City of Zacatecas
State of Zacatecas
United States Protectorate of México
June 15th, 1917, 1917(B)

T his is a bit of a change," Luz O'Malley Aróstegui said with a reminiscent chuckle as she came back from the ladies' WC.

She stood for a moment before the observation car's curved stern of knee-to-ceiling windows, reluctant to get back in the perfectly comfortable chair. Luz loved to travel . . .

Except for all the sitting. *Right now I would kill . . . or at least maim . . . for a brisk three-mile walk.*

Standing here gave at least the illusion of personal motion.

"A change, dearest?" Ciara Whelan asked, glancing up from the book she was reading and putting a finger to mark her place.

Luz had a trained spy's ability to read quickly, at a distance, and upside down. The finger rested at a line that went:

$$Ca_3(PO_4)_2 + 5C + 3SiO_2 \rightarrow 3CaSiO_3 + 2P + 5CO$$

Whatever $Ca_3(PO_4)_2 + 5C + 3SiO_2 \rightarrow 3CaSiO_3 + 2P + 5CO$ *means!* Luz thought affectionately.

Luz wholeheartedly admired her partner's extraordinary self-taught grasp of the practical sciences without in the least envying it.

The cover of the weighty tome in Ciara's lap proclaimed it to be *Outlines of Industrial Chemistry*, written by one Warren K. Lewis, Ph.D., Professor of Chemical Engineering, Massachusetts Institute of Technology (Third Revised and Enlarged Edition, 1916), useful as background for their current assignment and also something she might well have read just for the fun of it, though electrical engineering remained her first love.

And like the man Luz called *Uncle Teddy* and the rest of the world knew as President Roosevelt, Ciara could read several books a day at speed and remember them verbatim years later.

"Quite a drastic change from my most vivid memories of this stretch," Luz said.

"Good for you," Ciara said, rolling her eyes with a sigh of very mild sarcasm.

They'd be at their destination soon; she inserted a ribbon and closed the book before she went on:

"Because *I* can't see that anything's changed since we got east of Riverside the first morning out of Los Angeles! Golly, but America is *big*! And a lot of it is full of bushes and sand and rocks and lizards and buzzards and underfed livestock!"

Wet steel rails receded endlessly behind them as the *Mexico City Express* ground away the miles between El Paso and the Protectorate's capital. The metal gleamed and then vanished over and over again, distance fading into the murk beyond the cone of light. This was a comfortable train and fast, if not as fancy or fast as a luxury hotel on wheels like the *20th Century Limited* or the new *Aztec Chief*, which ran from Chicago to Mexico City four times a week. But photographers tended to show up where those stopped, seeking fodder for the society pages of national newspapers.

Which the two of them very much did not want, even if they were only tiny figures in one upper corner of a shot centered on cinema celebrities like Chaplin and Mary Pickford, or Party bigwigs like Jane

Addams and Herbert Croly. The enemy read the newspapers too, read them very carefully, and they had people who could recognize Luz's face, and Ciara's.

"We always were big enough that getting around took time," Luz said; she'd traveled all her life.

She put her hands on the brass rail and took the opportunity to stretch discreetly, using a routine that set muscles working against each other. Then she sat, gripping the arms of the chair rhythmically and unobtrusively, pushing herself backward and relaxing, then lifting her body just a little on one foot against the foot rail, holding it until the muscles began to quiver and hurt, and then the other, then both . . .

"But a lot bigger now, thanks to *el jefe,*" she added.

That was the way Black Chamber operatives usually referred to President Theodore Roosevelt, or less often with the English equivalent: *the Boss.* The Chamber was his personal creation, begun even before his landslide victory in 1912 and operating months before he was back in the White House; that had been before the amendment that moved Inauguration Day from March to January, of course. Things had been moving fast as people abroad and at home realized that the new Theodore Roosevelt and the New Nationalist movement and the new-minted *Progressive* Republican Party meant a change of regime, not just of names and faces and policy, and there hadn't been time to wait on formalities—which was the Chamber's modus operandi to this day.

"The United States has nine million, six hundred forty-eight thousand, three hundred ninety-five square miles currently," Ciara said, in the voice she used when quoting some card file in her head.

Luz found it fascinating; the finer points of human speech were *her* field of interest and expertise. And Ciara was never wrong when she spoke like that, not about anything quantitative.

Unless her source *was, I suppose,* Luz added to herself. Ciara went on:

"As opposed to three million, eight hundred sixteen thousand, seven hundred forty-two square miles before Mexico and Canada, umm . . ."

Her voice went from information-transfer to ordinary-conversation mode.

". . . joined us. And then we . . . umm, bought . . . Greenland and Iceland from Denmark just now."

The price had been ten million dollars, accompanied by destroyers and battalions of Marines as real estate agents.

"It's understandable that the Danes let the Germans resupply U-boats in their waters, given that Berlin has a gun to their heads, but . . . Uncle Teddy certainly makes things *happen*. Never a dull moment with *him* in charge!" Luz said.

Ciara nodded, but not entirely in agreement:

"Not geopolitically dull, but if you've seen one mesquite or cactus, you've seen them all. Or glaciers in Greenland, I suppose."

"We're just about on the edge of that, says the voice of experience! The shrubby and dry bit, not the glaciers."

South of here fifteen hundred miles of very-to-somewhat-arid land gave way to the fertile, closely tilled upland basins of the Bajío, and the gleaming cities the Spaniards had built on silver and Indian slaves in the days when their rule spanned continents and kings in Madrid dreamed of universal empire.

Ciara laid the chemistry textbook aside with a regretful glance; she'd been making little sighs of contentment and *ah* and *oh* and murmurs of *Yes, I see!* as she read.

And reading a textbook in public is merely eccentric, Luz thought. *Reading a set of Black Chamber briefing files with the Winged Dagger and All-Seeing Eye on the page headers would be both conspicuous and reckless, so in the secret compartment they stay. I do wish we'd had more than a few days' notice for the mission. I'm starting to worry that the Director and Uncle Teddy have an even higher opinion of us than I do.*

On the arm of Luz's chair was *her* choice of recreational reading, when she wasn't indulging her weakness for French symbolist poetry by the likes of Baudelaire, Mallarmé, Verlaine, and Rimbaud: the latest *All-Story Weekly*, with a tale by Edgar Rice Burroughs set in California and involving hobos, a missing heiress, a mysterious Gypsy girl living in the woods, private eyes, a car chase, a puzzling body, disguise, mistaken identities, and a grizzly bear named Beppo by someone very eccentric who was keeping it as a pet.

It was enjoyable blather, but then she and Ciara had done things *almost* as wild themselves . . .

Hijacking a German airship to escape from Berlin with a secret electronic range-finding device, for instance . . .

"So what *do* you remember differently?" Ciara asked. "This landscape looks as if it's been the same since it had mastodons on it."

"Not the scenery, the circumstances," Luz said. "I was remembering coming down this line through Zacatecas to Mexico City in June 1913, when Pershing took First Army across the frontier and we were running interference ahead of his Brute Squad, keeping the enemy confused and slow and helping him trap them. And again about six months later, after I'd done some . . . work . . . in Mexico City and Puebla and Cuautla with . . ."

Done *things* to *might be more accurate.*

". . . the *revolucionarios* and Zapatistas. And it was *different* then.

"*Solo un poco,*" she added with ironic understatement; *just a little.* "That winter and spring were the worst, when it looked as if the Intervention might fail and take the Party and the movement down with it. Not like this at all."

She waved a hand at the comfortable and not overcrowded car as they clacked south through the rainy night at a steady fifty miles an hour behind the American National Railways' workhorse Pacific Standard 4-6-2 locomotive, with a smoothness that told of recently relaid track and a good roadbed. The table between them held cups of steaming Mexican coffee—brewed strong with *piloncillo* sugar and cinnamon and orange peel and topped with melted chocolate ice cream, the rich dark scents overcoming the leather-polish-fuel-oil smell of modern rail travel. And also a plate of crumbly, cinnamon-rich *polvorones de canela*.

"That was when we all had to become . . . hard."

If they spoke quietly, they were effectively as private as a locked room.

"What *was* the trip like then?" Ciara asked; they were still learning each other's pasts, though no longer trying to swallow decades at a gulp.

"No pastries, I imagine!" she added, as she finished off her own buttery cookie, dusting her hands and brushing off a few crumbs from the front of her blouse.

They'd missed dinner so far today because they planned to eat at their destination and there had been a scheduling problem. And also to get their bodies accustomed to Mexican rhythms. Down here local custom kept the old pattern with the main meal, the *comida*, in the early afternoon and a *cena*—a dinner-snack—quite late.

Soldiers could afford to live in a bubble of home they carried around with them; spies could not.

"We were living on stale tortillas and dubious beans we scavenged," Luz said. "And Libby's canned corned beef when we were lucky— every supply convoy from the north had to fight to get through. It was like swatting clouds of wasps while they tried to sting you to death."

"That must have been . . . exciting," Ciara said, giving a good game try at hardened indifference to risk.

Two very eventful missions together was more than enough for her to pick up the principle that *excitement* wasn't a desirable quality in their line of work.

"Very exciting," Luz admitted ruefully. "But . . . we all got very good at swatting wasps before they could sting. Well, the survivors did."

The main annoyance for the Black Chamber operatives *this* time had been from men who thought two attractive young women traveling by themselves must be wasting away for want of male company, which had necessitated a number of chilling set-downs and one smacked face.

"And at that, it was better than . . . the last ocean cruise you and I took back from Europe," Luz said with a smile.

Ciara rolled her eyes in agreement; they'd made *that* under false pretenses on a German U-boat last year, one of the fleet sent to destroy the East Coast cities, and to add a little irony they'd nearly been killed by the depth charges of U.S. Navy destroyers before they got to Boston and broke free in a hail of gunfire to alert Uncle Teddy to the Breath of Loki. The next assignment, undercover in Berlin, had been just as stressful.

This year had been much more pleasant so far, mostly training and planning in San Francisco, with Ciara enjoying herself immensely doing courses at Stanford and very discreet consulting stints at the plants in the Bay Area that General Electric and Westinghouse were setting up to manufacture an American version of the German Telemobiloscope they'd stolen and doing it as far away from Germany as possible. Nobody on either side hesitated to copy the other's inventions anymore, beyond giving them a new name or even just a lick of paint in the national colors.

This mission was supposed to be an important job, but not really hands-on dangerous.

Which I will believe afterward, if it turns out that way. I seem to have some sort of malignant field around me, like those all-pervading electro-magnetic forces Ciara talks about, one that attracts wretched violence into my life.

"Sometimes getting there isn't half the fun," Ciara said. "But"—she inclined her head to indicate the outside—"this . . . In the adventure stories it's all lions and tigers and bandits and going over waterfalls all the time. Or magnificent glaciers and storms at sea . . ."

"Nobody would read them if they left in the seven weeks of flies and sore feet and runny guts. My family went through this way too many times when I was a girl," Luz said. "My *papá* built some of the branch lines!" she added proudly.

Ciara's turquoise-green eyes showed a quick sympathy, and she leaned forward to give Luz's hand a squeeze. She knew those travels had ended when Pancho Villa's men had butchered Luz's parents during the sack of the Sonoran hacienda where they were staying, while Luz herself hid at the back of a wardrobe in the same room with her pistol pressed under her own chin in case they found her. And crawled out afterward beneath the smoke of the burning *casa grande*, through sticky congealing puddles of their blood. That had been . . .

¡Dios Mio! Luz thought. *Going on six years ago now! Another* world, *not just another time. Before the Great War, before the Party, even.*

She smiled as she returned the pressure of her lover's fingers for a moment. The memory was still bitter, but it didn't paralyze her inside with cold murderous rage as it had for so long, and it had been months since the last nightmare about it.

Killing most of the men who did it helped. Catching Villa and watching him die did too. And love . . . maybe love doesn't heal all, but it certainly helps.

Ciara released her hand with a final squeeze. "I don't think I've told you how much I admire the way you didn't let that . . . that awful thing you went through make you hate all Mexicans," she said. "I hated the English, after they killed Colm in Dublin last Easter. And that killed my da, as surely as a bullet. Oh, I hated them, and it was bitter."

Luz reached out a finger and playfully tapped the air in front of Ciara's snub nose, which was set in a round freckled face, fresh and pretty rather than beautiful by most standards.

Entrancing by mine, she thought, and went on aloud:

"But you didn't hate them enough to go along with the Breath of Loki, sweetie, when you found out what was planned," she pointed out; her partner had been there in Germany as a courier from the . . . extravagantly . . . illegal Irish Republican Brotherhood before she switched sides.

Ciara waved a hand dismissively and shuddered a little: "*That?* Killing all those women and little children in London, and all the poor common workingmen who had no politics and only wanted to get enough for the rent and food for their families and a pint at the pub now and then? That would be . . . like spitting on my brother's grave! *He* died fighting openly for what he loved, against armed men."

"Still," Luz said. "Mind you, sweetie, I hated the Mexicans who actually *did* it."

She shrugged. "After that I fought Mexicans I had nothing personal against because my tribe was at war with their tribe, and because Uncle Teddy was my war-chief and he told me to fight. I liked Germany and the Germans I knew at school there . . . and I liked some of the ones we met there on our last mission . . . but I fight them too for the same reason."

And frankly, because I enjoy fighting . . . or maybe it's the winning *part. It makes me feel* alive, she thought. *In a way only* you *do otherwise.*

Aloud she continued:

"Human beings have always had tribes, and they always will, and the tribes have always fought for land and booty and power . . . and they always will. So the important thing is to *win*."

"Well, we have *nations* now," Ciara said, uncertainly.

What Luz had said wasn't *exactly* Progressive rhetoric, though large parts of the New Nationalist brand of national-social Darwinism could be boiled down to about that. For a naturally jovial, genial man of deep affections and strong friendships . . . who'd once walked all around the White House neighborhood cradling a stray kitten he'd saved from dogs until he found it a good home . . . Uncle Teddy had a rather combatively bleak view of human nature and history.

Luz spread her hands. "Nations are tribes writ large with fancier names and machine-guns instead of spears. It's not usually about right and wrong—"

For her, close reading of *Beyond Good and Evil* and *The Genealogy of Morals* in her late teens had confirmed long-held inchoate doubts about whether those concepts had any real substance beyond local custom and personal preference.

"—it's just Us and Them, which is a lot more common. I actually like Mexico, and a lot of its people. I'd much rather live here than . . . oh, Illinois, say. I've . . . let it go. There's a time to heal."

And especially since meeting you, my heart, my darling. Which reminds me . . . I've been putting this off . . . let's get it over with . . .

"Ah . . . there is one thing you should be aware of, *mi amor*, about the station chief in Zacatecas, Julie Durán."

"It's very Progressive, a woman holding a job like that," Ciara said enthusiastically. "What an age we live in!"

Well, every word of that's true, but . . . this is going to be awkward . . . I really should have bitten the bullet and said something earlier . . .

"She's the *only* woman who's a station chief, so far, I'm afraid, out of fifty-three domestic stations, six in the Philippines, and a round dozen and climbing abroad," Luz said. "Though there are two more as *assistant* station chiefs . . . Alma Michaelis in El Paso, and Theresa Baez in Merida down south, if I remember the current roster correctly."

"Bob . . . her husband . . . is . . . remind me . . ."

Her perfect memory doesn't work quite as well with people, Luz thought, and filled in:

"Executive Field Operative Roberto Durán. He's New Mexican—old ranching family from up north of Taos, and they own land in the San Luis—southern Colorado—too. He was the first station chief in Zacatecas, and Julie was his assistant—they were the ones who made sure there wasn't going to be a 'marriage bar' in our outfit—"

Many organizations public and private made women retire when they married, or used the prospect as an excuse not to hire them in the first place; not, however, the Black Chamber. Everyone got paid the same according to their rank, too, which wasn't at all common even among Progressives.

Yet, she thought, and went on:

"—because he flat refused to take the job without her staying on the rolls officially, and I backed him up and got Uncle Teddy to put a word in and he talked the Director around. The fact that Bob's a cousin of the governor of New Mexico didn't hurt at all. The Director has him off doing something hush-hush now, so Julie got the job, to maintain continuity. She'd been doing most of it for a while anyway, while he got roving assignments."

"A cousin of State Governor Miguel Otero, he would be; and Otero was territorial governor too," Ciara said, showing she'd been paying attention.

New Mexico had only become the forty-seventh state in 1912 . . . though there were fifty-nine and rising now. The starry flag was getting crowded.

"Yes; Otero's influential in the Party because he was one of Uncle Teddy's early backers in '12, when it was risky. *El jefe* never forgets that sort of support. The Durán family are very well-to-do but not really rich . . . not by East Coast or Californian standards."

Ciara snorted quietly, and Luz made an acknowledging dip of her head; that was a matter of perspective. To a shopkeeper's daughter from South Boston *Luz* was rich, though she'd never seen it that way herself. Her father's business as a consulting engineer planning and running projects had meant contact with people who really *were* rich—which in those circles didn't mean *having* millions, it meant being able to *spend* millions.

"Bob's *papá* was in the Rough Riders like mine, so we met and hit it off in our teens when our fathers were at the reunions; a lot of the Rough Riders were from the New Mexico Territory, as it was then, and the Duráns are just the sort of frontier-baron-rancher people Uncle Teddy likes—he was at Julie and Bob's wedding. I put in a word for Julie when she wanted to join . . . our organization . . . in late '12, when we were just getting going, and the three of us worked together a good bit afterward. I introduced them, in fact . . . she was Julie Foederer then, of course . . . and they fell for each other like a pair of bricks tossed down a well. It was obvious by then that there was going to be war soon."

"Yes, I remember how angry people were."

Plenty of Americans had been killed in Mexico by that time—including her own parents, and very nearly herself—and tens of thousands driven out, and there had been deaths on American soil. Scores of volunteer Rough Rider regiments had sprung up in response to Uncle Teddy's call even before the election was over.

"Julie was in her senior year at Bryn Mawr when I arrived in '08, though; her people, the Foederers, are from Philadelphia. She took me under her wing . . ."

. . . her elegant, batlike, old-money, been-to-Paris-and-met-Natalie-Barney wing . . .

". . . there."

Get to the point, Luz, you're dithering, she thought.

"I'm sure we'll all get along well on this job, then!" Ciara said happily.

"Ah . . ." Luz said, glancing upward as she summoned all her reserves of social tact, not to mention courage, and cleared her throat. "At Bryn Mawr Julie and I were, um, close . . . extremely close . . . for a while. That ended with a few tears, but no anger, and we've been *friends* since."

In fact, we had a brief but extremely torrid affair, Luz thought, as she saw Ciara frown and then drop her eyes and flush beneath her transparent redhead's skin as she caught the implications.

"Oh," she said.

Luz carefully did *not* smile at rather fond memories; that *oh* was quietly pained.

Third person I'd ever been to bed with, and the first woman. ¡Ay, but that was fun! And an eye-opener.

It was her turn to reach out and take Ciara's hand for a comforting squeeze. One of the many reasons she was glad she'd been born female was that women, even Anglo-Saxon ones . . .

Which, gracias a Dios, *I am not*, she thought. *Though I can fake it if you hum a few bars.*

. . . weren't expected to act with the sort of perpetual bottling-up and emotional constipation that men had to show, especially in public and especially with each other. It also made discretion about certain things less difficult and irritating than it was for men in the same situation, though you had to be somewhat careful, and annoyance at the world's idiocies never entirely went away.

"I'm yours forever now, *querida*, but I can't abolish the time before we met," she said softly. "And I *am* a little older than you."

"I wish you'd told me earlier!"

Luz met her eyes. "Did you *want* me to? I didn't think you did. I'm sorry if I was wrong about that."

Ciara hesitated. "No," she said. "I didn't . . . but I'm . . . well, I'm a little angry now you didn't anyway!"

"So you're angry now that you weren't angry earlier?" Luz said. "If I had told you, would you have felt better on this trip?"

"No," Ciara said unwillingly. "I'd have been . . . anxious."

"And I was *afraid* you'd be angry and that there was nothing I could do about it, so I hesitated," Luz admitted.

"You? Afraid?" Ciara snorted.

"Different type of *afraid*, sweetie. There aren't many people whose anger I really fear, but you're one."

Ciara's smile died. "You really mean that, don't you?"

"Yes."

"I . . . I'll never be that angry with you, Luz. Never angry enough to *hurt* you."

They were silent for a moment, and then Luz nodded and spoke more lightly:

"Throw in that we couldn't possibly turn down this assignment for personal reasons!"

The Director and el jefe *certainly know about Ciara and me*, Luz thought; they'd been moderately discreet, but they *were* living together. *And as long as we deliver the goods, they'll look the other way. If it started interfering with business, though . . . and they could certainly* find out *about me and Julie back in the day, if they started someone tapping into the ever-grinding Bryn Mawr alumni gossip mill . . .*

Ciara took a deep breath and smiled, though it was obviously a little forced. "No, of course we couldn't, love. Thank you for explaining. It might have been awkward if you hadn't. At . . . at least we know she won't be shocked about . . . us."

"Well, no. But she's a bit of a jokester and teases people sometimes," Luz said, and added to herself:

Everyone. Incessantly. Mercilessly.

The fact that Julie was married now, and was triply a mother, and that Luz had introduced her to her husband wouldn't have much impact on the way Ciara *felt*, though her basic sense of fairness would; she didn't *dislike* men, but Luz strongly suspected that when it came to matters of romance, they just didn't exist in Ciara's emotional universe. Until she and Luz met she'd assumed that was because she was a good Catholic girl and God was saving the spark for a husband, but she'd learned better in a hurry.

Whereas I . . . well, Julie and I used to travel à voile et à vapeur, *both by steam and by sail, as the French say. Now I'm just happily monogamous.*

Ciara was silent for a moment, then went on: "I'm . . . it's very odd, looking inside . . . me."

Which she does much better than most people her age, Luz thought. *Much better than I did. I was smart back then, but also a tight-wrapped bundle of rage with a hair trigger and a knife in my pocket.*

Ciara went on: "I really *am* sort of . . . of *angry* you didn't tell me earlier! I knew there must have been . . . before me, I mean . . . But I didn't *want* to know the details! So now I'm angry you did tell me . . . and that you didn't. It's . . . it's illogical!"

Luz chuckled; for Ciara that was a serious self-accusation, since she was one of the most spontaneously rational people Luz had ever met.

"The heart has its own reasons the head knows not!" she said. "That's jealousy you're feeling, sweetie. You haven't met the green-eyed devil much before, which says something good about you."

Ciara made a shocked sound of denial and Luz gave her a fond smile. "I'm not blaming you, and *I'm* not angry! It's not a rational emotion, and it never feels nice."

"The locomotive's slowing," Ciara said with relief, her head coming up.

She was reading clues in the machine sounds, seconds before even Luz's acute senses caught the feeling of deceleration, and a long melancholy hoot from the steam whistle followed on the heels of her words.

Shortly afterward the conductor came through, announcing their arrival in Spanish and good, though accented, English just before the train took a steep downward slant toward the valley that held the town, a glowing snake of electric lights amid darkened hills. They went back to their compartment and packed and closed their cabin bags and hat-boxes to be ready when the train halted for the fifteen-minute stop.

They stepped down quickly at the cry of "Zacatecas! All passengers out for Zacatecas! *Todos los pasajeros con destino en Zacatecas!*"

And ducked their heads for a moment to avoid the sideways drive of chilly rain in the narrow gap between the train and the overhanging roof that covered the platform. The moderately sized station here was brand-new and well lit, built or at least faced in the local *cantera* stone, which came in a dozen shades of pink and rose-red, all in a restrained Spanish Colonial style that wouldn't have been out of place in California or the American Southwest either these days. But it and the small city it served weren't nearly big enough to extend to the giant glassed-roof shed over the tracks that major centers had.

Luz smiled again at the contrast with her memories of previous visits, ones of bullet-pocked walls in the bright light of noon, barbed wire and machine-gun nests and the stink of smoke and, faintly, of rotting bodies. Now it was nine o'clock and the sky was black with the drizzling clouds, rain still pattering on the roof over the sidings and reducing the metallic burnt-oily-steamy smell of petroleum-fueled locomotives and sharp tang of creosote tar from the sleepers in the roadbed.

There were American soldiers this time too, but only a dozen, a squad's worth of young conscripts from someplace where, judging by the name-tags on their left breast pockets and the faces under their steel helmets, most of the people had four Swedish grandparents, directed by a corporal who looked as if he was old enough to shave but only just. They were spruce and heavily armed and doing everything just as they were supposed to do, right down to never putting the index finger inside the trigger guard.

But under their discipline they were obviously profoundly bored amid a bustle of people disembarking and meeting friends or family and trundling off to the baggage claim, and they were talking quietly among themselves about an impending reassignment, which couldn't come too soon.

One idly whistled the tune of an officially discouraged marching song that dated back to the Philippine Insurrection, a ditty titled "Little Brown Brother" that Luz knew well:

Social customs here are few
The females they all smoke and chew
The men do things the Padres say are wrong;
So kill beneath the starry flag!
Let's civilize 'em—with a Krag!
And return us to our own beloved homes!

There was even a local band dressed in vaguely nineteenth-century quasi-uniforms wandering through and wheedle-de-dumping out a brassy march in the background . . . a very Latin version of "There'll Be a Hot Time in the Old Town Tonight"; street music was one of the features of these highland towns, often leading to impromptu dancing, and they were probably in the station because this was a good place to get out of the rain and get a few tips.

Mexicans who could took a long leisurely midday rest with their *comida*, and then stayed up much later than Yankees generally did. It often drove the efficiency-worshippers endemic in the Progressive movement mad with frustration, especially if they were the sort of obsessive who pursued *efficient citizenship* by doing time-and-motion studies of the best way to put butter on toast to avoid wasting precious time at breakfast that could and should be spent building the nation instead, but long exposure made the adjustment easy for her. It also made the streets lively in a way Luz liked. An equivalent small city in most parts of America would have rolled up the sidewalks by now on a weekday, with a late-night bridge game considered hot stuff.

"Brrrr!" Ciara said, shivering a little at the contrast with the heated train.

They set their hatboxes and coach suitcases down on the colored tile of the floor for a moment to await the redcap who would bring their trunk out to the street entrance; the air was around fifty degrees but felt more chill than that with the damp.

"I see what you meant about packing some warm clothes, darling! In *summer*, too. How did that story about Mexico being hot all the time get started?"

"At sea level, *mi amor.* In places like Veracruz or the Yucatán or Tampico, where you stew amid the bananas and mangoes and your shoes rot and fall apart like damp cardboard and fungus grows on you in embarrassing places you can't scratch in public," Luz said. "We're at eight thousand feet here; *tierra fría*, the cold country. Warm days and cool nights in summer, cool to cold in winter. It's a different world down there in the *tierra cáliente.*"

"Nice traveling with a native guide, that it is!"

Luz laughed, but there was a real pleasure in showing Ciara the places she'd known. She was looking forward to the chance at a long vacation in Boston, for the reverse.

"Oh, and watch out for being short of breath. It happens sometimes when people come up from sea level. Don't try to ignore it, just rest when you have to and adjust gradually. And drink lots of water, the air here sucks it out."

There was adequate warmth in their quietly modish but not excessively eye-catching summer traveling suits of knit wool fabric, whose cut was among the fruits of Coco Chanel's first American year, which had included ordinary streetwear as well as high fashion. Luz was quietly proud of suggesting to Director Wilkie that it would benefit the American economy if a message was sent to Biarritz offering asylum to Luz's favorite *modiste.* With lightning-quick wits and a ferocious concentration on the main chance, the young designer had set speed records through the deadly chaos of the French collapse for the nearest American outpost waving the letter overhead.

She was now sleekly ensconced in a splendid apartment in the El Dorado at 302 Central Park West, laying down the law on fashion to the wealthy barbarians of the New World with steely French arrogance, charging heavily for the privilege, and accumulating socially prominent male hangers-on. She'd also—somehow—found out who was responsible for her good fortune and gave them special deals on her output. Luz and Ciara both had the V-necked silk blouses over a chemise, tunics, slightly flared shin-length overskirts and four-pocket vaguely military-style overcoats with natural-waist belts that she'd produced in this spring's season, in maroon and dark green respectively, and plain low-crowned brimmed hats with only a little Chantilly lace for trim.

The clothes suited their covers as Protectorate upper civil servants with good Party connections too, specifically a roving inspector looking for new places to put all-female technical training institutes and her assistant. Their youth was credible enough; the civil service hadn't expanded quite as fast as the military since the change of regime in '12, but it was close—and closer still here down in the Protectorate, where Plenipotentiary Lodge had had to start from scratch. Promotions came fast and seniority meant very little, since nobody actually *had* any relevant experience.

That cover gave them good and legitimate reasons to meet with anyone, including government officials, and to wander around being inquisitive and asking people questions, whether local or gringo. People might suspect they were government secret agents, but they'd suspect that of any newcomer anyway. As an added bonus the clothes were comfortable, gave very good freedom of movement even by modern standards, and made it easy to conceal bits of gear, especially with some subtle modifications.

In Luz's case the gear included a chamois leather sap filled with fine lead shot, a wire garrote with cocobolo-wood handles, a set of lockpicks, a miniature camera in the handle of her purse, a .380 Browning FN automatic pistol her father had given her as a twelfth-birthday present, and a beautiful, authentic, and viciously effective six-inch folding *navaja* with a Toledo-steel blade in the classic *sevillana* style.

She'd learned to use *that* semiclandestinely in her childhood from an ancient and very disreputable retainer-coachman-bodyguard of her mother's known as Pedro El Andaluz, who'd told her once that she was the sort of girl who'd need it very badly someday. She gave a reminiscent smile at the memory of the evil old *baratero*, whom she'd loved like a cross between a grandfather and an accomplice, and then shouting caught her attention.

A score or so of young men were huddled off in one corner of the station's platform, none older than her own mid-twenties. They were Mexicans, ordinary local mestizo peasants from their looks, their loose off-white clothing, the colorful fringed serapes they wore cloak-style against the chill, the sandals or less on their battered feet, and the tall-crowned, broad-brimmed, and often ragged straw sombreros on their heads. All of them had small bundles of possessions tied up with cord on the ground beside them, so they must be traveling as a group. They were staring at—and some of them were starting to mutter resentfully back at—an American soldier who was waving his arms and pointing to a clipboard in one hand while he used loud fragments of what he thought was Spanish over and over again to tell them they had to wait; for a train, for dinner, or simply wait in general. The repetitions got more confusing as he went on, and they'd started out badly.

"Just a second, *querida*," Luz said.

The tall lanky soldier had sergeant's stripes on the loose-cut and infinitely drab brownish-gray-green modern U.S. Army field uniform, a color designed to blend into nearly anything except snow, and a Thompson gun with a fifty-round drum slung over his back. He also had a Deep South low-country gumbo accent, a flushed sun-red cracker complexion, and sandy hair cropped close under a turtle-shaped oblong steel helmet with a few raindrops running down its dull grit-finished rustproof surface. His Spanish wasn't nearly as good as he obviously thought it was, and what he did have sounded as if . . .

As if he'd learned it from someone in the Yucatán. ¡Madre de Dios!, *he said* pibil *instead of* horno *for oven . . . make that he learned Spanish in the Yucatán from someone whose own first language was Mayan! And he's saying . . . I* think *he's saying . . .* it go in oven-ing big long long time *instead of just* wait be-cause it's cooking now. *It's like a Russian peasant trying to talk to farmers from Maine in bits of English that he learned from a Chinaman in the Bronx.*

Nor did yelling make you more comprehensible, despite the fact that people the world over seemed to think so by instinct.

Luz sighed. Besides being a good deed, stepping in was entirely in concert with her cover role; Party functionaries usually loved setting situations . . . and people . . . to rights with a brisk efficiency that sometimes slopped over into what unkind souls called being bossy self-righteous finger-wagging scolds. Their much-delayed dinner would have to wait a little longer.

"Sergeant?" she said, stepping close.

And with an effort of will she dropped back into her native Californian-style general American English, crisply leavened by European finishing schools and Bryn Mawr. She and Ciara had been talking mostly Spanish and German for months, to improve the younger agent's skills.

Then a little louder: "Sergeant!"

The man wheeled on her, face and fists clenched with anger and frustration and eyes red with a long day that had probably started before dawn, obviously trembling on the brink of telling her to go mind her own business, with embellishments.

She gave him the Bellamy salute—coming to attention with the right hand placed over the heart, then the arm extended at a forty-five-degree angle with the palm up. It had started as the gesture used by children and teachers during the Pledge of Allegiance each morning at school, and had more recently become commonplace for civilian adults at patriotic occasions: during the national anthem or a flag-raising or a parade on a public holiday and at official speeches and the like. Here she was technically saluting the American flag patch on his shoulder.

It wasn't *officially* a thing only Party zealots did in an everyday one-on-one encounter like this, but that was the way to bet. He straightened as he took the gesture in, that and her clothing and a manner that also reeked of upper-middle-class status and probable connections to powerful people who could start a chain of chewings-out that would end in the painful gnawing of his very own personal buttocks.

"Ma'am?" he said tightly.

"I don't think they understand you, Sergeant."

Tactfully, she added with a friendly smile: "I can hear you were stationed in the Yucatán. Spanish here is different from what you're used to—it's like the different ways people talk in Alabama and in Massachusetts."

His brow cleared; evidently he hadn't thought of it that way, but he'd certainly have had experience with regional dialects of his own language in the Army.

"I'll translate, if you tell me what the problem is. What's going on here?"

"They're Army recruits, ma'am," he replied. "Fo' this-here new Mexican voluntary enlistment program."

She nodded and smiled encouragingly; it was *very* new, and it promised Mexicans enlisting in the U.S. armed forces citizenship for themselves and their immediate families and a land grant of a hundred sixty acres after four years or the duration of the war, with help to stock it.

Luz suspected it was going to be very popular, too. The dollar-fifty daily wage of a buck private in the U.S. Army was four or five times what a *peon*, a country laborer, made here, not to mention the separation allowance for dependents, and the rest of the package was very attractive indeed. That was enough land to make you someone of considerable substance in these parts, a man of respect, what their neighbors would call *el gran ranchero de por aquí*. Those were a class the Protectorate administration wanted to expand and tie to the new regime and the United States, which would be a useful by-product of the Army getting more raw material.

And the Army's used to dealing with rustic young men who don't speak much English, she thought.

The machine took them all—Norski farmboys and Finnish lumberjacks from the Upper Midwest, Lithuanian Jews in the pushcart-and-tenement sweatshop warrens of the Lower East Side, Sicilian fishermen in San Francisco, anything you could imagine—and turned out a standardized crop-haired, shoulder-braced product at the other end, able to read, write, and speak the national language well, understand a map or written orders, handle machinery, swear with vivid obscenity and scatology in good Anglo-Saxon fashion, make a neat cot in barracks, and brush their teeth American-style after chowing down for years on the bland abundance and vaguely Midwestern-cum-Southern uniformity of mess-hall food.

Same principle here. It worked for the Romans, no reason it shouldn't work for us.

"I'm tryin' to tell these-here gre—"

He checked himself. Using the word *greaser* was against regulations, on the principle that it was better to expend a little courtesy than a lot of ammunition; a safe enough rule to break among his own kind, but not here with some prim censorious Party functionary on hand.

"... ah, these here *boys*, the train north is delayed, and they'll get fed when the vittles I spent the expense money on get delivered, ma'am," the sergeant said. "And then they got all upset. Hell*fire*, they're supposed to want to be so'jers! Late for dinner? Ain't nothin' nohow t' what they-all be getting."

"It's not that; they're used to being hungry. I think *they* thought you were telling them they had to go and find their own dinner if they wanted to eat at all, Sergeant."

Meaning they thought you'd pocketed the money that was supposed to feed them—which if you grew up poor in Mexico is the first reason that would naturally come to mind dealing with anyone *in authority.*

"Let me help," she added.

"Uhh ... thank y'kindly, ma'am," he said.

"You're serving America, Sergeant, so I'm just helping the country," she replied.

Realization showed on his face as if a lightbulb had gone on over his head; now he wasn't going to have to explain a screw-up to an officer after all, *or* admit that he didn't have the command of the language he'd claimed. For obvious reasons soldiers stationed in the Protectorate got substantial bonuses for being bilingual, especially ones on detached duty.

She turned to the men and switched back to Spanish, using the clipped Mexico City variety she'd learned there at private schools and social engagements in her teens, different from the lively bounce of her mother's Cuban dialect and even more so compared to *abuelo* Pedro's *d*-dropping Andalusian drawl.

"Señores, be calm!" she said, making a soothing palm-down gesture with both hands. "There has been a misunderstanding here. Let me explain."

Those crisp tones would be familiar here in the central highlands, and sounding like a great landowner's daughter down from the capital would be all to the good, giving her authority. Languages had always come easily to her, and their variations and varieties.

The *peones* straightened up too, as they would for the lady of their *patrón* back home; just because a man was illiterate and spoke only one language didn't mean he was stupid, or couldn't pick up on the clues of dress and accent or notice the respectful way the American sergeant had talked to *her*. Their square brown faces relaxed in relief as she made the message clear. As she'd said, hunger was as familiar to them as daylight; their anger was at the thought of being cheated.

One of them removed his hat and held it before him in both callused hands as he gave her a little bow.

"Thank you very much, Doña," he said, using the formal *usted* and the word for *lady* that paralleled the respectful male *Don*, as he tried to be as polite as he knew how.

It was the careful courtesy of a proud man who had nothing else to give in return for a favor.

"You speak most excellent Spanish, Doña," he added.

Unlike that noisy gringo went unspoken in the flick of his eyes to the noncom.

Luz gave a very slight nod in return, maintaining a cool *de-haut-en-bas* distance toward strange men not of her family or social circle, in accord with local custom. What Americans considered ordinary friendliness could be badly misunderstood here.

"Good Spanish? How not, when Spanish was the language sung to me in my cradle, the tongue of my own dear mother?" she said, crossed herself, and added:

"Que Dios la tenga en su Gloria."

Which was the local equivalent of saying: *May God rest her soul.*

That brought broad smiles, and most echoed the pious gesture; they probably thought she meant her mother was Mexican.

It was perfectly plausible, and she'd often passed for a local on undercover missions south of what used to be the border; her long-limbed build was from her father, but otherwise her looks favored the Aróstegui side of the family, who were criollo Cuban-Spanish. With an unadmitted but inevitable dash of Taino Indian and God-knew-what, almost certainly including the odd quadroon, all picked up in the three and a half centuries since they'd moved from Santander in the Basque country to Santiago de Cuba and started accumulating sugar plantations. She had a smoothly olive complexion that darkened quickly to light wheat-toast brown in the sun, straight silky hair of raven-wing black, eyes that were very dark save for narrow blue streaks near the pupils, and a face that was a little high in the cheekbones, straight-nosed and full-lipped above a small but square and slightly cleft chin.

It was a set of features that could pass unnoticed save for unusual comeliness in most places from the Rio Grande all the way to southern Chile, or for that matter anywhere around the shores of the Mediterranean, north or south.

Several of the men whispered to the one who'd spoken and nudged him. He moistened his lips and went on:

"Doña, with all respect, may I ask you a question?"

She nodded, and he went on:

"These promises that *el Presidente Teodoro* makes, can they be trusted? Will the gringos treat us honestly?"

Luz thought for a moment and decided that even for a spy sometimes honesty *was* the best policy. Occasionally, at least, and especially when nobody was in hearing range except men who'd all be a thousand miles away getting yelled at by drill instructors in a day or two.

"That is two different questions, señor, and requires two different answers. As to *el Presidente*, yes. He is a hard man with a hard hand if you stand against him—"

There were nods at her short punching gesture with a clenched fist; nobody who'd lived through the Mexican Intervention was going to doubt *that*.

"—but he is a good friend, a good *jefe*. He was a brave soldier himself in the American war with Spain when we were children, one who always led his men from the front into the teeth of the bullets and the steel. Afterward he defied his own superiors to get care for them when they were sick or hungry. When he rose to great power, those who had fought by his side were never turned away from his door, however poor they were or whether they were Anglo or *Indio* or of Mexican blood. Above all things he respects and honors brave and loyal men, and he does not forget those who followed him and supported him, whoever they are. You will get the pay you were promised, and the land and tools and animals, and the citizenship papers. Or quite likely death in battle, but you know that, eh?"

That got a chorus of smiles and nods and instant understanding; the bonds between a patron-boss, a *jefe*, and the clients who supported him in return for protection and favors were something people here absorbed through their skin in childhood. And nobody who'd ever fought Mexicans really thought they lacked sheer guts. She went on:

"As to your second question, some of the gringos will deal fairly with you if you do your best. Others will despise you and treat you badly from spite, or will insult you because they do not know or care about your customs. May you meet few such, but you *will* meet some and they *will* give you trouble."

The nods were sober this time, though they weren't surprised. If any group of people on the whole round Earth knew what it was like to be stuck at the bottom of the social sewer pipe where everything nasty eventually fell on your head, it was Mexican *peones*.

"Thank you for your honesty with us, Doña," the man said.

The sergeant was looking at his watch and over his shoulder, obviously wondering fretfully where the hell the food he'd ordered was but unwilling to go look himself lest the situation unravel in his absence. Luz made an instant decision and spoke to him:

"I'm going into a bit more detail, Sergeant."

Then to the recruits: "Let me tell you a little story, señores," she said, and they watched her intently, a few squatting on their heels and lighting hoarded cigarettes. "My father's grandfather came to America . . . to a city named Boston . . . seventy years ago, fleeing from a famine that killed most of his village."

Grave nods at that; they all knew what a time of hard want was like, and had felt it in their own bellies and seen it the faces of gaunt children when war and drought passed over these lands.

"He was like you, a *campesino*, a peasant who had always labored on the lands of others for nothing but scraps and kicks. He was Catholic, spoke not one word of English, and he could not write even his own name. The people of Boston were all Protestants then, and all of English blood. They looked down on those like him, spat on them, mocked their holy things, called them stupid apes and dirty drunken savages fit only to live like pigs and work like mules. He did work, at first carrying a hod of mortar up ladders, then learning to lay the bricks himself; and he taught himself English and his letters in the evenings after long days of toil. He saved pennies for years, and bought a horse and wagon, and by the end of his life had his own little house on his own patch of land, and a few men and boys working for him and beside him. He saw that *his* son attended school."

She made a gesture with both hands palm up and slowly rising.

"That son did better, and became a man of property in a small way, and *his* son, my father, went to a great university with the children of the *ricos* and outdid them by wits and hard work. He became an educated man, an engineer who designed and built mills and railways and canals that gave food and work to thousands. You have chosen a dangerous road, señores, but one that may lead to a good place if you do your best and have some luck. And may God and His Mother and your patron saints watch over you."

She crossed herself again and turned away toward the waiting room and the exits in a murmur of thanks. Ciara took her arm and smiled beside her as they passed a handcart going in the other direction that held the promised dinner, judging from the appetizing smell of the *frijoles refritos* and eye-wateringly chili-rich local *birria de cabra*—goat stew—and the round baskets of tortillas, festival food by peon standards.

"That was kind of you, my darling," she said quietly.

Luz shrugged. "Well, it was good for them *and* for the country," she said, slightly embarrassed. "Build your body and your mind to build yourself, but build yourself to build America," she added, falling back on a basic Party slogan.

If there was one thing the New Nationalist movement agreed on, it was that you had to put duty to the whole first. That was why extending rights and education for all was policy. Not for the sake of individuals, who were only cells in the body politic, but for the welfare and future of the nation and its people, because it made each citizen better able to contribute to the country.

As they reached the arcade facing the street, a hand beckoned from the window of a plain Model T.

THREE

Sierra de Cardos

Near Jerez

State of Zacatecas

United States Protectorate of México

June 15th, 1917, 1917(b)

Röhm grinned at them and held up the odd-looking rifle; another lay at his feet, on top of webbing bandoliers of ammunition.

"This, example of one, a von Dückler StG-16 is, a *Sturmgewehr*, a . . ."

He seemed lost for the Spanish word for a moment, his scarred face working. Horst filled it in:

"*Fusil de asalto*," he said: assault rifle.

That wasn't an established term in Spanish, but then until late last year it hadn't been one in German, either.

I coined it myself because nobody would have taken something named Federov Avtomat *seriously. Now I'll get the credit, even though all I did was arrange to steal the weapons and machinery from the Russians after we beat them. It makes you wonder about the official versions of history, it really does. Though it looks like they've made a few improvements—the sights, and the grip on the forestock is farther forward and the machining is smoother, probably better steel too.*

"Correct, assault rifle," Röhm said. "Let me what it can do *ge* . . . be showing."

He held the weapon with the butt on his right hip and pointed with his left hand.

"These rocks there."

The StG-16 leapt to his shoulder. *Crack! Crack!* and two rocks the size of a man's head leapt off a boulder four hundred yards away. There was a murmur, but Horst thought it was for the shooting, which was impressive, rather than the weapon; the Mexicans were familiar with being on the receiving end of the Yankee R-13 for years now. Horst had taken his from a guard at the POW camp in El Paso, who didn't need it after his head acquired a 180-degree turn to the rear in Horst's grip, thus illustrating the old saying about there being no dangerous weapons, only dangerous men.

Weapons can certainly help, *though.*

"Now that," Röhm said, pointing to a similarly sized lump of pinkish stone.

It was much closer, but still around two hundred yards from where Röhm stood. His thumb flicked a little lever down at the back of the trigger guard, and then he shouldered the rifle again, leaning into it a bit.

This time there was a stuttering crackle, a *raakkkk* sound. Brass flew out of the ejection port as the German officer fired a series of short bursts, three or four rounds each. The rock jumped into the air and shed fragments in a peening, hammering circle. Each following burst struck just as it landed, until the assault rifle clicked empty.

There was another murmur from the Mexicans as silence fell and he quickly switched in another magazine and repeated the process.

An excited murmur this time—except for Pablo, who was lying where he'd fallen and now snoring in the way men who'd been clouted in the head often did, bubbles of blood growing and popping on his smashed nose, along with the inevitable flies. This time the guerillas were impressed on a more technical level; they were familiar with the American machine pistol, the Thompson, and how its heavy .45 pistol rounds could blast men to bloody sausage meat . . . but two hundred yards was about twice its effective maximum range. Some of them looked extremely thoughtful.

Nothing on a battlefield was ever easy, but the Great War had proven attacking was *hard* for a malignantly and mutually reinforcing mass of reasons. Defending was hard too if you didn't have access to a regular army's crew-served heavy weapons. Sometimes a compromise like the assault rifle gave you the *best* of all possible worlds. All the Mexicans were excited, and the more thoughtful ones were running possible scenarios of attack and ambush through their minds.

They started to crowd around Röhm, their questions louder and louder as they stumbled over each other's eagerness. Horst's head whipped up.

"Silence!" he shouted.

It fell in seconds, and then there were yelled curses and a few crossed themselves. There was a faint sound in the air they all recognized, a snarling buzz—radial engines, the nine-cylinder models the U.S. Army Air Corps preferred. That shook Horst fully back to alertness, like a jolt of cold water on a hot day. It came from the north, though that was hard to judge amid the echoes from steep rock-faces all around, and it was definitely getting louder.

"*¡Ay, chingao!*" someone yelped. "*¡Aviones gringos!*"

Nobody needed to say a word after that. The guerillas and the muleteers ran the animals upslope until they were under a brushy overhang of rock, then started frantically stripping their pack saddles.

Everyone who wasn't helping with that ran for cover themselves. Horst did too, but he paused to snatch up his R-13 and then the semiconscious Pablo, throwing the man over his left shoulder as he ran back uphill to the spot where he'd waited for the mule-train half an hour ago. Röhm arrived at almost the same moment Horst tucked Pablo under a bush without wasting time on gentleness, either because he'd been following or because he had as good an eye for ground as Horst did, a survival trait in a fighting soldier; he had both the assault rifles and their ammunition.

"I suppose you think that because you beat him and then rescued him, Pablo there will become your most faithful vassal and blood brother?" he said sardonically as he found a place with overhead cover.

Horst didn't turn his head away from the direction he expected the aircraft as he answered; there would be more than one, from the sound that was echoing off the mountainside. It was very pleasant to speak his own language again, after more than half a year living in English and then Spanish.

Even speaking with Röhm, he thought, and went on aloud:

"Hauptmann Röhm, do I look like a complete idiot? Or Old Shatterhand?"

"Not like a *complete* idiot, no," Röhm said, with a chuckle of recognition at the reference.

That *was* the sort of thing that happened in a Karl May novel; May was a writer of adventure stories set all over the world, but mostly in a highly colored version of the American West, where the German frontiersman known as Old Shatterhand and his Apache companion Winnetou wandered around, slaying enemies and animals and waxing poetic about their feelings and the landscape in fine subromantic style.

Very few German men of their generation—Röhm was about four years older than Horst—had grown up without reading them in their teens. Horst still did occasionally, or had back in Germany, for relaxation and nostalgia's sake. Though he knew that despite May hinting it was all true and that he *was* Old Shatterhand, the author hadn't even crossed the Atlantic until he'd written most of them and had never gotten closer to the wild Western lands than a good hotel in Buffalo, New York.

"Incidentally, I'm not a captain anymore," Röhm said; that was what *Hauptmann* meant. "It's *Major* Röhm now. The *Sturmgewehr* did very well—all the *Stoßtruppen* use them now. Ten magazines each, grenades, a Lewis or two per squad, and you're ready for anything—twice the firepower we had before for less weight. They're thinking of re-equipping the regular infantry the same way. You may be sure I wasn't shy about how I got them for us, and my battalion and regimental commanders were very impressed."

"*Ach, so*," Horst said, a usefully noncommittal verbal placeholder. "Congratulations. Well deserved, I'm sure—we heard about the Yankees running out of France with their tails between their legs."

Christ and His Mother! He was hard enough to deal with when we were of equal rank.

From his taunting grin the Bavarian knew exactly what Horst was thinking, and let the moment stretch out before going on:

"You're a major too, now. I've got the paperwork here with me somewhere."

Horst grunted in surprise; they were both extremely young for the rank in prewar terms, and fairly young for it even after two years of very heavy casualties—in proportion to their numbers German combat officers always had higher casualty rates than their men, up to about battalion command level. Before he went back to intelligence, at one point Horst von Dückler *had* been commanding a battalion for a little while . . . or what was left of it . . . as an *Oberleutnant*, simply because nobody more senior was alive and unwounded to do it. But on a personal note . . .

"I got promoted for that *beschissene* mess in Berlin? Or that *was* in Berlin until the enemy spies sabotaged the Annihilation Gas works and then escaped in the confusion with one of our naval airships and the secret radio-range-finding apparatus."

"Escaped with you and me in valiant pursuit all the way to the front in France!"

"I recall taking a Navy semirigid at gunpoint to do that," Horst said dryly.

"Exactly! Why waste precious time with bureaucratic formalities when you can grab a man by the throat and stick a Luger up his nose instead? I was impressed. You may be sure I upheld your credit manfully when I debriefed," Röhm said. "After all, I was involved too, so it was *my* credit as well. I emphasized my observations of the enemy *tanks*, too, and that was one of the first contacts—we're calling them *Panzerkampfwagen*, Panzer for short, by the way. Everyone's worried about them, and the War Projects division of the Emperor's Institute has a new crash program."

Horst gave a curt nod of acknowledgment. Röhm could have blamed everything on Horst, who wasn't there to defend himself, but that was the *cautious* move: deflecting blame while admitting a disaster. Claiming *credit* for what happened and trying to make it all out as an epic of heroism was much riskier . . . but it did require giving a share to Horst, as well, and if they'd both been promoted he must have done it very skillfully. Horst supposed that someday his career would mean something to him again, and in any case there was now a debt.

"Your Colonel Nicolai . . . I'm seconded to Abteilung IIIb too, now . . . managed to throw most of the blame on the Navy. They deserved it, too, the bumboy twits—they never even realized something was going on until we warned them, and did nothing about it until we came in at the last minute. Right now there's a lot of credit going around for everyone. Except the Navy, and even there the U-boats are stars. You're due major kudos for the *Sturmgewehr*, too, since your name's on it. These last few months everyone's polishing their medals and kissing arse and angling for a château . . ."

"Happy as God in France," Horst said, quoting an old German saying for ease and plenty.

"Precisely! Nicolai says you can have a nice one with a good vineyard, if you want it, by the way—the Custodian of Enemy Property is a very good friend of his."

"The colonel looks after his people," Horst said—truthfully.

"Though he's just been given an estate south of Kiev himself, three thousand hectares of black earth," Röhm added with a sneer. "He'll build a *Schloss*, I suppose . . . Schloss Spionage . . . and play at being a Junker in his spare time."

Horst looked over his shoulder for a moment and gave him a brief cold smile; Nicolai was no more of noble birth than Röhm. The von Dücklers were *Uradel*—nobles as far back as written records went, into deep time.

"He deserves his share. What's the point of winning a war if you don't plunder the defeated? And land, land is the best booty of all because in the end all other wealth comes from it. As for playing the Junker, did you think our lines sprang by magic from the loins of Wotan in the mists of time? Every *Hochgeboren* family tree starts with a lucky soldier—a commoner, too—planting the acorn with his sword, watering it with the blood of his enemies, and fertilizing it with his plunder."

"A point," Röhm said grudgingly.

"And you? I didn't think you'd give up a combat command for intelligence work."

Röhm wasn't just a competent professional soldier; Horst had pegged him as a war lover, one of the rare breed who simply reveled in combat and were very good at it.

"The war's over. It's been over since I walked into the Mediterranean up to my boot-tops," Röhm said casually, then grinned. "And then unbuttoned and pissed in the direction of the Yankees and the *Parlewuhs*."

"That was a campaign, not the war," Horst said, puzzled.

Röhm shrugged. "The real war, the main armies hitting each other head-on, the war of massed divisions and the Western Front and the Eastern Front . . . *that* war *is* over, all but the armistice and the negotiations. We're demobilizing now that the Yankees are out of Europe. Twenty-five divisions' worth of troops—all the older year-classes, a lot of skilled workers, the married men . . ."

"We are?" Horst said, shocked.

I think some part of my mind assumed the war would go on forever, he thought, contemplating that sensation.

"We need more aeroplanes and submarines and Panzers, not masses of infantry," Röhm said. "And to repair the railroads and five dozen other things we let slide because we had to, and then there are the new territories to whip into shape to yield what we need, since the Navy has *Scheiße gebaut*—"

Which was roughly equivalent to the English phrase *fucked up royally*.

"—and the Yankees and Englanders still control the oceans. With V-gas around on both sides, that big-war game isn't worth the candle, not until someone comes up with a defense, and the scientists say that won't be soon. We'll be putting down rebels and partisans for a generation inside our wonderful new Greater German Empire and that's better than nothing, but a bit boring. And God did not make me to be the founder of a line of Junkers!"

He cocked an eye skyward. "That little affair where we chased the Yankee spies and hijacked the airship, that wasn't boring at all. And this . . . *this* isn't boring either. Colonel Nicolai keeps his chosen men busy!"

The engine noise was much louder now, and all the guerillas were thoroughly concealed.

"And Colonel Nicolai didn't send me alone, magnificent German warrior that I am," Röhm said. "I came with presents besides your promotion papers, and little helpers . . . because the longer the Yankees take to get their own V-gas plant going, the better our negotiating position will be at those armistice talks sooner or later. It's all code-named *Alberich*."

Horst made an intrigued sound. That was the name of the king of the dwarves in the *Nibelungenlied*, the legends that Wagner had used as a basis for his Ring cycle. Alberich's tribe had made the magical swords and rings and invisibility capes of myth.

"Where?" he said.

"Had to stash them some distance away, far too bulky to drag into the mountains, and the helpers are technicians, not fighting men."

"*Ach, so*," Horst said with satisfaction.

He wouldn't get any details until he really needed them, of course. And working with Röhm might be difficult . . . but Röhm needed him, his superior command of the language and even more his local contacts and knowledge.

Röhm looked skyward again. "We can have fun with the toys, assuming we don't die today. How are your *Lumpenpack* of brown clowns here for fire discipline, by the way? They *hide* pretty well, but you learn that quick when you're attacked from the air. If you survive the first time or two."

"They're surprisingly good," Horst said—again, truthfully. "The incompetents and absolute brainless fire-eaters are all dead or in labor camps or back in their villages hoeing beans and hoping the Yankee secret police never find out about them. Darwin got them, you might say. The few still in the field know their business—natural selection eliminating the unfit."

Röhm grunted. "There must have been a lot of them to start with, then," he said. "In my regiment we were laying bets on whether the Yankees would give up on it and pull out, back just before the war in Europe started."

Horst shook his head. "Roosevelt doesn't give up on a fight once he's in it, and neither do the ones he picks for command, like Wood . . . Wood pacified the southern Philippines back after the Americans took it from Spain. That was as bad as Mexico was in 1914. Here . . . the Yankees killed three hundred thousand of the Mexican rebels and caught and executed all their best leaders, and made it plain they weren't going anywhere and would go right on killing until they got things quiet, and that discouraged most of the rest. Then the Yankees gave an amnesty, and they've been surprisingly mild to those who don't fight.

They like to hand out candy and pats on the head to children, and build new wells and schools."

"Stick in one hand, carrot in the other," Röhm said. "I prefer sticks in both hands . . . each of them wrapped in barbed wire."

You would, Horst thought.

Röhm gave another of those infinitely cynical grins. "And most of these here, they're the ones their own families would . . . how do the Yankees put it . . . I have been studying that abortion of a cross between *Plattdüütsch* and Froggie called English and what I'm thinking of is a lot like *jemanden verraten . . .*"

"*Rat out*," Horst said, dropping into that language's American version for a moment; he spoke it well, though with a noticeable accent.

"*Ja*, that's it, the ones their own families would *rat out* if they went home. Americans are great ones for coining a vivid phrase!"

It was perceptive of Röhm to figure that out so quickly—he must have come across by U-boat, one of the big new cargo carriers, and paddled ashore in a rubber raft to some deserted beach not more than a couple of weeks ago, to meet locals able to help him transport and hide Nicolai's *toys* and their operators.

U-boats are so very useful. To think of all the money we wasted on battleships! Thank God we started developing them seriously a little *before the war, at least. The Kaiser insisted on outdoing everything Roosevelt tried . . . and imitating a smart man's actions is* almost *as good as being smart yourself.*

"And here are our Yankee friends, ready to shit on our heads like pigeons in the *Englischer Garten* back home," Röhm said.

They were talking normally; neither was the sort of man who whispered simply because he felt anxious.

The aeroplanes were a flight of four Curtiss Falcons, two pairs flying in a loose gaggle along the front of the mountains and banking in to hug the curve. Röhm had a pair of small field glasses out, little ones the size of a palm that he held inside his hand to shield them from reflections—you *could* see the glint off a lens from the air.

"Falcons," he said, and grunted thoughtfully. "The latest model, with the three-hundred-fifty-horsepower engines. They gave us hard trouble in southern France whenever the fighting scouts couldn't keep them off, like artillery firing over open sights from the sky when you didn't expect them, bombing and strafing our front-line positions . . . and the artillery and the supply columns. I'm surprised to see them here away from the front lines . . . No, damn me, I'm not! Why cross the Atlantic through the wolf-packs to sit on their backsides in Corsica or North Africa, and lose more ships supplying them?"

Horst studied the enemy aircraft through the scope. They were neat twin-engine biplanes with spatted landing gear, a bit larger than a fighting scout but not much, four Browning machine-guns built into the pointed nose, a shark's mouth and staring eyes painted below, and two more machine-guns on a ring mount manned by the observer who sat back-to-back with the pilot. Bombs were slung under the lower wing, two large or four smaller ones on either side of the engines.

They were close enough now that he could see the heads of their pilots and observers, encased in leather helmets and goggles and with their scarves fluttering in the slipstream, turning from side to side as they looked at the shrubs and rocks and trees below. Horst examined the loads of the war aeroplanes through the x3 sight of his rifle and swore to himself before shouting a warning in Spanish:

"Gas bombs!"

A volley of colorful curses came from various places of conceal-ment, rippling farther away as the warning was passed on. Even Mexi-cans allowed themselves to show that they were frightened by poison gas, which you could neither see nor fight back against . . . and none of them had masks. One of the Falcons had green or yellow crosses painted on the noses of its load, four of each; the Yankees used the same color-coding as Germany, since they'd copied it along with the war gases themselves.

Green cross meant diphosgene mixed with a little chlorine to help it spread, and it could blind you but mostly killed by destroying your lungs. Sometimes at once, sometimes you started choking and it got worse and worse, and sometimes you just abruptly dropped dead hours later; it was nearly invisible, and detectable only by a slight smell like new-mown hay; as an added bonus it quickly corroded the filters in gas masks of the sort they didn't have.

Yellow cross was even worse news. That meant a newer weapon called nitrogen-mustard introduced last year; it was a viciously effective invisible vesicant smelling like garlic or horseradish that burned every part of your body it touched, soaking freely through cloth, the wounds swelling into huge and agonizing liquid-filled blisters, crippling and blinding and killing like third-degree burns inside and out . . . or like being flayed alive in a tub of acid.

Röhm and Horst had both seen them in action and Horst felt his mouth go dry. Neither was as bad as Annihilation Gas, of course. But dead was dead, and V-gas was at least quick: Green cross and yellow cross were both as painful as the worst sort of belly wound for a slow hard passage to oblivion. Or to the afterlife he no longer really believed in at times like this. Gas was feared more than other weapons because it didn't just threaten you with death, it threatened you with death by slow torture.

"*Himmihargodzefixsaggramentallelujamilextamarschscheissglumpvarregts!*" Röhm shouted, a thick Bavarian dialect mixture of blasphemy and scatology that couldn't even be translated into standard German well, much less English.

"What is it?" Horst said.

"Look at the last pigdog in the arsehole chorus line of pigdog flying Yankee swine farts," Röhm said.

Horst swung his rifle. The four bombs under *that* one's wings were just long smooth ovals, painted black on top and light gray below.

"You know the stuff we put in *Flammenwerfer*?" Röhm asked rhetorically; flamethrowers were a German invention and used modified fuel oil. "Well, just lately the ingenious inventive Yankee swine took that and made it worse—gasoline thickened to jelly with soap, with powdered magnesium and aluminum so it'll burn underwater and *something* that makes it stick like glue and burn you to the bone. I've had it dropped near me twice now and that's twice too many."

"Well, damn that," Horst said mildly, despite feeling his scrotum clench. "Of course, weapons are *supposed* to hurt."

"How philosophical, you Junker cunt!"

"I have to tell you that I love you too, Ernst, just this once before we die," Horst replied, and they both laughed in a harsh bark.

The aeroplane bearing the firebombs had a personalized sigil on its side, a red fire-breathing boar's head with horns, and under that the legend *Hellpig.* That made more sense now.

It seemed to be a theme of this *Schwarm*, what Americans called a *flight*. The others had names too: *Satanfist* and *Hellhammer* and *Mr. McBeelzebuddy Flies*. The last one took him a moment to figure out—humor was one of the last things that came across as your command of a language got better.

"The other two have four HE fragmentation bombs each, standard forty-kilo models," Horst added.

Which since aircraft bombs didn't need thick heavy casings meant each bomb had an explosive load equivalent to four or five shells from 210-millimeter heavy howitzers.

"Fucking joyous Christmas Day," Röhm snarled as they waited motionless for the aircraft to sweep by; at least it wouldn't take long, not at a hundred eighty kilometers an hour.

"Let's hope none of the Mexicans gets a wild hair up his ass," he added.

None of them did . . . but the mules were much less disciplined.

One broke free of its handlers, probably spooked more by the smell of the fear in their sweat than by the racketing buzz of the engines as it built to a climax. The animal danced sideways away from the cliff overhang, braying and bucking and kicking in a circle, then dashing away down the slope toward the path it had climbed only a few minutes before. One of the handlers *did* lose his head then, running out to follow it, waving his arms and shouting, which let another break loose as well.

"You don't notice it!" Horst said in what was nearly a prayer. "It's just a mule . . . it looks like a deer to you, your president loves wild animals, he'd crucify you if you machine-gunned a deer from the air . . . it could be running wild . . . oh, Holy Mother of God!"

One of the Yankee aeroplanes had spotted the mules running down the narrow path; it turned away from the mountains and then up and over in a showy Immelmann turn that left it flying straight back toward the path; the others went into a circle at slightly higher altitude, waiting. It dipped lower, until it was skimming the slope, and the pilot squeezed off a burst from the forward-facing machine-guns, walking them toward the target with the forward motion of his craft.

The sound of the short burst hammered at their ears in an overwhelming *BRAAAAPPPP!*

The sharp nose of the Falcon disappeared for an instant in muzzle flash as the tracers stabbed out. The mule nearly disappeared from sight in the dust the burst raised as well. When the debris from a hundred-odd rounds blew away, it was lying shredded on the ground in a pool of blood and parts and scattered cornmeal and dried beans from ruptured sacks, and giving its last dying kick.

The mule driver was just behind it. He survived the burst unharmed by some freak of ballistics and might have passed unnoticed if he'd simply leapt for cover or even just frozen, but in what was either hysteria or reflexive courage he brought up his rifle and began firing at the thing that had killed his animal.

The pilot certainly noticed *that*, and the observer swiveled his twin weapons and gave him a half-second burst as the aircraft banked away; six or seven of the heavy high-velocity bullets hit the muleteer, tossing him aside in an instant's jinking dance like a loose-jointed wooden doll shaken by an angry child. The second mule shied violently around the bloody corpse of its companion, then disappeared down the slope at a gallop.

The aeroplane went by overhead looking close enough to touch, pulled up and looped again to avoid the cliffs, and soared out over the basin to the east. The others approached it; Horst brought up the rifle and saw broad gestures exchanged as they circled, ending with the flight leader waving his right arm in a circle overhead and then chopping it toward the mountainside with a striking motion, the edge of his palm forward like the blade of an ax.

"For what we are about to receive . . ."

"May the Lord make us truly fucking thankful," Röhm finished.

Horst thought of shooting—there was less point in concealment now—but warned by the muleteer's futile gesture all the American aircraft kept higher, enough to make that a waste of ammunition, especially since he knew the latest Falcons had light armor around parts of the engines and the crew's seats. Which didn't prevent all twenty-odd of the guerillas from blazing hopefully away, but Horst thought a similar number of Germans would probably have done about the same thing. Once one man shot, most found joining in irresistible.

Mr. McBeelzebuddy Flies came in first with the gas bombs and released all eight *behind* Horst's position as it climbed, so that they arced out gracefully . . .

Upslope, Horst thought suddenly. *Against the cliffs* above *us.*

"*Rennt!*" he screamed: *Everyone run!*

The bombs detonated with a muffled liquid *thump* of dispersal charges, precisely placed to flush anyone downslope out of cover. Horst jumped to his feet and just barely remembered to make his yell in Spanish this time:

"*¡Huyen! ¡Huyen!* Run for it! Poison gas is heavier than air! It'll flow down toward us like water and saturate the whole area! Certain death! *Run! Run!*"

Pablo was awake enough to be cradling his injured head. He screamed in pain and surprise as Horst grabbed him again and threw him over his shoulder before dashing away down and across the slope. Röhm loped not far away, but the Mexicans were a little slower. He heard the snarl of engines again and a Falcon was heading straight for him . . .

Hellpig swept by overhead and released its load of fire, the flame bombs tumbling by above them, turning end-over-end. Horst risked a single backward glance and saw that the target was a clump of fleeing guerillas unfortunately close behind. He wrenched his attention back to the rough ground as he stumbled and recovered with a hard twist against the uneven weight on his shoulder and flogged himself to run even faster, grunting with effort at each long stride.

"Don't just run, scatter!" he yelled. "Don't give them big—"

There was a hiss like a dragon's coughing roar, then a rumbling thunder of flame and acrid chemical reek; the back of his neck felt as if it were on fire. Pablo shrieked like a gelded hog, and gobbets of fire *did* fly past, landing on brush with malignant hisses and setting it aflame. A man ran by, a pillar of moving, howling fire, and then collapsed ahead of him. Others shrieked like damned souls behind. Horst leapt heavily over the burning corpse and his trousers were only smoldering when he landed, coughing in the bitter chemical smoke underlain by a roast-pork stink.

"—big targets!" he choked out to himself.

Machine-guns chattered in the air, the tracer rounds stabbing down like twisting corkscrews of death as the aeroplanes circled above their foes, the observers using their twin weapons to squeeze off bursts at anything they saw moving.

CRUMP, and a hundred-pound bomb exploded, shaking the earth under his feet.

Fragments of hot razor-edged steel went by with a malignant whine, and the blast made him stagger on the edge of a fall that would mean death. The ground opened up ahead; he went down the side of a ravine in a half-controlled fall, and for a wonder it was narrow enough that trees along the edge above gave good cover. His mind sketched distances.

"Just . . . a minute," he wheezed, and halted.

This wasn't a pace men could keep up for long, particularly not carrying heavy burdens. He set down—dropped—Pablo and scrambled for his canteen, half-coughed and half-spat out a mouthful. Carrying that much weight at speed was something he *could* do, but it wasn't easy. Some of the water came out through his nose, and he coughed and spat again to clear his mouth. The Brownings were still chattering behind him, as if the American gunners feared ammunition would be outlawed tomorrow. It was maybe a thousand meters or so behind him now, and they were thoroughly out of view. Which gave them a few precious seconds of safety, perhaps a minute or two, and the ravine would take them a kilometer or more under cover.

Röhm was sobbing for breath not far away, fumbling to lay his StG-16 down so he could get to his own canteen and then bend over with hands on knees before he caught enough breath to speak:

"That . . . was *too much* of not boring," he managed to gasp.

He'd moved very fast over the short distance, but only by pushing himself to ten-tenths of capacity and a little more. Röhm had the sort of build that was a knot of muscle on muscle under field conditions but would go to hard bulging fat if he had ease and plenty of food, especially when . . . if . . . he reached middle age. Horst weighed about the same as the Bavarian, between eighty and ninety kilos give or take, but his long limbs and runner's constitution gave him the advantage here.

But Röhm is death in a fight; don't forget that.

Horst choked on the second swallow, kept it down, and followed with another. Then he could talk:

"One of them will have a wireless set," he said. "There will be more aeroplanes like flies on dead meat, and there's a garrison of Rangers in

Jerez. They have motor trucks and the roads they've made down there are good, so they can get to a spot an hour's walk from here in twenty minutes. Did I tell you how happy I was to have you show up and bring me the good news of my promotion, Röhm?"

Before the Bavarian could reply, Pablo stirred. "Gringo pig, I kill you soon now," he gasped, and began to vomit half-digested tortillas and beans over Horst's boots.

The two Germans looked at each other.

"Hello, *Major* Shatterhand," Röhm said, and they both began to howl with gasping laughter.

Things were moving. If luck was with him, he might get a chance to deal the enemy a stinging blow . . . and while it was a very big war, the part of it people like him fought was much smaller. So he might get a chance—

I might get a chance at . . . her. He knew it was obsession talking, but he couldn't make himself care about that. *It will be her. It must be.*

FOUR

Black Chamber Station HQ
City of Zacatecas
State of Zacatecas
United States Protectorate of México
JUNE 15TH, 1917, 1917(B)

This is a lovely home, Station Chief Durán," Ciara said politely.
And sincerely, Luz thought. *Though she's been very quiet. I hope this isn't going to be a problem.*

Ciara patted her lips with the linen napkin and put her fork down for a moment. She'd been making an occasional wordless sound of appreciation as she ate, though the assault on her delicate Irish taste buds waged by the chilies warred with a healthy appetite to bring beads of sweat to her brow and frequent sips at the tall cool glass of Carta Blanca beer that accompanied the meal.

"And a lovely dinner."

The Black Chamber headquarters in Zacatecas was also the station chief's residence, common enough in a backwater like this, or what *had been* a backwater, and her extremely capable cook had laid on a late working meal here in her office. There were platters of *gorditas*—crisp fried corn pancakes stuffed full of onions and pulled chicken or the tangy soft local cheese or *chicharrón* pork cracklings; *asado de boda*, a slow-cooked pork stew with a long-simmered sauce made from dried guajillo chilies, almonds, peanuts, raisins, cumin, cinnamon, mashed garlic, dark chocolate, and yellow onion; and pinto beans, red rice, and tortillas on the side, all scenting the air pleasantly.

"The layout reminds me of our home in Santa Barbara," Ciara went on.

"The Casa de los Amantes? That's flattery, Miss Whelan, albeit we've tried," Julie Durán said.

Luz winced slightly, as Ciara's eyes narrowed just a bit at the reminder that Julie had been to the *Casa* first.

Though we had separate rooms and nothing untoward happened apart from a few stolen kisses, not with my parents there, Luz thought. *But I can scarcely say that in public. Damn you, Julie, you always did have a fine hand at needlework.*

The station chief was thirty, with pale blue eyes, a long regular windburned Anglo-Saxon face that would have been horsey if it weren't for a strong-boned prettiness, dense pale flaxen hair done up in a practical bun, and a trim athletic figure much like Luz's, though she was closer to Ciara's five-four than Luz's five-six.

"And do call me Julie. A friend of Luz is a friend of mine," Durán went on to Ciara. "Luz has needed someone she could really rely on as a true . . . partner . . . for a while. I'm very glad you're there for her now."

The slight hesitation before *partner*, and the glance at the *Claddagh* pledge rings Luz and Ciara wore on their left ring fingers, showed she understood the situation without being too blatant. What wasn't openly named didn't have to be officially denied.

Julie can *be unobnoxious. When she wants to be, and she believed me when I told her back in the spring that this was dead serious for me.*

"It's Ciara, then, um, Julie," Ciara said, thawing a little.

She emphasized the *K*-sound, being a little sensitive about the proper pronunciation of the uncommon Irish name, which sounded like *Keera*, not *Sy-ar-a*. Erse-Gaelic spelling accomplished the difficult feat of being just as nonphonetic as English.

"And the way it's built around a courtyard here *is* similar to our home," Ciara said . . .

Laying the very slightest emphasis on *home*, as if to say *and she ended up with* me*, so there, you vamp.*

"The legacy of Greece, via Rome, via the Moors, via the Spaniards," Luz said; architecture was a much safer topic.

This arrangement of rooms around a central arcade-court had been born and elaborated around the Mediterranean and points east; it made for a very private, easily defensible home that kept out heat, drafts, prying neighbors, thieves, unauthorized boyfriends, tax collectors, and other such vermin.

All the old colonial-era mansions on Zacatecas's narrow, winding, hilly streets had been built to that pattern, with wealth wrung out of the sweat of *indio* laborers in the silver mines. This one was two flat-roofed stories of reddish stone with grillework over the outside windows and a stout door, now topped by a brass plaque reading *Universal Imports, Inc.* Since 1913 the Chamber had cut passageways through to the remodeled houses on either side that held more office space and staff accommodations, and doubtless there were the usual clandestine tunnels and deliberately sinister underground holding cells and other fruits of a long gradual sprucing-up process.

"It certainly has nicer atmospherics than the Black Palace," Luz added with a grin.

El Palacio Negro de Lecumberri was an ill-omened pile on the outskirts of Mexico City, a prison of dark repute for political enemies of President Porfirio Díaz until 1911, and the southern HQ of the Black Chamber since August 1913. Mexico hadn't been the Chamber's *exclusive* focus since the Great War started, but it was still crucially important.

"Lecumberri?" Durán said with a snort; they'd both worked out of the place and neither had enjoyed it. "Just *going* there makes me want to cackle like a wicked witch in a fairy story—"

She gave an unnervingly convincing laugh redolent of insane evil.

"—and commit atrocities on random passersby. I should *hope* Bob and I could do better than *that*!"

Working spaces in the Black Palace were mostly repurposed cells, since the client list was still extensive but more select than in Díaz's day. Julie's office *here* was a high-ceilinged second-story room done in pale plaster, uncrowded even with the long oak table at which they were seated as well as a big desk with telephones, a smaller typist-secretary's station with a massive Underwood, a Dictaphone machine and its wax cylinders, bookshelves and map hangers and filing cabinets.

A brown tile floor was scattered with colorful Zapotec rugs from Teotitlán del Valle, and windows opened onto the interior arcaded walkway that ran around the courtyard at this level. Roses and wisteria and jasmine vines climbed trellises on the pillars and arches outside, scenting the damp air that came through the half-open windows now that the rain had stopped.

"You *have* done better, Julie," Luz said. "Pass the tortillas, please, Miss Colmer?"

There were four of them at the table, since Durán had included her confidential secretary in the dinner-cum-meeting, someone Luz knew only from a quick run through her file. At the beginning she'd known everyone in the organization at least by sight and name, but that was years ago, years of constant expansion. Not to mention heavy casualties.

Henrietta Colmer was a striking young woman from Savannah, Georgia, with smooth dark-brown skin, softly curly black hair held back with a red ribbon, full handsome features, and a quiet manner. Luz didn't know if she'd picked up the personal dynamics at all . . . but she was willing to bet that was the case. Julie most emphatically did not tolerate dimwits, so she was undoubtedly sharp as well, given that she'd reached such a responsible position so quickly. Plus being around Julie sharpened whatever wits you started with; you had to run fast to keep up.

And that's a haunted look in her eyes, Luz thought. *Not surprising, with the load of sorrows she got handed by fate and the Germans.*

Colmer's dossier said she'd been away in Baltimore learning office skills and about to graduate from one of the new Department of Education's even newer vocational scholarship schools when the U-boat launched its load of horror-gas at her home city. That was the only enemy submarine in an American harbor that hadn't been captured or destroyed when Luz and Ciara brought the plans for the Breath of Loki back from Germany. There had still been some warning, but her parents and five younger sisters had been among the unlucky minority who couldn't evacuate in time.

It was Party policy to help the relatives and survivors. Through some combination of chance, desire—Luz suspected a wholesome lust for revenge—and circumstance, she'd ended up in the Black Chamber's CSS—Clerical Support Section. And probably assigned here in Zacatecas by some woman-hater who thought he was playing a malicious joke on Julie by saddling her with a "charity Negress" she'd be reluctant to refuse.

Though the joke's on him, not her. It's a sign of good strong character and a fundamental sense of duty that she's dealing with her grief through action and service to the country, not going passive and sucking her thumb because her feelings hurt so bad. Action's what I did, and Ciara did . . . and what Uncle Teddy did when his wife and mother died.

"The food's better here than the refectory in the Palacio Negro, too," Luz added.

The local dishes were very different from the Cuban style she'd learned from her mother, but she'd spent long stretches here in Mexico from childhood on, and shorter ones in Central America as her father built plantation railways and sugar mills and coffee factories. Her parents had always tried the cuisines of the places they lived—as her father said, if he'd enjoyed boredom and long winters he'd have stayed in Boston.

"Not hard. *They* use Army cooks," Julie said. "God have mercy, creamed chipped beef on toast in *Mexico City!* No wonder the prisoners all talk!"

Well, there's the Water Treatment too, Luz thought as she chuckled; that was a more scientific and efficient version of the Water Cure used in the Philippine Insurrection.

Julie waved again to indicate the building. "Here it's more a matter of living over the shop, but I do want to hand it on in good order to whoever my successor turns out to be."

Her voice in English had a Philadelphia Main Line sound, similar to but not quite the same as Uncle Teddy's Hudson Valley patrician tones, with a crisp -*oah* sound at the end of words like *four* strained through slightly clenched teeth. They were speaking mostly in Spanish, though, and Luz noted . . .

"You've shed the last of that antique *nuevomexicano* accent you picked up from Bob and his family, Julie," she said.

In central Mexico the Spanish of people from Taos sounded very rustic and very old-fashioned, roughly the way the rasping twang of hillbillies did in California or New York. She'd heard Appalachian English described as "Shakespearean," which wasn't even completely untrue . . . if Shakespeare had lived and died as an illiterate peasant from the hills of Northumberland or Galloway.

Luz added: "Now, if only you could walk around with a bag over your head, *mi amiga*, you could go undercover here easily."

You also had to learn to push back a bit at Julie, or she'd walk all over you without even trying.

"Or I could pretend to be a leper," the station chief added. "Speaking of disguises, are you two wearing *wigs?*"

They were: close duplicates of their natural looks and chosen hairstyles, a raven-black, shoulder-length high-style bob for Luz, long and bright strawberry-blond for Ciara. She looked slightly alarmed, and Luz touched her shoulder.

"Nobody but a trained observer would notice, believe me, except at very close range," she said.

Then to Durán: "Close crops for operational reasons, on our last field mission—about seven months ago. Damned inconvenient, but in the line of duty."

That was an oversimplification. Luz had had her hair cut down to the stubble to fit in with a group of French forced laborers in Berlin. Ciara had dyed hers to be less conspicuous, and when they got back it had been simpler to cut the mouse-brown result off and let it grow out naturally, avoiding a spell of startling half-and-half. The specialists the Black Chamber kept on retainer made the best disguise wigs in the world, lace-based and hand-tied, with methods culled from everything from the theater to modern medical science.

Durán and her secretary were both in businesslike shirtwaist outfits with turn-down collars and man-style neckties that would have been perfectly normal for women working in offices in Washington or New York, and with the jackets off it showed their shoulder holsters.

"I see they finally got around to designing a set of shoulder rigs for *us*," Luz said. "Bless the Technical Section!"

Conventional ones simply didn't go with having breasts, even her own middling-sized bust, much less a deliciously full figure like Ciara's.

These were like the back half of a skeletonized sleeveless bolero jacket fastened with an elastic strap across the sternum; they had the pistol on the left, presented nearly horizontally and butt-foremost just under the bosom.

"I had two made up to your and Miss Whelan's measurements when I heard you were coming; you can adjust it to be snug with the buckles," Julie said.

"Thanks! And those aren't 1911s you're carrying," Luz said, naming Browning's famous Colt .45 and the Chamber's field pistol of choice. "But there's a family resemblance? Like a little sister."

"It's designed by Browning, pretty much the same mechanism except for a double tilting link instead of single. And a four-inch barrel. Made for concealment and clandestine work, not as a soldier's pistol. They're calling it the Browning Amazon."

"*¡Ay!* So that's where the rumors of a new standard issue came from."

"Right you are. The round's new as well, a .40, or 10 mm if you want to be European about it. Hundred-and-forty-five-grain hollowpoint bullets at eleven hundred feet per second, which gives nearly as much wounding power as the .45."

She nodded to Henrietta, who fetched two wooden cases of blank polished ebony about the size of a volume of the *Encyclopaedia Britannica* and put them by the plates of the visitors. Luz slid hers open; one of the pistols rested in a molded recess in the lining of black velvet, along with three magazines, thirty-six rounds resting point down in shaped holes, a small flask of lubricating oil, a multitool, pull-throughs, and other oddments. Luz picked the weapon up, reflexively worked the action, and eye-checked the chamber with the muzzle elevated—she had been well taught, starting considerably before her father gave her the cherished Belgian FN automatic in its special pocket.

Then she extended the new pistol. "Nice," she said, judging and relishing the balance and heft; guns didn't delight her aesthetically the way blades did, but she had a professional's solid respect for her tools. "Light compared to a .45!"

"Framed in a new airship-grade aluminum alloy," Julie said, and Ciara's eyes lit with interest at the metallurgical note. "Which is corrosion resistant, too."

"How's the kick?"

The 1911's .45 ACP round was a brutal knock-down man-smasher, but it had always felt a little too heavy for her. A light bullet that *hit* was infinitely more effective than a heavy one that missed, and she was usually very accurate.

But this might be a useful compromise.

"My wrist reads the recoil at about three-quarters of a .45's," Julie said. "Unscientific, but there you are."

"Hmmm, I like the finger grooves but the butt's a bit wider than I'd have expected . . ."

"Staggered-row clip, twelve rounds, the *very* latest thing," Julie said, rather as if it were a new hat—she'd always been a bit of a fashion plate.

"*¡Ay!* That could be useful! And the .380 *isn't* very much bullet. There's no margin for error with the light cartridges designed for straight-blowback guns. Thanks very much, Julie. I'll shoot this in as soon as I can."

You don't need a pistol all that often in this line of work, but when you do, you need it very badly and you need the target to stay *down. And there may be more than one target.*

"Thank you very much, Station Chief Durán!" Ciara said in turn. "This pistol is a beautiful piece of work!"

Julie and her secretary both blinked a little as they realized that while Luz spoke, Ciara had unfolded the cloth tucked into the inside of the lid, spread it out, disassembled the automatic, laid the parts out neatly with mathematical exactitude, examined each closely, and was now putting it back together with cheerful interest and no hesitation at all, despite it being the first time she'd touched the pistol.

"Mr. Browning is *so* talented!" she said. "His designs are so . . . are so . . . *so* crisp! *Elegant.* But not *fancy* at all. No extra weight! No unnecessary parts or complications!"

She shook her head and made a disapproving clucking sound. "I had to disassemble a damaged Lewis gun last winter and replace a broken return spring and put it back together, and in a terrible hurry with my fingers cold—"

In a burnt-out French farmhouse with Stoßtruppen *about to attack us with machine rifles,* Luz thought fondly. *And it was the first time you'd touched one of those, too.*

"—and it's *much* too complex. It's . . . fussy. Fiddly. And too many of the operating forces are redirected instead of keeping them in line, lateral stresses that weaken metal parts and make them likely to crack . . . that circular return spring below the action, just like a clock's . . ." she said.

Her eyes rolled in disdain.

"All you'd need to do is put a coil spring and hydraulic buffer in the butt instead and you'd cut a pound of weight *and* make it more reliable *and* reduce the felt recoil even with less weight."

Luz smiled to herself with a glow of pride. Ciara wasn't particularly interested in weapons or fighting skills in themselves, though she practiced assigned lessons dutifully and diligently, despite a tendency to murmur *Oh, sorry!* when she hit a sparring partner.

Machines interested her, though, very much, and she had an uncanny ability to put a working model into her mind very quickly indeed, as if its parts and the way they moved together were the notes of a piece of music she could play and watch and halt or put into reverse.

She did it even better with electro-magnetic fields, which Luz knew were real but couldn't mentally visualize at all.

"You're very welcome," Julie said, taken a little aback by the casual display of technical virtuosity.

Then she dismissed her surroundings with another wave and a charming smile for Ciara:

"But this place isn't really a home, of course. Bob and I have bought a ranch down near Jerez . . . that's—"

"A country town about thirty miles west of here and a little south," Ciara said absently, showing she'd done her homework.

"I was surprised when you told me, Julie," Luz observed.

Though I wasn't at all surprised you didn't want to rusticate for long on the Durán estancia *north of Taos dancing attendance on the* abuela *and four widowed great-aunts*, Luz thought. *The older part of Bob's family didn't really think you were* at all *the sort of blushing virgin bride their gallant boy deserved, though I'll bet the great-grandchildren thawed them a bit.*

Aloud she continued: "And even more when you started talking about barns and sheep-dip and seed selection and the family trees of bulls in your letters. You being the most completely urbanized human being I've ever known."

"Urbanized or not, I've always liked Hesiod and Virgil and an occasional picnic in the country," Julie said, in a slightly defensive tone.

"Those are classical poets who wrote about rural life," Luz said to Ciara. "Though I doubt either of them did much of the pitchfork-and-shovel work themselves."

"Well, I've never wanted to go *that* far either; μηδὲν ἄγαν—nothing in excess," Julie said. "The *casa grande* there was a bit battered and scorched, which made it affordable—a little tiff between the Huertistas and the rebels."

"Which rebels?" Luz asked with interest.

There had been about five major armed factions in the field in 1913 when the Americans crashed over the border and ashore in Veracruz and Tampico, and all the self-proclaimed saviors of Mexico had been living off the land and what they could levy as *loans* and *contributions* and with a shifting set of alliances and betrayals and splits and mergers. Plus the minor players, ranging from overambitious would-be *caudillos* with a few hundred thugs to plain old-fashioned bandits taking advantage of the chaos and yelling *vivas* in the name of whichever leader was most convenient while they robbed, killed, raped, and burned. Doing said leader's popularity no good at all, especially when someone hired the gangs on officially . . . which had happened fairly often.

In two years of slaughter and destruction they'd made a fair start on wiping out the painfully achieved progress of the thirty-two-year reign of Porfirio Díaz.

"Huerta's men versus Villistas, basically—this was just a few weeks before the Intervention, and . . . well, all the stock had been looted and the workers dead or fled and the fields were growing up in weeds by the time we bought it."

"That was back in January of '14, wasn't it? Quite a declaration of faith!" Luz said, remembering vividly what that month and year had been like.

"*Who has* faith *in the future*, makes *the future; who* makes *the future* takes *the future*," Julie said piously, quoting yet another Party slogan. "And it paid off handsomely; the previous owners being men of *little* faith, so we got it for a song and they took the dollars and ran for it. *It* being Laredo, Texas, and living there is *just* the punishment the cowards deserved. Now it's worth five or ten times as much as we paid, even without counting improvements."

"How much land?" Luz said.

Luz had been very busy personally and professionally for the last year, not to mention out of the country for long periods, and the two friends' abbreviated dealings had been heavily focused on the Chamber's work or on Julie's children. She'd been vaguely aware the Duráns had bought property but not the details. Though from the letters she hadn't thought it was a small vacation place acquired just for the countryside quiet and space for little Alice's pets, but she still blinked when Julie said:

"Twenty thousand acres to start with. Fourteen after we deeded six thousand to the Protectorate."

Serious acreage! Luz thought.

"You gave away a third of it, Mrs. . . . ah, Julie?" Ciara asked in surprise.

"Not precisely *gave*. It's called the *one-third ranchero* program," Julie replied. "The Protectorate gives big landowners a really generous line of credit at low interest to modernize their operations provided they donate a third or so of their land, and then divides that into good-sized family farms, which are . . . were . . . thin on the ground here. Twenty to thirty farms eventually from what *we* gave them, for example. Mexican hacendados are, um, *strongly encouraged* to participate . . ."

"If they ever want to get contracts from the government or credit from any bank that wants to stay on the government's good side ever again," Luz said, defining *encouragement*. "Plus the revolution scared a lot of them into seeing that giving up something is better than losing everything, not to mention avoiding getting killed, and the smart ones lean on the dinosaurs so they don't get the benefits without paying the costs."

"But it's pretty much compulsory for Americans with large properties here," Julie added.

"Very Progressive!" Ciara said with a smile of approval.

She had a typically Irish dislike of landlordism, and was obviously imagining sturdy independent farmsteads with neat kitchen gardens and healthy children around well-stocked dinner tables and cats drowsing on the windowsill . . . though being four generations away from the land herself via Dublin and South Boston, probably not the sodden sweat and calluses and ground-in barnyard stinks that went with the lives of working countryfolk, even ones who owned their own land and made a decent living.

Luz was *also* imagining twenty to thirty more families each with a rifle over the mantel and a deep, visceral reason to be ready to fight for the new order, which was a strong policy point.

Henrietta nodded vigorously too—her father had been a customs clerk, but probably a fair number of her relatives were sharecroppers and no better off than the *peones* here.

"And the line of credit was very helpful," Julie said. "We can use every penny of it, *and* what our families sent us, *and* we're working on getting more loans from the bank; we're just starting to get some real returns out of the place this year. They reap wheat with *sickles* here! Oxen! Oxcarts with two solid wheels! Oxen pulling *wooden plows* and turning norias to lift water! It's . . . it isn't even medieval . . . it's *biblical* and Old Testament at that; I keep expecting to meet the Prophet Eze-kiel, or Judge Deborah. We took one look and ordered a dozen tractors and a dozen Ford motor trucks and a well-drilling rig and a bunch of wind pumps, just for *starters*."

"Works-and-days, back-to-the-land, Julie?" Luz said, amused.

Roberto Durán had been raised as the third son of a genuine if very affluent working rancher, but his wife seemed to have a convert's en-thusiasm.

"It's catching, particularly when you have children, and we think we can make a very good thing of it, using modern, efficient Progres-sive methods."

Luz chuckled. "A client of my father's near Santa Barbara once told him—he'd just commissioned an irrigation system—that it was very simple to make a small fortune as a gentleman farmer."

"How?" Ciara said, interested.

"You start with a *large* fortune, buy land, and shovel the rest of the money into a farm-shaped hole in the ground."

Julie made a rude gesture involving thumb, nose, and waggling fin-gers and continued:

"The *casa grande* has good bones, eighteenth-century, and I've been overseeing the renovations while Bob's away. They have plenty of fine stonemasons and carpenters here. You two must come and visit when you have time."

"And perhaps some interesting people could be there at the *same* time," Luz said, and added to herself:

That our cover identities need an excuse to meet.

"Hmmm . . . yes," Julie said, glancing upward slightly.

She'd had the same thought, of course. They'd always been able to fill in the blanks with each other.

The station chief went on: "Jerez is worth a look for the architec-ture, and it's pretty country, very much like northern New Mexico but not as dry or rocky, lots of interesting rides, and we have good horses.

There are orchards, and we're putting in a vineyard; the area has produced wine for a long time. Not very *good* wine, but Bob thinks we can do better, and we've gotten a French vintner. And the hunting's good up in the mountains just west of there."

"Too good, ma'am," her secretary said.

Luz cocked an eyebrow, and the younger woman—she was still short of twenty-two, within a month of Ciara's age—went on:

"We had a report of a contact with bandits in those mountains today."

It was official policy to refer to all guerillas, rebels, and other opponents of the Progressive project down here as bandits; the context made it clear they weren't talking about ordinary rural thieves.

Julie Durán frowned, and then shrugged. "A flight of four Falcons flying . . . try saying that really fast ten times . . . out of the air base near there spotted movement in the interdicted area . . . a pack mule . . . and shot it up. Then someone on the ground shot at *them*, they did a bombing run, and many someones shot swiftly . . . try saying that . . ."

"Naughty! Papá Noel doesn't bring sweets for *los niños traviesos*!" Luz said.

Falcons were bombers or two-seat fighting scouts depending on the mission, fast and heavily armed. Shooting at a Mk. V Falcon with a rifle while it did an attack run was rather like a field-mouse making an obscene gesture with the middle digit at the very last owl it ever saw; it might relieve the luckless rodent's feelings a little in the painful, violent concluding moments of its life, but wouldn't accomplish much else.

"Oh, Santa brought the naughty children presents—green cross and yellow cross bombs, firebombs, high explosive, and then machine-gun fire . . . that sort of present," Julie said.

"Even better than coal in the stocking," Luz said approvingly. "As *el jefe* says, if you're going to hit at all, hit hard, not soft. Follow-up?"

Air surveillance and air power were wonderful things, fruits of the new Progressive age, but there was still no substitute for close-range work on the ground.

"We have some of the 2nd Philippine Rangers in Jerez just now—their A Company. They're Bugkalot."

The Ranger regiments, American and Filipino, were the military partners of choice that the Black Chamber called on when it needed muscle beyond what its own operatives could furnish. The Federal Bureau of Security had its own in-house Intervention Battalions, which Luz considered wasteful and inefficient . . . and which the U.S. *Army* viewed the same way a bad-tempered bull mastiff did a stranger dog it found peeing on its fence line. Not entirely by coincidence, the Army liked the Black Chamber much better than it did the FBS.

"They sent a platoon to do a ground check," Julie said, and explained to Ciara:

"The Philippine Rangers are recruited from mountaineer clans like the Bugkalot back in the Philippines, pagans, from remote areas the Spanish never really got in hand. The Army is the only way they can earn much cash, and they like to travel, so we have regiments of them here in the Protectorate. Worth their weight in gold for small-scale work in rough country."

"Luz has mentioned that they're very hardy and brave," Ciara said. "And good trackers."

Luz chuckled reminiscently. "Also, headhunting is their national sport, and they find life boring now that we insist on them not waging blood feuds with their neighbors or raiding the lowlands. Collecting heads was how their young bucks impressed the girls. And paid their brideprice, too. They weren't slave raiders like the *Moros*, they just wanted household decorations as tokens of social worth . . . rather like lace curtains and a piano in the parlor, only with them it's human heads hanging in nets from the thatch over the fire pit instead."

"Does that give many problems, Julie?" Ciara asked the station chief. "That headhunting business?"

"Not as long as we let them pack the heads in salt here and send them home parcel post for free to impress the neighbors," Julie said cheerfully. "That really helps with recruitment back in the islands; the Army get a new rush of volunteers every time there's a mail delivery."

Ciara started to laugh, and then stopped when she realized none of the others were treating it as a joke except Julie; Henrietta was quietly rolling her eyes with the air of someone well used to the station chief's sense of humor. Luz sighed and gave a small nod of confirmation; that description was essentially the truth, though Julie was being a bit more blunt and showing a lot more levity than was usually considered politic when talking about it.

"Well, our ancestors were headhunters once too, *querida*," Luz said. "In the *Táin*, the Cattle Raid of Cooley, Cú Chulainn is always whacking off heads and tying them to the rail of his chariot by their hair or nailing them over the door or leaving them at river crossings for the heads' friends and relatives to find and be peeved at."

Ciara nodded, since that was true enough—and her Fenian household had been brought up on the old Irish hero-cycles. She was looking very slightly green at having the Iron Age epic poetry translated into modern life, though.

Julie chuckled. "*Our* ancestors?" she said. "Speak for your Cubana-Celtic self, Luz. *My* ancestors were much more reserved and dignified and pious: They sacrificed their enemies to Wotan by hanging them . . . from ash trees, mostly . . . and then spearing them. Or drowned them in a sacred lake for the goddess Nerthus."

"Mine built the pyramids and invented medicine and astronomy," Henrietta said, and they all laughed.

"Funny, you don't *look* Nubian," Julie added.

Ciara's eyes widened, and Luz gave the young Negro woman a quick glance, but Henrietta was laughing harder still. She and the station chief were evidently on joking-teasing terms . . .

And that is one very attractive young lady, person and personality both . . .

Luz caught her old friend's eye and then flicked hers sideways at the secretary, raising a brow. Julie replied with a narrowing of her eyes and a brush of her left thumb over her wedding ring, conveying:

No! Emphatically, no!

Luz shrugged slightly—*just asking*—and touched her pledge ring with the same gesture, to say she shared that opinion of the virtues of monogamy. The whole exchange took around one and a half seconds and passed unnoticed by the others.

Julie has changed. Well, we all do with age and responsibilities, I suppose.

The station chief went on smoothly aloud: "The Rangers counted either ten, eleven, or twelve bodies . . . Hundred-pound bombs, well . . ."

Luz nodded; if one of those burst right next to a human being, the liquefied results got sprayed over half an acre along with bone chips and sticky bits of sinew and connective tissue and the odd booted foot. You ended up having to count toes or teeth if you wanted forensic detail.

"And about a dozen dead mules . . . that was the gas and machine-guns, mostly . . . and the loads from the pack saddles, evidently mostly corn and beans and chilies and dried fruit and jerky and salt."

"Weapons?" Luz asked. "Ammunition?"

Guerillas always tried as hard as they could to salvage those from their dead. How much they left behind was a good marker for how fast they'd run away, which was an excellent proxy for how badly you'd hurt them and how frightened they were. Depending, of course, on how determined they'd been to begin with, but the few Mexicans still in the field against the Protectorate in the summer of 1917 were likely to be genuine *chicos rudos*, the local idiom for tough guys. Or to have burned their bridges behind them beyond possibility of forgiveness by anyone whatsoever, or both.

"Four Winchesters, six old Mexican Army 7 mm Mausers, and a Colt .45 single-action revolver, model '73. That one was probably used by Wild Bill Hickok before he got shot in the back in Deadwood—

somebody had filed off the foresight and cut away the trigger guard. Around twenty rounds per weapon counting spent brass, plus enough assorted cutlery to start a pawnshop. No ground contact yet, so no live prisoners, and the spent cartridges all fit the weapons captured. Except for one variety we haven't identified yet—we only got them this afternoon. Plenty of them, though, about as many as the others together."

She inclined her head; Henrietta fetched a small brown paper bag, folded and held with a rubber band, spread out a clean handkerchief from a stack kept in her desk, and carefully shook out over a dozen spent brass cartridge cases.

"We're going to forward these to Mexico City . . . Lecumberri . . . for the Technical Section detail there to look at," the secretary said. "The closest match I could find in the catalog was *Japanese*, of all things. Arisaka 6.5 by 50 mm semi-rimmed. But surely that can't be right? They're *not* semi-rimmed, fo' . . . for one thing. And the book says Japan doesn't do headstamps on their cartridge bases and these have them, see?"

She flicked one of the cases around with a pencil and pointed with the tip; on the brass disk surrounding the dimpled primer was stamped *S/L/01/E17*.

"Japanese? That's *almost* right," Luz said. "If you're consulting last year's catalog."

Luz took a pencil herself from the holder on the table, inserted it into the empty mouth of the cartridge, and lifted the shell. Bringing it to her nose brought the sharp scent of nitro powder, and a strong smell like mustard and horseradish as well, one that made her move it away sharply.

"Mustard gas," she said, and got her hankie out just in time as she sneezed.

"*Perdóneme.* Not enough to be dangerous, but I wouldn't lick this if I were you, Miss Colmer, and I'd wash my hands if I touched it. Which shows why nobody was going to linger to police it up. It *is* the Arisaka round you mentioned, but made in Germany and modified to be rimless as of January. They use it in their new machine rifle . . . the *Sturmgewehr*, they call it," Luz said.

"*Assault rifle*," Julie said; she was almost as fluent in German as Luz. "I suspect that's the usage that will catch on."

"Ah!" Henrietta said, and Ciara made a similar sound.

Luz nodded, remembering the peening hammer of rounds on the ragged stone of the ruined farmhouse above her head, pinning her down like a whole battery of Maxims. Everyone who'd been following the war news in detail had heard about the *Sturmgewehr*; one more nasty surprise in the first major war of the modern industrial-scientific era.

And the Great War has had as many nasty surprises as there were pieces of roasted peanut in Mima's turrónes de maní *at Christmas*, Luz thought.

Many of the surprises were almost as lurid as the ones writers like Wells and Burroughs dreamed up—in fact, some of them were the *same* surprises, translated from wild fiction to reality, like Wells's *The Land Ironclads*, which had prefigured the tank. Though it should be past tense for Wells—he had almost certainly died in the horror-gas attack on London, which was ironic, because he'd predicted that too, with his *The War in the Air*.

"The stamp would be *L* for *Lindener Zündhütchen-und Tonwarenfabrik*, they're in Hanover," Luz went on, with Ciara nodding beside her; this was an area where their talents overlapped. "*S* for *Spitzgeschoss*, pointed bullet; *01/E17* is the date—made this January."

"Yes, now that you point it out," Julie said, with a resigned sigh; she could do at least half of that herself if she tried, and perhaps all of it. "Oh . . . that's . . . really unfortunate. Because now we know that Germans were involved, but we don't know how many, or if they're still alive. The bodies not being very recognizable, and I doubt they were in *Feldgrau* to start with."

"It's amazing how similar people of different nationalities are when they've been blown to bits," Luz said, which produced startled laughs from Ciara and Henrietta and a rather different one from Julie.

"Not the usual argument for the Brotherhood of Mankind, but cogent," the station chief said.

"We didn't get one of these assault rifles, or even identifiable bits of it, just the cases, ma'am," Henrietta pointed out. "I think we better assume that *if* there were Germans there, and not just weapons they're supplyin' to the bandits, one of them got away, carrying it."

Julie sighed again. "Or it could be a Mexican with an assault rifle carrying it away, but you're right, Henrietta, we should assume the worst. We do know they land agents and weapons, occasionally. Too much coast to prevent calls from U-boats if they only surface after dark, and some of their new cargo-resupply models can carry quite a lot, multiple tons."

"We . . . may have a handle on that soon," Ciara said. She glanced at Luz, and went on after a slight sideways flick of her index finger: "A method of detecting ships at night and at great distances. It hasn't been widely deployed yet, but it will be soon."

A quick nod convinced Luz that Julie had been briefed about the American version of the Telemobiloscope, but that wasn't directly relevant.

"The survivors ran and ran fast," Luz judged.

"Right. Whoever it was were probably moving through; we haven't had any actual attacks near there for over a year," Julie said.

"That's what we *hope*," Henrietta said stubbornly. "The Rangers say that-there was just too rocky to be sure, but they think there were some who lived. And there were the mules and supplies, that means a lot of mouths, I'd say. Twice the count of bodies, the stepped-on count, maybe more."

She had an educated woman's vocabulary and grammar in both languages and a moderately strong low-country southern accent, which was something Luz had always found rather pleasing. But from hints on her vowels and diphthongs Luz thought that she'd grown up around someone . . . perhaps a grandmother . . . who spoke Gullah dialect. In Spanish she was slow and careful, and the accent was stronger, but it was very creditable and showed a quick learner. She switched back to English for:

"Wishin' don't make it so, Lord knows. Not with that, ma'am, not with anythin'."

Julie sighed. "You have a point, Henrietta. And evidently someone *was* feeding them, whether *they* are actual Germans or just the recipients of their damned U-boat-born largesse. We can't have that."

To Luz she went on: "The Rangers are looking for tracks, though it's nightmare country, all up and down, not much surface water and a lot of cliffs and bare rock. And I'm pushing my sources in the area. I turned a couple of PNR types early this year, a warehouse manager and a barber in Jerez . . ."

"Ah, good," Luz said.

A barbershop was a perfect cover for clandestine work, as good as a cantina or *pulqueria*; people came and went, and hung around to gossip. Ordinary shops weren't quite as good, but a warehouse did give you the chance to move goods around and make deliveries and have people working and visiting at all hours.

"Right, I'm using them as ant-lion traps, but very carefully to stretch out the time before they're detected. I don't think either has been blown on yet. I'll drop in on our ranch—lay on a dinner party for the new divisional commander, say, I was going to do that eventually anyway—and on the way make contact and in a just sort of mildly, more-in-sorrow-than-anger way ask why they didn't tell me about someone smuggling food to holdouts in the Sierra. That'll sweat them into finding out even if they don't know, because they really, really don't want to be identified as working for us."

"That's good craft," Luz said approvingly.

When you were running hostile informants controlled by threats—

blackmail, for instance—appearing to already know everything was demoralizingly effective. And Julie's sources would be suspended between the entirely realistic horror of what their former friends would do to them if they found out they'd been turned and an equally rational terror of the Chamber, so they'd be doubly zealous to keep Julie's protection. She'd probably promised them and their families comfortable new identities somewhere up north eventually, which they would really get . . . eventually . . . if they survived long enough. The Black Chamber always honored that sort of promise, just as they always carried out their threats; it was policy to be as remorseless as a machine about both.

"I'd send a surveillance airship to work with the Rangers if I could pry one loose from the Navy, and the Ranger battalion commander concurs," Julie added a little wistfully. "Strongly concurs. Two would be ideal. Fat chance, as they say. Antisubmarine work has priority over internal security, since we already had things well in hand here before the declaration of war. We only have the Falcons because they're not useful for anything but shooting down other aeroplanes or attacking ground targets."

"Are there airship support facilities at the Jerez Air Corps base?" Luz said, drawing maps in her head.

"Just the basics, a docking tower and an electrolysis setup for lifting-gas, and patches for the cells. Fuel and engine maintenance and general repair are the same as for heavier-than-air. No sheds closer than the American National Airways fields in Mexico City, though."

Airship sheds were enormous, and would be costly enough even for the smaller semirigids that Air Corps bases wouldn't have them without regular need.

"The basics are good enough. I've got a code you can send to the Director and he'll get two of the latest *Constitution*-class patrol semirigids sent up from Tampico and you'll get them *muy pronto*."

Both Henrietta and Julie reacted to the promise; the Negro woman's eyes went a little wider, while the more experienced station chief merely blinked. Luz had just revealed that her tasking's priority was high enough to let her simply skip all the usual channels, forms, requests, and interservice bun-fighting. Authority like that came only from the very top.

The *very* top; even Director Wilkie couldn't override the admirals just on his say-so, not that fast.

Luz went on: "You'd better see that the Army puts observer teams from the Rangers on the airboats. The *Constitutions* can stay up a hundred hours at a time, longer if they drift occasionally with their engines off."

The local Chamber operatives looked puzzled, and Ciara explained: "They have onboard pneumatic starters so they don't need to be spun up by ground crews."

"Ah! Silence is *golden*," Julie said with a broadly delighted predatory smile, immediately picking up on the implications.

Heavier-than-air craft had to loudly advertise their coming, and guerillas all knew to dive for cover at the first sound of engines. If an airship could *restart* its engines at will, it could get upwind of the area it wanted to cover and then go free-ballooning across it without letting anyone know it was around, like an aircraft gliding . . . except that it stayed up by inherent lift, not aerodynamics. A quiet approach would be much more likely to catch targets on the ground unawares.

Luz nodded. "And they're steady enough to use high-powered telescopes. But the crews are used to looking for periscopes and snort-tubes from submerged U-boats, not naughty little boys leaping and gamboling through the woods where they shouldn't. And check the communications. I wouldn't put it past the Navy to have different wireless frequencies just so they don't have to lower themselves socially by actually *talking* to grubby uncouth nouveau riche *soldiers* standing on dry dirty dirt."

"What about muddy dirt?" Henrietta asked, and Ciara chortled.

"Mud? That's why they have Marines," Luz said . . . dryly.

"In the Navy, they think soldiers on dry land evolve into Marines wading in mud, and Marines evolve into fully aquatic sailors . . . which is to say, into human beings. It's the Annapolis version of Darwinism," Luz said.

The two younger Chamber members laughed, but Julie only smiled wryly.

"You'd be surprised how close that is to reality, youngsters!" she said.

Luz went on: "You won't need me to put the brute on the captains of the semirigids, they'll be fully briefed on priorities before they get here."

Julie's eyebrows went up. "Many thanks, Luz! The Navy hates risking them where there might be a combination of thunderstorms and sharp pointy mountains, especially in high country like this."

"War is risky," Luz said. "Things wear out and break and people die."

Henrietta was making notes on a pad. Luz added: "And Miss Colmer, add that we've positively identified *recent* German equipment in conjunction with a bandit incident here; give the date on that just to be specific. It'll be in the situation reports at HQ and the usual incident reports circulated down here, but it doesn't hurt to make sure the right eyes back home run over it."

Julie leaned over to check what her secretary had written, made an approving cluck, and pushed it over to Luz to have the appropriate one-day code appended from the list in her head. A trained memory was indispensable for spies and, to the limited extent there was a difference, to the secret police.

"I'll get this encrypted for the eleven-hundred return to HQ," Colmer said; she'd do that and burn the original before she left the room, that went without saying. "If the orders are cut fast, we should have the airships within . . . oh, two days if we're lucky, three if we're not, dependin' on their readiness rate and how long it takes the Navy to reschedule things. I'll alert the Air Corps to expect them too, of course."

I thought *she was bright,* Luz thought. *And bold, not afraid to argue with Julie. That's a very good estimate, both on distance and the time it'll take the wheels to grind, considering how new to all this she is; not many secretaries would have picked up the background this quickly. Julie should see about getting her transferred to the Operations Section if she wants it—there are circumstances where someone with her looks could be very useful, though she'd need a mentor to look after her. Really good clerical work is valuable too, but it might be a bit selfish to keep her just for that.*

"That ought to make life an ordeal for some deserving candidates," Julie said with satisfaction, blotting up the last of her *asado de boda* with a tortilla. "I can feel their pain . . . and that feels so very, very *good.*"

"The airships and the Rangers between them should take care of this incident in the mountains," Luz agreed. "I'd like to go over and do some interviews in a few days when they've had a chance to comb the Sierra and possibly make more contact. Interviews with the Ranger officer and with the pilots, for starters."

"We can combine it with introducing you to the new garrison commander and his intelligence chief at my little soiree. Plausible cover all 'round. And nobody local is going to spot you at the air base, probably."

Luz nodded. "Good thought, thanks. I'll hunt around to get more of a feel for the situation here in the interim. A prisoner we could sweat would be ideal, of course, but . . ."

The reputation of the Bugkalot and their cousins was usually a considerable asset to the Protectorate government, but it did make people very reluctant to surrender to them. Though the rumors about ripping out the livers of prisoners and eating them before their eyes were, as far as she knew, grossly exaggerated.

Or at least somewhat *exaggerated.*

"The security for the Dakota Project is supposed to be impenetrable, but—"

". . . but the *Titanic* was supposed to be unsinkable and we all remember how *that* went," Julie said to complete the sentence.

FIVE

Sierra de Cardos

State of Zacatecas

United States Protectorate of México

JUNE 18TH, 1917, 1917(B)

*P*ablo may be hasty, *but he's determined enough for two*, Horst thought.

Pablo was breathing through his mouth as silently as he could while they moved in single file through what passed for dense forest here, moderate stands of a pine called *ocote* averaging about eighty feet high filling the air with the spicy-sweet scent of their sap, and with the soft warm sough of the breeze through their branches and needles. It was beautiful upland country if you viewed it objectively, steep blue slopes fading into the distance all around, interrupted by streaks of bare cliff that were often pink . . . and though objectivity was rather hard when you were being hunted and were half-starved, Horst still tried. Not least, it gave him something to think about besides the hunger; the cargo those mules had brought had been badly needed and they'd left it behind at high speed three days ago.

He was impressed with Pablo's willpower; the nose had to be hurting badly under the improvised splint, and it was still too swollen and full of blood clots to pass much air, but the Mexican hadn't let it slow him down. The path beneath them was narrow, winding across the steep hillside with that exact attention to the slope that only careful surveying or the instincts of wild animals could produce. He was also impressed by the Mexican's endurance in this thin air and up-and-down landscape, which had Horst's lungs and legs aching a little even now. The four of them had been moving over rough country since dawn, with nothing but a few stale tortillas and some pine nuts, though at least they had plenty of good water.

His own belly growled, and it was getting harder not to daydream about things like *Schlesisches Himmelreich*, a particular favorite of his that his family always had on his birthdays as a boy—smoked pork belly cooked slowly with dried pears, plums, and apples, spiced with cinnamon and served with sour red cabbage and bread dumplings. Horst swallowed the rush of spit at the memory and was about to suggest that they stop to wait out the hottest part of the day and eat some of their meager hoard. It would be the same vile mess, since they'd been too hard-pressed to stop for much hunting or foraging, but as the old soldiers' saying went:

Altes Brot ist nicht hart. Kein *Brot,* das *ist hart.*

Old bread isn't hard. *No* bread, *that* is hard.

Pablo's head came up as Horst drew breath to speak. The guerilla knocked back his sombrero with the back of one wrist and looked up, sweat running down his brown face and making his mustache limp. The other ex-muleteer—he went by *Chango,* evidently something to do with his ears, which were juglike—nearly ran up on his heels.

Horst and Röhm silently went to one knee on either side of the trail; Horst lowered the rolled blanket that carried his camping gear and share of the food to the ground and carefully switched off the safety of his rifle. He was still carrying the R-13; he preferred it, and had passed on the second assault rifle to Pablo. That had been a case of love at first sight, and had *slightly* decreased the Mexican's hostility to Horst.

Chango started to complain, and Pablo silenced him with a thick hissed:

"Bájate, simplón!"

Which meant *Take cover, fool!* and had Horst's entire approval.

They all waited, while birds chirped and warbled and insects buzzed . . . and sometimes stung as they went after the salt-rich water of the humans' sweat. Pablo's injured face twisted in frustration, ignoring the pain the expression must cost him to pay attention to instincts that had kept him alive through years at the focus of a clever, unceasing, and utterly merciless hunt.

"There is something wrong," he said softly. "I thought I heard engines, very faint and then a very little bit louder, but now there aren't any. I do not know what's wrong, but they should have been getting *fainter* before I lost them."

Just then Röhm's face turned westward, toward the narrow cleft in the mountain wall they were heading for, and he swore . . . also softly. The others all followed his eyes. A finned orca shape was drifting forward there, just clearing the pass and then rapidly gaining altitude by virtue of the way the ground dropped steeply away beneath it to the east. The airship was a hundred meters long . . . a hundred American yards, or near enough . . . and a quarter that at its broadest point, and a few minutes put it nearly at a level with their position high on the mountainside. The long aluminum-and-glass gondola slung below was a third of the length, suspended from the interior bracing keel that gave semirigids their name, and it had a ball turret at each end with twin machine-guns.

Horst knew the type well, since the German Navy had outright copied it—both sides had been doing that with various gadgets since the war started or even before—and it should have been accompanied by a continuous racking snarl from the two big radial engines that stuck out from the gondola on stubby winglike projections on either side. They were silent, and the very modern three-bladed aluminum propellers—most aircraft still used wooden ones—were visible and motionless.

"It must have been disabled," Röhm said quietly in German. "Yankees put off fixing things."

Horst grunted; that didn't *feel* right, and it was too much of a coincidence for it to be right over their heads. Americans *were* sloppy at maintenance by his meticulous Prussian standards, but you had to admit they were good with machinery in their own way. Yet what other explanation could there be? Aircraft engines were started by spinning the propeller, and that had to be done by hand or by truck-mounted engines before takeoff, very much like cranking an auto.

Except for the very largest airships, von Dückler, you dumb-head! Horst told himself, mentally slapping his own skull. *And more autos have self-starters all the time, and the principle is the same!*

The newest, biggest zeppelins were *much* larger than the one he was looking at; three times as long as this semirigid, truss-framed goliaths with up to ten engines each. *They* could stop and start their own engines using compressed-air motors, and some could bring them inboard for repairs. There was no reason the starter mechanism couldn't be built small enough for lesser craft.

Don't expect things to stay the same in fields that didn't even exist *when you were a youngster! Keep up with the pace of change or die!*

He unslung his R-13 and slowly brought it to his shoulder, resting the forestock in the crutch of a twisted pine and holding his left hand to shadow the end of the telescopic sight so that there would be no chance of a reflected flash of light from the lens to catch the eye of the crew of the airship. The semirigid sprang closer. It was mostly painted in a light blue-gray so it wouldn't stand out from the sky to a surface observer at sea; for the rest it bore U.S. Navy markings, a white five-pointed star on the tail fins and an identification number, ZNMP-22.

The name painted across the blunt bows was some obscure Yankee joke: *Sock-Two-Pussy*, showing an octopus with a boxing glove on each of its tentacles punching at two cats with *Pickelhauben* on their heads— the spiked cloth-covered leather helmet German troops had worn until the more practical coal-scuttle-shaped metal *Stahlhelm* replaced it last year, and which was still used on ceremonial occasions when your skull wasn't likely to meet shrapnel or shell fragments.

More importantly, the crew seemed perfectly at ease, three of them on either side leaning out of the gondola windows, scanning the valley below with heavy binoculars on flexible mounts—the airship must be steady enough for that, particularly without the vibration of the engines to make everything a blur as the optics moved . . .

"At a guess, they've got a model with self-starting engines now," he said, and repeated it in Spanish. "So that they can switch them off and drift when the wind is in the direction they want to go—it extends the range for surveillance work. And you can't hear them coming."

Röhm grunted and nodded; there was nothing wrong with his wits, especially on matters military. Pablo wasted his breath on a long sequence of liquid insults mostly involving the airship's and its masters' mothers and sisters, asserting their lack of morals and the thousand unknown fathers of their offspring to the last generation, also alleging bestiality, blasphemous hostility to God, His Mother, and the saints, and intimate relations with devils and domestic animals and siblings.

Pablo finished cursing and added: "I hope Miguel is keeping a sharp lookout. He is a good man, but he gets into a rut and thinks of nothing but the task before him."

The guerilla party had split in two after the attack on the mule-train, to leave fewer tracks while they put as much distance as they could between themselves and pursuit; a couple of drenching afternoon thunderstorms had helped, but they could *feel* that someone was dogging their trail relentlessly, and they didn't have the numbers to split off an ambush team to buy time.

It wasn't much like combat as he'd experienced it in Europe . . .

More like hunting, he thought. *From the game's point of view. Or like undercover intelligence work, or like something halfway* between *that and fighting.*

Miguel and ten others—two painfully wounded, with blisters from the mustard gas or the clinging muck from the firebombs—had taken the easier, lower path while the fittest went along the mountainsides. That kept the two groups roughly level, the easier passage balancing the greater strength, and the upper party had a better view along their back-trail.

Horst turned his attention to the valley as soon as he'd checked that they all had good overhead cover. It was steep-sided and there was little in the way of flat land at its bottom; there was a seasonal stream, which had pools now and a trickle between them, and heavier overhanging trees, oaks and other broad-leaf varieties he didn't recognize. Except that one type looked a little like poplars and were letting fly with seeds attached to some odd downy cottonlike stuff that floated on the breeze like warm snow. He scanned along the stream, slowly and carefully; it was five or six hundred meters away and about the same distance lower, though the x3 scope brought it much closer, close enough that hummingbirds—little living jewels like crosses between birds and dragonflies and like nothing he'd imagined before he first set foot on this continent—showed as tiny blurs going past.

Ja, he thought. *There they are.*

Miguel was in the lead, a rifle in his hands and his head swiveling alertly . . . but unfortunately only at ground level. The rest followed him, the *soldaderas* helping along the worst-injured, and several more armed guerillas bringing up the rear. They were doing well . . .

Except that they haven't noticed what's hanging over their heads. Pablo is right: Miguel is used to listening for aircraft and it's going to get him killed and possibly me too. Because if I can see them from here, then the airship . . .

As he watched, a set of blurred streaks shot out from the gondola, the *thumps* running up the rock and pine woods of the mountainside, and an instant later echoing back from the other side of the valley. Then the streaks burst with harsh *crack* sounds that echoed likewise, turning into round puffs of blue and red smoke.

Signals, Horst thought grimly.

"*Miguel, Miguel, du bist total am Arsch*," Röhm said.

Horst saved his breath; Miguel *was* utterly fucked, but there was no need to make a joke of a brave man's impending death.

At the same time the airship's engines coughed, sputtered, shed wafts of smoke, and settled to their usual droning roar. It turned as purpose came back to its drifting passage, heading into the wind from the west and then throttling down until it hung nearly motionless above the party of guerillas. The machine-gun turrets flexed and turned, but it didn't try to come down low enough to use them, not yet. Individual rifle shots weren't much threat to a giant bag of hydrogen, but Horst was grimly certain they didn't need to take any risks.

Miguel visibly started and probably cursed; Horst could see his mouth moving, and his fist shaking at the great shape hanging in the sky above him, and behind him the others ran into the forest and took cover. Then the guerilla jerked around, ignoring the airship and grasping his rifle as if it were a life ring at sea. A perceptible instant later Horst heard what the man down in the valley did. Human voices, distant but shrill and loud for all that, a shrieking with a barking chant in it:

"*Kie-kkkkkkk-oooooOOOOOOhhhh-ak-ak*," endlessly repeated, a saw-edged rising and falling ululation; he instinctively knew it was a hunting cry made as men burst into an all-out sprint to close with their prey, howling every time a foot struck the ground.

"*Cazadores de cabezas!*" Pablo shouted.

Headhunters, Horst thought; he'd heard enough to be fairly sure it was truth, not just slandering an enemy.

Pablo turned and began a plunge downslope, toward his fellows, the assault rifle in his hands.

He really is a hasty man, *but there's nothing wrong with his guts or instincts*, Horst thought. *Though it's a wonder he's still alive. There are old soldiers, and bold soldiers, but few old, bold soldiers.*

In the same moment he grabbed the collar of the guerilla's shirt and jerked him back—tensely and cautiously, ready for a rattlesnake-swift knife strike. He wasn't worried that Pablo would turn the rifle on him; the Mexican was too good a soldier at this peculiar type of fighting to fire and so pinpoint his own location with a pursuit closing in.

"No!" the German barked. "Think, man! If you kill a headhunter or two before they kill you, do you think Roosevelt will rage and weep? Will they mourn in the streets of Chicago or New York?"

Though some woman might weep and scream with grief for a husband or a brother or a son, in a hut far away amid hot jungle hills.

"We are here to do the Yankees *real* harm! We cannot do that if we die in some meaningless skirmish!"

Pablo did *start* to go for a knife, then stopped himself with an effort that left him shaking and wet with harsh-stinking sweat.

"You are right," he grated in a voice of utter hatred as Horst released him. "Fuck your mother, you are right. I will stay here with you and your friend the murdering *jodedor*. But do not speak more now, or I will kill you."

He stalked away and melted into cover, nearly invisible even though Horst knew where he was. Horst slid back to his own watching position; considering that men who'd been Pablo's comrades for years were now certainly doomed, it said something that the Mexican was able to overcome his impulses. Or possibly the prospect of hurting the people he hated was what tipped the balance, more revenge than he'd thought possible in years.

"We need him," he said warningly in German. "We need him very badly. Chango is as brainless as one of his mules but Pablo is cunning, he knows the area well, and he has contacts in Jerez and Zacatecas."

"Yes indeed," Röhm replied, good humor in his tone.

Horst looked over; the Bavarian had laid his small binoculars down on the brown rock before him and was unfastening his canteen.

"Were you afraid I would be angry with the good heroic Pablo?" he said.

They were speaking softly, but not whispering. The distance would make even a bellowing shout faint. Röhm went on:

"No, no, we *do* need him. Besides that, first, while I might be angry if you, my dear comrade, said such hurtful words . . . nothing any of these chattering brown monkeys says really matters except as *I* choose. And second, hmmmm, what was it the old Greeks said, about self-knowledge?"

"γνῶθι σεαυτόν," Horst said, who'd had the classics drummed into him like any upper-class youth. "*Gnōthi seauton*. 'Know yourself.' One of the maxims inscribed at Apollo's sanctuary at Delphi."

"Exactly. Just what I was thinking of! Clever, clever fellows, those Greeks! Though the language wasn't my best subject at the *königliches Maximiliansgymnasium*."

Röhm grinned. "And in fact I *am* a murdering *jodedor*, as our good friend Pablo said. Why be angered by the truth? And now the Yankees are putting on a lovely show for us on this fine day after a walk in the clean country air, though the refreshments could be better. A nice tall mug of *Rauchbier* and a plate of *Thüringer Rostbratwurst* with more of the beer sprinkled on while they cook, and done on a hot grill rubbed with bacon, I think, by preference. And a heap of fried potatoes. But even without beer and sausage and potatoes, life is good, Horst, *mein Bruder*. Life is very good."

Horst turned his head to hide a grimace of distaste and put his eye to the scope on his rifle. He didn't fear Röhm, which he suspected put him in a distinct minority among those who knew the man, but he couldn't afford to fight with him either.

You use what you must for the Fatherland, he thought.

His mind called up memories, flashes and glimpses. The rambling ancestral *Schloss* of the von Dücklers, the village and church huddled close by as he rode back across the fields, with the snow of an iron winter creaking beneath the hooves of his horse. The windows glowed yellow in the dusk through leafless trees and the chimneys trailed smoke up to a gray sky . . .

His father's quiet blaze of pride and the hand on his shoulder with a brief *Like a von Dückler, boy!* when he'd come home from the Marne with a captain's insignia and the Iron Cross on his tunic.

His mother's face in lamplight and her touch as she sat by his bed while he tossed with fever as a boy.

A stab of unexpected wistful envy as he watched his older brother Eric kneeling and laughing as his child made his first staggering steps away from his mother and toward his father's outstretched hands, waving and crowing triumphant laughter as he stumped and staggered on chubby legs through mown grass starred with fallen petals of cherry blossom.

They need me. My Heimat *and the Fatherland need me, need men like me, in this new world of ice and fire. For them I will endure anything . . . and do any-thing. Anything at all.*

He put his single eye back to the sight. For long moments there was nothing but branches and pine boughs moving in the wind, and what followed was more a thing of sounds rather than what he could see.

But the sounds painted a vivid picture for someone who had the experience to interpret them, them and the occasional glimpse of muz-zle flashes.

A flurry of shots—the familiar slow *bang-bang-bang* of bolt-action rifles, yelling, the swifter snapping *ptank-ptank* crack of the American semi-autos like the one he carried, the typewriter crackle of machine pistols, the muffled *bumpf!* of a grenade and then another, a brief red wink visible through the branches of the trees in the shadow they cast. The distinctive rattlesnake stutter of a Lewis light machine-gun squeezing off neat professional short bursts. A high thin screaming, pain this time, cut off in a way anyone who'd been on battlefields would recognize. Silence fell for a moment, and then the yammering exultant brabble of the headhunter war screech again.

One of the *soldaderas* broke into view, dashing across the clearing with her skirts kirted up and her rifle at high port. A flash of steel came from behind her, pinwheeling through the air and striking in her thigh. She went down with a scream of shock and tried to rise and fell again and lay scrabbling at the earth. Miguel dashed out of cover from the other side of the opening, obviously trying to rescue her and drag her back to his position.

"*Dummkopf*," Röhm said crisply, watching through his binoculars. "And a *dead* stupid-head, soon enough."

Horst nodded agreement, unconscious of the gesture until it disturbed his sight picture and he had to set it again, though he sympathized more with the guerilla leader than Röhm probably did. You hated to leave one of your own down and wounded, but tactical necessities had to take precedence. He'd seen times where four or five men were lost trying to go after a single casualty crying for help on ground raked by enemy machine-guns, and where whole companies could have been decimated by chain reactions of unthinking heroism if a leader hadn't clamped down an iron discipline.

You had to be ready to die for your battle comrades, just as a good company commander had to love the unit he led like his own sons, but the mission came first and to accomplish that you had to be ready to kill the thing you loved.

He'd expected someone to simply shoot Miguel as he ran for the bait, but instead a figure broke cover across the oblong clearing. It was a blur, moving very fast and casually wrenching free the blade that stood in his first target's leg as he passed without breaking stride, bringing a fresh but weaker scream from the *soldadera*.

There are a lot of big veins and arteries in the thigh, Horst thought clinically.

He didn't like killing noncombatants, though it didn't bother him overmuch when necessity demanded it, but a woman who took up arms *was* a combatant. And as he knew from experience—he touched his eye patch reflexively—sometimes a dangerous one.

Dead in a few minutes at most with a wound like that.

Miguel had a pistol in his hand, an old-style revolver where the hammer had to be thumbed back for each shot. He managed to get off two, both missing. Which was no surprise; most men *did* miss in combat, even at close range. Horst didn't and he didn't think Röhm would either, or Pablo, but they were all unusual types in their own ways.

Miguel threw up the revolver to block the arc of steel that came at him. Instead his hand flew free still clutching the weapon, and he had a fraction of a second to stare at the spouting stump before there was another flash across his throat and he fell and flopped like a landed fish for an instant. The one who'd killed him ran on, halting and crouching low in the shadow of a tree for a long moment.

That let Horst see him clearly. He was a little man—that was clear from the relative size of the R-13 rifle slung over his back—who seemed to be built out of wire and sinew, a quivering readiness for motion clear despite the bagginess of the American-style uniform. His hollow-cheeked face was brown, browner than most Mexicans Horst had seen, his narrow black eyes darting around in utter wariness, with high knobs for cheeks and a button nose, and a rat-trap mouth open wide for a gasp or a grin.

His filed teeth showed blood-red, and so did the spittle that drooled down his chin. Objectively Horst knew it was just the juice of the betel nut that people in the man's part of the world chewed the way Europeans used tobacco, but something in his mind recoiled at the sight. That wasn't helped when the headhunter raised the dripping blade in his hand and casually licked it; the weapon was twenty inches of broad steel blade curved like a saber, but sharpened on the *inner* side, with an odd-looking flared hilt curving inward more sharply still. He'd heard that it was called a *Ginunting* in those far-off isles. Besides that the man wore a floppy canvas bush hat over a red headband that held frondlike feathers at the rear to dangle down his neck, and around that neck a string of small bones with a tuft of fur or hair. Long ornaments dangled from the upper lobes of his ears on both sides.

The silence stretched, and then a whistle sounded, three short blasts and a long one. Evidently that was the *all clear* signal, because the man Horst was watching relaxed—at least as much as he ever did—and walked back into the clearing. He was definitely grinning as he raised Miguel's head by the hair and chopped it free of the neck with one swing of the inward-curved blade in his hand. He threw back his head and gave that barking, moaning shriek again, and a dozen more like him faded out of the brush, like figures appearing in a magician's act. Many of them carried heads of their own and the blade they'd reaped them with in the other hand; they formed a ring and began a hopping, hip-pumping, stamping birdlike dance, wheeling in circles with knees deeply bent and arms outstretched to either side. Miguel's killer danced in the center, stopping occasionally to hold the head high, yelling with glee.

An American officer stalked into the open space, a tall man with a red mustache and a rifle held muzzle up with the butt on his right hip, but nevertheless wearing the same necklace and headband and ear-ornaments as his men. One of them passed him a bloodied weapon, and he absently licked it before returning it to the man who'd offered it; the headhunter visibly swelled with pride as he strutted off.

"Arse-licking teacher's darling," Röhm chuckled; he was watching the same scene through his binoculars. "I bet he always brought an apple to school."

The officer's whole posture and wagging finger spoke of a scolding. In similar circumstances German soldiers would have braced to attention, and Horst thought American regulars would have done the same—though even Yankees *probably* wouldn't have been dancing around waving severed heads amid sprays of blood in the first place. The Rangers shuffled their feet and looked down with sulky pouts instead; one was kicking his toe into the dirt like a schoolboy caught throwing spitballs at a rival. At a final decisive gesture they wiped and sheathed their steel, stuffed the heads into bags that closed with drawstrings and put those in their knapsacks, unslung their rifles and machine pistols, and trotted off in a springy, tireless, businesslike fashion.

"The Yankees' little brown monkeys are *serious* little brown monkeys," Röhm observed. "Ah, they're bringing the airship down."

The red-haired American officer raised a flare pistol and fired into the air, the shell bursting green. In response the airship hovered overhead and dropped a cable; men on the ground secured it to a huge boulder, and a winch whined until the craft was down below a hundred meters, its nose much lower than its tail and not far above the tips of the pines. A bosun's-chair arrangement was dropped next, out of an open door that had a boom and pulley; wounded men, bodies, and bundles of gear began shuttling upward, and other bundles that probably held food and ammunition came down.

"Efficient!" Horst said. "They'll lose a lot fewer of their hurt if they can get them out fast by airship like this. The first couple of hours are the crucial ones with a serious wound. And bringing in supplies like that means lighter loads and faster movement."

"Wouldn't be practical if anyone was shooting at them," Röhm remarked, rising and slinging or tucking away his gear.

"Right," Horst said, picking up his own rolled blanket and slinging it from left shoulder to right hip. "Time to go."

He called to Pablo: "Let's get some distance before the headhunters are after us. That pass the airship came over is open now and they haven't caught *our* trail; we can go west and circle back farther south. With some luck they'll never know we were here."

They moved off briskly, but with due care for cover, the men with the assault rifles before and behind for emergency firepower at close range, Chango behind the leader and Horst second to last. He spoke over his shoulder to Röhm.

"Someone is extremely sensitive about guerilla activity in this area—that wasn't everyday precautions we just saw."

Röhm nodded. "Colonel Nicolai was right. The Americans have put their V-gas factory in Zacatecas and they're ramping up security in the area. They're calling it the Dakota Project—the time we wasted sending men to that stretch of nowhere! For a while Nicolai was convinced it was in that place where Teddy the Cowboy had his ranch! That let them get it nearly finished while we were rushing around an empty steppe and they picked our men off. But they're about finished and that's the best time for an attack, and they know it."

He paused and said thoughtfully: *"Wahrscheinlich haben sie dafür einen Großkopferten aus dem Stab geschickt."*

That meant he thought they'd probably sent in a hotshot trouble-shooter from HQ to oversee it—though *Großkopferten* meant literally "big-head."

Röhm used an English idiom next, rather badly, with malice afore-thought and a grin in his voice:

"Or maybe a *Großkopfjäger*, a big headhunter. But the headhunter won't know about the toys I brought. The Yankee Big-Head-Hunter doesn't want to be our brother, so we'll use my toys to . . ."

"So schlag' ich dir den Großkopf ein," Horst said with a slight cruel smile; that completed an old saying Röhm had been playing on, with an appropriate modification. "Smash his Big-Head."

The original went:

Und willst du nicht mein Bruder sein
So schlag ich dir den Schädel ein.

Which meant: If you don't want to be my brother, I'll crack your skull.

"Exactly, Horst. Exactly."

SIX

City of Zacatecas
State of Zacatecas
United States Protectorate of México
June 19th, 1917, 1917(b)

Luz followed her usual morning routine, developed since she and Ciara started routinely sharing a bed: rise first, start breakfast, brew coffee, and wave a cup of it near Ciara's nose until her eyes blinked blearily open, before kissing her.

"Up! Up, slugabed!" she said, retreating and holding up the cup. "By the Power of the Omnipotent Bean of Wakefulness I conjure and command thee to arise from the inky depths! *¡Adelante, mi corazón!*"

The younger operative staggered into the breakfast nook of the little apartment in the government guesthouse, managed to tie the belt of her robe over her nightgown on the second try, and slumped into a chair, blinking in the bright morning light from the courtyard. Luz set the coffee in front of her and poured in thick yellow Jersey cream—which must be from the Durán hacienda—and two spoonfuls of sugar.

"What do we do today?" Ciara asked. "More studying of the files?"

After she swallowed a mouthful of the coffee; her morning persona grew rapidly more lively with caffeine.

"No, I think we've got all that. Today we play tourist, mostly; that means a lot of walking up- and downhill, so wear good stout shoes."

"I will . . . oh, my goodness, that smells wonderful! Seafood and onions and . . . what on earth is it?"

"You *are* waking up," Luz said with a grin, whisking a small ceramic dish that bubbled gently in from the small kitchen with its compact, efficient modern gas range and icebox. "It's something my mother liked for breakfast."

"Cuban, it is?" Ciara asked.

"Sort of. *Huevos a la Malagueña*. Shrimp in lime juice, sweet red pepper sautéed with onions and garlic in olive oil, stir in tomato paste, wine, saffron, and bay leaf, put it all in a dish and break the eggs on top, sprinkle some cilantro on them, and bake for twenty minutes or a bit more. There was a baguette—someone must have opened a French bakery in town, of all things—so I toasted some of that to go with it. There's a Copeman Electric Stove Company automatic toaster, the very latest thing."

"Shrimp and wine and olive oil and saffron and French bread? And our hostess said she had *a few basic things* put in the kitchen here!"

Luz took a bite herself, making no comment. She detected a slight tinge of the hum of the wasp in the words, and it wasn't even really unfair. Julie had been cheerfully uncomplaining of hardship, filth, and squalor back when they were in the field, but she had old-money ideas of what constituted the *civilized basics* at home.

Instead Luz turned back to work:

"I need to develop a sense for this place again—it will have changed a good deal since my last visit—and you need to pick one up. Besides, it's what our cover identities would do if they were really traveling around scouting places for technical schools for girls. *And* we'll make contacts. You can't say ahead of time which will be useful, but *some* of them will be. And *you* need to take it easy for a little while to get acclimated to the altitude—that hits some people hard. Say so if you feel you can't catch your breath."

Ciara frowned a little. "It's a pity we're *not* looking for places to put technical schools for girls," she said. "How I could have used something like that when I was younger! Secretary Addams is *so* wise to set them up, and they need it here even more."

Luz grinned to herself. She agreed that the program was very worthy, but she also very much doubted that any vocational institute, even those established by Secretary of Education Jane Addams, could have outdone what her lover had accomplished by self-education and correspondence courses and the help of her aunt Colleen the unofficial accountant and amateur mathematician, and honorary auntie Treinel the certified high school teacher. Students at a conventional coeducational high school might well have mocked and frightened her out of pursuing her native talents in science and technology, which would have been a crime . . . and was also an unofficial reason Secretary Addams was establishing separate institutions for young women.

Though Stanford's engineering faculty, as the war allows . . .

"Fear not, *mi amor*," she said. "There *is* exactly such a program just getting started now down here, and we can probably swing something for Zacatecas if we feel it deserves it. Uncle Teddy and the Director tend to smile when you ask for favors for someone *else*, so it doesn't draw down our . . . line of credit. We need as much of that as we can get, frankly, being circumstanced as we are."

Ciara swallowed convulsively, stopped, and sat upright, her busy fork halted in midair as a realization struck.

"Does . . ." she almost squeaked, and went a little pale. "Luz! Does the *president* know about . . . about you and me?"

Luz's eyebrows went up. "Well, I'd be extremely surprised if he didn't, sweetie. He's a brilliant man, a polymath genius, the smartest president we've ever had bar none. Brilliant about people, too; I've never met a better judge. You *danced* with him at that barbecue we had at the *Casa* on New Year's! And we haven't exactly been hiding our light under a bushel."

"A lot of men don't pay . . . pay attention to women?" Ciara said hopefully. "If you know what I mean. They miss things?"

"I certainly do know," Luz said.

She'd taken advantage of that weakness more often than she could count in the unforgiving trade she plied. It had helped keep her alive, and made quite a few oblivious men very dead.

"But Uncle Teddy?" she went on, shaking her head. "He *looks*, and he *listens* and *notices*. Did you think he didn't know about . . . oh, Secretary Addams and Mary Smith? Uncle Teddy and Addams have been close political allies for years now—she gave the speech putting him up for the nomination at the convention in 1912, and people are *still* talking about how daring that was!"

"You think he wouldn't mind, then?" Ciara said hopefully.

"Not a chance, sweetie. He's a sincere and honest Victorian prude— I'm morally certain he's never touched a woman he wasn't married to, for instance, and as rich, powerful, handsome, charming men go that makes him a prodigy—so I very much doubt he *approves* of us, or of her. But she's useful to the country and the Party, and as for us . . . my *papá* went to Cuba with him in the Rough Riders, he was good friends with my parents after that, and he watched me play with his children as a little girl and told me stories. And most of all you and I have both done the United States very great service, and with Uncle Teddy the country always comes first. After the Breath of Loki . . . and Projekt Heimdall on top of that . . . nothing else even comes *close*."

"Oh," Ciara said, breathing out and taking a big gulp of water. "You frightened me a bit there, darling!"

"Sorry, sweetie. I wish we didn't have difficulties that way, and in an ideal world we wouldn't. But in *this* world we do—and you are so utterly worth it."

That got her a brilliant smile, and Ciara returned her attention to the spicy richness on her plate.

"I'll want to look at the Dakota Project plant site, and the construction," Ciara said after a few moments of consumption. "Plans are one thing, actual machinery another. I'll need to walk over it to see the potential vulnerabilities—hopefully starting soon while it's still new-built. I don't see what you and I can do to increase security at the plant, but maybe something will come to me."

"We'll need to arrange excuses for that. We don't have to do *exactly* what our covers would do, but we have to retain their general rhythm. And we'll have clandestine meetings ourselves with various panjan-drums, but discreetly, also to avoid blowing our cover. I'm going to avoid the FBS as long as I can—in terms of concealment, they have trouble remembering to button their flies after using a toilet."

Ciara giggled and then looked thoughtful. "Speaking of covers, how has Julie kept the station secret?" she said.

Luz chuckled. "Since 1913? She hasn't, that's how. You can't, not when you're operating out of a stationary HQ in a city of forty thou-sand. Not everyone knows, but everyone who's *interested* knows, or strongly suspects. She can keep *some* things secret, though: the identity of sources, safe houses like this, and so forth. And it helps to keep the *pretense* of Universal Imports up; you don't have to ram something into people's eyes. Can you just imagine putting the winged dagger over the door?"

Ciara rolled her eyes in agreement. The Black Chamber's blazon—produced by *el jefe* himself back at the foundation, and fitting his ro-mantic, boyish love of adventure—showed a double-edged dagger point-down between eagle's wings, with the All-Seeing Eye in a pyra-mid over the blade.

From the shadows, steel . . .

"We don't even have that at headquarters," Ciara chuckled; they'd gone there for a second debrief on the Heimdall mission a few months ago, mostly for her to talk to scientists. "Not outdoors! It's . . . it's *ostenta-tiously* plain there. But what if someone saw us at Julie's?"

"Sometimes a visible outpost can be useful as a trap," Luz commented.

"So you can sneak up on people while they're looking at it and kick them in the backside?"

Luz smiled and took a bite and picked up one of the papers.

"Exactly! And it's not a problem for us; part of Julie's job is to keep an eye on newly arrived gringos in her territory, particularly Protectorate employees, so being invited there when you get in is par for the course, though most won't get a nice dinner and a chat about old times and a complimentary pistol. And she's openly part of the social scene here; the people we're supposed to be would need to liaise with the local power structure. If everyone's suspect, nobody in particular is."

The papers included the *Mexican Herald*, the English-language newspaper from the capital; nowadays it was the Protectorate's unofficial official organ along with its Spanish-language equivalent, *El Progresivo*, also helpfully provided. Luz propped the first up against the saltcellar, unlikely to be needed with this meal. It was important to keep up with the world and not get too locked into professional tunnel vision. Things were changing, and very rapidly indeed. The world where she'd have to spend the rest of her life was in the process of being born.

Let's see . . .

"Greece and Portugal are dropping out of the war," she said. "The Portuguese and the Spanish and the Italians are forming a League of Latin Neutrals. Or *Brotherhood of the Utterly Terrified*, really."

"I don't blame Portugal—the British left the Portuguese division behind in France," Ciara said; she was never going to like the British Empire.

"And the British are handing over most of Africa to the USA," she said, then winked at Ciara's surprise and went on: "The Union of South Africa."

"That must cark Lord Protector Milner, giving all that to Botha and Smuts," Ciara said, with a degree of *Schadenfreude*. "They having fought the English back when I was a little girl and they made them look so silly, the whole great empire taking all those years to beat a few little farmers riding about on ponies. And Milner was so cruel to the poor Boers!"

If the British Empire had invaded hell, people of the Fenian persuasion would have raised volunteers to aid the satanic host against the Saxon aggressor. She didn't explain that the union was getting millions of British refugees as well as millions of square miles of—mostly already inhabited—territory, and wouldn't be run by Boers much longer, thus finally fulfilling one of Milner's fondest dreams back when he'd been Imperial proconsul there at the turn of the century.

Instead Luz held the paper up and tapped a headline: "And Ireland, including Ulster, is to get a Home Rule parliament," she said.

"*Éirinn go Brách!*" Ciara said cheerfully: "Ireland Forever!" Softly: "Colm and Da would be so happy. They'd have preferred a republic, of course, but this is . . . very good."

"Lord Protector Milner says Britain, Australia, and South Africa are all to have local parliaments too," Luz said, reading on. "And India. The five will be of equal standing, and have equal representation in an imperial parliament set over all to deal with the Army and Navy and trade, the currency and other joint matters . . . it'll be meeting in New Delhi in January 1920 . . . suitably out of bomber range of Germany. Kipling's there writing a poem about it."

The rest of the war news amounted to inconsequential skirmishing, mostly in southern Palestine and Mesopotamia between the British-Indian forces and the Ottomans, and some air fights over the English Channel and raids with bombers carrying what were coming to be called *conventional weapons*; all unpleasantly final for anyone killed there and their relations and friends, but small-scale.

Plus the grim and endless naval guerilla between the U-boats and the USN and Royal Navy. It was an odd feeling, to have the Eastern and Western Fronts both shut down after three years of epic bloodletting . . .

The remainder was filler. One article extolled the success of the Burnham-Duquesne plan to introduce hippos in the bayous of Louisiana as a solution to the high price of beef. Which was at least more interesting than Governor Haynes's promise in California to work with the Bureau of Reclamation to create fifty thousand new family farms in the Central Valley and Imperial Valley irrigation projects—very worthy and very dull, unless you wanted to start a farm near Bakersfield and grow raisins while turning into one yourself. And an artist's conception of what the giant new Boulder Dam would look like when it was finished had a certain grim majesty, with a seven-hundred-twenty-six-foot-high American eagle spreading its twelve-hundred-foot wingspan in low relief across the face.

And last but not least, a triumphant article proclaiming that ninety percent of the butter in Wisconsin was now made by farmer-owned co-ops, those pillars of the Party's Country Life Program.

"*¡Dios Mio!* Think of that, ninety percent—the millennium is at hand!" Luz said sardonically.

Ciara frowned thoughtfully. "That isn't important?"

Luz chuckled. "Oh, it's important, it's why I told our stockbroker—"

Ciara shook her head and said with lingering disbelief: "Me having a stockbroker!"

Luz had made a will naming Ciara her heir after their first mission, when they moved in together; after their exchange of pledge rings and their return from the second operation, she'd set up a joint trust for her considerable and pleasantly compounding inheritance with both of them as co-trustees holding an undivided half-interest. It had taken a bit of effort to convince Ciara she was serious and wouldn't take no for an answer; just about the same three weeks as it had taken the lawyers in San Francisco to draft something unbreakable and minimally taxed in the way of a transfer inter vivos.

"—told *our* stockbroker to sell our shares in all those milling and meatpacking companies and International Harvester and Dow Chemical's fertilizer company. Eventually the farmers' co-ops are going to own all that . . . though then *they'll* have to deal with the Amalgamated Foods Union and the United Chemical Employees, and much joy may they have of each other. So it's very *important*. It's just not *interesting*, as far as I'm concerned."

Like Uncle Teddy, she found money and finance rather boring . . . which might be due to the fact that they'd both gotten considerable though not huge chunks of property from parents who were working-affluent but not really wealthy by the standards of the *really* wealthy, and so had never expected to have to think much about earning their daily bread.

Unlike him she'd avoided losing her inheritance on harebrained schemes like the ranch in the Dakotas that had cost him his shirt and left him dependent on book royalties and writing for the magazines until he moved into the White House for good.

She patted her lips with her napkin before she went on:

"Let's clean up and get going. We'll see some sights, tour the Plaza de Armas, visit the *mercado* . . . and let some information roll downhill toward us."

"And make contacts?" Ciara said.

"Different forms of the same thing. Something will come up, one place or another. The trick is recognizing it when you see it, and seizing the fleeting chance."

Luz and Ciara both removed their hats, letting them fall down their backs. Then they pulled the white lace mantillas they'd brought over their heads and threw one end to the side and over their shoulders to frame their faces before they entered the local cathedral—technically, the Cathedral of Our Lady of the Assumption of Zacatecas. The infinitely familiar Sunday scent of old incense enveloped them as they touched their fingers to the holy water in the font and crossed themselves, murmuring, "*In nomine Patris et Filii et Spiritus Sancti,*" and then "*Adoro te devote, latens Deitas*" as they faced the tabernacle and bent their right knees to the ground for a moment in the genuflection, that graceful almost-curtsey gesture you learned as a girl, one that briefly left your skirts pooling around your feet.

"Very pretty," Ciara said softly, looking around at the gold-and-white splendors of the interior rising to an octagonal dome. "Not very much like the outside, though!"

Luz nodded. It was more neoclassical than baroque, though elaborate not enormously so since it had been plundered by the anti-clericals during the endless Mexican civil wars of the last century, before Don Porfirio gave the place a generation's respite, and only partially restored since.

Parts of it down in the foundations were nearly four hundred years old, dating back to the original parish church when this was a Spanish outpost in the country of the wild northern Chichimeca barbarians, and the present building had taken a century to complete.

Zacatecas had been a city sixty years before Englishmen started dying like flies of starvation and Indian arrows in their first settlements in Virginia, and it had had mansions and a baroque governor's palace and a Jesuit academy with a library of twenty thousand volumes before a few ragged, quarrelsome Puritan sectaries came ashore in Boston and started hitting each other over the head with ironbound Bibles in their new cod-scented wilderness shantytown.

The original altarpiece had been lost a few generations ago, but there was a very handsome marble-and-gold-foil replacement in a modern European style, contributed according to an inlaid plaque by one Gobernador Don Carlos Seelmann, with Julie Durán clandestinely kicking in help from the Chamber's Special Operations fund, a perfectly legitimate use of the money since it would be intended for public relations purposes. It was Protectorate policy to maintain a formal separation of church and state, as the laws of the Mexican Republic had done, but in a way that was ostentatiously polite and respectful to the faith of the overwhelming majority here.

That had probably done as much as several divisions of infantry to aid in restoring quiet after the main fighting ended; Luz knew it had also been policy set from the top to see that American Catholics were well represented among those in the Protectorate's administrative posts, and to firmly quash any too-public displays of militant Protestantism.

It helped that Uncle Teddy himself was barely even a deist, profoundly uninterested in theology and utterly disdainful of the squabbles between denominations, though he valued religion highly as a tool for spreading proper morals and fellow-feeling. He'd been careful to mention the contributions of Jews and Catholics—and men of Spanish and Indian and part-Indian blood—to the Rough Riders when he wrote his famous regiment's story, and he had bluntly stated more than once that America would have Catholic and Jewish presidents before the century was out.

There weren't many people here early on a weekday, though there was a priest kneeling in silent meditation before the altar, and a few worshippers in the pews telling their rosaries. A group of about a dozen more, women of all ages from their teens through their fifties and dressed in respectable middle-class fashion, were reverently taking up and folding the altar cloths before the images of the saints and the Virgin in the side chapels, and gently placing and smoothing new ones, intricately crocheted and embroidered. They would be taking the old ones to be cleaned and repaired; doing that was a devotion volunteers made in many Catholic countries. And they also seemed to be supervising the much more humbly dressed and much darker women who were sweeping and cleaning, and who were almost certainly their servants.

Luz was conscious of their glances but did nothing more than give a courteous nod in return. She and Ciara lit votive candles before a side altar to the Virgin on the southern side, portrayed as Our Lady of the Assumption, knelt silently with their heads bowed over clasped hands, then respectfully signed themselves with the holy water again as they faced the altar before leaving.

"I do miss going to Mass, sometimes," Ciara sighed when they were outside in the bright midmorning sun, giving the façade another look.

"I too, *mi dulce amor*," Luz said; which was true, though apart from a romantic spell in her early teens she'd never been more than conventionally dutiful, and that had faded. "At least we can look, though!"

The façade of the cathedral was worth any amount of careful attention, though oddly enough it faced the street, with a small plaza where you stepped down. The usual center of a town anywhere in the old Spanish Empire was a square called the Zocalo; Zacatecas had the Plaza de Armas instead. It ran along the *side* of the church and was faced by the old governor's palace. This mining town in the hills of a tough frontier had never had the usual elaborate grid plan imposed on it.

Doing a slow tourist tour of the town fit their cover identities. In contrast to the relatively spare interior, the dusky-rose stone front of the church was a riot of ornamental carving, with engaged statues of Jesus and the Twelve Apostles standing in niches, the Virgin over the entrance, and every inch of the pillars and arches stretching up and up done in a regular froth of Churrigueresque symbolic sculpture, in a local variant of the style even more ornate than its Spanish and Mudéjar originals.

"Though it does look just a bit like Balboa Park in San Diego, where we had that lovely stroll in May," Ciara observed, her eyes methodically memorizing and cataloging dimensions and facts.

Luz smiled at the memory of a carefree holiday. "It's the sort of thing that Goodhue and Winslow copied for the San Diego part of the Panama-Pacific Exposition back in '15, *querida*," she said. "Possibly the very one. Extremely popular nowadays, though personally I think it should be kept for churches and big public buildings—Spanish Colonial is wonderful for houses, but not this particular subvariety of it."

"The Casa de los Amantes is absolutely perfect," Ciara said, threading her arm through Luz's and grinning. "Because it's *our* home."

"Agreed!" Luz looked up again. "You know . . . this reminds me . . . somehow, I couldn't definitely say how . . . of the Aztec Calendar Stone, the Piedra del Sol, they keep in the Museo Nacional in Mexico City. Possibly just the intricacy of the carving."

"I've seen photographs . . . a great round thing, it weighs twenty-four tons. Is it like the pictures?"

Luz shook her head. "No. They don't get the detail, the depth, the subtle effects—whoever did that carving knew what they were doing, knew it right down in their souls, just like the ones who did this. And . . . it has this sense of *impact*, like the cathedral here. It hits the same part of the psyche, but in a completely different way."

"Different? How?"

Luz made a gesture of uncertainty: "I don't think it was actually used as a calendar by the ancient *Mexica*. I think it was an altar to their demon gods, an altar of sacrifice, and it still stinks of blood and fear, not to the nose but to the soul. Even after all these years, you can still feel it. Or possibly I'm being overimaginative."

Ciara shivered and hugged her arm as they turned to go. Nobody thought anything of young women walking arm-in-arm, or usually even hand-in-hand in the United States, though you had to be a little careful about that sometimes; and if anything even less so here in Mexico. It was one of the advantages of femaleness.

Someone cleared her throat. Luz turned smoothly, her cover persona falling into place with effortless ease.

"Yes?" she said politely, smiling and meeting the other's eyes for a moment and then glancing slightly aside. And remembering to keep the appropriate distance, which was a bit less than she would have in, say, New York or London.

When there was a London, she thought with a mental stutter; it wasn't something you adjusted to overnight.

"*Buen día, señora?*" she added, starting the conversation as was appropriate from younger to elder, from the petitioner to she who could give or withhold acceptance.

"*Buen día, señorita*," the woman said, smiling also though less broadly. "*¿Viene de visita?*"

Which was a polite way of asking what she was doing here in town: Open curiosity about a stranger didn't violate local custom.

"*Pues, sí. Hé venido a trabajar a Zacatecas. Y pensé venir a visitar la famosa catedral.*"

Which meant she'd come to work here, and wanted to see the famous cathedral.

That appeal to local pride got her a broader smile; the woman was one of the volunteer ladies from inside, all of whom had followed her in a flock, along with their scrubbing-and-dusting servants putting their gear in bags or baskets.

In her case she was middle-aged and also *socially* a lady, and probably a widow, judging from her mourning black and rather old-fashioned but high-quality dress and from the lack of the weather-beaten and prematurely aged look lower-class women usually had here. Her face had a grim strength, though, obviously in the process of becoming one of those formidable *abuelas* who ended up running so many Mexican families with iron will and hand. Mexican men liked to think they were always in charge of the females in their lives, and in some senses they were. But she'd rarely met one who didn't regard his grandmother with a mixture of love and fear, and dread her disapproval like a small boy.

There was a moment's silence. Luz nodded to the embroidered cloths in the older woman's hands.

"*Habra un festival?*" she said, asking if there was to be a festival.

The *mozas*—the much-more-Indian women who'd been scrubbing the floor; nearly everyone in Zacatecas was a mestizo, but some more so than others—were hanging back listening avidly, and the whole little flock of respectable females were gathering around, trying *not* to appear avidly curious and failing. Though they left the actual speech with the strangers to . . .

Give you odds her husband was a doctor, Luz thought. *Or a notario or something of that order.*

. . . to La Doña del Doctor, as was her right and duty.

"Have you come to hear Mass here?" the widow lady asked, establishing her bona fides before answering the question.

"Ah," Luz said, casting her eyes down and looking sad. "I have fled the battlefield; I have not yet felt ready to come to Mass."

Which was a diplomatic way of saying she didn't plan to, ostensibly at least because she felt too sinful to be worthy.

"But today, today, me and Miss Cavanaugh felt the need to come to see the great church at least," Luz went on.

Ciara smiled and said in her careful Spanish, which was now fully fluent but still distinctly accented, with her *b*-sounds too strong and the flattened *r*'s of a foreigner:

"Such a lovely cathedral! And inside one really feels the presence!"

Luz nodded. "I have seen larger ones, in Mexico City and Puebla, but none finer anywhere," she said, which was quite true and more importantly useful.

That led to an exchange of names; the formidable lady turned out to be a doctor's widow in truth, and named Dolores Gutiérrez y Coa. Luz gave her own as Graciela de Jesús Calderón Menéndez, and Ciara's as Mary Cavanaugh; Irish names were exotic but not altogether unfamiliar in Mexico, since Irishmen had been frequent in Spain's service and some had settled here since, and were known mostly as coreligionists. Nodding once more at the colorful folded cloths in their hands, she asked again:

"Will there be a festival, Señora Gutiérrez?"

"Oh, yes, soon there will be La Fiesta de San Juan Bautista. We take these home to mend and make perfect for the Lord before the celebration."

The celebration of John the Baptist would be toward the end of the month, on June 23 and 24. It had been a safe bet; there weren't any months *without* a saint's day, and a lot of them had festivals attached. It was another thing that drove the more puritanical sort of American crazed down here.

"Would you like to see them?"

"Oh, very much, Señora Gutiérrez!" Luz said.

Ciara nodded enthusiastic agreement. It was more genuine in her case; they'd both had sustained exposure to needlework, as any respectable girl did, but Ciara had enjoyed it more, or at least accepted it as necessary to keeping life going in her milieu, where a lot of clothing and household linen was still handmade or heavily taken in and altered, and everything was repaired and had its life prolonged as much as possible. Lower-middle-class respectability required a world's worth of hidden female labor.

"That is very kind of you, to two strangers such as we," Luz added.

The other women were informed by Señora Gutiérrez, as if they hadn't heard already, that the two strangers were interested in seeing the altar cloths, which made them suitable to talk to. A chattering flock swept up from the plaza and the side of the hill to an iron door in a pink wall that led into a patio, much like Julie Durán's except that it was about half the size and didn't have an active fountain, though there were plantings and flowers and shade in the arcaded corridor that ran around it. There was a bustle of shawls and hats and servants, and brisk commands for water of oranges.

Luz saw Ciara's eyes darting to either side at the remarks that were being made—*Skin like transparent alabaster! So perfect! Those eyes, like fine Chinese jade!*—and the fingers reaching up to touch her hair, obviously itching to pull it down and brush and redo it. It was all perfectly respectful, in fact a mark of friendly, companionable interest and acceptance, just a difference in custom. Those could be startling, though.

"Ladies!" Luz said, smiling and preempting any shocks. "I must make a confession for both of us! Seven months ago, late last year, we were both very ill with fevers, and had our hair cut. Yes, these are wigs! But wigs made of our own hair—see, I will show you."

She reached out and parted Ciara's wig, down to the ultra-fine lace skullcap that underlay it. That exposed a lock of Ciara's own red-blond hair, drawn out through the lace to mix with the wig's tresses and hold it firmly. Half a dozen crowded close to look, exclaiming.

"As you see, exactly the same shades; and the same for me."

That got more exclamations, this time of sympathy and also of admiration for the lace and the superlatively fine needlework that drew the individual hairs so densely through it. The thought of a woman having to crop her hair short was genuinely shocking here, but they recognized the folk treatment for a high fever. They were also interested in the newcomers' clothes, impressed by the workmanship and materials—wool knits weren't common here—and intrigued by the cut.

"These were designed by a French lady. From Paris, but now living in New York," Luz said. "One who escaped recently from the war there."

"*¡Ay!*" one of the younger women said, though she was a childless widow and expected to stay in the background.

Luz's memory picked María Luisa Muñoz Herrera out of the list of introductions.

"The unfortunate one, what she must have gone through, before she found safety! So terrible, what has happened, is happening, in France. All those poor people! Killed by surprise, unshriven, with no chance of the last rites or anyone to bury them in holy ground or mourn them or set out offerings on the Day of the Dead . . . and *los niños* in their cradles."

"Surely God will take the little ones to Himself and Our Lord will comfort them," another said, crossing herself; everyone present followed suit. "The Lady of Sorrows, herself a mother pierced by grief, will intercede for them."

"May it be so." Luisa nodded, but continued: "And Paris gone, the beautiful city, with its cathedrals and churches and great buildings of the past, all gone to nothing . . . War is very hard, war is suffering and loss and grief, we all know that, hasn't Mexico suffered over and over since the time of our grandparents? But this that has happened to Paris, that is a new thing that has arisen and is very bad, very evil. It will beget nothing but more evils."

There were nods and sighs at that; someone mentioned St. Thomas and St. Francis. Another was thankful that old Don Porfirio had died naturally in his Parisian exile, before the disaster. A third crossed herself and murmured that surely God would protect them in the end.

Señora Gutiérrez cleared her throat. "Let us examine the *manteles*, the altar cloths, ladies. We must find all the things that need repair. All must be perfect for the fiesta and for God and the good saint."

The cloths were set out on clean tables in the broad patio, where the strong natural light would reveal any faults, and the gear for repairs was brought out.

All the cloths were on a foundation of fine white linen; many were white-on-white, with broad central areas of drawn threadwork. Ciara helped smooth one. Diamonds, arranged in a lattice pattern, were filled with finely worked designs of spider monkeys, mermaids, women wearing hats and wide skirts, birds of many kinds, flowers, sacred hearts, crosses, and hands.

"This is marvelous work!" Ciara said approvingly, bending close. "So subtle, and so regular. The stitching is very even . . . I cannot see any gaps or mistakes even in this bright sunlight!"

"*Es trabajo devocional*," Señora Gutiérrez said, meaning that it was done as a devotion, an act of worship between the maker and God, a prayer in thread and cloth. "Human eyes may not see it inside the cathedral, but those of the Lord do."

And to be sure, also done for the maker's honor before her family and friends, Luz thought, smiling; most men might not notice the work much, but other women would see a good deal more even in dimness . . .

Other images were done by couching, with gilt threads and purl, very fine gold or silver wire, laid across the surface of the ground and secured by a succession of small stitches, a technique that required an infinite capacity for taking pains to do well, not to speak of creating the images in the first place. That was an art as exacting as oil painting.

Splashes of wax or other stains brought out cloths and bowls of warm water and patient care. Needles were threaded to repair spots worn or frayed, and after a while the strangers were allowed to help with the simplest parts. Conversation didn't stop during any of that, involving a good deal of gossip and teasing, and the two outsiders came in for a cheerful grilling. There were occasional pauses for more water of oranges, little glass cups of *arroz con leche*—which was a sweet creamy rice pudding seasoned with cinnamon and bits of fruit, and biscuits and coffee. Luz had never been invited into a Mexican home, however humble, without being offered something to eat.

"Yes, my father was an engineer in California," Luz said; the best cover stories played with the truth rather than simply trying to cover it up. "My family has lived there for a long time; a hundred twenty years, since the days when it was ruled by Spain. My grandfather's grandfather was an officer in the king's army and received a grant of land when he retired, near the town of Los Angeles. El Pueblo de Nuestra Señora la Reina de los Ángeles de Porciúncula, in full, a very small place then but a city now. Quite a lot of land, fine grazing and good for crops too, but he was blessed with many sons, and his *sons* were blessed with many sons, and so"—she shrugged—"we are not poor, but we are not rich, either."

That put her right in the middle of this middle-class gathering, avoiding the chilling effect of great wealth and the condescension directed at the lower orders.

"Your family kept their land when the gringos came?" someone asked.

"About half of it; there were quarrels, and cheating, but not always, and alliances too."

"Alliances like Concha de Moncada," someone said with a laugh, and there were more sighs, dreamy ones this time by the younger women. "Don Carlos, what a catch. The governor!"

Luz's spying ears pricked up; the governor of this state was a midwesterner named Carl Seelmann, and the de Moncadas were rich mine- and landowners.

I'll have to get Julie to fill me in on the details.

"And so handsome, such a real man, so dashing and brave, a true *caballero*, but *locamente enamorado*—ready to tear out his heart with crazy love for her."

That was accompanied by a dramatic heart-ripping gesture and an expression that was the speaker's idea of romantic agony and looked to Luz more as if something furry and large were biting her foot.

"And a baby coming already! No wasted time!"

The love lives of the upper crust were as much a cherished spectator sport here as anywhere.

Señora Gutiérrez sniffed. "Earthly love is but a path to love of God at best," she said. "So through her, Don Carlos was brought to the Church, to the salvation of his soul, and so his children will be brought up in the true faith."

"Yes, alliances like that," Luz said, blessing the vagaries of Governor Seelmann's heart. "My father's mother was a girl from Maryland . . .

Catholic, of course . . . and his father's sisters married among the new-comers; my cousins in those families do very well now."

Which was true enough in Santa Barbara; half the big ranchers around there had a *Californio* girl in the bloodline, which was regarded as rather chic nowadays provided the *Californio* was sufficiently wealthy and not too dark. In the last days of Mexican California, when a growing stream of Yankee adventurers had already started to settle in, there had been a popular saying that thirty thousand acres of dowry added amazingly to a young lady's charms . . . and that a big ranch was worth a Mass. She was basing this identity partly on a daughter of Francisca De la Guerra she'd gone to school with.

Eventually: ". . . and as the eldest of five girls, I must find work to help them and my mother, when dear Papá died so young," she said.

Which gave her a good daughter's excuse, centered on her family, for being unwed well past the usual age in Mexico. Spinsters weren't unknown here, though they were pitied, especially when they ended up living with relatives as hangers-on, often no better than an unpaid upper servant.

"Mary Cavanaugh" was supposedly an orphan from Chicago, raised by an aunt who acted as housekeeper to a group of priests who taught in a church school, hence the recipient of an excellent education that included tutoring in Spanish.

"So you are here to find locations for schools?" Señora Gutiérrez said.

"Yes, señora. Schools for girls, teaching skills such as nursing, or as accountants and telegraphists and telephone operators—"

And pharmacists and X-ray technicians, but let's not get too esoteric.

"—and the like, to provide respectable employment."

That was routine enough in the United States now not to be much of a novelty anymore, but still a very recent development here.

"Surely girls should marry," Señora Gutiérrez said. "Or take the veil."

"Oh, of course, and most will marry no doubt, such is the way of nature and God's will," Luz said, getting thoroughly into character. "But think, señoras, so many lost their intendeds, or those who would have become their intendeds, in the war here. Others lost their prospects when their families were ruined and have no dowries now. Some such will take the veil—one of my sisters is a novice of the Discalced Carmelites—but not all have a vocation. I do not, and it is a great sin to pretend one falsely. Surely there should be a way for them to win their bread, a way that will not mean hardship for them or their families."

That brought a buzz of interest, especially when she mentioned the wages that sort of work could command—nothing out of the ordinary north of the border, but still very generous here; it would be some time before incomes found a level across the vastly expanded domains ruled from Washington. Though the cost of living was lower here too, not just compared to New York or Chicago, but to places like Little Rock or El Paso.

As Julie pointed out, here it's all a pyramid based on men with oxen and wooden plows, Luz thought. *Even the peak can't get very high on that.*

"I would have thought such things would be put in the capital," Señora Gutiérrez said.

"Ah, the capital already has several," Luz said. "Also it is policy now to put things elsewhere—so that taxes will not always flow from places like this to be spent far away. And there are fewer temptations, problems, *distractions*, for young ladies away from the capital."

That brought a pleased chorus of agreement; one young matron clapped her hands in glee. If there were two things you could usually expect a middle-class audience in a Mexican provincial center like this to agree on, it was that Mexico City was a vampire sucking their blood, and that it was a den of iniquity and sin besides. Fortunately, the Protectorate actually had such a policy and program; the Black Chamber operatives were simply impersonating its agents.

And of course the Mexico City crowd think of these people as rubes, hicks, and dullards who deserve to be plucked, Luz thought.

———————

"What a charming group of ladies!" Ciara said a few hours later, waving over her shoulder. "And so friendly to two strange Americans."

"Well, it helps that we're Catholic," Luz said. "Which incidentally is hard to fake convincingly. And that my assumed name was Mexican, and of course that we both speak the language. Señora Gutiérrez is too shrewd and too strong-minded to be safe to be around much for honest spies, but I think a couple of the others might be quite useful as sources."

"That young widow, Luisa Muñoz, for example?" Ciara said.

"I liked her . . . You think she might be pro-American?"

"Do I think that she wants us to rule Mexico? No. I doubt a tenth of them are, in *that* sense of the term, and that's being optimistic.

"I did get the distinct impression she didn't actually dislike us, and that she thought the Germans were much worse," Ciara said, with a shudder. "Which is true. That horrible thing at Castle Rauenstein . . ."

Luz nodded; they'd seen the horror-gas demonstrated there on a regiment of captured Czech deserters, while they were both under-cover as German assets—as a Mexican and an Irish-American revolu-tionary respectively. Though that had only recently become pretense on Ciara's part.

"And she mentioned her husband was killed in the fighting before the Intervention," Luz said. "I'll see if she has a dossier, and which of the factions he was fighting for."

"There's a possibility that she's pro-American in the sense that she thinks we're the best of a bunch of bad alternatives, including some Mexican alternatives. It's just a hunch . . ." Ciara said.

". . . but a hunch is your mind working where you don't notice it."

And that part of my mind has a lot of hands-on experience, she thought; she didn't think that was vanity, but it wasn't something you said aloud. *Nice to see my beloved educating hers.*

"I see what you mean, but even if she is, what would she know?" Ciara said.

"Possibly nothing, possibly more. Men tend to dismiss women's gossip for the same reason everyone tends to forget servants have eyes and ears, but tapping that telegraph can be extremely revealing. We should cultivate those ladies if we can, inconspicuously. In particular, take any opportunity you have to get to know Luisa. I think she liked you, too."

Ciara laughed a little self-consciously. "I was never much of a mixer . . . You're the one with the charm!"

Luz shook her head. "Don't underestimate yourself, *querida*. You just didn't have much opportunity, busy as you were."

Running a bookstore, caring for an increasingly ailing father, and self-administering the equivalent of at least a university degree would do that.

"I've noticed that people like you, especially when you're being spontaneous."

"Spontaneous under an assumed name?"

"That's just a matter of living the part. You only need to say something specific from your cover when it comes up—don't volunteer information much, it sounds suspicious."

Ciara nodded gravely; she was always serious about work. Then: "What next?"

"The *mercado*," Luz said, naming the main town market as opposed to the periodic street-and-square variety. "The Jesús González Ortega Market, to get technical. We need to do some shopping . . . and it's where the whole city comes together. I've found it useful before, but nobody will put this identity together with the covers I used then."

The *mercado* was only a block from the cathedral and the Plaza de Armas, a handsome building reconstructed after a fire early in the century, then rebuilt and reopened in the last prosperous days before the revolution, and of which the locals were immensely and rightly proud. The frame was cast iron, the nineteenth century's idea of modernity, but much of the facing and all of it on the Beaux-Arts single-story frontage of square windows and pillared portico on the Avenida Hidalgo was pink stone; the ground dropped away steeply behind, leaving the lower level two stories high and featuring a covered section with a roof supported on cast-iron columns and lacework that had been the last word about the time Luz was born. Every detail had been copied from somewhere else, but the ensemble was intensely Mexican.

They walked in amid the thronging crowds and a white waterfall of noise, buying two *henequén* shopping bags for a nickel from a vendor at the entrance and putting them over their arms.

"Now, this is lively, as lively as the produce stalls down by the Haymarket back in Boston!" Ciara said. With a smile at Luz: "And it's such fun, doing the marketing together!"

"It is, *querida*," Luz said sincerely.

And a bit like old times, she added to herself, looking around.

At butchers' stalls, bakers', and quite literally candlestick-makers', piles of strange gaudy fruits and the first small sweet local peaches and baskets of cherries, piles of potatoes and beets and onions and nameless roots and strings of chilies, vendors of street food tending their pots of beans or vats of hot oil, porters trotting by under enormous stacks of anything at all and everyone shouting their wares or bargaining at the top of their voices under the high arched ceiling . . . which echoed so that you *had* to shout to be heard.

In July 1913 she'd shot a man named Felipe Ángeles, a Mexican commander who was far too honest, popular, and capable to be allowed to continue as head of the city's defenses against the approaching Americans, in a crowd even more densely packed than this, at high noon, not twenty steps from where she stood almost exactly four years later minus one month. She'd faked a stumble with her little FN pistol muffled in a serape folded and pressed against his chest, and then lowered his body to prop him sitting against the wall and drape the colorful rectangle of woven wool from chin to knees. Next to—ironically—a butcher's stall with strings of sausages and piles of chops and tripe and pigs' heads on hooks, which neatly covered any smell of blood.

And all the while she'd loudly berated her supposed husband for spending their money on *pulque* while she did all the work, with a final shrill yell advising him to sleep it off before he came home if he didn't want a *comal* broken over his worthless, lazy, drunken head. The sugar skull had been inconspicuously tucked into his hand beneath the woven wool . . .

None of the few to notice her at all had done anything but laugh at the little bit of street drama while she tucked the cloth around him. Then she'd bought a *gordita* stuffed with pork-rind *chicharrón*, lime, and salsa from a vendor standing beside her nearby tub of hot oil. The seller had given her an approving grin at her treatment of the worthless male of the species, and Luz strolled away eating it with a hand held to keep it from dripping on her blouse, passing between two men assuring each other that General Villa would stop the gringos far north of Zacatecas . . . at the worst, no closer than Torreón, surely . . .

The screams and commotion started when she was crossing to the other side of the road in front of the cathedral just off the Plaza de Armas, probably because someone had seen more blood flowing out between the iron pillars of the market arcade than legitimately deceased porkers could account for.

Luz blinked herself back to the present. "Let's get some greens, chat with some of the sellers, and share a *gordita*," she said to her partner. "And then drop them off at the icebox; I want your green salad nice and crisp, to help your lovely hair grow back."

There was a message waiting on the table of their dining nook, probably courtesy of the secret passage.

"*¡Aja!*" Luz said, as she read the three cryptic lines. "Well, I'll be taking the salad along to a potluck, it seems."

Ciara looked at her and raised a brow. "And when you say *Aha!* in Spanish, it bodes ill for someone, darling. What is it?"

"We're dining with the station chief again, late, and via the confidential entrance. It seems that the airships arrived promptly, and the Rangers made contact with bandits. She'll need to brief us; apparently it's not clear whether they got them all."

SEVEN

Horst von Dückler walked forward along the side of the road, a strip of sacking tied across his eyes, tapping ahead of himself with a staff cut from a mountain ash in the heights a day's walk behind them, and his hand on Ernst Röhm's shoulder. It was mildly, pleasantly warm, a perfect bright summer morning after the rain shower that had drenched them a little earlier, and the air was heavy with the scent of wet new-laid dust from the road and damp turned earth from the fields to either side, of dung from the animals pulling carts and wagons, and now and then the acrid exhaust of motor vehicles or the rattle of bicycles . . . and always of the sweat of steady hard effort from trudging men and women with heavy burdens on their backs.

Odd, he thought. *My sweat smells just a little different from the Mexicans'. And so does Röhm's, even more so. Heavier and . . . thicker. Probably because we grew up eating different foods? I don't imagine Bavarian* Käsespätzle *or Silesian* Himmel und Erde *are too common here!*

Horst heaved a silent sigh at the thought of savory black pudding, fried onions, and mashed potato with apples. He wasn't hungry now, but he found that he was longing for the tastes of home nonetheless.

And the weather, and the buildings, the pale quality of the light and the sound and sight and even the *smell* of his own people.

What he was missing bitterly now was his *Heimat* . . .

Heimat meant homeland in a much more particular and local sense than *Vaterland*, the place where your heartstrings were sunk into the earth, where your ancestors from time out of mind had lived and worked and begotten and given themselves back to the soil that bore them, and where you had grown to manhood in turn.

I am missing my that *rather badly*.

He'd agreed to Pablo's scheme for a disguise even though wearing a bandage across both his eyes brought back unpleasant memories of the nightmares he'd had after waking up with his left eye shot out . . . and convinced it was *both* eyes and he'd be blind for life. It had been very dark and the medic on the U-boat had kept him floating on morphine all the way back to Wilhelmshaven . . .

Waking up screaming again isn't a problem here, they've had their war too.

War smashed minds and souls as surely as buildings and bodies.

Waking up screaming in German, *that would be a problem here.*

A woman who had remained nameless had come in the dark when they left the mountains and dyed his hair with some local herbal juice, and his skin too, and left a similarly nameless bottle filled with more of it. Not too much dye, just enough that a glimpse under his long, baggy, and authentically dirty and smelly *campesino* clothes wasn't going to reveal the almost translucent paleness that was his natural color where he wasn't sun-touched to a honey-hued tan.

He supposed he should be glad the von Dücklers didn't tend to burning and peeling over and over again under a southern sun, or turning permanently brick-red as some did. His oldest brother Karl had fought in China against the Boxers at the turn of the century, and in the German colonies in Africa during the Herero War and the Maji-Maji uprising about a decade ago, postings he'd lobbied and pulled strings and activated family connects to get because he'd been bored to tears with peacetime garrison soldiering. Horst recalled how when he came back from German East Africa his forearms and face and neck had looked theatrically, unnaturally dark against the rest of him when he stripped for a swim.

And now authorities all over the American imperial sphere would probably be looking for a tall fair man with one eye, maybe even the British too, and the French, who were Yankee lapdogs these days. The U.S. military and the Black Chamber *certainly* would be. Fortunately, men with facial injuries were ten for a Pfennig here.

Horst could see reasonably well through the coarse burlap that covered his good eye; the hardest part was remembering to *act* as if he were blind, and tap with the walking stick. A glimpse at the ruined socket of his left eye was enough to prove his bona fides, and a fixed stare made the other look as if it wasn't functional.

Röhm was supposed to be a Mexican combat veteran too—his facial scars made it gruesomely credible—and one so damaged inwardly that he couldn't speak beyond a stammering growl and who acted as his blind brother's guide dog. That would cover his thick German accent. Horst's Spanish was good enough now that if he was very careful and kept to simple things he could pass as a native speaker . . . from some other part of Mexico, and if he gave no reason for people to pay special attention to him; there were nearly as many regional dialects here as there were in Germany, and war and revolution had set people moving.

There were plenty of war cripples too. He'd seen a dozen or more this morning on the road, and anyone who'd been around the detritus of battle would find the physical and mental damage credible enough. Röhm thought the whole thing was hilarious, and occasionally gave a tittering laugh that was both in character with his cover identity's shell shock . . . and entirely sincere.

There is courage, and then there is insanity. I know which I think Röhm suffers from.

The road that led eastward to the town of Jerez was new, made of well-cambered dirt with good ditches on either side and a surface of compacted gravel. It even had modern concrete culverts and small bridges over watercourses—seasonally flooded ones, mostly, which meant they had water in them now—to keep the occasional heavy rains from damaging the surface, which would have made it an excellent road in any rural part of Silesia. The whole thing reminded him of marching through France, down to the trees growing on either side and casting a little shade that felt like a flicker of coolness as they walked by; they were older than the road, twelve-foot saplings transplanted from elsewhere, though about one in ten hadn't survived the process and were being replaced. It was all very un-Mexican, and Horst asked a tactful question.

"Gringo military road, for their troops and wagons and motor trucks," Pablo said quietly.

Which was undoubtedly true, though there were plenty of Mexicans using it right now. For that matter, he thought that Mexicans—some prisoners, and others just poor men glad to swing picks and shovel dirt for their food—had probably done most of the building, with American engineers to direct.

Horst had regretfully shed his German marching boots, but by now his authentically dirty feet had adjusted to the sandals, though they didn't fully share the local peasantry's battered look. Nobody would think the odd machete or knife anything out of the ordinary—they were tools a *campesino* or muleteer needed for his work—so they kept those rather than sending them anonymously in loads of produce as they did the firearms. At least now he had a sound excuse to shave every day, to keep the fair stubble from showing.

"Checkpoint!" Pablo said under his breath. "*Rurales*. And gringo soldiers. They're *mallates*," he added.

Which was an extremely unflattering local word for those of visibly African descent.

The traffic thickened as it slowed, and Horst peered through the coarse fabric. It didn't come to a complete stop; the policemen were waving a good many through. The dozen gendarmes were all Mexican, all uniformed in a baggy outfit much like American Army uniforms but in a khaki-brown color and bearing the marks of the recent rain, and all heavily armed with Colt .45 pistols and R-13 semi-auto rifles or Thompson machine pistols. The local traffic went past the checkpoint at walking pace; now and then *el rural* examining them would motion someone aside for further questioning.

Horst had more than half expected they would be, and he wasn't particularly alarmed when a preemptory wave set them aside to wait.

We're out of the ordinary, and that catches the eye. No way to avoid it.

He squatted on his hams, a posture he'd had enough practice at recently that he could do it without his muscles seizing up, and pulled his sombrero down over his eyes and threw the serape back over one shoulder. Röhm did likewise, taking out a battered packet of cigarettes bearing the picture of a Frenchwoman of the turn of the century smoking a cigarette with pouting lips, and the proud label *El Numero 12*.

Smaller print showed that it was manufactured by a firm calling itself *El Buen Tono, S.A.*, which meant something like *The Fashionableness, Ltd.*

The other German lit three and passed one each to Pablo and Horst, who remembered to wait until his hand was nudged to take it. They were workingman's cigarettes, strong as the devil and biting harsh in his mouth and lungs compared to the Bulgarian and Turkish blends Horst preferred, but vastly better than the *Ersatz* wartime rubbish most people in Germany had been smoking when he left, which smelled and tasted as if it were made of the dried sweepings from the stall of an undernourished horse with a necrotic bowel disease. They had a chance to smoke them to butts and start another before the policeman waved them forward, and by then cool breezes and gathering clouds to the west hinted at more rain to come.

Horst spent the time he had to wait looking over the American soldiers, straining to inconspicuously pick out details through the burlap. There were about a *Zug's* worth, a platoon—a full forty-eight, as specified by the regulation U.S. Army table of organization, unlike the formations of the German army, chronically understrength after years of savage fighting. The gendarmes were horsemen and had picketed their mounts with feedbags on their noses, but four Model T trucks and a Guvvie—a type of little car with all four wheels driven—showed how the U.S. Army troops had arrived.

Horst felt a snarl of envy deep within. Only a few elite units of the *Deutsches Heer* had their own motor transport, even though both the internal combustion engine and the automobile were German inventions; his country had been critically short of petroleum until the recent conquests in Rumania and Russia, and it was still so short of rubber that vehicles in German cities mostly rode on wheels of resilient steel. Though Röhm had told him there were talks underway with the Japanese to supply that and other tropical goods, now that the Trans-Siberian Railway was running again under the new management.

But different *new managements east and west of Lake Baikal.*

He felt a certain amount of resentment at the thought. Germany had broken the Czar's forces, whereupon the Japanese had leapt in to tear off juicy chunks of the defenseless carcass, facing no real resistance, in exactly the same way they'd annexed the French and Dutch colonies in Southeast Asia. Even the Americans couldn't really object, since the Japanese were theoretically their allies and theoretically taking those lands over to keep the Germans out.

Well, we got the better *half of Russia for our pains, and the Japanese are a useful buffer against the Americans in the east. Remember the fable of the dog losing its real bone because it tried to grab at the reflection in the water! There will be a time to deal with them when we have mastered and settled the lands we've taken. Them and the Yankees and the English. Europe is what matters, and we hold that from the Atlantic to the Urals.*

As Pablo had said, the Yankee soldiers were all dark-skinned in varying degrees. Most of them were young, even the lieutenant bent over a map spread on the Guvvie's hood, though the slightly older platoon sergeant had the air of a man who'd *seen the elephant*, as the Yankee saying went. Many were big strapping muscular youngsters, one bigger than Horst himself, just the sorts you wanted to carry a machine-gun or cans of ammunition around a battlefield at the run. Röhm said the Yankees had done surprisingly well in France for green troops, with tactics obviously based on careful observation of the first two years of the war; they'd fought very aggressively too and had learned fast from that bloody experience.

Of course, by then everyone was out of those verdammt *trenches.*

These men had the cocky strut and snap of those sure of themselves, their comrades, and their training; he recognized it . . .

Because that's the way we felt in 1914. And we were almost *as good as we thought we were. Almost* meant two years and a million dead to do what we thought would be over by Christmas.

And they were certainly splendidly equipped, down to the ingenious folding tools they'd used to dig shallow fighting positions in the muddy dirt, what the manuals called hasty entrenching . . . and it was interesting that they had the discipline to dig automatically and uncomplainingly when they obviously wouldn't really need it and it meant soiling their uniforms and more work later going over their gear.

Digging in whenever you stop moving . . . that's good practice. Sweat saves blood. And the right habits keep you alive when you don't have time to think about it.

When another Guvvie arrived towing a two-wheeled trailer that had a smoking chimney, he realized it was what his own army had invented in the 1890s and called a *goulash cannon*, a mobile field kitchen . . . but motorized too.

Which made both Horst and Röhm give grunts of envious *disbelief*; he doubted there was one single motorized field kitchen in the entire German army. A more personal envy struck again when soldiers fetched pails of stew and sacks of cornbread to their comrades before it drove off . . . and a pail of soapy water for them to scrub out their gear when they were through, which was a nice touch. Three of them, the team of a Lewis light machine-gun, were close enough for the travelers to smell the food as they dipped it into their mess tins, and it had more meat in it than anything he'd eaten recently, probably pork.

When you were on the move in heavy fighting, soldiers would sometimes bark, meow, or neigh as they lined up at the goulash cannon, and with good reason. The cooks often replied with a cheerful *No, it's your granny, stupid-head.*

This pork stew also smelled . . .

"Whooo lordy, dat hottah 'n *hell*!" one of them burst out.

Chilies, Horst thought. *They're using local cooks and these Mexicans even put chilies in* chocolate, *by God's Mother!*

What the young men were speaking was about as far from the standard book-English he'd learned as the thick *Schwäbisch* of peasants from the banks of the Neckar was from his own Silesian aristocrat's *Hochdeutsch*, but Horst could follow it more or less. Mostly it was standard soldiers' talk about food and drink and women—they thought highly of the local girls and he was *nearly* sure one had said that tequila was dirt cheap and like being hit up . . . or beside . . . the head with a piece of timber—but there were other things as well, about their last posting, in Jackson, Mississippi.

". . . an' dis offay wid de string tie and de big hat, he say: *You cullud boys sure gots plenty of dem machine-guns*, an Ah say, all polite an respekful laak de standin' orders say: *Yassuh, we does and we knows how to use 'em. We's American fightin' men now, ready to lick Germans an' de whole damn worl' besides!*"

"An' whut he say den?"

"He doan' say nuthin'. But his face pucker up like he take a big bite o' de green persimmon."

The other two soldiers laughed, and the one who'd spoken first kissed his fingers and used them to pat the flat horizontal ammunition drum of the Lewis gun in an affectionate gesture and said:

"De bottom rail o' de fence on top now!"

"Haw! Dat de truf!"

"De Lawd save an' keep Teddy! Do Jesus, I prays he be pres'dent foevah and evah!"

"Aaaaa-men, brutha! I likes dat testifyin'!"

The *rural* finished with the group before them and jerked a thumb.

"You three!" he called. "The ugly stupid ones!"

All three of them dealt with the cigarettes they'd just lit the way a working-class local would, pinching them out with callused fingers and stowing them away. They rose and walked over to where the man stood with his thumbs in his waist belt. He extended a preemptory hand, snapping his fingers, and Röhm held out the pack to him; the *rural* took it, pulled out a cigarette, lit it with a little American gadget, and stuck the rest in a tunic pocket of his jacket.

He was a man in his thirties, with weather-beaten light-bronze skin and narrow black eyes and scars that were only a little less spectacular than Röhm's, though Horst thought they were from knives rather than shrapnel and the white tissue gave him a perpetually angry sneer that seemed to fit his personality. He was stocky and strong-looking, with a clipped mustache and the very beginnings of a paunch; a billed cap on his head had a flap to cover the neck, and he carried a Thompson slung across his belly.

Not much like what rurales *wore before the Americans came,* Horst thought.

He'd run across photos and paintings of those during his work in Mexico in early 1916 while the United States was still neutral in the Great War, making contacts for Abteilung IIIb. The gendarmes of the Porfiriato had been decked out in a version of vaquero garb, based on the *platero* costume of bandits of the 1870s . . . some of whom had been recruited by Díaz for his police back then, under the slogan of *bread or the club*; they got the bread, and swung the club on their former associates. Tight brown leather pants with silver coins sewn up the seams, high-heeled riding boots, broad felt sombreros, bolero jackets . . .

This looks much more businesslike, but I suspect the basic arrangement is similar, he thought.

"Papers!" the gendarme barked.

They handed the little identity booklets over; Pablo had a genuine set, and Röhm had brought expertly forged blanks along for himself and Horst, which had only needed a few details filled in and then some crumpling and rubbing with dirt to show—bilingually—a history of poverty and transient migrant labor. Once he'd glanced through them the *rural* casually dropped them in the mud, and Pablo and Röhm bent humbly to retrieve them and stow the precious things away, carefully wiping them and wrapping them in scraps of cloth. Horst took his when it was nudged against his hand, thanking God silently that he'd remembered not to react.

Perhaps after the war, I could go on the stage . . .

"So, who are you sons of whores really, and where do you think you're going?" the policeman said.

Pablo took off his sombrero and held it in both hands as he glanced down at the man's booted feet. There were big-roweled star-shaped silver spurs on the heels.

"I am Pablo Ramírez, señor. My cousins Diego and Alejandro and I are looking for work," he said quietly. "Our village is . . . was . . . near Calvillo, in Aguascalientes. It was burned in the fighting, and we lost everything."

Pablo had told them Calvillo was a region a bit south of there known for its guava orchards and hot springs, and also for having more fair-skinned men than most places.

"Since then we have moved about, trying to find food and a place, as our documents show, Your Excellency. We have heard there is much work in Zacatecas and Jerez; work and a roof and food is all we seek."

"Cousins?" the policeman said, going over their faces.

All showed the tracks of violence in their different ways.

"They don't look much like you, they're even uglier. And less *indio*."

Pablo sighed and scratched his head. "Well, sir, my aunt . . . the ma-jordomo of the hacienda was a cruel man who took what he wanted . . . you know how it is for a poor defenseless girl of the people . . ."

The *rural* laughed. "So your mother *and* your aunt were whores," he said. "Those ugly cripples don't look like they can work. We've got enough useless beggars around here already, whining and stealing and taking up space an honest goat could get some use out of. And then you can eat the goat."

"Alejandro is big as you can see, and he is still very strong, señor," Pablo said. "For many tasks he does not need his eyes, and Diego can help him . . . Diego does not speak well now, and he has bad dreams, but together they manage, with what help I can give."

The policeman reached out and pushed up Horst's bandage, grunted at the scars over the empty gaping eye socket, then took a pull at his cigarette and blew smoke up into his face. Horst carefully kept his remaining eye's stare blank, blinking only when the smoke stung slightly.

"That was a bullet, right enough. And your crazy *chueco* bastard brother there got his wits blown out by artillery, I know the look. Who did you fight for?" he said.

Röhm gobbled and stuttered convincingly. "Eh . . . Eh . . . El Gen-eral, El General . . . wuh . . . wuh . . ."

"General Huerta, sir," Horst said, still staring ahead.

Pablo went on: "Oh, yes, for General Huerta, señor. For the forces of order and respectability against Villa's evil bandits. We all went home with our wounds before the gringos . . . that is, before the *Ameri-canos* came."

The policeman bellowed mocking laughter. "Do you guava-sucking *hidrocálidos* know how many men I've asked that question? Hundreds, by the Virgin! Thousands! And do you know how many said they fought for Villa? Or Zapata? Or for the PNR *anarquistas*? Not one! And just *one* said he was Carranza's man, a *constitucionalista*. If I believed that pack of lies, even Villa and Zapata wouldn't have fought for themselves!"

He took another pull on the cigarette. "And I've seen thousands of war cripples. You know how many admitted they'd been *jodidos* by the Americans? None! It's amazing—the gringos killed three hundred thousand men or more, but from what people tell me they're such good shots that there isn't a single *güey* still crawling around who was just *crippled* by them. Even their artillery killed every *cabrón* it was aimed at, if I believed what I was told. So only we dumb Mexicans just fuck someone up for life instead of killing him outright, eh?"

"I am only a poor and ignorant man, señor, and know nothing of such things," Pablo said, his voice still soft.

I wouldn't like to be that policeman if Pablo ever caught him alone, Horst thought.

"Now me," the *rural* said, "*I* fought for Félix Díaz, the old man's nephew. Don Porfirio ruled for thirty-two years and gave us peace at home and built railroads and bridges, and he kept the foreigners quiet. Madero and Villa and Zapata and Carranza all talked big and made big promises that fools believed, and what did we get from any of them? Bullets up the ass and a sky raining shit!"

Pablo spoke again: "Excuse me, señor, but what did you do before the war?"

The policeman grinned. "Me? I was a *rural*!" He slapped the automatic weapon slung across his body. "Whoever sits in the palaces, there's always work for men like me!"

The mocking amiability dropped off the man's face like water off greased iron. He gave Horst and Röhm another long look, obviously feeling a mental itch he couldn't scratch. Horst put on an ingratiating smile to go with his blind stare over the policeman's head.

"Just work, señor," he said softly. "Work and food."

The *rural*'s eyes flicked to the young American lieutenant studying the map on the hood of the Guvvie, and equally obviously thought: *Not worth the trouble of talking to the damned* mallate *and making sense of his bad Spanish.*

"Now get going!" he said instead. "And pray to the Virgin and your saints that you never see me again."

As they trudged away there was a crack of thunder, and it began to rain again. Horst sighed quietly, but soldiers were at least as accustomed to working through rain as peasants were.

"At least that fucking traitor gets wet too," Pablo said, shrugging his serape across his shoulders and keeping his head down as they trudged through the storm. "And the *mallates.*"

EIGHT

City of Zacatecas
State of Zacatecas
United States Protectorate of México
JUNE 19TH, 1917, 1917(B)

Your idea about the airships was inspired, Luz," Julie Durán said. "Results almost immediately—and thanks to them, the Rangers got back quickly, too, so the information's available."

Luz looked at the contact report. "This isn't very detailed," she said.

"You should be able to quiz the commander of the detachment at my soiree tomorrow," Julie replied. "It would be next week if he'd had to *walk* out. And on a personal note, and speaking of hunting, thank you so much for those superb Purdey side-by-sides you gave us for Christmas, Luz—Bob loved his and promised me an African safari after things settle down. Though the way it's going, by then we may both be drooling in bath chairs pushed around by our great-grandchildren."

She nodded to a rack behind the desk, which held a very practical Thompson, a cut-down Remington assault shotgun, a number of hunting weapons, a scope-sighted Springfield sharpshooter, and a pair of gleaming double-barreled big-game rifles from the famous English gunsmiths, their high-polished walnut stocks discreetly inlaid with ivory and mother-of-pearl, chambered to Luz's order for the new .338 cartridge that fired a 250-grain bullet at nearly three thousand feet per second. Purdey & Sons wouldn't be making any more of those bespoke masterpieces, since their shop had been in central London.

The desk also had a wooden rest with a strip of brass of the sort usually used for nameplates, engraved instead with a saying old Porfirio Díaz had made famous in the three decades of his rule in Mexico:

Cogidos en flagrante, mátalos en caliente y después averiguamos.

That meant more or less:

When you catch them in the act, kill them on the spot and get the details later.

Cheerful maxims of that sort were a tradition; Luz had heard of one station chief in southern Mindanao who had a polished skull on a mahogany base on his desk, one with a neat .30-06 hole above the left eye, most of the bone at the back raggedly missing, and a plate with:

Here lies a Moro *who wouldn't do what I told him to do.* Sic transit Gloria mundi.

"Where *is* Bob, if you're allowed to say?" Luz said. "I know the Director likes to use him as a mobile troubleshooter since you took over as station chief here."

"Officially, he's in New York. Unofficially, but not really secretly, he's in Algiers getting our operation there going and cooperating with the French. If and when they'll cooperate, he says they're *very* touchy. Foch even more than Lyautey, who's the smoother one on their Committee of National Salvation. An understandable attitude given what's happened to . . . is happening to . . . France. It's delicate work."

There was pardonable pride in her voice; that was a very significant job indeed, since Algiers was obviously going to be an important listening post and forward base for Chamber operations in German-ruled Europe and points south and east. Over the next few years at least and probably for longer.

"Oh, and he gave me an unofficial and extremely tantalizing message for you from one of their brighter intelligence people: *Traveling Chilean feminists? I can't believe I fell for that. Congratulations!*"

Luz grinned, or at least showed her teeth, remembering the disconcertingly sharp dark eyes in that customs shed in Tunis.

"Another milestone in our European theatrical careers," she said cryptically, sharing a glance with Ciara.

Julie snorted. "And the rest went: *We know it was you in Amsterdam and on the train, but all is more or less forgiven.*"

"That's nice," Luz said calmly.

In fact she was irked; the survivors from that skirmish must have put two and two together with annoying intelligence—starting with the fact that someone in a skirt was shooting and throwing grenades and escaping with two Germans in one of their hijacked cars. They'd probably also figured out since then that she was somehow involved with thwarting the Breath of Loki attacks on the United States . . . but *not* the simultaneous one that had destroyed Paris and broken the Western Front.

Julie's raised eyebrow prompted Luz to review what could be said and she explained . . . somewhat.

"I had a bit of a run-in with the Deuxième Bureau—"

The Second Bureau of the General Staff was the French intelligence and covert-operations organization.

"—on my *next*-to-last trip to Europe in '16. That was before the 6th, before everything went to hell. I was deep undercover . . . penetrating an enemy operation . . . and their people on the spot thought I was a German asset and I could scarcely explain it to them, now could I? Unfortunate things occurred, errors in judgment, hasty and poorly considered actions. There were misunderstandings that produced hard feelings on both sides."

Those hard feelings *would have gotten us both unpleasantly killed . . .* much *more unpleasantly than most uses of the word* killed *imply . . . if they'd made us in Tunis in November. Things are different now; they don't dare get the Director's goat that way anymore, or Uncle Teddy's.*

Durán laughed, a quick hard chuckle. "How many of them did you kill in . . . Amsterdam, was it, Luz?" she said. "And on a train . . . probably a train to Germany?"

Between six and eight, depending on whether any of the ones I pitched the grenade at lived, Luz thought. *Fortunately they're not a sentimental people, the French, particularly their spies. But I will be very careful around them for the rest of my life.*

Aloud she said quellingly:

"Well, that's water under the bridge now, Julie. Best not to dwell on old, unhappy things. The spirit of Progressive Americanism under the New Nationalism means a unified, disciplined focus on the future."

"Imitating Secretary of Public Information Croly now, are you?"

"Oh, that's just low!"

She was naming, and insulting, Herbert Croly, Secretary of the Department of Public Information—overseer of the press and propaganda—and the Progressive Republican Party's chief ideologist, as well as the author of the shatteringly dull and turgid Party bible, *The Promise of American Life,* a much-bought, little-read book in which the phrase *the New Nationalism* had been coined and struck Uncle Teddy's attention like a thunderbolt about eight years ago. It wasn't surprising *he* liked the book, which had used him as an exemplar of a new type of leader who embodied the popular will and the national destiny.

Sometimes Luz thought Croly must feel like the sorcerer's apprentice, but her sympathy was underwhelming.

Julie's smile grew wider and she winked at Ciara: "The opposition here used to call her *Santa Muerte,* and they swore she could see in the dark, turn herself invisible, and walk through walls," she said.

"So does Colonel Nicolai of Abteilung IIIb these days," Luz said with resignation.

Julie's on a tear.

"And I hear they called her *Mictēcacihuātl* too, sometimes, down in Morelos," Julie said. "There are more people who speak Nahuatl . . . that's the old Aztec language . . . down there."

"*Mictēcacihuātl?*" Ciara said, butchering the Nahua word even more than Julie had.

"The Skull Goddess," Julie said. "The Swallower of Stars, Lady of the Land of Bones. Queen of Hell and Death in the old religion, basically."

Luz made a dismissive gesture. "That was my fault for being too flamboyant," she said. "What can I say? We were young, and our souls were on fire."

In fact she'd played up to that identification with the old Aztec monster-goddess, leaving little Day of the Dead sugar-paste skulls behind as a trademark and calling card.

"We *were* young?" Henrietta chuckled, and looked ostentatiously around the table. "Don't see many gray hairs here even now, ladies."

"A little flamboyance was a small price to pay for youthful energy and flexibility," Luz said.

"Nobody had much *experience* at what we were doing with the Chamber, anyway. We got that on the job. Or died. And we took a lot of our ideas out of books," Durán added.

"There were manuals then?" Ciara asked, puzzled because she'd read all the current ones and memorized them, including their publication dates.

"No, from adventure fiction. Things like *Kim* and Richard Harding Davis's stories."

Luz nodded at Ciara's *Is this real* glance and went into detail:

"And they often worked. Sinister gestures were useful to keep the enemy nervous and looking over their shoulders, for instance," she said. "Style is important here. It's a lot like advertising or popular fiction in some ways—manipulating people's conceptions. For example, you don't have to have spies everywhere and that's impossible anyway. You just have to make people *believe* you do."

The station chief's elegant blond brow arched a little further as she ignored the subject-changing. "And both of you getting the Order of the Black Eagle!" she said. "Nonposthumously! And I notice you're an *executive* field operative now, Luz."

"We earned it. I credit enormous talent, Ciara's magnificent bravery, and lots of luck," Luz said.

Their eyes met in an instant of perfect understanding. Julie would have guessed that the medals had something to do with thwarting the horror-gas attacks, and that the details were in the *Most Secret* files and would stay there for a long long time. So would their subsequent excursion to Berlin to penetrate the secrets of the Telemobiloscope, the revolutionary German radio-range-finding apparatus.

Though rumors had inevitably spread about the final bit, which had involved escaping the capital of Germany by hijacking a German Navy semirigid airship . . . equipped with the Telemobiloscope. And the role of then-Colonel and now-Brigadier Ted Roosevelt Jr. in the final rescue—a man they both knew socially as well as professionally—that had captured it intact.

And who, if he lives, may well be president someday.

"How's Algiers otherwise?"

"Bob's sent me some really magnificent little French objets d'art, which are going cheap there if you can pay in dollars."

Luz sighed heavily; there were times when Julie could wear on you.

Particularly with her clothes on, which is why it didn't last; that isn't enough, she thought, and went on aloud:

"We were through part of French North Africa not long ago, a little *after* the 6th that time, and it was already . . . rather bad."

"While traveling as Chilean feminists? It got much worse, Bob hints cryptically. That made me do a little research—call in some favors for information—and apparently it's the Entente's very own Armenia, though we're not supposed to say so."

"I suspected it would be something like that," Luz said with a sigh, and Ciara grimaced slightly and looked aside.

"Well, you did *ask*," Julie pointed out.

Shoving thirty-odd million refugees into an area that only produced a modest food surplus for its twelve million or so natives and million French *colons* even in years of peace and good weather was something that just didn't have any possible pleasant outcomes. Not with food short or just not there at all everywhere from Normandy to China. And shipping even more so, what with the U-boat packs and conflicting priorities.

Julie shrugged and went on: "Though the French have their news blackout clamped tight and it's mostly working, which is more than the Turks ever managed. No photographs, and I suspect no internal documentation that isn't burned as soon as possible. Our very own Public Information is helping, of course, lest excessive truthfulness confuse the public."

Julie added: "Their new public slogan is *Ce sont les Français qui font le sol français, pas le sol les gens.*"

"'It is the French people who make the ground France, not the ground the people,'" Luz murmured. "Fair enough."

"The Great War is Moloch the Devourer come again," Ciara said with a sigh and a troubled look, which was indisputably true. "It destroys everything it touches."

"It's a long ways from the first time," Henrietta said.

When they all looked at her she quoted softly from the Book of Joshua, her eyes distant:

"'So Joshua smote all the country of the hills, and of the south, and of the vale, and of the springs, and all their kings and peoples; he left none remaining, but slew all that breathed . . . the young and the old, the male and the female, and the ox and the ass and the sheep, with the edge of the sword, as the Lord God of Israel commanded.'"

Then in her own voice: "And mostly nobody even remembers their names."

They were all silent for a moment, and then Luz sighed and decided to change the subject; there was little point in brooding on what you couldn't affect.

"How's your little Alice, Julie?" Luz said. "I hope she remembers me; I feel a bit guilty I couldn't see her more often lately."

Luz wasn't more than a nominal, family-tradition type of Catholic these days. If nothing else, things in her personal life she wasn't prepared to change made confession and going to Mass impossible unless she simply lied truth out of creation, which she wouldn't do unless it was required in the way of business. But she'd been raised to consider being a *madrina*, a godmother, an important link and *compadrazgo*, coparenthood, a serious business and lifelong bond. And children were looking cuter with every passing year. She knew Ciara felt the same way, only more so.

A flash of thought went through her: sitting on the patio back home in the *Casa*, sipping a glass of wine and watching Ciara playing with a toddler . . .

Julie beamed and reached over to the desk to pass them a colortinted photograph that showed a curly-haired tot in a pinafore cradling a kitten. The kitten looked a little sulky at being beaten in the adorability sweepstakes, or possibly at the determined grip of the plump little hands.

"She's healthy, flourishing, pretty much toilet-trained, and *asleep* now, thank God. But she celebrated turning two and a half back in the spring by learning how to say *no*. Very loudly, over and over. Bilingually."

Luz grinned at the painful pun; the word was identical in the two languages Alice was being raised in. She and Ciara cooed appropriately over the picture. Luz had to admit the coo-wattage was high; she found children *much* more appealing past the oozing, belching larval stage, though Ciara liked babies too.

"And the twins?"

"Eduardo and Catalina are asleep too, thank God, but *they're* at the age where everything lying on the ground gets picked up and crammed in their mouths if it's small enough and gnawed on where it stands if it isn't . . . including garden shrubs, chair legs, and various ankles . . . I think Bob's side of the family must include some maidens from the werebeaver tribes of the Sangre de Cristo mountains. Thank God good staff is easier to get here."

"Even with security checks?" Luz asked, amused.

Julie was actually talking about the *servant problem*, probably the only Black Chamber regional commander who did, and in much the same way that her mother or sisters might with a few additions like making sure no enemy infiltrators entered disguised as cook's assistants and housemaids.

"Even with. Anita is an utter treasure . . ."

"And the *revolucionarios* burned her house and killed her husband, and the rest of her family only survived because our troops came along." Luz nodded, remembering.

The post as family nanny to the Duráns had involved citizenship, schooling and patronage for her own teenage children, as well as a place and a comfortable wage for herself.

"I'd have gone mad long before this trying to juggle everything without her. How my mother did it with six of us I don't know . . . no, I do, it was dear old nanny Maggie, bless her and κούφα σοι χθὼν ἐπάνωθε πέσοι—"

Oh, still quoting Euripides, Julie! Luz thought, and translated:

"Which is classical Greek for 'May the earth rest lightly upon her.'"

Julie sometimes forgot people who'd gone to university and done the classics were a tiny minority.

"—but even so. Secretary Davenport says three is the absolute minimum you owe the American nation if you have *good germ plasm*. Three is what he's got, I notice, not the great thundering herd of seven or eight he recommends for other people. Unless he's disqualified for *responsible reproduction* by feeble-minded, epileptic, drunken microcephalic dwarf aunts in the attic he hasn't let anyone know about."

Everyone chuckled. It was notorious that eugenics fanatics were not very progenitive themselves, on the whole, including the Secretary of the Department of Public Health and Eugenics. They were given to *do as I say, not as I do* pronouncements, when it came to the Party's slogan:

The Three Duties of the Citizen: Work! Fight! Beget!

At least Uncle Teddy practiced what he preached, since he and Aunt Edith had a swarm of boisterously impressive and healthy offspring.

And an ever-increasing roll call of grandspawn. Even Alice Longworth née Roosevelt is expecting, which is several types of miracle, though I'm not entirely sure even she *is sure who Daddy is, except that it's not Ambassador Nicholas Longworth III. And that's why she paid him a short and literally flying visit in Tokyo on the American National Airways inaugural run in March: to make the arithmetic at least a bit credible. Alice is what Uncle Teddy would be if he didn't have a conscience.* ¡Dios Mio, *what a man-trap, though!*

"And apart from the little incident in the Sierra, how are things going here in general?" Luz said. "I've read your situation reports, of course, but . . ."

The maid set out coffee and plates of churros and a bowl of melted chocolate for dipping the long skinny deep-fried pastries. Julie opened a box—Luz thought it was certainly French and probably Napoleon III—lacquered in a mellow shade of old gold, with a vignette of an eighteenth-century romantic couple dressed in shades of pink and turquoise on the top, framed with a gilded swirling acanthus leaf border; the corners were decorated with gilded scrollwork interspersed with tiny, intricate carved flowers. Its gilt-speckled interior of brown walnut was full of cigarettes, Egyptian ones of a brand named *Mogul*, and probably more expensive than ever, with the near-total collapse of world trade.

Julie put her cigarette in an ivory holder and lit it from a granite-encased lighter on the table, waving gracefully at the box as she leaned back in the heavy chair like a lounging cat. Henrietta took one, without a holder; Ciara declined and so did Luz, though she was hiding a smile at the memories the scent brought.

"I still agree with the Boss," she said.

The president notoriously detested tobacco in all its forms, which made using it very mildly daring for Party members. He was an extremely moderate and strictly social occasional drinker, almost but not quite a teetotaler; he'd quashed the Prohibition movement for alcohol because he thought it was stupid or unworkable or both, but he made up for it on cigarettes, which he was convinced were filthy and unhealthy at any dose. He'd found statisticians at the Department of Public Health and Eugenics who thought there were disturbing correlations with various loathsome diseases. That was enough to make Luz glad that she just didn't like the stuff to begin with, though you could prove anything with numbers if you tried hard enough.

"Teacher's pet," Julie said without resentment.

When the maid had finished clearing the table and left—the household staff might have been carefully checked but you didn't take unnecessary risks—Durán resumed her answer:

"Well, *officially*, everyone here except German spies and a few of their dupes just absolutely *loves* us to *bits* because we invaded Mexico for Mexico's own good and for the sacred cause of Progress and we are all happy and friendly and cozy as be-damned, tra-la, tra-la. If you don't believe me, just read the *New York Times*! Or those articles in the *Saturday Evening Post* and *National Geographic* with pictures of adoring Mexican kids getting handed chocolate bars by soldiers or Plenipotentiary Lodge and his wife opening a vaccination clinic."

Ciara's smile was a little pained; the other three Americans laughed heartily.

"That's not *el jefe*," Luz said.

Uncle Teddy had never made any bones about the fact that while he expected Mexico to benefit eventually, the Intervention had been launched to protect Americans and their interests, not to mention avenging their wrongs.

Which is absolutamente *why I was there from the beginning, lusting for revenge with all my soul and enjoying every moment of getting it.*

"It's that little toad Croly's smarm and soul butter," she went on aloud.

"And underneath the Department of Public Information's soul butter?" she asked.

Julie nodded. "*Un*officially, things are . . . not bad at all, compared to the way they were a couple of years ago. Steadily improving, I'd say. Most people are just glad the fighting's over and there's enough to eat, though God knows how long that'll last once they get used to it again."

"Ah, but you forget the universal power of enduring gratitude," Luz said with owl solemnity, and Julie snorted as she continued:

"The Army's cooperative . . . we have a new regional commander, Major-General Young, but he seems very competent . . . and the FBS . . . well, they're the FBS."

All four of the Black Chamber operatives smiled or shrugged at that; to them Federal Bureau of Security meant *plodding bureaucratic second-raters* at best and opinions went downhill from there. Plenty of sulky resentment of *reckless cowboys* and *lunatics* came back their way, along with pouting on the order of *Daddy loves you best and that's NOT FAIR!*

"Though I admit the FBS *did* get the local police up to the mark on suppressing ordinary crime, and they've even cut the corruption."

"Honest Mexican police?" Luz said skeptically, having lived in the country during the Porfiriato.

"No, no miracles; they just cut it down to, say, traditional Chicago or New York or St. Louis levels of corruption . . . which on second thought *is* a miracle and it's much appreciated and gets us a lot of credit."

"The local cops still take bribes, but no more shakedowns or demanding the maidenheads of daughters or shooting people because a personal enemy of the shootee paid them off or because they're bored and it's a hot day?" Luz said.

"About that. Crops have been good the last few years too, there's plenty of work with all the construction projects—even the hacendados have taken to investing with deranged optimism—and of course there's plenty of demand for everything the place grows or mines or makes, what with the war, and now that Mexico's inside our tariff wall. *And* we've managed to keep basic food prices reasonable. By shipping in subsidized corn from the Midwest, sometimes."

Luz nodded, happy though not surprised to hear it. "Neglecting that was one of old Don Porfirio's worst mistakes, there at the end when he started to lose his grip. You *don't* want people cursing your name every time they go to market or make a tortilla or hesitate to take a bite for themselves because their children are looking at them but have to do it anyway because they need the strength to keep their job."

Ciara nodded vigorously too. She'd grown up in a working-class neighborhood where food took more than half the average family's budget, and a breadwinner's accident on the docks or the mass layoffs that followed a trade panic like the one in '07 could mean going from meat every day to living on potatoes and wearing shoes an extra year, holes in the soles or no. Her own family had always been a little better off than that, but in daily contact with those less fortunate.

Julie waved agreement with the chocolate-dipped piece of churro in one hand and drew on her Egyptian cigarette and blew a smoke ring toward the ceiling before she continued:

"Wages are up more than prices, not least because of people working up north and sending money home, which is one reason the landowners are buying American-style farm equipment, a lot of it second-hand. There are still Carranzistas—"

"Even though he's dead?" Luz asked curiously.

She'd helped track Venustiano Carranza Garza to his final hiding place near Saltillo in early 1915, part of the steady grinding-down and tidying-up process, though the FBS had made the actual arrest.

"Still. A lot don't believe he just dropped dead in custody. The irony being that for once it really *was* just natural heart failure."

Heart failure was to the Protectorate what *shot while attempting to escape* had been to Don Porfirio's government. They were linked; being shot did make your heart fail.

"And we didn't get quite all the PNR anarcho-communard *revolucionarios*, and there are plenty of common or garden don't-like-the-gringos types mouthing off in cantinas when they think nobody's listening."

"They could find out they're wrong about that someday," Luz said with a grin.

She cleared her throat and sang a snatch from *The Mikado*, a Gilbert and Sullivan operetta she and Julie had both appeared in as members of the drama club at Bryn Mawr:

"As some day it may happen that a victim must be found
I've got a little list—I've got a little list
Of society offenders who might well be underground,
And who never would be missed—who never would be missed!"

Julie laughed, thought for a moment to summon memory, and then completed it in a pure well-trained soprano:

"The task of filling up the blanks I'd rather leave to you.
But it really doesn't matter whom you put upon the list,
For they'd none of 'em be missed—they'd none of 'em be missed!"

Then she continued: "There aren't any active cells that we've found for the last eighteen months, but there are probably sleeper groups hiding in the hills and among the public and waiting for a chance, or for us to get sloppy and let down our guards. They've learned to keep their heads way, way down, which is good enough."

"Pro-German activity?" Luz asked.

"Some but nothing serious, the odd *¡Viva Alemania!* or *¡Victoria al Kaiser!* written on walls, on the enemy-of-my-enemy principle, but the Germans didn't help themselves by boasting about London and Paris rather than denying it. And of course Public Information had plenty of really, really ugly pictures to show. Moving picture newsreels too, there was some screaming and fainting and vomiting among the audiences. They bothered *me*, and you know I'm not at all tenderhearted."

Henrietta nodded, stone-faced and silent for a moment, with a quiver so slight that Luz wasn't quite sure she'd seen it. When the woman from Savannah spoke, her voice was flatly calm:

"I know up here the horror-gas can't kill you deader than a bullet."

She tapped her head and then the spot below her sternum: "But your heart an' stomach don't necessarily follow along. Granted that's how my family died, but I don't think I'm bein' softheaded because of that."

Sentimentality, or even worse, *Victorian sentimentality*, was not an attitude the Party encouraged. You were supposed to cultivate a hard objectivity, to be an engineer of your own life and soul.

Ciara gave her a sympathetic glance, then frowned as something struck her. "Would anyone have *believed* the Germans if they had denied it? With the pictures and such?"

"Some would have pretended to, at first, and then actually started really believing it because they wanted to so badly," Julie said.

Ciara blinked a bit at the overwhelming cynicism, but Luz nodded; it fit precisely with her observations of how human beings acted. In fact, that type of selective memory was something she regularly checked herself for, despite the unpleasant mental sensations doing so gave you.

"It does help that the Germans are so reliably ham-handed. It makes it easy to look good by contrast," Luz noted. "They just have no capacity to put themselves in someone else's shoes, even for tactical reasons. Look at that medal they put out after they sank the *Mauretania*, with the passengers buying tickets from a skeleton!"

"And they never had any earthly idea why the British made thousands of copies of it and distributed them all over; it's the same thing that makes them such terrible spies," Julie agreed, and then went on: "We worried that the declaration of war on Germany might start something, but it depressed the holdouts instead. We lost the half of the 15th Minnesota Infantry division assigned here, they're just pulling out of this military district—"

Which consisted of four states that covered much of north-central Mexico.

"—as part of the general mobilization plan, but we got a new division at full strength instead, the 32nd Infantry, Regulars. The switchover's about complete now. They're mostly green in terms of work in the Protectorate except for some of the officers and noncoms, but they *look* menacing enough and the commanders have them out working hard across the countryside and up in the Sierra Madre Occidental."

"Green . . . the 32nd . . . that's a Negro division," Luz said, her eyes going up slightly as she consulted her mental files. "Major-General Young got them last October . . . West Point, Class of '89 . . . fought in the Philippines, then was military attaché in Haiti—he did good intelligence work there, I've seen the reports and they're models—fought at Veracruz and Puebla in 1913 as colonel of the 10th Cavalry, brigade command in Morelos and Chiapas, then chief of staff for the 32nd . . . He's the first Negro ever promoted to general rank, too."

"Yes, ma'am," Henrietta said neutrally. "Judgin' from the fact that they were used in the Gulf states during the martial law period, the 32nd was probably sent here because *el jefe* is absolutely sure they're reliable."

Yes, she's quite sharp, Luz thought.

"And because the General Staff and the White House thought well of General Young's ability to handle a delicate situation. This is a high-priority posting now."

Then to Julie:

"And because we *couldn't* send them to Europe. Without the horror-gas we'd be driving the Germans back through Belgium right now and we'd be across the Rhine before the end of next year. There'd be a massive butcher's bill, but we could do it."

That got a nod; they both knew the plans and the balance of forces. If the American army had been able to funnel itself through Britain and the Channel ports, attacking along the old Western Front with intact French and British forces by its side . . . but it hadn't.

October 6ᵗʰ—changing everything again, Luz mused, knowing they were all thinking the same thing, that everyone who'd been an adult on that day would go on doing so all their lives, and went on aloud:

"But as it is, the Army's all dressed up with no place to go—the General Staff are still racking their brains about it in the Iron House, and so is the Boss."

"Better *el jefe* and the Iron House than me," Durán said. "I've got quite enough to do cultivating my own garden, if you want to invoke Voltaire. Fortunately, the civil government in this state has been doing quite well too. Governor Seelmann's been doing well implementing Plenipotentiary Lodge's program here—roads, tube wells in the villages, clinics, forestry . . . The death rate's down, there are more kids in school, a lot more paved roads, a couple of small factories have opened this year, that sort of thing. Just as importantly, people are getting to believe there will be more of the same to come while we're in charge, which also gives us added prestige."

Ciara nodded happily, Luz noticed; that was more the *sort of thing* she wanted to hear, being basically inclined to carrots rather than sticks. Durán went on:

"He speaks the language well, which is appreciated . . . I know it's supposed to be compulsory for permanent upper-level administrative types here, but a surprising number seem to be baffled at anything more than the *pass the salt* level . . . and he married a local girl this spring, which was popular. Except with the people who really, really hate the hacendados, and they're not going to like us anyway."

"I heard her mentioned by some local gossips. Details?"

"One of the de Moncadas; María Concepción Ursula de Moncada y de Camino. Seelmann y de Moncada now."

"The de Moncadas . . . land, of course, and silver and lead mines," Luz said.

She recognized the surnames of the local elite, but not the young woman specifically.

"The de Moncadas have been here and rich for centuries," Julie said. "Younger son Catalan *cavallers* originally, arrived in the 1530s, successful free-lances during the Chichimeca Wars . . . ennobled under the Bourbons . . . rode out the independence war and the First Mexican War and the French occupation, and then did very well out of the Porfiriato. The *revolucionarios* scared them into our arms along with all their followers, clients, and hangers-on. Concepción's a nice girl, very pretty indeed if you like the Latin type, which I do—"

"Your name *is* Durán these days," Luz pointed out. "Why, you might as well be a damned dago yourself."

She did *not* add aloud: *since you've slept with so many of us*, though she was sure Julie had caught that in the smallest quirk of an eyebrow.

"Exactly. Concha's quiet—"

Concha was the standard short form for the rather formal Concepción. She'd go by that, because as the local joke went, if you walked out the door and shouted ¡María! here, half the women in the street would turn and look at you.

"—but no fool, and she was educated at private schools in Mexico City and by good European governesses . . . English and French and Swiss, not German, I checked . . ."

"Not that someone named Seelmann would have anything to say to that," Luz noted.

An amazing number of Americans with German surnames had paid quick visits to registry offices lately and emerged to bland Anglo-Saxon anonymity; going for patriotic handles on the order of Lincoln and Jefferson and Washington and Grant and Sherman was popular, and the number of Roosevelts would have soared if Uncle Teddy hadn't put his foot down. Governor Seelmann had apparently decided the *Governor* part and his military record were more important than an unquestionably Fritz moniker.

"Agreed. She speaks English and French and has passable general knowledge as well as the accomplishments, and her family took her along on trips north . . . not Europe, she was too young before the war started, but St. Louis and Chicago and New York. She's just nineteen now, in fact, which is a little bit young for him if we were up north; he's a childless widower and thirty-five."

That sort of age gap between bride and groom was nothing out of the ordinary among upper-class Mexicans, particularly when a man married for the second time.

"Was it political?" Luz said.

Julie and Henrietta both grinned and glanced at each other as if at a shared joke, and the station chief continued:

"No, it was a love match. Really. Carl was smitten in the grand fashion, though her family most *certainly* didn't object to having the governor as an in-law, and neither did their innumerable relations. They started inviting him over all the time as soon as they knew his intentions were honorable, which was obvious from his stunned-ox look and the way he treated her as if she were made of spun glass and silk and went babbling on about her keen wits and natural gentle charm and beautiful laugh and deep, kind nature. Honestly, you'd have thought he was sixteen from the way he shuffled his feet when she smiled at him. And he started asking *me* for advice on how to court her, which was flattering, but . . . sad, in a way."

"What about her?" Luz said. "Or did her parents just lean on her?"

Henrietta sighed melodramatically and put the back of one hand to her forehead while patting her heart with the other in a quick *vibrato*:

"Oh, he *talks* to me," she said, obviously quoting what she'd heard from Concha, with Julie's company rendering her socially invisible. "Oh, he's the only man who ever *listened* to me. The others *flatter* me but they don't *talk* to me, they're such *boys*, all they want to talk about is love. He's interested in what I *think* about things . . . oh, he has such depths of *soul*, he's so *lonely* and misunderstood, and he knows *Wordsworth . . .*"

Julie joined the general laughter. "I remember those conversations. I think she meant 'he's not *just* interested in getting his hands on *mis chichis*' and 'likes the same poets.' Granted, that would be a contrast with most boys her own age; her duenna could keep them at bay and polite but not control the direction of their hot panting gaze . . ."

Henrietta nodded. "God's truth, judging by the ones *I* meet. You feel like puttin' an arrow on your blouse and a note sayin' *My eyes are up here.*"

Everyone sighed or groaned.

"There are worse reasons for a nineteen-year-old to decide a man is interesting than the fact that he listens to her," Luz said.

Ciara nodded. "Especially if the girl wasn't one of those who think flirting is a sport like baseball and spend all their time on batting averages and trading cards, so to say."

"No, she's serious-minded," Julie said.

"He converted?" Luz asked. "I don't suppose the de Moncadas would let their grandchildren grow up outside the Church, governor-in-law or no."

Julie had done just that when she married into the Duráns; Luz knew she paid exactly as much attention to the Catholic Church now as she had to the faded, attenuated post-Quaker Unitarian wishy-washiness of her parents as a girl, which she'd once described to Luz as the Church of GAAVEB—God As A Vague Elongated Blur. And also as a form of inoculation against ever taking religion seriously, like the weakened virus used in the vaccination against smallpox.

"Converted? I'll say he did! He went Catholic publicly, and well before he got a *yes* from her."

"While they were still talking Wordsworth and he was revealing the depths of his soul," Henrietta said. "Maybe she tried to *save* his soul—she's very regular about confession and going to Mass."

"If she'd been a satanist, he'd be wearing a crucifix upside down now and intoning the Lord's Prayer backward," Julie said. "But if the hierarchy has a passkey, Carl's through the Pearly Gates already. The ceremony was overseen by the archbishop. In the cathedral, at the Easter Vigil . . . he spent the night on his knees . . . with her parents as *padrinos*. Baptism, confirmation, and first Eucharist all in one. And then a procession, with piñatas full of silver quarters hung up in the streets, dedicating a chapel to the Virgin of Zacatecas as Our Lady of the Assumption and a new altar for the cathedral . . . which incidentally mysterious sources helped pay for . . ."

"*¡Ay!*" Luz said, startled. "That's going the whole hog!"

Julie went on with an ostentatiously evil smile:

"I managed to convince him that doing a serenata during the courtship would help. In full *charro* fig, underneath her balcony, with two mariachi guitarists also in full fig backing him up . . ."

She strummed an invisible instrument, threw back her head with an expression of exaggerated blissful torment, and sang, quite well, but with a deliberate cat-on-a-fence-seeking-love overtone:

"Despierta
Dulce amor de mi vida,
Despiertaaaaaaa . . ."

"In a charro suit?" Luz said; that was what folk singers wore, an exaggerated version of old-fashioned Mexican cowboy garb. "Oh, Julie, you didn't talk him into *that*!"

Henrietta wiped her eye. "Yes, ma'am, she did—I heard her do it, as solemn as a judge. And when she told Concha about it at the reception, the poor girl flushed like a beet and began hitting the station chief here with her fan and calling her an evil triply cursed daughter of Satan and saying: *I hate that song!*"

"*¡Dios mío!*" Luz wheezed. "I'd forgotten how diabolical you could be, Julie."

Ciara was smiling but looking a little uncertain. "I don't quite understand . . . it all sounds so sweet? Except the bit with the fan."

Luz recovered. "It is sweet, *querida* . . . but . . . oh, my goodness, let's say a man went to Ireland and moved into Wexford or Cork . . . or the village of Skibbereen, for that matter . . . and tried to *fit in* by wearing knee breeches and buckled shoes and a green tailcoat and a weskit with brass buttons and a top hat and smoking a little clay pipe like a pottery leprechaun. And carrying a shillelagh and starting all his sentences with *begorrah* or *bejabers* or *top o' the mornin' to ye!*"

Ciara winced, and then started laughing too.

"Oh, it's not *nearly* as bad as that." Julie grinned. "Though one of my informants *did* report a spectator saying during the procession after the wedding that he hadn't realized that Don Raul's daughter was marrying the king of Spain instead of just some gringo. They do like a performance here, but there's a certain sense of proportion."

That set everyone off again. When she could speak coherently, Luz asked:

"No, seriously, as a professional, what was the reaction?"

"Affectionate and indulgent, more than anything—he got real points for trying and for meaning well and for being so desperately in love—particularly from our half of the population. It would have been different if he weren't respected for being firm when he has to be, but he is, and he's a very good horseman and was a champion fencer at West Point and has a couple of combat medals and some nice small romantic scars, which also gets him credit for being a *real man*, as they say here."

The actual phrase she used was *un varón de verdad*, which had a rather . . . earthier . . . connotation, something more like *a complete stud*. Julie went on:

"Don Raul gave them a hacienda west of town as a wedding gift, not far from our place, as a matter of fact—it was part of Concha's *herencia materna* from her grandmother's sister anyway, who died without issue. She's expecting, by the way . . . Concha, not the dead great-aunt . . . and that's popular too. Protectorate HQ has quietly let it be known that Carl can be governor here as long as he wants, and *that's* popular, since people know they're not going to get a stranger who doesn't know them dropped on their heads and they like the idea of a governor who's tied his fortunes and his bloodline to the place and to their people."

Julie turned sober and cleared her throat. "And he's getting credit for snagging this Dakota Project they've been building since January out east of town . . . Everyone loves the government money that's gone into circulation here."

Silence fell; Julie was carefully not mentioning the risks involved in having a V-gas plant that close to town. Luz said, a little defensively: "Well, it has."

More silence, and she went on: "Julie, *mi amiga*, this decision was made far, far above my pay grade or yours. You can imagine how urgent the priorities are, and it has to go *somewhere*; that it's here shows the men at the top think you . . . and Carl Seelmann and General Young, I suppose . . . have things well in hand. All we can do is try to make it work safely. Do you want me helping with that, or a stranger doing it? Someone who'd tell you not to worry your pretty little head about it? I can call in some markers and get us assigned to something else, if you'd rather."

Julie sighed. "That is a point. All right, let's do it. Oddly enough, I've started to think of this place as home . . . certainly more than Taos or Santa Fe. Or Philadelphia!"

They shook hands on it, a firm grip. Ciara yawned involuntarily behind a hand, and Julie said:

"The altitude here makes people sleepy until they're used to it. Let's have a toast, and then back through the tunnel and off to bed."

She produced a bottle from a cabinet, and Henrietta set out the four small glasses. Luz smiled when she saw the label; it was tequila, but not the usual silver variety, double-distilled and unaged. This was from Don Eladio Sauza's property in Jalisco, just outside the *town* of Tequila, and he'd taken to aging it in Tennessee white-oak barrels lately—originally simply because he was the first to export the liquor to the United States and could get them cheap and used from the bourbon distilleries there, and then seizing on it when he discovered how different it made the drink. This *añejo* variety had a slight golden tinge and a much mellower taste, and returning soldiers had spread its fame north of the former border and bade fair to make Don Sauza fabulously wealthy.

"He still sends you and Bob bottles?" Luz asked.

"Regular as clockwork, Christmas and the birthdays. And to you and James, I suppose?"

"Well, the four of us did save his life and his hacienda. It's rather charming, in a way. And it is the best tequila in Mexico—the Sauzas were the first to use only the *agave azul.*"

"To gratitude—not *quite* as rare as the passenger pigeon," Julie said, and they all raised their glasses and sipped.

"I hear *James* got married," Julie added, dipping back into Chamber gossip. "Who's the unfortunate Mrs. Cheine? He's quite scrumptious and dreamy, I admit, and rich as sin too, but *marrying* him? The man's a shameless tomcat, and a heartless one too."

"It's a Frenchwoman of my acquaintance, Yvonne Perrin . . . Yvonne Cheine, née Perrin, now . . . and a very strong-willed lady, pretty much a match for him, I think. A refugee—she saved his life, under circumstances . . . well."

They both made a gesture that involved pinching the lips together.

"He's effectively adopted the baby, too. Though nothing official was necessary, little Eléonore wasn't *quite* born yet at the marriage, though it was close, but you know what I mean. I'm . . . well, Ciara and I are both *madrinas*."

"And he has *officially* adopted Simone—she's a young girl, about six years younger than me, who escaped with Yvonne and the others," Ciara said enthusiastically. "A really nice girl, and smart as a whip, too."

She and Simone had become fast friends during that last mission in Europe, which had involved rescuing Yvonne Perrin and *her* circle of friends from German captivity and more or less certain death. There had been good operational reasons for it, but it had been done; all of them had settled in San Francisco, where Simone had been ensconced in a private girls' school with good mathematics and science teachers, she having decided that Ciara was a heroine to emulate.

And there are certainly worse models, Luz thought.

"They seem quite happy, the Cheines," Ciara added. "Well, not Mr. Cheine's parents, but they and he have never gotten along anyway, I understand. Politics."

Julie's brows went up, but Luz confirmed it with a nod.

"I don't understand it either," she said. "I always agreed with you about James . . . brave and clever, and a highly polished piece of Knicker-bocker old-money cad *pur sang*. But people can surprise you."

"Well, *I* never saw him do anything ungentlemanly, darling," Ciara said. "Except deceive and kill people, of course, but that was in the line of duty—they were all Germans."

They all shared a chuckle, and Henrietta's eyes showed a flicker of grim satisfaction. She raised her own glass:

"Confusion to the Kaiser!"

They all echoed it and drank the last drops, and Julie refilled the glasses.

"To *el jefe* and absent friends!" she said.

That was the usual concluding toast; *absent friends* were the Black Chamber's dead, of course.

"*El jefe!*" they all chorused, and drank. "*And absent friends!*"

"And three times three, to the Boss!" Luz thought she heard Henrietta Colmer say under her breath as she drained her glass.

Which wasn't surprising, considering what had happened down south since Luz and Ciara came back with the news that the reborn Klan was conspiring with the Kaiser's men. That panicked response to the collapse of the power of the Democratic Party, and hence of Dixie, in Washington and the growing strength of the federal government under the New Nationalism had spectacularly backfired. Not least by activating Uncle Teddy's old-fashioned Lincoln-loyalist, Union-forever side, and while Party activists weren't usually much concerned with the plight of the Negro—even those who didn't actively dislike them mostly wished deeply that they just *weren't there*—they were also very happy to use them as a handy political stick to beat the Bourbon Democrat opponents of the Progressive project.

They were calling it the Second Reconstruction now.

They all parted, and Luz and Ciara took the tunnel back to their apartment; they'd walked in from the street the first night here, to fit with their covers, but this time the whole visit was in secret.

The guesthouse had started out as a mansion much like the Black Chamber HQ; it had been split into six apartments, each of four rooms plus a small bathroom with a shower-bath and modest kitchen complete with icebox. Nobody knew—hopefully—that the Black Chamber actually owned and ran the place, and that one particular suite had a neat little tunnel connection running into the back of a wardrobe in the bedroom, disguised in the best adventure-fiction style.

A seventh apartment housed the large local family that did the maintenance and provided maid service and laundry and deliveries; the other suites were occupied by groups of engineers busy with the Dakota Project, or in one case an engineer and his wife and two small children, all of whom would move out when they found more permanent quarters or the Dakota Project was up and running and they moved on to the next project.

When Luz flicked on the electric light within, their night-things had been laid out on crisp lavender-scented sheets, and a cheery fire crackled in the tile-bordered hearth behind a screen of pierced brass. A fire at night was almost always pleasant here, even in high summer when days could be hot.

Ciara was slightly unsteady; a large beer and two quick shots of tequila were more than she was used to.

"Julie . . . Mrs. Durán . . . is very elegant and sophisticated," she said. Then: "You two . . . really are still good friends, aren't you?"

Luz met her eyes. "Yes, darling, we are," she said. "Bryn Mawr and what happened there isn't the biggest part of that. Afterward we . . ."

Her own eyes glazed for a moment: She smelled death again, and tasted fear and pain and an exhaustion that was pain in itself.

"We went through a good deal together."

Ciara blurted—probably due to the tequila: "I *am* jealous!"

Luz reached out and took both her hands. "I know, darling, and I know it feels . . . rotten. And it doesn't help that Julie never did know when to stop teasing."

"You're not angry?"

"No, I'm not—not at you. And I'm *used* to being annoyed at Julie!"

We've been friends for . . . *¡Dios mio!* Eight years now! And I can't recall ever being in her company for any length of time *without* being annoyed with her about something, except when we were both in peril of our lives or concentrating totally."

"I'm doing better than that!"

"Infinitely! I want to live with you for the rest of my life. I'd kill her within a month, or vice versa."

"I know who I'd bet on!" Ciara said stoutly. Then, softly and looking down: "She made me feel such a . . . such a schoolgirl! And a *frump!*"

Luz didn't reply in words; instead she swept Ciara into a clinch and a long kiss that tasted of tequila and chocolate and spices. That went on for some enjoyable time.

"Oh . . . my!" Ciara said, breathless. "Let's do that again!"

They did. "There's my opinion on who is or is not a *frump*," Luz said softly a long minute later.

They helped each other undress—even wearing Coco Chanel's latest, that was still easier with some assistance, and besides that it made a pleasant little evening ritual—and Ciara carefully removed the lace skullcap of her wig before the tall mirror, set it on a folding stand, and ran her hands through her six-inch mass of fine red-gold hair, rubbing her fingertips vigorously into her scalp. Her hair was straight or very gently wavy when it was long, depending on the weather, but right now it had a tendency to stand out in all directions like a glorious silky sunset or a very colorful dandelion ball. It also made her roundish, freckled, snub-nosed face look rounder than it was.

"I hate this!" she said. "It makes me look like a boy!"

"No, it *doesn't*," Luz said sincerely; hers was an ear-length cap of midnight now. "Nor do I."

"You look dashing with short hair, darling," Ciara said. "Like Artemis or a dryad or Queen Maeve. But . . . oh, Mother of God, it would have been awful as the dye grew out . . ."

Not least because everyone would have seen that she'd dyed her hair, still rather fast behavior in the circles she'd been raised in; she could scarcely pin a note to it reading *Done for Patriotic Reasons.*

". . . but . . . I do look like a *boy*. Or one of those bug-eyed dolls . . . only a *boy* doll."

Her hair did look a little strange like this. Luz had been bobbing hers to shoulder length for several years now, a look inspired by the French actress Polaire, and it wouldn't be long before it was back to that, but Ciara wouldn't be content until hers fell to the small of her back again. Bobbing was still a minority habit and a bit daring though spreading fast . . . but not yet in the intensely respectable lower-middle-class circles Ciara had inhabited until recently.

Luz came up behind her, smiling over her shoulder into the mirror and touching a finger to each side of her garter belt below the chemise she still wore. Ciara was two inches shorter than her, weighed about the same, and had an hourglass figure that would have been much more fashionable back at the turn of the century before an athletic slimness became the female ideal.

And she's got this underlying conviction she's not desirable. ¡Qué absurdo! *Well, if persuasion fails, there's always demonstration. It's almost embarrassing how I look at her sometimes . . . or just smell her hair, or see her smile or laugh or tilt her head or vanish into a book . . . and my mind leaps into bed and the toe-nibbling stage. Love and lust are both wonderful things, but when you put them together . . .* ¡Ay! *Fire!*

"*Mi amor,* you don't look *anything* like a boy, *gracias a Dios* . . . not above the neck and even less below it . . . but . . . well, if you wanted to, we could *pretend* to be two boys together . . . that might be interesting . . . You can be Kevin and I'll be Lucio . . ."

A peculiar expression came over Ciara's face as she parsed what Luz had just said, followed by a crimson blush and a laugh. Then:

"*Luz!*" and a poke in the ribs delivered backward. "Oh, *you!*"

Her face grew sober. She turned and gripped Luz fiercely.

"I wish . . ." she began. "Darling," she said into Luz's shoulder. "Would you do me a favor?"

"Anything, my heart," Luz said gently, a little surprised.

"Right now . . . would you make me forget everything but you for a while?"

NINE

City of Zacatecas

Hacienda of the Sweet Arrival, near Jerez

State of Zacatecas

United States Protectorate of México

JUNE 20TH, 1917, 1917(B)

Luz called "Good morning!" through the open kitchen door, as Ciara came yawning into the dining-room-cum-breakfast-nook of their suite. "If you're following the coffee, it's by your plate!"

No, she's not the sort who springs out of bed bright-eyed unless woken by something much more emphatic than the smell of bacon frying; an explosion might do, Luz thought, lifting the bacon out of the pan; she'd started the process this morning with a kiss on the back of the neck.

The arrangements didn't include a cook's services, but Luz didn't mind that. She'd always found cooking soothing and a good way to relax and think, almost as much so as music.

And feeding my darling gives me an absolutely absurd degree of pleasure, Luz thought.

Luz—who woke completely in an instant like a cat and at whatever hour she'd set her internal clock—slid the last of the pancakes onto the plates; set them on the table with the whipped cream, honey, and strawberries; and put the platter of crisp bacon and spitting sausages and mushrooms fried with them between. Then she brought a pitcher of water—you had to be careful to drink a lot of that in this climate. The scents of cooking and the coffee filled the space agreeably, with the fresh crisp air of a highland morning coming with dappled sunlight through the slatted louvers of the windows that overlooked the courtyard.

"And good morning again, my sleepy and adorably tousled . . . *Kevin*," Luz said.

She also deepened her voice on the last word.

"Good . . . *arrghpht!*" Ciara said, nearly choking on the coffee as she realized what her partner had just said.

Luz helpfully thumped her on the back.

"You are *impossible!*" the younger woman croaked after a moment. "And *shameless!*"

"I plead *merely improbable* on the first count, Your Honor, and guilty on the last, but I throw myself on the mercy of your heart's own court."

Ciara laughed, unwillingly at first and then with no restraint, and threw an arm around Luz's waist and hugged her; Luz rested her head against the top of Ciara's for a moment.

"And what has my love made for me? Oh, that looks heavenly!" Ciara said, managing to take a whole sip of the coffee this time.

She fell on to the stack of pancakes, carefully slathering each with butter and local honey and strawberries and stiff whipped cream before she stacked another on top, and helped herself from the sausages and bacon. Luz took a moment to stand smiling before she ducked back into the kitchen, set the pans to soak—dishwashing service *was* included— and returned to sit across from her partner and eat, admiring the way the shaft of morning light fell across Ciara's face.

"And today?"

"Today we buy an auto, then drive out to the hacienda later in the day," Luz said. "The rest . . . depends on circumstances."

Well, well, Zacatecas *is* becoming more modern," Luz said. "This part's different from how I remember it, at least."

They got off the trolley into the mild warmth of midafternoon and walked through the southwestern part of the town past streets crowded with traffic, where its serpentine S-curve valley grew a bit wider and the bare hills drew back. The buildings here were more recent, the streets broader and laid out on something close to a grid, and some had sidewalks and small roadside acacia trees; farther away from the main avenues and up the slope were patchy warrens of self-built *jacals* of adobe and rock and mud plastered over poles and grass and patched with flattened tins and corrugated iron, where rural migrants fleeing violence and just lately the very beginnings of mechanized farming had settled with their families and chickens and goats.

Women with braided black hair and dressed in colorful striped skirts and wrapped in loose fringed rebozos woven in geometric patterns were fetching clay jugs of water from the public standpipes and carrying them back toward those neighborhoods on their shoulders or heads, often leading a child by the hand or carrying one on their hip as well. More children and skinny dogs were running around on their own and anonymous laborers in sombreros and ragged off-white shirts and trousers plodded by, dodging the thick roadway traffic of cars and wagons and carts and bicycles.

There was a smell of dust and waste and sweat, but there were also important-looking—or self-important-looking—men striding along with watch chains across their waistcoats, and women with some pretensions carrying parasols and trailed by servants carrying bundles, lottery ticket sellers with trays at their waists crying their wares, women with dubious sweets or *pan dulce* well acquainted with the local flies doing likewise, a crowd of men talking and laughing around an open-fronted barber's shop and the barber making dangerous-looking gestures with a straight razor above a client whose face was buried in soapsuds, a blue-uniformed policeman in a cap with a leather bill whistling and swinging his truncheon from a loop around his wrist as he sauntered along . . .

"*How* is it different, darling?" Ciara said; she loved facts and details.

I'm an Impressionist painter, and she's a Pointillist, Luz thought, before she went on:

"No *aguadores*, no water sellers, now that we've extended the pipes within reach of everyone. The municipal supply here was always fairly good, but you didn't buy from the men with leather water bags if you valued your intestines. Particularly if you were an outsider! More autos and motor trucks . . . but my last visit in peacetime was six . . . nearly seven . . . years ago, so that would be true anywhere, even New York or Los Angeles."

Motor vehicles had gone from a few thousand to nearly a million in the United States during the last decade, from toys for the rich to a staple of everyday life.

"More bicycles. More mule and horse carts, too. Not as many porters carrying loads on their backs like that," she said.

She nodded toward a man bent nearly double under a huge net of clay jugs, trudging along with his hands braced on the tumpline across his forehead.

"All the delivery work would have been done by porters back then unless the load was just too heavy for a man to lift. They've patched up all the battle damage . . . mostly putting things back the way they were, people are conservative about their houses here . . . but there are more wires now too, more telephones . . . and *those* are new . . ."

At the edge of vision when the streets pointed west of south were a couple of blocky structures with big windows, skylights, a water tower, and the other tokens of manufacturing. The files said one was a shoe factory . . . though most of what it made was sandals . . . and the other made tack and harness. A cement plant was under construction, swarming with workers.

"When I was a girl visiting here, if you needed shoes or mule harness you went to a cobbler or harnessmaker and had it done to order; I remember my *papá* going into one to get a bridle repaired the first time we came through . . . that would have been 1903 . . . and how it smelled like new shoes and I was fascinated by the scars on the harnessmaker's hands . . . And some of the posters are different, of course."

The familiar ones were colorful advertisements for bullfights with matadors swirling their capes, or for plays at the Teatro Calderon, or perfectly ordinary examples advertising various brands of household goods. But there were some for moving pictures, from studios in Hollywood or Mexico City. And also the newly inevitable Department of Public Information type, some of them the same as you'd see in the north. Many others showed a heavily idealized Mexican peasant shaking hands with an equally stalwart and muscular American worker or soldier or farmer, or their female equivalents doing the same, or working side-by-side on dams and canals and roads to build the future, along with teachers and doctors and engineers.

That was the Progressive message, though of course it rather clashed with the attitude summed up in a standard local benediction on parting: *Que no haya novedad*—may no new thing arise.

One she nodded at showed a prosperous-looking man with an upturned mustache looking grave, with *José Luis Yaguno for Alcalde!* above the picture of the would-be mayor and *More jobs—Honest municipal taxes—Efficient cooperation!* below it; both were done bilingually.

"Efficient cooperation?" Ciara asked.

"Cooperation with us. That one over there has just *cooperation*, which means if you elect *him* he'll be cooperating too . . . but with *as little as I can get away with* tacked on the end."

They weren't the only gringos on the street; there were skilled workers and technicians from the Dakota Project in town for one reason or another, and businessmen or bureaucrats striding along—their bouncy walk made her self-conscious about the gliding local pace she'd fallen back into automatically—a brace of Negro soldiers seeing the sights with local girls on their arms, all four eating ice cream cones, and even a family of prosperous tourists, tow-haired all the way down their stepladder assortment of children running at three-year intervals from fifteen to a youngster clutching a stuffed Teddy bear. The parents were consulting a guidebook and looking more than a little baffled. Before the war they might have been equally bemused in France or Italy.

Luz stepped over to them. "Excuse me, sir, madam, are you having trouble finding something?" she said.

"Ah . . ."

Mr. Probably-from-Racine-Wisconsin-or-possibly-Indianapolis looked at her dubiously, and then visibly totted up her respectable clothing, impeccable Californian General American accent, and extremely Celtic-looking companion, and nodded. He had the beginnings of a potbelly, but the formidable shoulders said he'd done something physical as a young man, farming or lumberjacking or the like.

"Thank you, miss . . . we're looking for the, um, cathedral?" he said, confirming her second guess with his Hoosier rasp.

"Ah, you're in the wrong section of town, sir, but it's not far. If you turn around and go *there*—"

"I'd have been just as lost a little while ago," Ciara said with a smile as the midwesterners walked off.

"No, you'd be able to read a map." Luz looked around again. "All these new shops, too . . ."

Not all the new structures were flat-roofed either, as had been the custom in this town; many had pitched tile roofs, including one that looked as if it had an apartment over a shop, with a sign reading, in French:

Boulangerie—Patisserie—Confiserie—Creperie

And beneath it:

Café Chaud

Followed by:

Anciennement Rue Jean-Jaures, Paris

M. Teffeau, Propriétaire

With the Spanish equivalents, which included things just taken for granted in a Parisian setting:

Café y Panadería Francesa
Le Chaud
Pastelitos y Bebidas Deliciosas
Servidos en Nuestro Comedor y Patio

"Formerly of Jean-Jaures Street, Paris?" Ciara asked; her French was elementary, and mostly picked up from the female part of the Cheine household since the New Year.

"Yes, and I believe it," Luz said, laughing to herself.

Outside the door stood a dour, plumpish someone in an apron over a goodish dress who could only be Madame Teffeau. Her outfit would have been moderately chic in Paris when there still was a Paris; she was flanked by a daughter twenty years younger and thirty pounds lighter who had flour on her apron and hands, and talking to a skinny, wiry boy who could only be her teenage son. He was driving a delivery tricycle, like a three-wheeled motorcycle, whose box was heaped with paper-wrapped bundles and boxes. She was doing the talking in French with the occasional Spanish word thrown in, mostly street names, and . . .

"That's not just French, it's Parisian—she just said *n'pus jamais* for *don't ever.* Let's pick up something for dessert on the way," she said, as he darted off with a roar and puff of exhaust.

Once they were inside and the jangle of the bell over the door subsided Luz blinked; you could overeat just smelling the place, and she was surrounded by glass display counters backed by shelves on three sides, heaped with everything from baskets of plain but authentic baguettes through Kougin Aman—Breton pastries made with a croissant-like dough folded and refolded and baked slowly in rounds so that it puffed into many layers with a crisp crust of caramelized sugar ready to crackle under your teeth . . . and on to things made with candied orange peel and thin coats of dark chocolate . . .

Past the shop section was a small patio, set with eight tables under umbrellas and surrounded by chairs, all full in the bright midafternoon sunlight; in France they would probably have been out on the sidewalk instead, unless it was a shop in Provence. The customers were women, mostly youngish, including several they'd met repairing the altar cloths with Señora Gutiérrez. A door behind that led to the ovens—she could see a chimney smoking—where Monsieur Teffeau probably toiled, and the family quarters; there were large clay pots with gardenias and bougainvillea and oleanders spilling over their tops.

Luz waved and got a smile in return from her altar cloth acquaintances. The owner turned to her, and Luz mentioned a few places in Paris in her native-perfect arrondissement *huitième* version of French. That had Madame Teffeau wiping the corner of her eye with the tail of her apron and shoving a string-tied cardboard box full of edibles into their hands, and in what was very untypical behavior for a French shopkeeper refusing even token payment.

"We shall return, madame, and more than once, while we are staying in Zacatecas," Luz said on their way out. "And we shall repay your generosity."

"Did you see María Luisa having opera cake and coffee with some of her friends?" Ciara said. "I remember her from the altar cloths; a nice girl. She's the one who was so upset about Paris, and all the better for her!"

"Yes, she is a nice girl . . . and she's out in public," Luz said.

At Ciara's look she went on: "Except in the bigger cities and the capital . . . where they've got department stores and such . . . there *aren't* many places a respectable woman in Mexico can go just to have a cup and a bite and a chat with her *amigas*. She can't possibly set foot in a cantina or *pulqueria*, of course. Which incidentally means there's no place she can *pee*, if she feels the need away from her and her friends' houses. There are more ways than riveted iron of putting a ball and chain on someone."

"That's still a problem north of the border," Ciara pointed out.

"Yes, but not nearly as much as it used to be, or still is, here. This is a beginning! And while I admire the French more than I like them . . ."

"I *love* the smell coming from this box I'm carrying, Luz!"

"I didn't say I didn't love their *food*! Though sometimes you're better off not visiting the kitchen. But you've got to hand it to them for indomitability. The Teffeaus got out and got here and got this shop going in about the same time it takes to produce a baby."

"I wish I could just chat with someone like Luisa," Ciara said a little wistfully.

"I think you should make a chance to do just that, since we're not meeting Henrietta for a couple of hours and everything should look casual," Luz said.

"We'll go back?

"Not me, you. There was something about her . . . Yes, why don't you go do that now? Let her do the talking as much as you can; say I decided to take Madame Teffeau's gifts back to our guesthouse. We'll meet at that dealership in two hours."

The modest pink structure was next to an open lot behind a chest-high stucco wall and was labeled . . .

"Fred Foreman's Fords, Sales, Rentals, and Repairs," Luz read.

The Spanish translation below was understandable but a little eccentric: *Los Ford de Fred Foreman—Ventas, Rentas, Reparos.*

"A Ford dealership! The gazetteer said so, but it still seems . . . surreal."

They stepped through into an office waiting room decorated with dealership calendars and the usual patriotic prints, including one of Uncle Teddy riding up San Juan Hill with a bandana around his hat. A tall slim thirtyish man with carroty hair, jug ears, and freckles dressed in a rather loud checked suit and bow tie jumped up from behind a counter, smiling broadly.

"Fred Foreman, ladies!" he said in an overly friendly voice, radiating trustworthiness with an extended hand. "What can I do for you?"

"A Guvvie, please," Luz said, giving it enough of a squeeze to make him blink. "New, if possible."

She also gave their cover story and names, which by no coincidence whatsoever made it perfectly logical that a pair of young ladies would want such a rugged and masculine piece of engineering. Many of the local roads had been improved, but a lot hadn't yet.

Guvvie was short for General Utility Vehicle. A young man named Jesse Livingood had invented them a few years ago, just when the Intervention was getting underway, essentially by replacing the front axle of a Model T with a second back one, adding a front driveshaft, a differential case, and a few bits and pieces. It wasn't fast and even compared to a standard Model T it wasn't pretty, but with all four wheels pulling and the Model T's high clearance and ruggedness it could climb like a goat and take fantastic degrees of abuse.

"Well, I have three, but they're used, government surplus," the man said. "I have the Ford Model T touring car model and the light trucks new, but not that. Guvvies really move around here, ma'am—half the hacendados have one now. Why, the president himself—"

"Owns four, yes, I know, Mr. Foreman," Luz said.

Which was true. Ranchers and gentleman farmers and those with aspirations in that direction often did, especially those who'd used them in the Army. Uncle Teddy had been the first president ever to drive an auto himself, back in the opening years of the century, and he loved driving a Guvvie off the roads on western hunting trips.

Strong men blanched when invited to go along.

A plumpishly pretty mestiza in her twenties came through a door behind the counter to take Fred Foreman's place while he dealt with the clients. She wore a good American-style gray day dress with a lace collar and had a baby in the crook of her arm. A two-year-old in a sailor suit peeked out from behind her skirts; the paternal origin of both was obvious, and a younger woman, heavily pregnant, put her head through the door. She looked like a sister to the first, and took the baby when it was handed to her.

"I take care of desk, *Fede*," the elder of the probable sisters said in passable English, except for the last word, which was the local diminutive of Federico, exactly equivalent to Fred.

"Thank you, Señora Foreman," Luz said in Spanish. "We will not keep your husband longer than we must."

Most of the stock in the gravel-surfaced yard outside were rows of standard Model T roadsters or touring cars, in either the universal black or the Army's muted gray-green-brown, with plenty of the stretched light truck version as well, and a couple of the newest variety of truck, which had an extra axle and pair of wheels at the back. And half a dozen brand-new Fordson tractors, which ought to do well here with their stone-ax, low-maintenance simplicity.

Three Guvvies stood to one side, with prices on cardboard signs in their windscreens; the cheapest was three hundred dollars, and the other two were four hundred and six hundred. On the one hand, they were used; on the other, a Guvvie usually cost about twice what an ordinary Model T touring car did, and the current cost for one of *those* was five hundred fifty, a bit less than half the yearly income of one of the assembly line workers at Highland Park. On the third hand, *used* for an ex-military vehicle meant *used hard*.

"As you can see, the U.S. Army's finest creation—I drove one of these myself with the 7th Field Mortar Battalion—Miss, what are you—"

"This one is complete junk," Ciara said crisply, her head under the side-mounted flap of the hood and her *Baahst'n* accent a little stronger. "Three hundred? Parts and scrap value would be about fifty! The fuel line is split . . . and I think the block is cracked! You'd be lucky to get it out of the yard. Lucky if it didn't catch *fire*. And the tires are nearly bald."

"Well, now, Miss—" he began.

"Worthless junk," Ciara said again, without bothering to look in his direction.

Luz kept a slight, polite smile; inwardly she was chortling as Fred Foreman's freckled face fell.

Try saying that *ten times really fast*, she thought, gently mocking one of Julie's favorite running jokes.

Used-auto dealers were a new breed, but they'd mostly started out in the livery stable business as men who rented or dealt in horses, or learned the trade from those who had. You couldn't file an automobile's teeth to disguise its age or give it an opium-and-pepper suppository to conceal lethargy and sickness, but new mechanical equivalents of those ancient tricks were discovered every day.

And the cream of the jest is that he's flushing with rage that someone like Ciara is laying down the mechanical law to him, but he doesn't dare offend us. ¡Dios mio! How glad I am I don't work in sales! At least when I have to butter up annoying people in the line of business it's not because I want their money. Usually it's their information or their lives or both, and if it works I ruin them or kill them.

"This one's a bit better, but it needs work," Ciara said, after looking under the hood of the second Guvvie. "I'd better check."

The yard had an open-sided workroom with a metal ramp that let you drive an auto up onto a platform over a pit to give a mechanic access to the underside. Two men in grease-stained overalls *were* working on one; both were in their mid-twenties, around her age. One looked as if he were a close relative of Fred Foreman, and the other had a strong family resemblance to the man's wife and what were probably sisters married to the Foreman brothers. The redhead had a gold wedding band on his left hand and part of one protruding ear missing; his probable twice-over brother-in-law didn't have any visible injuries, but they might well have been trying to kill each other a few years ago.

They both unfolded broad smiles as Ciara marched into their workspace; the grins faded as she went right by them with a polite nod, examined and picked up a toolbox with an electric flashlight in it, and grabbed the rope attached to a little wooden platform on casters that she dragged along behind her.

"What is she *doing*?" Fred Foreman asked, honestly bewildered.

"Not buying a pig in a poke," Luz answered happily.

Ciara spent a few minutes guddling around under the hood with a socket wrench, then dropped on her back on the platform, took the flashlight, kicked herself under the high clearance of the Guvvie's wheels, and went to work there. Things banged and clanked, and Ciara invoked the Virgin and the saints when something rattled, apparently because she was shaking it. She'd never even been a passenger in an auto until she left Boston last summer, but she'd spent years helping her elder brother Colm the machinist on various jobs, and like all mechanically inclined youngsters these days they'd both studied autos just as hard as they could. Hands-on experience since had been nuts and cream to her.

Luz could clean a carburetor and do other running repairs; it was something she'd had to learn, working in the field. Ciara had a genuine affinity.

She pushed herself back out; by this time both the mechanics were standing nearby and offered her a hand up. She ignored it, not as a discourtesy but because she was in a state of total focus, tucked a foot underneath herself, and came up that way.

"This one's not bad but that engine and drive train needs to be torn down and put back together. Valves reground, everything cleaned out, and I think one of the magneto coils replaced. Probably new spark plugs too."

"*Sí, señorita,*" the Mexican-looking mechanic began, and continued in heavily accented English. "We were going to—"

His companion elbowed him and he fell silent.

Ciara moved on to the third. It was the newest-looking, had the double-width tires introduced on the latest model and a folding canvas hood for a roof—one that showed at least one round hole covered with a patch even in the down position. After a few minutes of careful appraisal, she nodded with a judicious pursing of her lips, wiping her hands carefully on a rag from the toolbox.

"This one's not bad at all," she said. "Made early last year from the batch numbers. Several important parts have been replaced and the frame was bent and then straightened with an air hammer and given a riveted reinforcement patch—looks like it was in a bad collision accident and then fairly well repaired."

Both the young mechanics nodded vigorously; the redhead listened with his head turned to put his unclipped ear forward. In the loud flat voice that people with damaged hearing often used he said:

"We did that. Finished yesterday, so we didn't have time yet for the others."

"But the price is ridiculous for an Army auto that was in an accident and sold out of service," Luz added. "And ridden hard and put away wet every day, too, that's how soldiers deal with equipment."

"You're government workers, ladies! It's on your expense account!" Foreman said plaintively.

As a matter of fact, it *was* on their expense account, but their cover identities would be careful about the amounts, which were rigorously checked.

"I'm not going to waste the American people's substance," Luz said primly.

The expression of unanswerably sound Party doctrine shut him up with a snap.

Technically she could report him, and *soliciting the corruption of a public servant* was a very serious crime these days. Uncle Teddy had gotten his start in national politics as an anticorruption civil service reformer, and it was a cause still dear to his heart. It was especially dangerous down here in the Protectorate, under martial law. Foreman wasn't frightened enough to suspect her of being FBS or even worse

Black Chamber, but being a Party member with obvious connections in Mexico City would be more than enough, especially considering that a used-car salesman generally had good reasons not to want a light shone under his rock.

Plenipotentiary Lodge was death on corruption too, in a cold, merciless Puritan Yankee sort of way.

"Country before convenience," she added, and he nodded frantically.

"I would never suggest otherwise . . . ah, five fifty, then?"

And besides, Mima had taught her bargaining, and taught it as a blood sport.

Ciara drove the Guvvie through the bright midday warmth southwest of the city at about twenty-two miles an hour—just a bit below its top speed—while listening carefully to the little twenty-horsepower engine's four cylinders hammering away with a ticking *tuktuktuktuktuk* sound.

"No problems," she said happily, weaving past an oxcart whose driver walked beside it; the traffic here wasn't particularly heavy, but its nature made driving an adventure in itself.

The little stick-sided two-wheeled thing in front of them was heaped high with some sweet-smelling green fodder that hid everything beyond it—including things in the oncoming lane, given the curve. Most of the animal-drawn vehicles stuck to the shoulders of the road, but not all. The white oxen rolled their great brown eyes as the Guvvie passed them, heading into the downhill turn without much problem.

Then Ciara saw what was just *after* the oxcart; a file of mules, tethered together and very close. Which *was* a problem, given the oncoming truck in the other lane, and she hit the brake and clutch pedals for a moment while wrenching at the wheel as the *A-ogoooogha! A-ogoooogha!*

of the Guvvie's horn sent mules skittering and their driver cursing and the auto weaving close enough to get the beasts' scent and for some slobber from their tossing heads to spatter on the windscreen.

"Gather at the river! *Lord Jesus spare a sinner!*" Henrietta Colmer yelped beside Ciara, rearing up in a way that showed she could drive too; she was stamping for the brake that wasn't there in front of *her* where she sat to the driver's right.

We designed these roads for motor traffic, but I don't think Mexico altogether agrees with that. Not yet, Luz thought, looking up from the file in her lap.

She also slapped a hand into the open attaché case beside her on the bench-style backseat to prevent the papers from going flying, as the auto lurched and swayed and skidded and then steadied down again in an empty stretch to cries of relief from the driver and passenger in the front.

Fortunately the road was two lanes broad with generous graveled shoulders even when it went through cuttings in this rocky ground just west of Zacatecas. Those surroundings looked even drier than they were, with barely enough pasture for goats . . . which didn't mean there weren't goats, herded or at least watched by ragged preadolescent boys as they wandered amid a clatter of bells. The surface was as good as any main highway back north, roller-stabilized concrete topped with a layer of asphalt pavement. Asphalt was dirt cheap around here, and the same vast oilfields on the Gulf that produced it helped finance things like the road net.

Standard Oil and its peers had learned not to complain at the taxes. There was plenty left over, and the roads helped them too in the long run by encouraging the use of autos and motor trucks, not to mention the contracts that had followed when all the locomotives on the new Mexican portion of American National Railways were switched to oil fuel.

Luz had the backseat to herself . . . except for the briefing files, a Thompson gun muzzle-down in a leather scabbard on the back of the driver's position, and their evening dresses in a long cloth bag hanging from one of the roof struts by a hook, though they'd kept the canvas hood down since it didn't look like rain and the visibly patched bullet holes didn't have the right optics. She took the time to think and plan while the two younger women settled back to chatting happily, laughing now and then, and occasionally dipping into a paper bag of candied peanuts set between them. They were getting along fine, which was pleasant in itself and in a small way a good thing in terms of her partner coming out of her shell and developing Chamber connections from the ground up as she went along.

Everyone needs connections and friends. If you're a woman, you need them more. If you're an offensively brilliant, eccentric woman who loves me, you need them even more than that. And Ciara will need her own at some point; being able to tap into my network is good, but it isn't enough. She can't spend her working life being Luz O'Malley Aróstegui's protégée.

The lively traffic and people going peacefully about their lives were a pleasure too, not to mention savoring the smooth ride, and she smiled into the warm wind smelling of plowed earth and road tar. Luz had put years of her life into the Intervention, blood and pain and fear, boredom and sweat, watching friends die and resigning herself to the often brutal and usually squalid necessities of her trade, and now the field she'd helped clear was bearing fruit.

"Turn right at the intersection up ahead," Henrietta said helpfully, as she passed the *bota* of warm, leathery-tasting, but welcome water they'd been sharing back to Luz for a moment. "That'll lead us straight west to Jerez and then through it."

The station chief's secretary had a folded map in her hand, staying in character with commendable consistency even with only the three of them in the little auto . . . and the fact that there were plenty of signposts, bilingual ones at that. You never knew who might be *looking* at any given moment in public even when you couldn't be overheard, and Henrietta was ostensibly their guide, having delivered an invitation from her employer at Universal Imports to attend a function at the Duráns' Hacienda del Dulce Arribo—Hacienda of the Sweet Arrival.

Quoting from Flecker's Golden Road to Samarkand *again, Julie,* Luz thought as she mentally translated the name. *Though at least it's not* Golden *Arrival—even Flecker thought that he used the word* golden *too much.*

Many of the local bigwigs would be at the party, American and Mexican both, and the visiting aspiring-middle-grade types they were pretending to be might well have been included; the Party disapproved of social snobbery and thought highly of team spirit and promotion by merit. A dinner party was an economical disguise, a way to discreetly introduce herself to several powerful men who needed to know her face-to-face while losing both herself and them in the crowd, and it also gave her a reason to be out of Zacatecas for the interviews at the air base and with the Ranger captain that the Chamber had planned for tomorrow. Many of the guests would be staying overnight and trickling out after breakfast, as was standard for country house affairs.

They'd left Zacatecas after a light snack—you had to pace yourself if you were expecting a ten-course formal dinner—and Ciara had had a possibly quite productive gossip with María Luisa and her friends at Madame Teffeau's patisserie, and felt that Louisa was *definitely* preoccupied with something she wanted to discuss with an American. That gave them more than enough time until sunset even at this time of year, assuming no serious problems . . . which in these parts was a fairly radical assumption. They were in traveling gear: bandanas around their heads beneath hats that had chin cords to keep them on, motoring goggles, cord jackets with lots of pockets, gloves, practical boots, and divided skirts of the sort that let you ride a horse astride and then fasten up with a row of ornamental-looking silver buttons to turn it into a skirt on foot.

It was all a bit daring . . . for 1907 . . . and a little old-fashioned in 1917, if you were south of fifty; these days American women frequently just gave up the ancient struggle to deny their own bipedal nature and wore pants where a special situation demanded it. Like many of those *north* of fifty you could tell Uncle Teddy flinched inside at the sight of women in trousers, for all that he'd encountered it occasionally in the lawless frontier crudity of the Dakota badlands a long generation ago. Though *he* at least rarely complained aloud. But things were different at the sort of elite bunfest they were heading for tonight.

They could at least wear their pistols openly on their hips in this upper-class-outdoorswoman gear. For that matter it was becoming common again in the United States proper, though much more so for men and a little more in the West than the East. Uncle Teddy had never made a secret of the fact that ever since his days as a rancher and deputy sheriff chasing outlaws and feuding with mad murderous French counts and their hired gunmen amid the Badlands buttes, he had always kept a weapon—currently a little FN auto pistol like the one her father had given her for her birthday as a girl—in the bedside dresser and slipped a Colt .45 into a pocket when he went out, a routine as set as putting on his hat. That had occasioned some surprise at places like the Harvard faculty lounge in the past when the shooting iron was transferred from an overcoat to a jacket, but these days if he did something in public millions imitated him, regardless of the occasional unfortunate accident.

Hence Uncle Teddy and Fred Burnham making firearms classes mandatory in the Boy and Girl Scouts to cut the carnage, Luz thought with a curve of the lips. *That and their utter horror at discovering how many red-blooded, rootin'-tootin' Americans didn't know which end the bullet came out of!*

The Scouts themselves were universal and compulsory nowadays, part of the common school system and a preparation for national service. So at least the *next* generation wouldn't be able to say nobody told them that walking around locked, cocked, and safety off . . . or twirling said locked, cocked pistol with a finger through the trigger guard was a bad . . . very bad . . . really, really *very bad* idea.

Though you could *argue that idiots culling their germ plasm out of the national heredity by fatally fumbling with a loaded piece is just what the Department of Public Health and Eugenics means by* negative selection. *Plus the
spectacle of bespectacled insurance adjusters in Chicago and plump shoe store pro-
prietors in Poughkeepsie playing at Bold Frontiersman is* definitely *amusing,
and life is too short and painful not to laugh when you can.*

By the time they were past the rocky section the road had dropped
about a thousand feet, and then they lost another thousand as they continued toward Jerez, a handsome farming town with a core of eighteenth-
century buildings something like a quarter-scale version of Zacatecas
City. The afternoon turned warmer as they lost altitude—not uncom-
fortably hot since it was still over six thousand feet and it would be cool
at night, but definitely more summery than Zacatecas's *tierra fría.*

The drop put them in a flattish upland basin, pastures with straw-
colored grass green-tinged from the first rains, and rectangles of
plowed land showing dark brown, or less frequently the golden-brown
stubble of reaped winter wheat with rows of sheaves. There were occasional though admittedly usually rather small and often thorny trees,
as well as the ubiquitous little patches of spiny, paddle-shaped nopal
cactus in neglected spots just now breaking into their big, showy flowers of yellow and red and white. And even an attempt at *planting* trees
by the sides of the road, which might or might not last depending on
how well the protective collars of wire mesh worked.

The Department of Public Works proposes, dem goats disposes, Luz thought.

Peones worked in the fields, the dirty-white costumes of the men
and the colored hiked-up skirts of the women showing against the dark
soil; around here getting the seed into the ground as soon as some rain
allowed was one of those rural things that had to be done *right now,*
quite literally "on pain of death" since local experience was that they'd
starve if the crop failed. The Protectorate's famine relief policies were
too new and peasant trust in government policies far too low to have
altered those assumptions.

The wooden plows and harrows pulled by pairs of the patient oxen Julie had mentioned were finishing up, but also more modern American-style machinery drawn by mules and horses and once or twice a tractor. Men and rather fewer women moved to a rhythm ancient before the conquistadores came, the tall-crowned sombreros bobbing as they made holes in the dirt with the pointed wooden sticks called *coa*, dropped in seeds of corn or beans from slung sacks or baskets, and covered them with a push of one foot.

Clumps of adobe huts or stone-stick-mud-and-cornstalk *jacals* were scattered about, with beehive-shaped clay graneries and ramshackle pens beside them. The greater whitewashed or stucco or stone bulk of a hacienda stood out on a rise now and then, a few burnt-out and abandoned, the rest still in operation with laborers' quarters and church tight-clustered around them and often a watchtower in a defensive circuit-wall, like a medieval fortified village . . .

Which is what they are, practically speaking, Luz thought.

Past Jerez were more fields, but the road turned to graveled dirt—still as good as any rural byway in gringolandia, and better than most; the Party had never met a road it didn't have a burning itch to straighten, widen, and improve, and here in the Protectorate they didn't have to convince reluctant local voters to fork out for it. Traffic was sparse in most places but busy in clumps, and it included things like a very large and very badly managed flock of bleating and comically newly shorn sheep that sidelined them and some other passersby for an interminable wait amid a smell of greasy lanolin and dung . . . until it turned out to be the collision of *two* large, badly managed flocks.

Traveling here could drive you insane unless you planned for unexpected delays and took them philosophically.

Ciara and Henrietta took advantage of the enforced pause by teaching each other some of the folk tunes they'd grown up with, trading spirituals and work hollers for Fenian fight songs and planxtyes and laments.

Ciara's singing voice was a slightly thin soprano though she had no trouble keeping a tune, since she played the piano very well, almost up to orchestral standards. Henrietta's was a contralto like Luz's, but of a deeper smoky-tinged coloratura variety. It sounded a little odd when they belted out the chorus from an old Gaelic clan march together at full volume, because while she did well with "The Rising of the Moon" in English, her Georgia accent grew stronger when she sang:

"Oró, sé do bheatha bhaile
anois ar theacht an tsamhraidh!"

Luz mostly sat and listened—with the Thompson gun cradled in her arms while they were stopped and by ingrained habit keeping an eye on her surroundings—but she joined in at the end, contributing a Cuban song her mother had liked:

"Sobre las ondas del mar bravía
puse tu nombre con que soñaba
y a medida que lo escribía . . ."

That one had the half-dozen pedestrians stopped with them listening closely, and applauding in pleased farewell as Ciara put the Guvvie in gear and drove off. Luz slid the big machine pistol back into its scabbard and sat back with a sigh. The Sierra de Cardos rose like a blue ripple on the western horizon, gradually accumulating clouds that climbed until they formed thunderheads towering dizzy-high into the blue, rose-colored as winds and shadows fell toward the west.

"This is the turnoff, my hapless newcomer friends," Henrietta said, pointing.

Ciara grinned as she hit the foot-clutch to downshift into low gear, throttled back with the lever on the column of the steering wheel, stuck out her hand to signal, and made the turn. Driving was still a sport to her, as well as a skill she was proud of mastering. There were two stone posts marking the entrance to the hacienda's lands, and a sign in English and Spanish.

"Look! We're on the Durán ranch without a dead sheep stuck to the radiator!" Ciara said. "No burro braying on its back in the backseat, waving its little hooves in the air and squishing Luz! No goat riding on the hood bleating prayers to Satan! A miracle, by Mary Mother and the Saints!"

The hacienda's fourteen thousand acres were a fair chunk of the planet, around twenty-two square miles, but the new internal laneways were about as good as the road they'd been driving on, though narrower.

Other things looked different too after a few years of well-funded and aggressively Progressive management. The fences were neater and much more uniform, all stout treated posts and tight-strung five-strand barbed wire from the Monterrey steel mills, around fields bigger and squarer than usual here. About a third of them were plowed and harrowed and planted and dotted with scarecrows or scarecrowlike ancients with even older shotguns to keep the birds from eating the seed corn—one advantage of good equipment and plenty of it was that you could do crucial operations faster.

The rest was in grazing, but there weren't any goats: Goats were officially considered backward and inefficient. The cattle and sheep the mounted vaqueros herded already showed the influence of the pedigreed red-coated, white-faced Hereford and golden Jersey bulls and square-built Australian Polwarth rams the Duráns had brought in from the family's ranches in New Mexico to cross with local grade stock bought cheap.

Which is metaphorical, when you think about it, Luz thought with a grin of her own. *Though they have generations a lot shorter than ours.*

In one of those plowed fields she saw three tractors with tall rear wheels of cleated metal drawing broad disk harrows to turn the last furrowed stretch to dark-brown smoothness. Four multirow planters followed along, each drawn by big teams of stout mules; it was all just like a first-rate farm in Missouri or Iowa. Closer to the center of the property were a number of deep wells, wind pumps, and irrigation channels, fields of wheat—reaped golden-brown stubble now—vibrant-green alfalfa, brand-new orchards of young waist-high fruit trees with their trunks painted white and enclosed in woven-straw sheaths, and what her Californian eyes recognized as a fair-sized vineyard on grafted rootstocks set out in spring and well into leaf now. Pencil cypresses would give the verges and tracksides a Tuscan look, if they survived beyond their current sapling stage.

Men and women were tramping homeward with tools over their shoulders, or in some cases riding that way crowded into Ford motor trucks pulling two-wheel trailers full of equipment, a jarring sight given her experience of Mexico.

Though I suppose it makes sense. Time they spend walking to work and back is time they don't *spend working . . . which is inefficient. Knocking off a bit early for farm laborers in the busy season, though, aren't they?*

Most haciendas had their *casco*—the complex of central buildings—tightly packed together, with rutted dirt and weeds right up to the outside wall. Such splendors as they had were within, in the patio and courtyard-centered owner's residence. The Duráns had taken advantage of the ruin that had come here with the fighting to open things out, starting anew on everything but the *casa grande* and the church. Those were eighteenth-century buildings on seventeenth-century foundations, and now with twentieth-century tweaks like electric light and piped water.

Barns, corrals, wool press, stables, equipment sheds and a winery under construction, a dairy, and—very modern anywhere and weirdly alien here—brand-new cylindrical concrete silos and grain stores were well off to one side in a direction that put them downwind, given the prevailing breezes hereabouts. Even with all the modernity and efficiency in the world there was no way she knew of to make a pigpen fragrant, or at least not in a good way.

The *calpanería* that housed the workers was rows of three- or four-room adobe cottages on concrete pads, plastered and whitewashed L-shapes with red tile roofs, each enclosed in a walled sixty-by-ninety yard that gave space enough for a chicken coop and a little truck garden. The living quarters were obviously intended to help enclose a central square when they were finished, and there were some larger public buildings as well, in the same plain but rather handsome generalized Hispanic style. More adult farmworkers were around than she'd have expected before the sun was fully down, as well as the expected swarms of children, and the smells hinted at pots of highly spiced *mole* and something good roasting, while an amateur but enthusiastic band warmed up.

Ciara slowed and gave it a look as they drove by; she had sensitive antennae for feudal oppression, having been raised on stories of the sins of the Ascendancy back in Erin, which were bad enough in reality and even worse as told to the children of a nationalist exile who'd made it out of Dublin one jump ahead of pointed questions from the Metropolitan Police, the Royal Irish Constabulary, and detectives from the Special Branch in London.

"Not so bad," she said, slightly surprised. "And better when it's finished and the plantings grow and it's not so raw."

Henrietta snorted laughter. "Ciara, honey, they got laid-on water here, a good store, a free ration of cornmeal and beans to every family every week, a clinic with a nurse, a school, *and electricity!*"

Only a few American country folk outside the edges of the bigger cities had that already, though the number was growing fast with the new rural utility co-ops and regional grids. The Zacatecas area had gotten a major power plant early in the year, built on a maximum priority by the Army Engineers with General Electric assisting, to serve the Project and incidentally the surroundings.

"People *fight* to get jobs on this place, and they live better than a lot of American-born folks in Georgia," Henrietta added, with a slight edge of bitterness.

The people she was talking about in her home state had tarpaper shacks or tumbledown one-room log cabins, some dating back to slavery days, with cotton planted right up to the door and often not even a vegetable garden to vary the diet of fatback and grits bought for extortionate prices, on credit, at interest rates indistinguishable from usury added on to debts they could never pay. Ciara sighed acknowledgment, then glanced over her shoulder for an instant.

Luz gave a nod of permission; what she'd heard via the Party-insider grapevine was going to be announced by the Department of Public Information fairly soon anyway, with all possible bells and whistles and rah-rah, probably via a presidential speech if Public Information could pry Uncle Teddy away from the war for a day.

To distract people from the fact that the war is frozen in place and our leaders are scratching their heads and wandering around asking each other What to do, what to do? *in plaintive tones while Hindenburg and Ludendorff drop their trousers and slap their withered Prussian buttocks in our collective face.*

Ciara said confidentially: "Henrietta, a little bird told me that the Department of Lands and Agriculture back home is going to start breaking up the plantations in the South, making the planters sell what they can't work themselves with their own equipment and hired labor, and hand the rest out to the tenants. To the sharecroppers, as they say down there."

Henrietta Colmer froze for a moment, and said in a voice that was soft and startled at the same time:

"Lord Jesus!"

The new regime had never been shy about making changes and stepping on toes—that was pretty much the New Nationalism's whole point—but this would take a third of the country and pull it up by the roots. Henrietta blinked, engaged in some obvious hard thought including math, and went on:

"That'd be better than half the cotton land on a big Black Belt spread anywhere . . . maybe two-thirds . . . and more over to the Delta country. Probably a lot of planters will just sell up and get out of the cotton business for good an' all if they can get a fair price for the land. Or switch to growin' something else: cattle, maybe, or peaches . . . pecans . . . truck . . . or goobers and hogs."

"Really?" Ciara said curiously. "They're going to get *paid* . . . paid something at least . . . for the land they give up—wouldn't that finance working the rest of it? Buy modern equipment and hire men to use it?"

The way the Duráns have here went unspoken.

Henrietta shook her head: "Reason they need lots of sharecroppers on a cotton plantation is to keep the hands for the *picking*. There's plenty of machinery already can plow for cotton and plant cotton and even do most of the chopping . . . weeding, you Yankees say . . . but the planters don't use it. They leave the croppers with one-mule walking plows and hoes like Granddaddy used in slavery days because nobody's made a machine can *pick* cotton yet. So you can't hire enough hands in picking season, not cash wage, not for a big property and still have it pay any profit."

"Why not?" Ciara said.

"Planter hires a hand for cash right at the busy time of year, he has to *pay* cash out of his pocket . . . and planters like money going *in* there a lot better. He has to pay a hand by the day, pay *before* the cotton's sold, and pay about the same if cotton's selling at five cents a pound or twenty-five. And a hired hand can walk away just when the planter needs him most, because that time of year everyone's looking to hire," Henrietta said.

"Ah, and the sharecroppers are stuck because they're paid only the once in a year," Ciara said, taking the point, and Henrietta nodded.

"Not one red cent until *after* the landlord sells the cotton for whatever it fetches that year; the planter gets paid by the commission buyer, and then makes the division—about half and half, mostly. That's *if* the planter keeps honest scales and honest books, and believe me, a lot don't. A cropper can't up and leave, either; he owes the planter money and it comes out of his share before he sees it, he owes the storekeeper money and *that* comes out of his share before he sees it. He owes money to every-damn-body in God's creation, all the time! Except for three weeks after the harvest, maybe, if he's lucky, and then it's back to borrowing against *next* year's share. He stays, and he picks, and so do his family, from can-see to can't-see."

She looked back at Luz, who was nodding in respect at the concise explanation of the economics that had kept that part of the country a seedy, backward, down-at-heel national embarrassment for decades.

"The croppers will be getting forty acres and a mule, ma'am?" Henrietta asked skeptically.

That half promise hadn't worked out well for her people after the Civil War, which she'd have heard about from her own grandparents.

"More like eighty acres, a team or a small Ford tractor on hire purchase, a line of credit from a credit union, and a co-op running the cotton gin and buying fertilizer and supplies, Miss Colmer," Luz said, and added: "It's not just for *colored* tenant farmers, of course."

"There are about as many white ones, *walkfoot bookra* they're called, gettin' treated near as bad by the boss-man," Henrietta observed, incidentally confirming Luz's guess at a Gullah speaker in her background. "Sometimes they even realize it, until the planters turn one of their bought politicians loose screaming *uppity nigra!* and their cracker brains turn to . . . buttered grits . . . and run out their ears."

"So it's not just altruism, either," Luz said.

"Good," Henrietta said dryly. "Altruism's not what you'd call real reliable, most times, ma'am."

Luz nodded. "The Party always thought that section was an anti-Progressive . . . medieval . . . drag on the country's economy. And now that Negroes have the vote again it's not enough to put down night riding and lynching, the Party needs to keep the planters and crop-lien storekeepers from putting the knuckle on them to vote for the Democrats."

"By twisting a noose made out of their debts around their necks, right? I suppose it helps a *bit* that the planters are all Democrats and *Bourbon* Democrats hot for state's rights at that. They spit whenever they hear *el jefe*'s name," Henrietta said.

Unlike the hacendados here, who we need, so we have to be easier on them went unspoken.

"If they're already enemies, the Party can afford to ignore it when they scream," Luz agreed. "Especially now, with this being wartime and that making it so unpopular and risky ..."

Make that lethally *risky*, she added to herself with tactful restraint, and carefully did not mention Savannah or what had happened to Colmer's family as she continued. It would be painful enough anyway.

". . . to be labeled pro-German. Which to be fair is mostly *un*fair to them; only a few went anything like that far and the rest were as horrified as anyone, but we're going to do it to them anyway to keep them weak."

Henrietta grinned, and Luz went on:

"The plan is to use this to peel the poor white tenants away from them and into the fold too; there will never be a better time to cut their bosses off at the knees."

"That's smart thinkin'," Henrietta said, and patted Ciara on the shoulder in thanks for getting her the news a little early, and then: "Here we are."

Here was a broad semicircular drive done in pink crushed stone up to the front of the *casa grande*. It too would be lined by imposing Italian cedars, presently six-foot saplings; there was a fair start at lawns and plantings around the house, a rarity in this land.

A fountain with water spraying around a cavorting of elongated elfin-looking bronze maidens and greyhounds in the modern style played in the open area before the iron-strapped oak main doors, but the building itself was a hundred feet of two-story 1750s Mexican baroque in dark-rose limestone masonry, pillars and arches over a raised tile-floored veranda, and a long *mirador* balcony much like it above. At either end were four-story towers, lavish with carving and with little ornamental white-and-green tiled domes above; you could just see an identical pair at the rear of the complex. The cross-shaped church a few hundred yards away had a dome of its own, in robin's-egg blue.

Though I think that glint is off the muzzles of aircraft-type twin Brownings inside the uppermost story of the casa grande's *towers, so they're not* just *ornamental,* Luz thought. *And I can tell why they've put in those Talavera tile surrounds on the windows—you can see the staining from a smoke plume on the stone above that one where the tile's not all on yet. As Julie said, this place didn't burn all the way* down, *but it did* burn.

It was only around six thirty, but there were already quite a few big Peerless, Reno, Owen, and Packard touring cars to show guests arriving, and several horse-drawn carriages owned by the more conservative local gentry that looked as if they had been splendid, back around the turn of the century. The vehicles included a massive six-wheeled staff car built on the chassis of a Mac AC truck, accompanied by a little Ferret light armored car and a few Ford trucks, enough to carry a platoon of motor riflemen. The soldiers were there too, a squad on alert and the rest at ease but with their weapons to hand.

They and the housemaids who'd brought out trays of coffee and varieties of *pan dulce* were chatting easily, trying out bits of English in return for badly pronounced Spanish from phrasebooks; some of the troopers actually had the phrasebooks in hand, leafing through them in a hurried hunt for something more appropriate to mild flirtation than: *Halt or we shoot!*

Or: *Tell me at once . . .*

—where the bandits are!

—where the weapons are hidden!

—where . . .

Uncle Teddy and General Wood had seen to it from the very beginning of the Intervention that the American military down here took being properly respectful to the local womenfolk very seriously indeed—originally by means that had included a few well-publicized summary executions after drumhead courts-martial in the field *pour encourager les autres*, to get the idea of discipline home among the first wave of enthusiastic volunteer Rough Rider–style regiments.

A pennant with two silver stars on a yellow-edged triangle of black flew from the bumper of the staff car, a major general's banner, the sign of a divisional commander.

"That's a guard detachment from the Reconnaissance Battalion of the 32nd Infantry," Luz said thoughtfully; the soldiers were all Negroes. "General Young must be here already. Good."

A man she recognized was also there, waiting at the steps and greeting guests and looking harassed if you knew him *well*, wearing the sort of well-cut sack suit and homburg you displayed just before changing to evening dress for a formal event. It was also fairly obvious he'd feel more comfortable in cowboy boots, chaps, and Stetson, though that might be her personal knowledge speaking.

"*¿Por qué tan triste en una fiesta, Alfredito?*" she said to Julie's brother-in-law as they came to the steps: *Why the long face at a party, Alfie?*

"*¡Lu—Graciela! ¡Ay!*"

Alfredo, or in some circles Alfred, Durán was her own age and only a bit taller, lean and hard and hawk-faced, with a mustache and cropped black hair and eyes as dark as her own without the narrow blue streaks, his skin a weathered outdoorsman-brown; he had a stiff left knee courtesy of a bullet in 1914, caught while leading his unit of New Mexican mounted riflemen as they fought their way out of a guerilla ambush.

"It looks like being *mayordomo*"—which meant manager—"here suits you, Fred," she replied.

They shook hands—the etiquette of that had changed a bit since she was a girl—and she introduced Ciara under her cover name. Hen-

rietta and he just shook without more than *hello*, since she was a familiar fixture here. Normally he would have given Luz a kiss on the cheek
and an embrace, as she was an old friend of the family and more or less
qualified as a family member herself by virtue of being his niece Alice's
madrina, which made her a *comadre*. That . . . more or less . . . meant
"joint mother" and made Alfredo her sort-of-notional brother.

"It does suit, or at least the parts I can do from the saddle, and it's a
good way to get experience . . . Graciela," he said, in his archaic-
sounding *nuevomexicano* hillbilly Spanish.

Julie had said she'd slip him a word. His last-minute recall of her
cover identity proved she had.

"Where's Julie?"

"She's in the kitchen, and she tells me I have you to blame for this
nightmare!" he said. "Noemi's there too."

That was his wife, and also third cousin. The Duráns were a
sprawling, expansive clan, affluent and well-educated, but still rather
provincial in some ways.

"Julie decided we had to do this at short notice, so she brought the
town cook and staff out here to *help* . . . So far, there hasn't been any actual gunfire or slit throats."

Luz chuckled; two head cooks and their staffs suddenly pitched
without warning into one *cocina* was a recipe for war to the knife if
she'd ever heard one, or at least for rolling chaos.

"And General Young's wife volunteered to help get things in order
too; his party got here a couple of hours ago and she was taking tea
with Julie and Noemi when the news of mortal combat came via an assistant cook's helper sobbing helplessly and falling on her knees and
kissing Julie's hand while she begged for aid," he said.

"Well, I regret that's a problem for our beloved Noemi, but . . ."

Alfredo visibly held on to his temper. "*Mi amiga*, did it occur to you
when you asked Julie to put this *do* on, that this is the end of the
summer-crop planting season? Which comes *right after* the wheat har-

vest, the sheep shearing, and the first cutting on the alfalfa? No? *And* we're putting in a hundred and sixty acres of sunflowers as an *experiment* this year, so it's completely new to everyone? Every delay after the rains start reduces yields! It couldn't *wait* another week?"

"No it couldn't, *Alfredito*. It's . . . business."

Which meant Black Chamber business; he sighed and shrugged acknowledgment. That was what his brother and his sister-in-law did; the hacienda was *a* business, but it wouldn't be the family *business* until they both retired. He planned to be running his own spread by then, of course.

"And it's not as if you're out in the fields yourself," Luz added.

"I should be, keeping things running smoothly, not standing around drinking cocktails in a penguin suit! And we have to give the people a fiesta if *we're* having one! Especially given how hard I suddenly pushed our workers when Julie gave me the news, we're finishing the last of the sunflowers *this afternoon*, three days ahead of schedule. Everyone had to give up unnecessary luxuries like sleep."

"We saw that, the tractors. Very . . . efficient."

Efficiency and *virtue* were more or less the same thing in the New Nationalist lexicon.

"They're roasting *old-fashioned* pigs and *inefficient* sheep down in the *calpanería* right now and rolling out the barrels!" he began. "All-out burst efforts like this are *not* efficient. The hangovers tomorrow alone will—"

TEN

Four of Alfredo's subordinates came trotting up, *caporales*—foremen—hats in hand, two of them in the usual *peon* dress and two in more modern blue bib overalls and print cotton shirts and smaller American-style Western hats rather than the huge local sombrero, and all obviously burdened with questions only Don Alfredo could answer. He held up a hand to them, turned over his shoulder to wave the house servants forward for the baggage—and one to take the Thompson gun and its ammunition to the *Casa's* armory, after Luz removed the drum and worked the action to make absolutely sure nothing was in the chamber—and Luz led her small party into the entry hall.

Fortunate for the mission that I never got down here since they bought this place, Luz thought.

She'd seen Julie often enough over the past few years, but that was usually while her old friend and her family were on visits north. In Santa Fe late last summer, just before Luz left on that mission to Europe that had led to her meeting Ciara, for instance, and then again this spring while Ciara was off doing technical consultant work at the Telemobiloscope plant.

So at least the house *staff here don't know me.*

They were in the upper corridor leading to their rooms before they ran into two people who *did* know her. Fortunately and almost certainly by no coincidence whatsoever, that was Julie's daughter—and Luz's *ahijada*—Alice, and her *niñera* Anita, who was about forty, sensible-looking in a good dark dress with her hair coiled over her ears, and could be relied on for discretion.

As the timing of the *chance* encounter here in a safely private part of the house and her use of a polite but distant nod showed, rather than the friendly deference that would have been the normal greeting to Luz in her own persona. As opposed to the we-work-for-the-same-boss smile she gave Henrietta.

The child she was leading by the hand was a few months short of three; she looked at Luz dubiously for a moment, searching her memory over massive depths of time that stretched all the way back to Ferris wheel rides and cotton candy in April—and to vomiting all over Luz's frock—then broke into a dazzling smile of recognition and charged full-tilt with her arms spread, caroling:

"*Nannnnaaaa Loooooz!*"

The projectile topped with brown-yellow curls ran into her at speed and enthusiastically embraced her leg, making her stagger. A bouncing golden retriever puppy a couple of months old and with about the same color of pelt followed, perfectly ready to be joyous if his deity-playmate Alice was and sniffing with vigor and lolling tongue.

"I gotta . . . *puppy!*" Alice informed her, looking upward from her waist. "Diego! *Diego licks!*"

Diego did, rather indiscriminately, when she offered her hand to sniff and at Ciara's and Henrietta's patting.

"An' I gotta . . . gotta *pony!*" Alice stepped back and threw her arms wide, jumping up and down twice for emphasis. "*Big!* All *fuzzy!* Lucero! Gotta . . . !"

She smacked a small plump palm on her own forehead to show where the star-shaped blaze was, which was what *Lucero* meant.

"Come see, Nanna! *Lucero eats!* Apples! An' ... an' ... carrots! An' ...
an' ... sugar! Big ... big ... *teeeeths!*"

The girl bared her own milk teeth in a grin that unintentionally
mimicked Uncle Teddy's as well as a horse reaching for a lump of
sugar, grabbed Luz's hand, and began to tug. Luz bent, gripped the
solid wiggling weight under the armpits, put a smacking kiss on her
face, and spun her in a circle until she was giggling helplessly and
breathless, and then settled her down on her hip, on the left side so
there wasn't an automatic pistol in the way.

"*¡Qué niña tan grande, mi pequeña ahijada ha llegado a ser!*" she said:
"What a great big girl my little goddaughter has become! Tomorrow
we will see your pony and feed him apples and carrots and sugar."

At that age, *tomorrow* had about the same impact as *next week* or possibly *never*, but Luz had cunningly concealed the last of the candied
peanuts against this chance. Now she did a stage magician's gesture—
the Chamber kept several prestidigitators on retainer for training purposes, along with the acrobats, cardsharps, and second-story men—and
apparently extracted it from Alice's nose. That left the toddler gaping
in delighted wonder and then going *Mmmm!* and chewing with a pleased
expression when her godmother popped it into her mouth. Diego's eyes
and nose followed the peanut with a rapt expression and a piteous
whine, showing he'd long since mastered the concept of *treat.*

The girl pointed at Ciara as she chewed, frowned in thought, then
smiled again as she found what she was searching for and brought out
the concept in a happy squeal:

"*Piiiink!*"

"This is my friend Ciara," Luz said gravely as she set the child on
her feet again.

Ciara, who *was* a bit sun-flushed, bent down and nodded with equal
solemnity, extending a hand that Alice grabbed with both of hers and
shook enthusiastically, but as much side-to-side as up and down.

"Now you must go with your nanny Anita and have your own dinner like a good girl while the grown-ups do grown-up things," Luz said.

"*Not* good girl!" she pouted. "*Bad* girl! Big, bad girl now!"

Then with a mercurial change of focus. "'rietta! 'rietta! Kiss! Keera-piiiink! Kiss!"

Henrietta and Ciara applied the required smacks, and Alice let herself be led off, waving and smiling over her shoulder as the puppy bounced at her heels, its claws clacking on the smooth brown tile of the floor. Ciara and Henrietta grinned back and waved to the child.

"And now to work. Half an hour, Miss Colmer," Luz said. "You'll be our liaison with General Young of the 32nd and set up the meeting. Do emphasize that we need to keep the numbers involved to a minimum; it shouldn't be hard, he's an intelligent man and he has experience of clandestine work as a military attaché."

"Yes, *ma'am*," the secretary said, shaking her hand and exchanging a friendly hug with Ciara before she left.

Luz chuckled as they headed for their two—discreetly connected—rooms.

"By that age they're actually *cuter* than puppies," she said, casting her eyes back toward the diminishing figures of Alice and Diego. "It takes a while, but all at once they are."

"Suddenly everything feels sunnier!" Ciara said, looking in the same direction with a long sigh.

Luz put her arm around her waist and squeezed.

"We can, eventually, if we want to; there are ways," she said.

Ciara laughed and gave her a look of mock wide-eyed astonishment.

"But not *that* way," Luz said dryly.

"And I'd like to give my da grandchildren, may it help him rest in peace and smile in purgatory," Ciara said, crossing herself and sobering. "With Colm dead, I'm the only one to do that for my parents."

"And me for mine," Luz said in agreement.

Just as individuals were a cell in the organism of the nation, they were also the link between past and future, in the families that were the next step up toward that greater unity.

"But not yet."

Ciara sighed. "No. First the war."

And surviving it, Luz thought, knowing the thought was shared.

Looking down from the head of the stairs, Luz could see why the big central courtyard of the *casa grande* was called the *patio del limón*: the potted lime trees that alternated with climbing red roses, blue-and-white wisteria, and purple bougainvillea. It had fountains that looked as old as the mansion at opposite ends with beds of white geraniums around them, but the pavement had been relaid with modern hydraulic tile in a repeating pattern of lilies and fronds around pale expanses.

There was already a fair scattering of guests under Japanese lanterns strung from lines overhead: American men in white tie or (in the case of the younger ones) black, Mexicans mostly the same, with a few instances of a self-consciously archaic local splendor that involved short tight embroidered silver-buttoned silk jackets, ruffled shirts, knee breeches, loose ascot ties, and red sashes about the waist.

The women were all in evening dresses, though of less uniform cut than they would have been before the destruction of Paris. New York was trying hard to become the fallen city's successor as unquestioned arbiter of fashion but hadn't solidified its position yet, and Mexico City—refuge for a good many displaced French *modistes*, feeling at home there since Frenchmen had long been prominent socially and in business in Mexico—was making a valiant come-from-behind challenge. Chicago and San Francisco were neck-and-neck for third place, and Rio and Buenos Aires were making noises and waving their hands to be noticed from far away southward.

Nobody outside the reach of German artillery paid any attention at all to Berlin's pretensions.

There were soldiers too, officers in the plain but sleekly tailored dress uniforms of darkest midnight blue and peaked caps the regulars used these days, with touches of color in the rank insignia and medal ribbons and the buckles of their pistol belts. One Ranger captain was in the same thing done in green, also showing his regiment in the polished tomahawk he wore through a loop in the back of his belt; it was ceremonial here, bleakly functional otherwise, as well as a symbolic link with Roger's Rangers back in the eighteenth century, the grim frontier guerillas of the French and Indian War. The Ranger was tall and weathered in the way fair-skinned men got here, with a red mustache to match his cropped hair. The half-dozen regular officers were all Negroes, and only one of them was anything as lowly as a captain.

A pleasant murmur of conversation sounded below the tinkle of falling water, and a fortunately restrained small charro-suited mariachi group in one corner was doing a soft treatment of "La Negra." It was much cooler than even an hour ago, and an occasional rumble and flicker from the west showed a storm over the mountains, but she didn't think it would rain here today.

Possibly tomorrow, which might be convenient. Rain can draw a veil, and it keeps people inside.

Ciara took a deep breath beside her as they descended the staircase from the arcaded *mirador* of the second story.

"You look wonderful, *querida*," Luz murmured, wishing she could give her hand a reassuring squeeze.

It was true; Ciara was wearing a modish but not extravagant modern green evening gown that flattered her hourglass figure with its wide neckline, long straight sleeves, and a loose dropped waistline above a shin-length skirt, together with a necklace of emeralds in disks of gold filigree that had belonged to Luz's father's mother. They looked much better on her than on Luz, bringing out the turquoise of her eyes, the alabaster complexion, and the sunset blaze of her hair.

Or her wig, Luz thought affectionately.

One advantage of their cropped state was that they could do a complex raised hairdo together with the wig on a stand and then simply wear it like an article of clothing. You definitely couldn't do it by yourself while the hair was growing on your head, and the whole thing could be a serious bother at times, which was why hairstyles had been getting at least a little simpler since the war started.

"And remember, your cover persona has about as much experience at this sort of occasion as you do—you're supposed to be a church-raised orphan from the South Side of Chicago!"

Which showed why cover identities were usually tailored as closely as possible to the real backgrounds of the people assuming them. Truth could be very convincing, and even more misleading.

"It's not important to the *job* if you feel a bit awkward, so you don't have to worry about it."

"It feels important to me!"

"Ah, but *you're* not here, *querida. Mary Cavanaugh* is here; just remember that."

Ciara nodded, then shook herself slightly and firmed her lips into a pleasant smile, though Luz suspected it took as much courage, if of a different kind, as facing gunfire and poison gas in Berlin had taken. The success of their mission meant not attracting attention from the enemy . . . and the enemy could be anywhere.

That's my girl! I knew she was a lioness the first moment we met!

To Luz this gathering was a variation on the infinitely familiar. The social side of her father's business had taken her into mover-and-shaker circles from her teens on, as soon as she'd been old enough for adult mingling; before that she'd mixed with the children of her father's clients.

You could even call those European finishing schools formal training for high-society espionage! It was supposed to be about status-seeking and husband-hunting, but the skills transfer surprisingly well.

She wore an underdress of black silk, with an overdress of soft black silk tulle, accented with black sequins, and dress straps of silk velvet over her bare shoulders; the only drawback was that it showed that her shoulders and arms were those of an acrobat, not a bureaucrat, but most people were surprisingly obtuse about things like that . . . and these days, most Americans at least would simply assume she was a bit of a fanatic about the Strenuous Life and *build your body.*

A faceted French jet appliqué with long dangling beaded tassels hung from the right bustline, and around her neck was a single large pearl in a silver clasp, a Tahitian drop of the genuine deep lustrous black that was the rarest of all colors. Her father had bought it for her mother on their tenth anniversary, and it flattered both of them.

Let's see . . . Luz thought.

The biggest clump was around Governor Seelmann and his bride, who wasn't showing much yet but had a definite glow in an elegant white tulle gown and tortoiseshell combs in her piled raven hair. *That* group included Don Raul de Moncada and his rather stout wife, both beaming approval, and a couple of their sons and *their* wives. The sons were in elegant but modern black tie; Don Raul was wearing something his great-grandfather might have taken to the court of the emperor Iturbide a century ago.

A bit like a matador's traje de luces. *Or vice versa if you know the history,* Luz thought.

That group also included Julie Durán, accompanied by her brother-in-law Alfredo, and looking extremely self-contained and dressed in the pale azure tint named Alice blue after Uncle Teddy's eldest . . . who now that Luz came to think of it had a very similar Nordic complexion. Her eyes . . . which perfectly matched that icy color and the blaze of diamonds around her neck . . . flicked across Luz's in a single second of acknowledgment without affecting her expression at all or the conversation she was having.

Luz and Ciara attracted quite a few appreciative male and appraising female glances as they came down the stairs, and a few self-introductions as they came to the patio floor, mostly from younger men or those of both genders fascinated by their Coco Chanel gowns.

Luz slid past them politely with only a few sentences exchanged— about the war, the dresses, the weather, the crops, the war, American bureaucratic intrigues, the war, hints about Mexican hacendado family dramas that sailed over her head, the war, the improvements the Duráns had made to the hacienda, and the weather and crops and the war over again—with the ease of long experience. They both took glasses of chilled white wine from a passing tray and nibbled on a few hors d'oeuvres—Luz's favorite was a piece of candied nopal cactus, a taste that took her back to her childhood, but the anchovies curled around mushrooms on tostadas were fine, and the little spicy sausages on toothpicks. Ciara's nerves had smothered her usual healthy appetite until she had to force herself to swallow one, which was a pity because they were worth paying attention to.

By the time they'd circled around to the officers of the 32nd Infantry Division, even an expert wouldn't have thought they were making a beeline in that direction rather than just dutifully touching bases; Luz had been using a mental equivalent of flipping a coin to pick directions, and only the lack of pattern might have been revealing.

Hopefully nobody is looking at the two earnest if well-connected bureaucratic do-gooders Ciara and I are supposed to be; but if anyone hostile is looking in general, they will *be looking at the divisional commander of the garrison and anyone who meets with him and his officers. So we need to be very careful about contacts with the military. The Black Chamber station chief has good reasons for occasionally talking to people with our cover identities; a general doesn't. His intelligence officer* especially *doesn't have a reason to be concerned with a schools program.*

Major-General Charles Young was at the center of the group, a striking-looking man in his early fifties and only a little gray at the temples of his close-cropped, tight-curled hair, with the broad-shouldered, deep-chested, lean-waisted build and ramrod West Point stance that the dress uniform showed off well, and a cleft square chin and somber eyes. They lightened as he looked down at his wife, Ada, and she said something that made him smile.

He has presence, and they make a handsome couple, Luz thought.

Henrietta aside, Ada Young was the only Negro woman present; the other officers probably hadn't had time to send for their families yet from their previous posting in Jackson, Mississippi.

She's a San Franciscan, I recall. Still short of forty; they met while he was stationed at the Presidio there, and it started with a common interest in music. Young plays the violin very well, according to reports, which gives us something in common.

Ada Mills Young's eyebrows rose very slightly as Luz and Ciara approached. General Young and his party certainly weren't being shunned, the way he probably *had* been in lonely frontier forts in the 1880s, when he'd been one of the grand total of *three* West Point graduates of his race. Quite a few of the American guests had spoken to them, mostly the men but including a long friendly chat by the governor and his wife. They also weren't being eagerly sought out, the way a new white divisional commander and his staff would have been, either, and the junior officers weren't circulating much.

Rather more of the locals had approached them, and less stiffly and not visibly *making* themselves do so, and none of them needing Julie gently chivvying them on from behind with the Black Chamber's fearsome reputation keeping the social smiles of her guests—or victims—fixed in place.

It isn't that Mexicans don't have racial prejudices, Luz thought; the social complexities were interesting in themselves, and understanding them was essential to her work.

She'd often heard upper-crust families down here gossiping with snide malice about each other's precise skin tint, nose and eye and lip shape and for the males the degree of body hair, listing them all with pedantic care . . . while often boasting about some ancient Aztec princess in their family tree with their next breath. And *mallate*, which was a misspelled Nahuatl loanword and how they'd refer to the Youngs if the Youngs weren't the powerful representatives of the current rulers, wasn't any sort of a compliment.

The original meaning of the word was "black dung beetle."

They just have slightly different *prejudices . . . and they're much more pragmatic about it. For example, if you put a man in a general's uniform with seventeen thousand heavily armed soldiers bristling with artillery and machine-guns and battle cars and fighting aeroplanes at his back, he suddenly becomes very socially acceptable indeed.*

Luz introduced herself and Ciara under their cover names; Young recognized them immediately, and Luz thought he knew her face too, probably from a file photo—and translating those to reality was surprisingly difficult, which argued for powers of observation and also that the Iron House had sent him emphatic orders about priorities.

The very young major with intelligence tabs beside him did as well, showing it only with a flicker of the eyes behind his round-lensed spectacles.

They exchanged pleasantries, and Young gravely agreed that the project setting up technical schools for girls was indeed extremely worthy. His wife agreed emphatically, and probably sincerely. The two Black Chamber operatives moved on after a polite interval, circulated for another ten minutes, then calmly walked through a doorway and into a corridor where Henrietta Colmer stood, as if they were looking for the ladies' toilets.

"This way, ma'am," Julie's secretary said quietly.

Her gown was tangerine-orange silk velvet, falling to lower calf length, horizontally gathered at the front waist with long scarflike folds at each side, and a bodice of gold lamé lace over a silk lining. Luz thought she recognized Julie's taste in clothes and she was fairly certain she recognized the gold-wire and ruby-chip necklace, but Henrietta had been smart to take the advice on the dress . . . and the loan of the necklace. They both went very well indeed with the confidential secretary's chocolate complexion and large dark eyes, though it would all have been far too bright for the station chief.

A *casa grande* this size had scores of rooms, built around several courtyards; the renovations had restored them all, but a good many were still very sparsely furnished. The one they were eventually ushered into was on the opposite end of the house from the kitchens and servants' quarters and other utilitarian functions, of modest size and pale white; there were stacked heaps of pipe and sacks of grout a little farther on. It had an exterior window barred with iron grillework, and a niche with an archaic-looking Madonna and Child of painted wood. The single table was massive and genuinely ancient carved oak, something Cervantes or Cortés might have been comfortable sitting at . . . unless they smacked a knee on the supports beneath. There was a very faint smell of drying plaster lingering in the air.

The 32nd's commander and his intelligence officer rose with gentlemanly courtesy from the equally massively antique leather-wood-and-brass chairs on the other side of the table, and inclined their heads. Luz nodded back; she thought she saw the younger man's eyes skim over the three of them and then click back to Henrietta for a second or so, taking in the impact of the gown and the way it went with the contents.

That one's about thirty. Even these days that's young for a major, Luz thought.

"And may I introduce Major Andre Dicot? Chief of my intelligence staff and a very capable man," Young added, as they all shook hands—with a very slight hesitation on his part, since women doing so man-fashion was still slightly *advanced*. "I have complete confidence in him."

A grin. "I was going to say *despite his youth,* but obviously that's not going to be a problem in this room, where I'm the Methuselah at fifty-two."

The American military had doubled or more in size every year since Uncle Teddy's return to power in 1912 . . . or to put it another way, it was now about twenty-five times larger than it had been in that eventful year and still rising, if not quite as fast. Added to that was the way the president and General Wood had ruthlessly purged the last overweight, aging barnacles who'd clung on since the Indian Wars in the upper ranks of the tiny, ossified force that had dragged out its days and decades in dusty forgotten frontier outposts, before the shambolic chaos of the war with Spain in the late '90s revealed the extent of the problem.

Back then forty-year-old lieutenants had been common; nowadays, the military combed the country for talent wherever it could be found and had an even younger command structure than the Party. The chief of the General Staff was the oldest general on active duty now . . . and Leonard Wood was all of fifty-seven.

Still, thirty and a major . . . he's either a hotshot prodigy, or has powerful patrons, or both. Probably both.

"Pleased to make your acquaintance, Executive Field Operative, Field Operative," the young officer said; his voice had a musical cadence and undertone that said *New Orleans* to her, and *probably raised in a French-speaking neighborhood, middle-class at least.* "And to see you again, Miss Colmer."

They sat; Henrietta had a small pad in front of her, but it was rather ostentatiously closed, with the mechanical pencil laid atop it.

"No names, no punishment drill," Young said approvingly. "I've met Miss Colmer briefly before, and your station chief here assures me she has full clearance in these matters."

Which means he appreciates she's here to report to Julie, Luz thought. *Julie and him and Ciara and I disappearing at the same time would catch too many eyes, given how many people know what Julie's job is. Nobody notices a secretary—probably a lot of the locals think Henrietta is some sort of personal lady's maid.*

Then *his* eyes swept over them with a slight expression of bemusement. "Though . . . I've also heard of *you*, Executive Field Operative. After Puebla and the explosion at the enemy HQ via the Army's rumor mill . . . Good *God*, but they were disorganized there when we hit them after that bomb went off . . . There was the capture of Villa . . . and more reports since last October, however heavily redacted, which I now realize were about you two ladies. You and your associate—"

He nodded to Ciara.

"—are . . . not quite what I expected, really."

"I can understand that things might look a bit unprecedented from your side of the table, General Young," Luz said smoothly, acknowledging that everyone on her side of it was wearing a skirt.

At the same time she made a small gesture that started with her hand pointed in his direction and then curled her fingers back toward herself, one that might have been construed as:

And the same thing from over here, for slightly different reasons.

The previously stone-faced and gimlet-eyed Major Dicot actually smiled for an instant, and Young laughed aloud.

No flies on either of them, and they're more mentally flexible than most regulars. Good. If there's one thing I abominate, it's working with . . . which means working around . . . high-ranking idiots. All the more so if their stupidity is self-inflicted because they let emotion override reason, rather like an unfortunate inheritance like a clubfoot.

"Not a comparison I'd immediately think of, but I do see your point!" Young said.

Dicot murmured something like *Touché* under his breath, the fencing term for a hit, and Young smiled a little before he continued:

"Perhaps Susan B. Anthony would have too, or the Grimké sisters!"

Luz remembered from his dossier that he was a friend of W.E.B. Du Bois, the Negro intellectual leader and nowadays irritating but influential Party gadfly, from the days when they taught together at Wilber-force College in Ohio; unlike most, he'd be familiar with the historical links between the women's suffrage and abolition movements.

And you certainly couldn't go through Bryn Mawr without hearing about it! she thought.

Then, soberly, the general went on:

"Ours is a very great nation, Field Operative, and in more ways than its size and power—though thank the Lord we have that! Not perfect, no human creation is . . . and even God had to allow for a serpent in paradise . . . but very great, and in the world as it is now the last bearer of the hopes of the human race. I was born in Kentucky a year before Lincoln's assassination. My father had to run for it even to enlist as a private soldier in that war, though Kentucky never left the Union; after peace came he had a little one-man livery stable in an Ohio town nobody outside fifty miles' distance has ever heard of, while he learned to read and write from my mother. Yet here I sit—"

His hand turned inward for a moment as hers had, indicating himself . . . and by implication the stars on the standing collar of his dress jacket.

"—a man born a slave, born in a place where the law forbade me even to learn my letters. It is an honor beyond price for any . . ."

He stopped himself smoothly before saying *any man*, a hitch in the words most people wouldn't have noticed.

". . . any citizen to serve that great nation as we do . . . as all of us here do."

"Agreed, General Young," Luz said sincerely, and then: "*Build your body and build your mind to build yourself; but build yourself to build America. And America can only be properly served . . . best served, served as she deserves . . . if the nation can draw on all her children, according to their ability and loyalty. We here are proof of that. Now let's concentrate on precisely how we're to deserve well of the Republic in this instance."

Dicot spoke: "None of us would be here if this weren't of a very high priority indeed; and that we were selected is rather flattering. And racking to the nerves, when you think about it . . . which it is to be presumed we all have."

Luz nodded, absently noting that while his English was very fluent there was sometimes a trace of French in the word order and turns of phrase he used.

"Operative Whelan and I have been involved in a number of, ah, significant operations, and your division was picked as most suitable . . . out of any number sitting idle at the present," she said.

Both the soldiers grimaced very slightly; nobody in the Army was happy with the way the horror-gas had frozen the chessboard of the Great War. Being too weak to fight was one thing and bad enough; having plenty of force and not being able to find a way to *use* it added insult to injury.

"I suspect many other factors went into the decision to put the Dakota Project here: everything from geography and railroads and wind patterns to the civil governor's record. But as you say, Major, high expectations are a curse as well as a compliment. America *must* have what the Project produces, and we must have it *soon*. The problem is that it's just as obvious to various people on the other side, most especially Colonel Nicolai and Abteilung IIIb, so that thwarting or delaying the operation of the Dakota Project is a high priority for *them*."

Young nodded. "I presume you're not just speaking of keeping this district nailed down as we've been doing, or the conventional security measures around the Dakota Project."

Luz shook her head. "No. The *bandits* are a spent force in terms of major operations around here, even with a few Germans possibly helping them. So in terms of raw *power*, we already have far more than we need. Packing yet more men around the plant and digging more machine-gun nests and putting up more checkpoints to ask people for their papers won't increase our degree of protection and might even decrease it."

Major Dicot gave a quick sharp nod. "Yes, exactly, Field Operative. More men would just get in each other's way."

Which marked him as an intelligence specialist rather than an infantryman in spirit. In Luz's experience few combat soldiers ever thought you could use too many men in an operation, and in conventional fighting they had a point. There was a sort of brutal basic arithmetic to head-on combat where more was by definition better . . . but this was a contest in sneakiness, not weight of metal.

"Doing that sort of thing tells of a poverty of the imagination," Dicot went on, confirming her estimate. "Or of doing things to look busy for the brass in the Iron House."

"Fortunately General Wood and the president have a low tolerance for that type of nonsense," Young noted, and made a curt *Go on* gesture to put the conversation back in Dicot's hands.

"Our enemies here most probably will not be so obligingly stupid that they try to fight us head-on; fight us on our own terms, that is to say, when that's been a disaster for them every time they tried it," Dicot said.

Young made a balancing gesture. "Though you can't always count on the other side being smart, either. I saw that in the Philippine Insurrection when I was a captain with the 9th Cavalry, on Sulu and in Mindanao and Luzon, and again here, in the first year or two, particularly in Morelos. They often did choose head-on confrontation, long after it should have been obvious to them it wouldn't work."

"Yes, General Young. But . . ." Luz let the word hang.

"But yes, that doesn't matter, because if they're that obligingly stupid the problem is self-solving with the measures already in place. We have to focus on the worst possible outcome, not the best."

"The more so as the Germans are involved," Luz said. "They don't give a damn about their local dupes' interests, short or long term, and they'll manipulate them into doing things that are stupid from the bandits' perspectives if it serves their purposes. Harming the Dakota Project is more than enough incentive to burn those assets to the ground."

"Good point," Dicot said.

Ciara leaned forward and spoke, the awkwardness she'd felt at being part of a high-society dinner party falling away as she moved into an area she was thoroughly comfortable with:

"The technical side makes our problem more difficult, General, Major, because you *don't* have to apply much force to a plant like this to wreck it. Just a tap in a precise place—nothing that one man couldn't do, if he got in and did it exactly right. As, um, our organization demonstrated in Germany last year."

Young's eyebrows climbed, and Luz shook her head as she said:

"*Our organization* in the collective sense; my colleague and I weren't tasked with knocking out the plant in Berlin, no. We did have a chance to observe it very shortly after the fact, one of those improbable things that happen more often in covert operations than you might think—"

"Especially as I would think they're probably kept hermetically sealed from each other," Dicot said shrewdly. "As much as possible."

Luz made a palm-up gesture of assent and added a slight wiggling movement of the fingers that emphasized the *as possible* part as she continued:

"—and we do know the field operative concerned. All the guards, barbed wire, machine-guns, and searchlights didn't matter at all, and believe me, the Germans did not stint in those regards."

Dicot's dark eyes narrowed. "And the filthy stuff is so damned lingering," he said. "I understand that's why the Germans took so long to get their plant back in operation. Everything had to be decontaminated by men in rubber suits."

"Or by prisoners and forced laborers," Luz said.

Ciara nodded. "But we were lucky there; they were starting a production run when we . . . our operative . . . managed to overload the valving and then blow the catalytic chamber."

Dicot frowned as he parsed the technicalities, but the general laughed. "So he didn't even have to use a bomb!"

"Yes, he used the system to create the overpressure by . . . by taking control of the controls, you might say," Ciara said. "Though I admit it *sounded* like a bomb at the time—we were nearly a mile away."

Now Dicot chuckled too, a sound that perfectly expressed the emotion that Germans called *Schadenfreude*.

"Much easier to walk in with a knowledge of the plant's controls than with sixty pounds of explosive in your pockets! Elegant!" the intelligence officer said. "Devilish, in fact. Worthy of . . . that organization you belong to!"

Ciara nodded, then doggedly returned to business: "V-gas doesn't store well . . . currently the impurity levels are high even with best-practice methods . . . so that's only done just before deployment. The damage would have been much greater if it had been further along, with more of the actual agent in the storage tanks."

And Ciara and I *would have been most certainly killed*, Luz thought with a slight inner shiver.

Remembering the effort of will it had taken to drive through the base at Staaken knowing that invisible, impalpable death might be pooling around them and they'd never know until the night went darker still and their hearts and lungs simply . . . stopped . . . or every muscle in their bodies convulsed hard enough to snap their bones. They'd both seen horror-gas used on human beings while they were in enemy territory under deep cover, at a demonstration for Germany's supreme warlords Hindenburg and Ludendorff. Ciara still had nightmares about that, sometimes, and woke crying out as the shell burst once more over the prisoners. It made the same danger for yourself unpleasantly . . . visceral.

"You can be sure *our* plant isn't vulnerable to *that* particular form of attack," she said as an aside.

Ciara went on: "Unfortunately, the whole process involves high temperatures, high pressures, and materials that are . . . are *conventionally* toxic even before the synthesis. It's at the very edge of what's technically possible with today's latest methods; that's why the Germans came up with it first, they're ahead of us in organic chemistry . . . ahead of the world, really. They started work on it just before the war, they had the production process on a laboratory scale, and even so it took two years to industrial production and field deployment, and the process and product are still very imperfect. Our *copy* of their process is even more improvised because our chemical engineers had to work backward from the material we captured, guessing and taking chances along the way.

"There were . . . accidents in the process. Losses. Some of them of people it will be hard to replace," she added gravely. "We had to . . . cut corners. We still *are* cutting corners, really. If it weren't wartime, this would have taken twice as long or more."

Young thought for a moment and spoke to Ciara.

"There are more ways of dying for the country than enemy bullets. Perhaps, Field Operative, you could give us an internal listing of the most vulnerable spots, places where a knowledgeable enemy agent could do the most damage, so that we could do more than hold a perimeter? And we'll compare it to what the plant engineers say, of course."

"Yes, of course, General," Ciara said with a smile. "Though I need a convincing reason to survey the plant personally. Plans are wonderful things, but observation is even better."

Dicot tapped thoughtfully at the table, turning his eyes up slightly in thought before saying:

"Sir, a good way to dispel the . . . ludicrous rumors . . . about the plant being dangerous would be to arrange tours. By yourself and your lady . . . the governor and his lady . . . officers of the division . . . selected civilians, such as a pair of visiting Department of Education employees . . ."

Ciara made a finger-in-the-air gesture to acknowledge the elegant solution.

"That would do nicely, Major Dicot. I've studied the plans in detail; what I need is to do visual checks."

"You have an evil mind, Major; I thoroughly approve," Young said. "And you should familiarize yourself too, of course."

"And we must have reaction squads within the plant area, men who've been thoroughly briefed and drilled in responding to any alarm with no lost time," Dicot said. "I think the reconnaissance battalion should be the unit tasked with that. Guarding the perimeter is one thing, but this requires quick thinking, keen powers of observation, and initiative. Scouts are selected for that."

"Excellent thought, at least initially," Young said. "Coordinate with Major Johnson of First Battalion, and get me a plan within twenty-four hours. It'll have to be constantly updated, but we'll have a framework to proceed from."

"Yes, sir!"

Luz spread her hands. "But that's a palliative. As Frederick the Great said about concentration on the *Schwerpunkt . . .*"

"*He who tries to be strong everywhere, is weak everywhere: He who defends everything, defends nothing,*" Major Dicot said, picking the appropriate quote easily.

"Our enemies only have to be strong in one place, and only for one moment," Young said. "While our position requires us to defend everything all the time."

Luz motioned agreement. "Fortunately, *our* responsibilities are more limited than yours, General. I'm still getting a feel for the situation here . . . but what bothers me most is this contact the Air Corps and then the Rangers had with a bandit gang in the Sierra."

"I saw the report. Air surveillance is probably the biggest single innovation in warfare since I was a young man, and air attacks on ground targets come second. A chance encounter, surely?"

"Yes, but the mules the Rangers found, and their loads of food, indicate that they're getting local support . . . from people who would presumably shelter them and help them move if they get closer to Jerez, or Zacatecas. The ammunition from an assault rifle—their StG-

16—definitely indicates a German presence. I learned long ago not to disregard that nagging feeling that something is going on and I'm not seeing it."

Young's smile was grim, and his eyes saw something far distant for a moment.

"I lost any disdain for *that* sort of feeling traveling up the Gándara River on Samar in the Philippines, jungle dense as a fortress wall on both flanks and swarming with *ladrones* out to slit our throats, thick as the mosquitoes and almost as dangerous," he said.

"So I'm putting some effort into dealing with it, General Young. The station chief is activating all local contacts and sources, we have interviews with the Ranger officer and the Falcon crews planned, and I'm pushing for vigorous action in the Sierra."

Dicot raised one eyebrow. "Reading the contact reports, I was surprised the Navy released two airships for action this far inland," he said. "And that it was done so quickly. The admirals are generally more protective of those patrol semirigids than they are of their children . . . and they're very fond of their children."

So that was you and *you have serious pull if you're able to override the Navy that fast* went unspoken.

It was a good thing that the airships had come up, because it meant both men knew she wasn't someone they could disregard without consequences even if they wanted to, and this way she didn't have to be blunt about that to the point of antagonizing them.

Young nodded confirmation.

"There are reasons for the naval high command keeping their patrol airships close," the commander of the 32nd said softly, looking at her. "The U-boats are a constant threat, and Tampico is a priority target for the enemy; they keep many of their newest and best long-range submarines on that route. Those semirigids are the best counter to submarines we've found so far. Men may die because they were diverted."

Die burning alive in torpedoed tankers, she knew he was thinking. *Die*

vomiting the fuel oil they'd swallowed before they were pulled out of the water.
Choke by inches in utter darkness, in air pockets trapped in the hulls of sunken
ships, with nothing for their kin to bury and nothing to remember them by but an
official telegram.

"Well, that's war, General," Luz said steadily. "Resources are always
limited, and priorities have to be set as to where they're sent. We've
both put our lives on the line for the Republic when our superiors told
us to, trusting that they knew the necessity . . . and we've both taken
command responsibility, which means sending others to die and never
knowing for certain if our decisions were the best ones. Men . . . and
women . . . die, but they die that the nation may live."

Young met her eyes for a long moment and nodded, murmuring:

"To every man upon this earth,
Death cometh soon or late.
And how can man die better
Than facing fearful odds
For the ashes of his fathers
And the temples of his gods?"

They ran through the rest of the details, including methods to con-
vey messages quickly through Dicot, and finished before the call for
guests to be seated. As they stood, the intelligence officer said casually
to Henrietta, with just the right shallow bow and respectful tone:

"If you have no escort for dinner, Miss Colmer, I would be honored."

"Why—"

Henrietta's eyes moved slightly toward Luz, who gave a very small
up-to-you shrug.

It was a pity that men didn't generally wear wedding rings, but she
thought Dicot probably single. General Young's indulgent smile was a
good indicator; much like Uncle Teddy he was rather straitlaced even
for a man of his generation. At least according to his Black Chamber

dossier, a type of document that gave details of rather different and sometimes rather more intimate things than the conventional service "jacket" in the Iron House files back in Washington.

And Henrietta's a big girl who can look after herself. And there's no job-related reason she shouldn't have a pleasant partner for dinner conversation, rather than sitting next to someone who thinks she should be out in the kitchen washing the dishes or that all Negro women are harlots, or both. In fact, a known social acquaintance between the two of them might be helpful because it's so plausible. It gives her a good reason to visit with him . . . which gives us a good way to communicate unobserved. I'll tell Julie, though she'll probably notice anyway.

"Why, that would be lovely, Major Dicot," Henrietta said. "Thank you so much."

After they'd left with the usual polite formulas, Ciara offered her arm to Luz with the same stylized gesture Dicot had used, and they both laughed.

"I need to talk to that Ranger captain," Luz added. "Business. Let's go see if we can do that naturally, or at least have Julie set up a time for going into details with him later . . . that would be better, in fact. He wouldn't be here if there weren't news. And we can enjoy dinner; Julie couldn't boil an egg herself, but she does have a very good nose for a cook."

ELEVEN

Town of Jerez
State of Zacatecas
United States Protectorate of México
JUNE 21ST, 1917, 1917(B)

The Jerez warehouse Pablo led the Germans to in the long rainy summer twilight was stone-built and centuries old, with carvings in the elaborate style of a bygone time on its pinkish-yellow exterior. The big main doors were sized for wagons but locked for the day. They filed through a smaller side entrance from an alley into the dim interior.

Pablo vanished into a series of hugs and back slapping and genial swearing and insults with the dozen or so men waiting to meet them, or at least with the Mexicans among them, only one of whom got something as cold and reserved as a handshake and a *Good evening.* He was the man with the keys and looked like a model of middle-class respectability next to the others . . . many of whom made *Pablo* look respectable.

As ripe a collection of unhung rogues as I've seen, Horst thought. *But we'll see. I think some good use for the Fatherland can be had from them.*

"Keep quiet!" the man with the keys said.

Everyone ignored him, until Pablo added a curt "He's right. Shut *up,* you fools. I want to kill more gringos and traitors before I die."

The darkened warehouse had none of that almost painful feeling of raw newness Horst had noticed so often in America; he doubted that this was the first time a gang of armed conspirators had met there—and probably it had seen bandits even more often. Even the beams supporting the second story well overhead were massive time-blackened things that bore the chisel-like marks of being hand-squared with adzes on top and bottom; the sides were left in the natural curves, though any trace of bark had vanished long generations ago.

Jerez had been founded in the same year that Martin Luther finished his translation of the Bible off in Germany, nearly four hundred years ago. First as a little fortified outpost on the road to the north during the wars against the Chichimeca nomads—the term was Aztec, and meant *dog people*. And then a market center for the haciendas whose grain and livestock fed the *indio* laborers in the mines, and their masters too.

The warehouse wasn't quite *that* old, but . . .

It smells *ancient*, he thought, as he stripped the false bandage from his face and pulled on his eye patch. *Though the wet air may be bringing that out.*

The relief unbinding his eye brought was even more profound than what he felt reclaiming his weapons, leaning the rifle nearby and tucking a .45 into the waistband of his trousers under the long shirt. It wasn't a gun that made him a man and a soldier; he'd proven that often enough. But pretending to be blind made the skin up his spine and across the back of his neck tighten worse than concrete physical dangers did.

Know yourself, he thought. *Something deep within me fears helplessness far more than death.*

A kerosene lantern on a cord running through a pulley on the ceiling was turned up after the alley door was closed, and Pablo's contact—whose plump fleshy face looked gray with fear, though part of that might be the light—led the way through a maze of piled goods; six of the men picked up rifles or pistols and dispersed to the entrances and second-story windows. The contact with the keys was going by the name Zacarías, which might or might not be anything his parents would recognize.

From the ancient smells, the warehouse had held many things through the generations, things whose scents had soaked into the mortar between the flagstones of the floor or the walls and rafters; leather and corn and peppers, the ghost of dried fruits, and things that gave off smells of minerals and chemicals, and tarry-spicy sawn pine wood. Right now what it mostly had was stacks of baled wool about four meters high and ten on a side, in a checkerboard pattern, with dirty-brown tufts sticking out through rents in the burlap coverings.

Horst suppressed a momentary grin. That smell was rather nostalgic, since the wool sheds on his family's estate had exactly the same greasy lanolin odor, one he associated with losing his virginity in an enthusiastic if smelly grapple with a Polish harvester girl about fifteen years ago.

And two more men who *weren't* Mexican followed the contact, looking relieved not to be alone with Pablo's brothers-in-arms anymore. Both were nondescript, one in his twenties with a bushy mustache that emphasized the unfortunate size of his nose, skinny neck, and large Adam's apple, and the other a thirtyish clerical type with ink-stained fingers peering through round wire-rimmed spectacles.

Like Zacarías they were dressed in suits with waistcoats and shirts with buttoned modern turn-down collars and ties. His were good quality but not new, and theirs the cheaper off-the-rack versions of the sort worn by town dwellers of the petite bourgeois anywhere in the Western world, more or less—dress varied much less by nation and region in towns than in the countryside, and much less among the middle classes than with laborers. Like Horst and Röhm they were much fairer-skinned than most Mexicans, but not implausibly so unless the four of them stood side-by-side—there was a lot of variation here, and their brown hair wasn't anything of note. Then they braced to attention and visibly *almost* snapped off salutes.

"At ease, you dumb-heads," Röhm said with soft venom. "Permanently. You're not in Germany now. You're not in uniform either—you do realize what the Yankees will do to you if they catch you?"

"Yes, sir—ah, yes," one of the two said. "That was made clear before we left, sir."

"Stop calling me *sir*!"

"Yes, s . . . ah, yes."

America and Germany both worked according to a set of rules that gave you certain protections—not rights exactly, more in the nature of mutual concessions—if you were captured. If the angry, exhausted, and frightened soldiers at the point of the spear didn't just shoot you anyway, which happened about half the time. And *provided* you were in uniform, carrying weapons openly, and enrolled in a recognized sovereign government's armed forces. According to the same set of guidelines, anyone else trying to fight a regular army—spies, guerillas, rebels without a state behind them, or civilians supporting any of those—were vermin and could be shot without trial if taken.

Or *tortured* and then shot, though that wasn't publicized as much. Or whatever other unpleasant fate the captor decided was expedient.

Even as a regular prisoner of war, Horst had gotten the impression from the questions his military interrogators asked that the Yankee army and the Black Chamber had waged a quiet little bureaucratic skirmish with each other over him, and he had no illusions as to what his fate would have been if the Chamber had won.

Fortunately, he *had* been in uniform when he was wounded and captured, fighting American and French soldiers in the company of other armed, uniformed German troops . . . including Ernst Röhm, who'd escaped with the remnants of his squad of *Stoßtruppen*. Horst's captors had been American soldiers themselves. The fact that he was working for Abteilung IIIb, the military intelligence agency, didn't matter to them and they were sensitive about preserving the niceties, lest it be their turn someday. And to be sure also for considerations of honor.

Fighting their soldiers as well as the bitch, he thought sourly; he'd been so *close* to killing her. Moments, seconds . . .

These two with Röhm aren't soldiers, not really, in uniform or not, which is probably why he's so short with them. Whatever his faults, Röhm is a soldier and a very good one. They're more like technicians, but that's what we need.

"Your names," he said to the two men. "And your occupations and military specialties."

"Otto Schäfer, si—Sorry!"

"Artur Kraus," the bespectacled one said; he seemed a little quicker on the uptake, or possibly basic training hadn't taken quite so well. "Herr Schäfer was at the Berlin higher technical school—"

The term he used was *Technisches Lyzeum* and was difficult to translate directly into English. Schäfer wouldn't have been conscripted in peacetime, when only about half the young men were called up, and less than that in the cities. Things were very different now, of course.

"—before the war. I was . . . ah, a documents specialist."

Whatever that means. Something I don't need to know, probably—you certainly meet all types in this clandestine business!

Schäfer finally spoke for himself. "I had been working in *Luftstreit-kräfte* electronic signals intelligence since I was called up, until I was transferred to the Alberich project last year."

"You can both speak some Spanish, I assume?" Horst said . . . in Spanish.

"My father was agent for an export company in Cádiz for many years," Schäfer said in the same tongue. "My identity papers say I'm a Spanish salesman for a firm there dealing in mining equipment."

He didn't have a German accent at all, but he *did* have a European Spanish—specifically Andalusian—one that a Mexican would probably place at once, and he made a perfectly convincing native of that kingdom. You found the same range of physical appearance in Spain that you did in Germany; it was the frequencies that were different, so that you could tell a crowd of a hundred Germans from a hundred Spaniards, but not two individuals. Spaniards weren't common here but they weren't rare enough to be a wonder either. Plenty had lived and worked in Mexico during the Porfiriato. Not all had managed to get out during the chaos and the American invasion afterward, and a trickle had come back since things stabilized.

They weren't much *liked* in Mexico, though that shouldn't be a major problem. Even larger streams were heading west from Spain recently, to Cuba or Argentina or Uruguay or Chile, or even here, since "European neutral" and "target on your forehead" were now roughly equivalent terms.

"I also," Kraus said, also in Spanish; he had an accent but was fully fluent, much better than Röhm. "That was a qualification for this assignment. I am supposed to be a Dutch engineer working for a Swiss company that makes telephone switchboards."

That showed Colonel Nicolai's attention to detail; in German Kraus sounded like he came from Oldenburg and had grown up speaking the local *Plattdüütsch* dialect . . . which was very close to the Netherlandish spoken just across the—former—border. *That* was what colored his Spanish. If the colonel couldn't get an accentless speaker with the necessary technical skills, at least he'd gotten one with a *plausible* accent. Not many Mexicans could tell the difference, but a lot more Americans knew German. And some knew its subdivisions as well.

"Show me the equipment, then," he said bluntly.

"We have one explosive payload left—the others have already been transferred to the ultimate location to match up with the rest," Schäfer said. "All the other gear is at the launch site; it is not nearly so heavy."

Pablo's contact Zacarías broke in: "That was very unwise! The gringos suspect something—more police, more soldiers, more searches. I warned you!"

One of the other *revolucionarios* scowled at him and spat. "I didn't notice you shedding much sweat," he said. "And there were only eleven of us for the whole job—we could have used an extra set of hands . . . *Doñito* Zacarías."

The warehouseman fell silent; that diminutive tacked onto the honorific *don* meant something like *little lordling* and directed at an adult male meant something like *worthless snob*. Pablo looked at him while Kraus and Schäfer went to work on a big plain wooden box, and the local man went even grayer. The scarred guerilla's face normally bore an angry sneer; Horst thought it was a little more pronounced now because Pablo disliked townsmen, disliked the rich—which the man Zacarías was, compared to a *peon*—and utterly despised cowards, and Zacarías was also in a pitable funk. Which was very odd indeed.

For years he's been a rebel with the American authorities—with the Black Chamber, for the Virgin's sake—hunting him. How has he gone on so long, if he crumples with fear so easily?

One answer was that if he didn't keep the flame burning, someone like Pablo, that seeker of blood and man without pity, would pay him and his family a visit, or one of Pablo's friends like the one scowling with his hand near the hilt of a curved skinning knife right now. That was only a *partial* answer, though.

Sometimes you had to shoot men on your own side who broke and ran in battle, lest panic spread like a contagious disease. Horst had himself. But not even a formal army could work that way very often if it was going to work effectively at all—as witness the fate of the hosts of Nicholas II, very former Czar of All the Russias, where common soldiers had been treated like serfs under a continuous rain of blows and abuse and sometimes fired on by their own artillery if they re-treated.

You cannot expect a man to be a frightened, beaten dog in peace and a lion in war, Horst thought.

In an underground force, sheer terror was essential as a deterrent but even less practical as a standard tool. Men had to *want* to fight under those conditions, where they were putting their families at risk, not just their lives.

He dismissed the matter from the forefront of his mind as the side of the crate came down. Inside was some sort of bomb, though without the fins at the rear that those dropped from zeppelins or aeroplanes had: a simple steel tube as long as Horst's body and a meter through with a single riveted seam . . . In fact, it reminded him of the canisters that had destroyed London and Paris and Bordeaux, though it was much smaller.

He looked a question at Röhm. The Bavarian smiled unpleasantly— Horst had yet to see anything pleasant in any of his smiles—and shook his head.

"That was considered, but no. Just high explosive. Though in the right place, it will release plenty of the Yankees' own V-gas, eh? They cannot even accuse us of violating the gentlemen's agreement not to employ the gas anymore—they did the same to us last November, you may remember."

Horst nodded at the dry understatement. He did recall the terror he'd felt in the control center of the gas plant in Staaken when he realized what the sabotage had done, and remembered it very vividly indeed, even compared to being underneath endless *Trommelfeuer* artillery barrages or in a U-boat under attack by depth charges. Invisible, odorless, and a lethal dose smaller than the dots marking the umlaut in *von Dückler*; as General Ludendorff himself had said after witnessing a demonstration on captured Czech rebels back last year, V-gas was a terror weapon of great frightfulness.

Röhm was even more frightened than I. But I think he enjoys the sensation, at least in retrospect. No matter. We both did our duty regardless, and that is all you can ask of any man.

A circle of six bolts was countersunk into each rounded end of the steel tube; the bolts stood out from the metal, with bolt heads at the end of a handspan of threaded shaft. That must be the way it was fastened to the frame before and behind; three more stood on either side.

"A hundred fifty kilos of explosive," Schäfer said, with that happiness Horst had often noted before in men explaining something they knew well to a neophyte. "You see, this is also structural—it is the central part of the fuselage."

A flying weapon? he thought. *Ingenious! But then, without Germany's scientists the Fatherland's soldiers could not have won her so much in this war.*

"The frame that holds the upper wing—there is only one, above the body of the machine—is bolted to the sides here and here, with booms carrying the tail fins stretching backward on either side. The engine and the pusher propeller to the rear, and the guidance system to the front. The fuel tank goes above the explosive—it amplifies the effect a bit, and every bit helps."

That was more explosive than even the largest shell or any but the largest bombs dropped from the newest four-engine aeroplanes.

The casing doesn't need to be thick to withstand stress the way a shell does, he thought. *And the wings and engine don't need to carry anything* but *the bomb. A flying torpedo!*

"Guidance system, you say?" Horst said.

"An electrical gyrocompass, *mein H . . .* señor. Connected to the control surfaces by hydraulic actuators and cables. The original idea was Yankee—an inventor named Sperry, a few years before the war. An altimeter controls altitude, and a counter records the number of rotations of the propeller—it can be set to cut off at any point. For range, you see? At that point the engine stops, the wings fall off, and the load continues on a ballistic trajectory until impact."

He beamed at the bomb, as if seeing it in flight.

"You establish the bearing and distance from the point of launch, the craft takes off and ascends to the preset altitude, and proceeds on that bearing until it reaches the preset distance; the gyrocompass corrects automatically for anything tending to push it away from the bearing."

"Range? Speed? Accuracy?" Horst asked.

There had been plenty of new weapons in this war, and some of them had been instant smashing successes like V-gas . . . while a rather larger number were humiliating failures, some succeeded but weren't worth the resources and effort needed to produce them, and a majority required extensive testing in actual use and then changes to be practical.

"Range is a hundred twenty kilometers! Well, a little more or less depending on the direction and intensity of the winds."

"*Ach, so!*" Horst said, a pleased, impressed sound.

The technician beamed as his child metaphorically showed off its paces; that was about seventy-five American miles, and it was much farther than artillery could reach. And with a bigger load of explosive than any but super-heavy siege guns like the Krupp and Škoda monsters that had shattered the Belgian forts in the opening weeks of the war.

So. It can deliver a heavy load to a great distance.

"Speed . . . about ninety kilometers per hour."

This time Horst's grunt was less enthusiastic; that was about the top speed of a good motorcar on a good road.

"Easy for fighting scouts to intercept, then. Or even for antiaircraft fire, since it can't maneuver."

"No, s . . . no, not at all!" Schäfer broke in. "They can be launched *at night* with no effect on accuracy! The guidance mechanism does not need light at all, you see. It is electromechanical."

"*Ach, so,*" Horst said, thoughtfully this time.

The technician nodded enthusiastically. Fighting scouts couldn't operate at night to any purpose, and darkness made even takeoff and landing very risky indeed. A Telemobiloscope might help, but they were far too large to be mounted in any heavier-than-air craft for now. Direction from the ground or an airship would be extremely cumbersome, given the short time available for interception and that wireless sets small enough for a fighting-scout aeroplane were still experimental, heavy enough to degrade performance, and unreliable to boot.

Again, for now, Horst thought, rubbing thoughtfully at his jaw. *Things change so fast in our times! What did that Marx fellow say ... all that was sacred is profaned, all that was solid melts into air? Perhaps he should have been a poet, not a failed prophet.*

He said aloud: "Speaking of accuracy?"

"Ah ... the air torpedo itself, sir—"

He nodded: *Lufttorpedo* was a striking term and caught the concept well.

"—has a circular strike radius of four kilometers at extreme range. The air currents, you see, we are working on that but ..."

"No, I don't see," Horst said. "That's an area-bombardment weapon at best, able to hit targets like a substantial city. Possibly very formidable if it were using V-gas—"

Which, now that I come to think of it, is an understatement; you could do raids of the sort that destroyed Paris and London that way, launching hundreds of these things at night, and it would be unstoppable. And at increasing distances, as the equipment improves in range and speed ... fleets of these things swarming over cities ...

"—but what use is it for *this* mission?"

The technician and the documents specialist and Röhm all smiled in eerie unison, and all looking equally carnivorous for a moment. Kraus actually rubbed his hands together in glee while he said:

"*Ach, so*, we have a little refinement."

He lifted the lid off another box. This contained a piece of electronic apparatus, with dials and switches and gauges on its surface.

"A wireless transmitter. With this the error radius is . . . Schäfer?"

"Ten meters. It must be placed very near the target, of course."

Röhm laughed. "You are the answer to that problem, Horst."

Kraus unfolded a cardboard container and passed him the set of identity documents inside; a folded American uniform lay under them.

"I have been working on these since we arrived," he said. "With information and models provided by our local allies, that was why I had to be here at all."

Horst glanced through the documents; they showed a Major Reitmann, U.S. Army Engineers, born in Racine, Wisconsin, and educated at the University of Chicago, commissioned in 1915 courtesy of the Reserve Officer Training Corps . . . who apparently looked very, very much like one Horst von Dückler, down to injuries incurred in a training accident with explosives . . .

His mind started sorting possibilities. "How to coordinate with the launch?" he said.

"The air torpedoes can be set up, and then launched either by timer or by the action of the transmitter itself, and the transmitter can be set to activate after a delay," Röhm said. "Setting up the launch is my job; I cannot plausibly impersonate a Yankee, even one of German stock, even for a few moments. But you, my dear comrade—"

"Where's Zacarías?" Pablo said suddenly. "He's been in and out since we got here like an old man with a weak bladder, but—"

He'd been waiting patiently through the German conversation, occasionally giving the bomb a glance that said he knew that it was explosives destined for the Americans and loved the general idea. His followers were doing the same; some of them actually patted it and grinned.

Now his head whipped around.

"Everyone, stay back and keep watching for gringos!" he snarl-shouted, and plunged away through the dim lanolin-smelling heaps, with Horst close by on his heels and Röhm not far behind.

The two technicians froze like deer in a strong light, bewildered by the sudden shift; the *revolucionarios* watching the windows and entrances called questions, to be met with obscene shouted commands to shut up and stay alert.

Horst had memorized the layout of the building when he came in, more or less automatically. The office for the warehouse was a cubicle built much later than the building itself, near the wagon-sized main doors . . .

And it has a telephone.

It also had a stout door, which was locked; Horst heard thumping and cursing as Pablo tried to break through. He had a pistol out by the time Horst arrived there, and was aiming at the lock—though at least he was showing enough sense to stand to one side and hold the crook of his arm over his eyes before he tried to shoot it out.

"*¡No!*" Horst barked. "Out of the way!"

At the same time he turned his motion from a trot to a sprint, then leapt into the air with his legs crooked. Both slammed out just before he struck the door, smashing his heels into the old warped wood right beside the latch and the lock.

There was a thump, a crunch of breaking board, and a snap of metal parting.

"*Scheisse!*" he snarled, and then "*Uhhhf!*"

His body had forgotten he was wearing rope sandals, not the stout hobnailed boots of a German officer. The eighty-eight kilos of bone and muscle and the strength of his long legs still broke the frame of the door in two places and ripped most of the lock out of the door and the jamb both, along with a bolt that had been shot from the inside. Pain shot up his legs at the same time; he'd come close to breaking his own bones too.

The grunt happened as his shoulders slammed into the packed dirt floor, and then again when Pablo stepped on his stomach as he dove into the room with a knife in his hand; fortunately he'd already tensed the muscles of his gut as he prepared to rise. There was a yell and a crash from within the office.

"No guns!" Horst barked as he raised his legs and jackknifed them down, using the momentum to flick him up into a crouch and then a forward stride.

He spoke in German, because Röhm was right behind him with a Luger in his hand, and they couldn't afford the noise. Jerez wasn't the sort of place that ignored gunfire in the night, even on a rainy evening in this commercial district. Too many people lived over their businesses, or next to them, and the Yankee-trained police reacted quickly to calls.

The office was big and cluttered and dark, but more of the twentieth century than the warehouse outside; desk, side-cranked adding machine, telephone, wooden filing cabinets piled with a clutter of papers and ledgers and invoices. There was an electric lamp on the desk, and the gloom was deeper because Pablo had overturned and broken it as he was kicked backward and fell in a heap. The hips and legs of the fleeing warehouse manager Zacarías still showed as he tried to wiggle all the way through the window—only half of it was in this cubicle built onto the inside of the original wall. And he'd somehow pushed the two vertical iron bars loose, despite the fact that they were set directly into the stone of the wall—like most Mexican windows, this didn't have a wooden frame.

Probably . . . almost certainly . . . he'd weakened them well before against just this sort of chance. Probably about the time he became an informer for the Black Chamber; the only people more insanely suspicious than secret rebels were double agents pretending to be secret rebels, because they had to look both ways at once, every hour of every day.

Horst lunged across the dimness of the room in three long strides. His right hand closed on an ankle and he hauled backward with a strength huge to begin with and multiplied by desperation, twisting as he did. Zacarías shrieked, high and thin as a trapped rabbit, a mixture of fear and pain as the leverage ripped at his knee and hip joints. Horst could feel the sudden resistance as the man grabbed at the outside of the window, scrabbling with blind desperation, and he heaved again as the scream of pain turned into words—though not intelligible ones.

Zacarías released his hold suddenly and popped out of the window like a cork from a bottle; there was a knife in his hand and he whirled and slashed as Horst staggered backward. The blade was broad and had a curved cutting edge and an eagle-headed hilt, the silver glinting in the dim light. It might have struck, if the man's injured leg hadn't given out as he turned and cut. Then Pablo was on him, a knife of his own in his hand, and the two Mexicans locked together for an instant. There was a flurry too swift to see, and Zacarías staggered back.

Horst grabbed his knife wrist and the hair at the back of his head. The man half turned, and blood gouted out of his mouth with a wet choking sound, pulsing in rivulets that looked black in the darkness. Horst grunted in disgust; he knew the signs, and he didn't need the sight of Pablo's knife hilt standing out of the waistcoat to know that the twenty-five-centimeter blade had gone up beneath the breastbone and into the lungs.

The German wrenched sharply. Neckbone snapped with a green-stick crackle, and Zacarías's body jerked and went limp with a sudden sharp stink. The blood slowed, no longer pumped out by the heart—that was why Horst had finished him, to cut down on the possibly dangerous and certainly inconvenient mess—and the German dropped the corpse. Faceup, which would also help with the flow problem. Pablo came over to retrieve his knife, which was fine now that the wound wouldn't gush. He had a cut of his own on the back of his left forearm, and worked the fingers to make sure nothing important was severed, giving a nod when his fingers moved normally. Sweat sheened his face, probably from pain as well as the sudden burst of effort.

Röhm paused in the doorway to call back that the emergency was over and to summon his two subordinates, then holstered his Luger beneath his long *campesino* shirt and—rather surprising Horst—gave the cut a dash of *mezcal*-cut water to clean it and a quick efficient field dressing with a swatch of rags.

"In a knife fight, the winner gets bandages and the loser gets a hole in the ground," he said, and then translated it into bad Spanish.

Pablo, unexpectedly, grinned at that. It made his scarred, bruised, and battered face even more like a caricature in a catalog labeled *sinister looks* than before.

Horst looked down at the dead Zacarías and bit back, *Did you have to kill him? We could have made him talk.*

He hadn't been the one facing Zacarías's knife, after all, and Pablo had. A face-to-face knife fight operated on a very thin margin, which was why you didn't have one if you had any alternatives—stabbing from behind was much safer. Horst knew both from experience; he had a cut-down bayonet with a knuckleduster across the grip, what *Frontschwein* called a trench knife, tucked away himself. And in any case the man's behavior had already answered the basic question.

"We'll have to get out of here, and quickly," he said.

Overriding a jolt of alarm as generalized danger turned in an instant into a specific, immediate threat, and feeling every sense sharpen, until the very air he breathed in was laden with knowledge.

"The traitor could have—"

The telephone rang, a harder, lower-toned sound than the one used in Germany. Horst stepped over to it and raised the old-fashioned separate receiver on a cord to his ear, using his free hand to wave the others to silence.

"*¿Bueno?*" he said, schooling his voice.

Which was the local answer to a call and asked if the *line* was good, not something you could count on here until recently. For standard phrases like that his Spanish was undetectably local; by now the European-Spanish accent he'd originally had was gone along with all or nearly all of the German one.

"*¡Sí! Bueno*," someone on the other end said. "*¿Se encuentra el Señor Sandoval?*"

Horst realized with an internal click that Sandoval must be Zacarías's surname. He tensed at the female voice, but it wasn't *her*; expecting that was illogical, but he couldn't help it, even if he didn't know her location to within a few thousand kilometers. She *might* be up to some deviltry in Europe or even Asia, and not on this continent at all; anything but sitting quietly at home was believable. American women had been insolently brassy and forward even before the new regime, and more so now.

"He is not in the room at the moment, señorita," he said, looking over his shoulder.

What he'd said was even technically true as Schäfer and Kraus dragged the body out by the ankles under Röhm's direction, both looking a little pale and green at the sights and smells.

The voice went on: "Find him and put him on immediately, then, please. I'm returning his call and it's urgent."

The Spanish was native-fluent, local even, but . . .

The tone is pleasant and the words are polite, but it's preemptory. Crisp, no-nonsense, commanding. That is someone talking to Sandoval or Sandoval's employees as if they were her servants.

Which since Sandoval had been turned and had apparently called out meant that this was, to a high degree of probability, his American controller. Probably his Black Chamber controller.

"*Disculpé, lo iré a buscar de inmediato, señorita*," he said, promising to look for Mr. Sandoval right away, a useful turn of phrase in Mexico where *inmediato* could bear the same relationship to "immediately" as *mañana* did to "tomorrow." He'd thought Yankees sloppy-careless about punctuality and exact performance of promises and orders, until he came here.

Then he set the receiver back in the cradle; that might buy them a few moments, but talking further would be futile at best, possibly harmful.

"We need to get out of here, *now*," he said, striding back into the warehouse, where there was a frantic bustle of packing.

I wish it had been her *on the phone,* he thought. *Even with the added risk. I won't say killing her would make me die happy, but . . .*

Then: *No. The mission comes first. Remember that, Horst! She's probably off somewhere doing something disgusting and evil far, far away. But maybe she will be here. It's not out of the question . . .*

"Stop that!" he snapped, as a clumsy octuplet of Mexicans and Germans started to back a wagon toward the *bomb* part of the flying bomb and others ran back and forth with crates and weapons.

"Do we have timers and detonators available?" he asked.

I shouldn't delay . . . but if it is her, how poetic to repay that bomb on Rapsstrasse back in kind! Diehl's headless ghost will laugh in heaven or hell or Valhalla.

The technician nodded uncertainly, obviously wondering what was going on. Röhm wasn't, and grinned his troll's grin as he spoke.

"*Ist der Papst katholisch?* My thought exactly, Horst. Pay the bitch back in her own coin."

TWELVE

Hacienda of the Sweet Arrival

Lieutenant Thomas Selfridge Army Air Corps Base

State of Zacatecas

United States Protectorate of México

JUNE 21ST, 1917, 1917(B)

Earlier the same day, Luz stepped back and removed the empty magazine of her new Colt .40 automatic pistol, letting it fall into her left hand and setting it on the shelf. She hadn't missed any of the targets that had popped up, and would have been shocked if she had, now that she was used to the new weapon. You still had to practice to maintain the skill, and there was a satisfaction to doing something difficult and doing it *right*. And in pushing yourself to do it better, which in her case mainly meant faster; it had been a long time since she missed much.

Rather like playing the violin, but less melodious, she thought, and removed her earplugs—light rubber on a cord that let you dangle them around your neck, yet another innovation of the Progressive era and a very recent one.

Among the renovations the Duráns had made to their new property's headquarters was a separate building with a gymnasium and *salle d'armes* for the *build your body* part of the Party's program. The latter included firing ranges of the very latest and most Progressive type. Luz checked the chamber of her .40—which was easy since the slide was locked back after firing the last round—slipped in another magazine, released the slide to chamber a round, snapped on the safety with her thumb, and waited with the muzzle carefully elevated. The machinery of the shooting range clicked and rattled as it reset.

That made her conscious of her surroundings again; it had just started to rain outside in blustery gusts amid a smell of wet dust. The building that contained the *indoor* firing range had only waist-high walls at its perimeter, with a high roof supported on pillars all around. It was shady but not dark, very comfortable on this early-summer highland day.

They'd spent the morning elsewhere, at the house stables helping young Alice stuff her plump and profoundly lazy but good-natured pony with treats, and then they'd led him around the corral with her perched on his broad, ambling back, kicking her heels and dreaming of headlong gallops on flashing-eyed Arabian steeds, and the pony walking just as little as he could, with deep martyred sighs when compelled to any effort whatsoever. That had kept them suitably out of the way while the guests departed. Now Alice was napping, and the adults could be about their business inconspicuously.

"I like this pistol," Luz said to Ciara. "The weight and recoil are very moderate, and it's a sweet piece of design, extremely well balanced; you're right about how talented Browning is. I'm already as accurate as I was with my FN .380. And the twelve-round magazine could be very handy in a tight spot."

"Sure, but don't you have a sentimental attachment to that little bitty Belgian gun, since your da gave it to you as a birthday present when you were a girl?" Ciara teased. "Rather than giving you ribbons for your hair, or a dolly . . ."

"Papá gave it to me to protect my life, and by then I was already a bit old for dolls," Luz said.

"Which is why you still have the one with the silk hair on a shelf in your old room from when you were a girl, and the stuffed bear with the mismatched button eyes?" Ciara laughed; they shared the master bedroom at the *Casa* these days.

"Well, I may need them again someday," Luz said, then cleared her throat and changed the subject: "So I'll keep the FN as a remembrance... or for when I need something *very* concealable ... and switch to this for every day. It's important not to get sentimental about tools."

This part of the complex was a pistol range, only a few months old but with the slightly bitter-acrid smell of nitro powder already in the fabric of it. From back toward the center of the enclosure came the grunts and fists-and-feet-on-leather of two of the Zacatecas station's operatives practicing modern all-in hand-to-hand combat as it had evolved over the past few years in the Chamber and the military—a mixture of Bartitsu, French *savate*, Japanese jujitsu, boxing, wrestling, and plain old-fashioned fork-of-the-crick riverboat-and-frontier no-holds-barred butt-stomp-and-gouge American dirty fighting. And over that Julie's sharp voice, only a little muffled by the wire-mesh mask she was wearing:

"En garde! Prêt! Allez!"

On the heels of the last command the soft scuffle and *ting-click* and panting of Julie and Henrietta fencing with the epée began again immediately. That distant descendant of the rapier via the gentleman's smallsword of George Washington's day might not have any direct application in combat these days, but it was very good general athletic conditioning and taught hand-eye control and quick reflexes and bone-deep physical self-confidence.

I must get in a few bouts if I have the time; Julie can really push me.

"Now it's your turn, *querida*," Luz said. "Nothing fancy, just tap two into each target's center of mass. Muscles of the arm engaged but not quivering-tight, squeeze the trigger, fire as you exhale with just a slight pause in your breath before. Bring the weapon up, sight, fire, let the sights fall to the next aiming point and then the pause in your breath for just a second as you take up the slack. Don't jerk the pistol around, don't force it, everything *smooth*. Fast you can build with time, but it comes after accurate—a slow hit is usually better than a fast miss."

"Though a near miss can make them keep their heads down, eh?" Ciara said.

"Quite right, and we'll get to that. But basics first."

Ciara stepped up to the line drawn on the asphalt floor—combat shooting rarely involved a convenient counter at waist height, unlike popping bottles at county fairs—and waited until Luz nodded. She raised her identical Amazon, visually checked that the safety was off, and kept it muzzle up with her right side presented, leaning forward slightly with her left fist tucked palm up against the top of her breastbone, her right foot advanced, the left at shoulder-width distance and pointing at a forty-five-degree angle with both knees slightly flexed.

Luz had first learned the pistol in a different and more genteel upright fashion, but she'd adopted that stance and taught it to her partner. It had become popular in the last few years and was known in Chamber and military circles as *the Andy*. It was based on actual nineteenth-century professional duelist styles and also recent experience in the field, but named after Andrew Jackson, who was Uncle Teddy's third most favored president after Washington and Lincoln.

Not least due to the fact that he'd greeted South Carolina's first rumblings of secession with a blunt promise to hang anyone who tried it from the nearest tree and *high as Haman* . . .

Ciara stood quietly, her face intent. There was a conventional bull's-eye down fifty yards from the shooting line, but that wasn't the main target. The gallery was floored with sand, fifteen yards wide, and enclosed by high adobe walls thick enough to stop a bullet the way a sponge did water. Ricochets were still possible, but then so were strokes and heart attacks—you took reasonable precautions and then went forward.

Luz raised her voice: "Live fire here! Ernesto, on my mark . . . one, two, three, *now!*"

The attendant Ernesto threw an electrical switch and a mechanism of gears and wires clicked into operation. Ten yards downrange the outline of a man snapped upright and began to move sideways in a curve along a rail at a walking pace; it was made of steel with a fronting of white plywood to absorb shots, covered in turn with a cutout of black paper.

Ciara's pistol came to the level . . . smoothly.

Crack! Crack!

The target fell down with a muffled clang, and two white flecks appeared on what would have been the center of a man's torso. Another flipped up closer, shaped like a man lying down with a rifle . . .

Ciara shot with steady regularity until the last of the moving targets fell, then fired the last of her twelve rounds at the bull's-eye and hit it in the upper right-hand corner of the outer ring. Luz shook her head as Ernesto dashed out to replace the paper covers, then to sweep up the spent brass, and Ciara checked the chamber by eye, snapped the slide home and reloaded, then holstered the pistol with the chamber empty and the safety on.

"*¡Extraordinario!*" Luz said.

Ciara was frowning; she was a perfectionist in her way. "I only hit five of eight," she said, slightly fretful. "Hardly better than half! *Counting* the end target, and I only barely hit that at all. It's just velocities and trajectories—why can't I do better?"

"You only started practicing in January, sweetie," Luz said. "I first fired a pistol with my father holding my hand when I was . . . seven? I think. And you're just not a born shooter, none of this comes naturally to you. But you're starting to *hit* quite often, which is what matters at the last, because you listen to the instructions and follow them precisely. Believe me, that's rapid progress. Offhand pistol shooting is *hard*, much harder than using a rifle."

Though how you'd do in an actual gunfight only time will tell, mi amor, she thought. *You've got plenty of nerve, but the edge is another matter, turning fear into rage and rage into a cold living drive to kill. Most people don't hit a tenth, or a hundredth, as often in a real fight as they do on a range, even a modern one like this.*

Ciara smiled, showing her dimples. "It's a machine, darling. I'm usually fairly good at operating machines with a little practice. Now show how it's *really* done again."

Luz actually shot better in action than at practice. She stepped up to the mark herself.

"Double speed," she said, and Ernesto twisted the handle of his switch. "Set for a walking shoot."

She thumbed the safety off and took the point-blank stance, the one you used when someone might pop up at your feet or be flattened against the wall beside a doorway you were going through and grab at your gun; you faced more to the front, with the shooting hand back and braced against your side. The left fist was clenched and held near the neck; in the real thing she'd have had her *navaja* in that hand, ready for a backhand slash or overarm stab down between collarbone and neck.

This stance required absolutely instinctive aiming, since you couldn't use the sights. She took three deep slow breaths and spoke:

"Live fire here! Ernesto, on my mark . . . one, two, three, *now!*"

As he threw the switch, Luz began walking forward, her mind a receptive blank; beneath that ran memories, of fear and stink and pain, of feeling her own blood running down her skin, darkness . . . death caught in the corner of the eye, channeled into an awareness as total as a scorpion's, and as automatic.

Motion. *Crack!* Motion. *Crack!*

Luz came to herself at the end of the range and shook her head, almost tasting the hot salt that spattered across your face when you shot at arm's length. She walked back and found Ciara waiting for her, with Julie and Henrietta in their padded fencing costumes and the tall redheaded Ranger officer. The man was in the normal baggy drab field dress now, where the tomahawk looked much more natural, and he was stone-faced as he looked down the line of prone targets with one brow raised. He was somewhere between her age and his low thirties, though the weathered look of someone who'd spent most of his waking hours out of doors all his life made it difficult to tell precisely, and his face had the long bony square-chinned look his ancestors had probably brought from the Scots border country via Ulster.

"Ma'am," he said after a long moment in a strong hill-country southern twang. "I reckon you can come hunt in the Wolf Valley country back to home just about any time you please."

Julie chuckled at his expression of thoughtful purse-lipped interest as Luz reloaded and set her automatic in the new shoulder holster.

I didn't plan it that way, but perhaps it's for the best, Luz thought. *Giving him something he can understand.*

Rangers were the usual partners of choice for the Black Chamber when they needed active muscle, but she hadn't worked with this particular man before, though his campaign ribbons indicated he'd been in the Intervention since the start.

It was a big war and this is a big country, she thought.

"Captain York, of Roger's Ranger Regiment, currently attached to the 2nd Philippine Rangers," Julie said in introduction; the Rangers provided the officers for their colonial equivalents.

Then to the two operatives from her station who'd been practicing all-in:

"Lee. McNaughton."

That was said with a flick of her eyes toward the entrance. Both men—they looked about Luz's age, or at least a little younger than Julie—went that way briskly past the weights and exercise machines, the vaulting horse and parallel bars and climbing ropes, ready to quietly head off anyone trying to get in while their superiors were talking.

Then she went on: "And my colleagues, Executive Field Operative Luz O'Malley Aróstegui and Field Operative Ciara Whelan."

"Ma'am, I am right pleased to meet you and Miss Whelan," the lanky hill-country soldier said.

They shook hands in the modern fashion; his were big even for someone who stood six-two, and felt like flexible rawhide wrapped around a hydraulic grab as he gave a brief firm grip.

East Tennessee, and a country boy, she thought. *And he recognized my name; not surprising, the Rangers are a small world and they gossip. Though those ear piercings for the Bugkalot jewelry aren't exactly hill-and-holler style . . . not unless you count northeastern Luzon as hillbilly country. And the Bugkalot* don't *let anyone use them unless they really* do *represent heads taken in front of witnesses. They must like him quite a bit.*

"Likewise, Captain York," Luz said, and took a look at one of the badges on his arm. "Ah, you're one of Fred's Children too, I see."

The alternative nickname for graduates of Burnham's scout-sharpshooter-wilderness survival school in the mountains near his Yaqui Valley estate in Sonora was *bug eater*, but that might not be entirely tactful on short acquaintance.

"You were at the Yaqui Base Camp, ma'am?" he said, smiling for the first time.

"Twice," Luz said. "In 1913, when it was just getting started, and then again in late 1915 for the winter version. Let's see what you brought us, Captain."

They sat at a rustic picnic-style table not far from the edge of the building, where it looked out over a dripping field of young grass big enough for an outdoor rifle range, amid gray light lit by an occasional lightning flash and rumble of thunder. The falling water would make it entirely private and the staff had already left out coffee and lemonade and a plate of various types of *pan dulce* under a gauze cloth and withdrawn. An electric light gave a puddle of brightness over the table.

"First, thanks for getting us those Navy airboats, ma'am," York said. "We thought that must be the Chamber, and it was a true help."

He pronounced the last word as *he'p.*

"You're welcome, Captain. It seemed efficient."

"My boys can move fast through rough country, none better, but it was purely a relief to be able to get our provender from above. And our men on them saw a good deal from up there too; with the eyes of eagles, as the Good Book says. And it kept some of our hurt alive to get them to the doctors fast, I reckon."

He'd been carrying a light haversack, one of greased leather that repelled water almost as well as rubber. Now he put it before them on the table and undid the straps; his long battered fingers were deft on the buckles.

"Them we were chasing, the ones the Air Corps johnnies bombed to start the whole thing, they moved pretty fast, 'specially considering they had wounded," he said. "They didn't leave much sign, which slowed us down, and they laid false trails—did it well, too, which slowed us more. We caught up with them when an airboat came at 'em from the west, over the pass they were heading for. If I were doing it again I'd have the boat drop a blocking party ahead of 'em. Live and learn in this here modern age. 'A course, some jest dies in it afore they *can* learn."

He took a rough pine box out of the haversack, about the size of those used for shipping cigars.

"So, we mopped up the ones we caught. No prisoners, I'm afraid, though we . . . well, really *I* . . . tried. My boys are crackerjack fighters and they can track a ghost over bare rock, even better than my folk back to home, but they're not really soldiers . . . more warriors . . . or hunters, in a way. Man-hunters. They see an enemy, they kill as long as the enemy's fighting back . . ."

Or if they want the head to show off at home whether they're begging for mercy or not, Luz thought.

"... and this bunch of *bandits* were pretty determined. The holdouts are, now, mostly. Them as had any givin' up in 'em have already done give up."

The box was filled with wadded cloth, apparently used bandages; a faint scent of pine sap and old blood rose from it. Two irregular flattish lumps of dried plaster of Paris nestled in the improvised padding.

"I had a sort of feelin' the ones we caught weren't all of 'em, so after we got our wounded out I had the boys search the mountains to each side. Up-and-down and rocky, even compared to Fentress County—"

Which confirmed her guess as to where he came from; that was on the Tennessee-Kentucky border, bloody ground since the Long Hunters came through before the Revolution and blood-feudist territory during the Civil War and the generations since.

"—but there are game trails, and old man-sign; campfires, the odd rusty buckle or spoon or a dropped coin. Just about gave up on it when we didn't find anything at first, but I knew we weren't going to have to walk out anyways, thanks again for the airboats, so I kept us all at it an extra day. All I got was these, from the south side of the valley, up a couple-two thousand feet above the stream."

He lifted the cloth padding with the plaster lumps carefully out onto the surface of the table. Both had been made by pouring liquid plaster into depressions in the ground, waiting for them to set, and then very carefully lifting them out and removing the dirt with a soft brush.

"Heel prints," Luz said thoughtfully. "Boot heels, not huaraches, not sandals."

"Right," York said. "Now, not all Mexicans wear huaraches—"

He pronounced the word correctly, even the initial *h . . . wwh* sound and the trilled *r*, both of which most English speakers found difficult.

"—but most of the country folk do. I couldn't say exactly when the man with the boots went through, but it's been raining a fair bit around there—"

He jerked a thumb at the drizzle outside; it was the right time of year, and the mountains got more than the upland basins like this.

"—and the prints were mighty sharp, so it couldn't have been *much* before we had our fight. I can't absolutely swear it was the same day, but that's what my belly tells me about the way they looked, though I couldn't prove it to a judge."

"It's lucky we're not trying to prove anything in court, then," Julie said thoughtfully, her fingers toying with the hilt of the epée she'd laid on the table, smells of sweat fresh and stale coming from the padded white fencer's plastron she still wore.

Luz looked at the heel prints, then drew a black ebony rectangle about four inches by two out of a pocket. She pulled open the telescoping action; one end held a magnifying lens, and she went over the plaster cast slowly and in detail. Then she handed it to Ciara, who did likewise.

"Pad, please," Ciara said, her voice with that odd inward-turned remoteness it had when she was concentrating.

Henrietta slid her pad and mechanical pencil over. Ciara did a sketch of each heel on separate pieces of paper, with a side view of each as well, and used the ruler marks notched into the side of the sliding case to get the precise measurements. She listed those with arrows indicating reference points, and then filled in dots to mark the places where the boot's hobnails had dug into the soil.

She slid it over to Luz, who used little crosses to show some hobnails that *weren't* there, completing the pattern. Luz could sketch fairly well, but it was an acquired taste and Ciara did it much better—native talent and correspondence courses in mechanical draftsmanship had made her machine-accurate. Beside the drawings Luz made quick printed notes, principally about the missing dots in the pattern and the shallowness of the marks.

"Check on this, please," she said.

The drawing was handed around; each of the five seated at the table studied it and then the plaster casts again.

"Seems right," York said last, after a long intent look at the sketches.

He had the patient attention to detail of a man who'd hunted for his family's food since before his voice broke.

And probably got the hickory switch on his back from Paw if he came back with a turkey where he'd spoiled the meat by shooting it in the body instead of taking off the head, Luz thought. *And another switching if he used more than one bullet.*

Aloud she went on: "How deep were the prints? Your notion on the man who made them?"

"Pretty deep, an' the dirt was some damp but not what I'd call soft," York said. "Those were the best marks I could find, but I could follow where he'd walked for mebbe a hunert, hunert 'n' fifty paces easy enough, 'nuff to match strides. My guess . . . man about as tall as me, mebbe a hair shorter—"

He held out his thumb horizontally to indicate how much by its width, the habit of a deeply rural man not used to working in formal measurements unless he thought about it.

"—an' mebbe just a trifle heavier-set. I put my own boots to that ground, and the prints waren't as deep by about this—"

He held out his right fist, with the little finger extended to show he meant about a quarter of an inch.

"—even when I walked heel-heavy a' purpose. Stepped about as long as me, hard to tell exactly 'cause there was so much rock there, but not more than, oh, two inches or so different."

There were raised brows around the table. He was describing a six-footer, heavy enough to be muscular but not massive. Mexicans who stood six feet tall weren't unknown but weren't common either, most especially among the badly nourished peasantry; at five-six, Luz was tall for a woman in the United States, but around average for a man here. The sort of height York was describing was much more common among North Europeans.

And to be sure, among their overseas descendants. Or people of African blood, but I don't think a Negro wearing German boots among Mexican guerillas is very likely.

Her eye estimated York's *weight* at about a hundred seventy-five or eighty pounds; he looked slender, but it was all muscle and sinew and he moved with a loose-jointed grace. The same on a man two inches shorter suggested . . .

Suggests someone I know.

"Whoever this feller is, he walks heel-down and toe-out, too, even more than most low-country men do—sort of a stompin' way of walking, I reckon. Not much like the folks hereabouts, either."

Luz had noted that the Ranger had a light, smooth, and even walk, with the weight put on the ball of the foot and the heel touching lightly and the toes pointed almost directly ahead; many country folk from his part of the Appalachians did, especially hunters from the real backwoods. Their ancestors had picked up that and a good deal else from their Indian predecessors, in the merciless generations-long wars that had ground and hacked the moving line of the frontier westward through the mountains and valleys, and in trade and occasional intermarriage between the spasms of slaughter.

"There was others with him, but the sign wasn't as good. Not more than three, I'd say, though. And they got out of there fast, a lot faster even than the big bunch we caught had been movin'. Four men total, all fit and movin' quick and not leaving much in the way of tracks."

"Right," Luz said, adding the estimate of height and weight to the notes. "Miss Colmer, have this transmitted to HQ, and get their forensics people on it, *por favor*," Luz said—they were speaking English, though she had the impression the Ranger had fair Spanish. "I expect they'll confirm my estimate, though. That's a German *Marschstiefel*— marching boot. The pattern of the hobnails is distinctive."

I will not say it is him.

Though her gut was convinced that it was Horst von Dückler indeed, and out for blood.

That's emotion speaking. Stay with the facts.

She pointed with Henrietta's mechanical pencil. "And see around the heel, like a reversed horseshoe? That's the iron heel plate. I think but I'm not sure that these are of the officer's pattern; I'm not sure because they're quite worn, and because there's some variation—German officers buy their own, and they're usually handmade. Some of the hobnails are missing and the rest are just barely dimpling the soil, they've been ground down; and there are gaps in the heelplate, where parts have snapped and worked free. These boots have been used hard and repaired locally. The heel-first walking style is German, too, especially their military men."

"Ah, now that's good trackin', ma'am, even if you're doing it at a table with coffee an' cakes," York said, finishing an apricot empanada in two bites and dusting his hands. "Happy to have been of service to our friends in the Chamber."

"Thank you, Captain York," Luz said. "And check with your battalion commander in Fresnillo. I've been given authority to draw on your company as needed, and you may very well *be* needed. Heads may have to be removed at some point, without too many questions asked or excessive formalities."

"Yes, ma'am!" York said after they exchanged a verbal code for that, raising a finger to his brow in salute. "Ladies," he added to the others with a nod as he left.

Luz looked around the table. "I'm going to operate on the assumption that there was at least one German with the bandits in the Sierra," she said thoughtfully. "One who survived both the initial air attack and then the brush with the Rangers that got most of the survivors. He's definitely not among the dead; he certainly still has Mexican accomplices, and possibly there's more than one German."

"Henrietta," Julie said. "You have that incident report we discussed this morning?"

The secretary nodded, and reached into the attaché case she'd kept within arm's reach even when fencing.

"Here, ma'am."

It was the standard record circulated to relevant persons—military commanders, governors, and FBS field leaders and Black Chamber station chiefs—in a given area. It also included the contact digests for the whole Protectorate, usually covering some time back, easy enough to do since there weren't very many anymore. Julie flipped through it and tapped an item, turning it around so Luz and Ciara could see it.

It was from the Navy and recorded a U-boat contact by a Naval Aviation airship, north of Tampico and quite close to shore. The semi-rigid had done a depth-charge run, but the submarine had escaped . . . and more to the point, hadn't been spotted again. Luz frowned; the Kaiserliche Marine's commerce raiders were always trying for the tanker convoys into and out of the great oil port. If the submarine had been heavily damaged, it would have run for home . . . but it would have attacked otherwise, unless that wasn't its tasking.

"The thing is, this was three weeks ago, and there haven't been any attacks since," Julie said, showing she'd been thinking along. "And while sinking merchantmen is their main occupation, U-boats are very useful for getting agents in and out—the flying boat spotted this one just after dawn. Now, was it going *in* . . . or going *out*, mission accomplished, let's head for Wilhelmshaven and beer and barmaids?"

"They have cargo submarines that can transport hundreds of tons, too," Ciara pointed out. "The ones they used for the Projekt Loki attacks were that model, with batteries of rocket-mortars in place of the cargo holds. They're not armed; they use them for resupply at sea, fuel and torpedoes and food and spare parts and so forth."

"And smuggling agents and gear into enemy territory when they need large tonnage capacity," Luz said grimly. "But it's risky bringing them close to shore in heavily patrolled shallow water, so they don't do it without a very good reason. Ordinary commerce raiders lurk in groups farther out."

Luz frowned more deeply and looked at the plaster casts again.

"That's an awful lot of wear on a boot for three weeks' walking," she said thoughtfully. "Whoever was wearing it didn't come in on a U-boat recently. Is there a connection, or are we seeing something that's not there? Is A connected to B, or are we being insanely suspicious about plots? Which is an occupational hazard in this line of work."

Henrietta spoke unexpectedly: "Remember the parable of the three blind men tryin' to describe an elephant? Seems to me we're in that position. We've got three pieces, but are they A, B, and C, or are they A, J, and X?"

They all smiled ruefully. You could fool yourself quite comprehensively when you tried to fill in the blanks from very little knowledge, but you had to do it anyway.

"True, it's important not to get too wedded to one explanation . . . I need more information!" Luz said.

Julie chuckled as she folded the remaining *pan dulce* into the cloth.

"Well, that's our business, now, isn't it?" she said. "We'll be seeing the pilots this afternoon and no doubt after that we'll be *even more* at sea."

"On to the airfield, then. *¡Ándale!*" Luz replied.

The Army Air Corps base outside Jerez was a dose of undiluted twentieth-century modernity, like something out of the 1920s or 1930s rather than their own decade, blazing with electric lights through the dimness of a rainy afternoon. It was also much bigger than it really needed to be, built to work as a training base as well as an operational one, in a place where land close to railroads and towns was cheaper than in the north and opportunities to drop explosives easier to come by.

Luz found it bracing and strange at the same time; it was odd to remember that not more than a mile away men were tilling fields with wooden plows drawn by oxen, and planting their corn and beans with pointed sticks and the soles of their feet. The runways were rolled concrete rather than the more usual graded dirt—to ensure that they were usable in wet weather like this—and so were the roadways. The concrete, plywood, two-by-four, and sheet-metal buildings were blocky and boxlike, painted the Army's uniform greenish-brownish wolf-gray, each one looking like a slight variation on the others, even the big hangars with their sideways-sliding doors and curved roofs.

There had been a school of avant-garde European painting just before the war that looked a little like this; the problem was that Luz had never *liked* that school.

"Everything prefabricated, everything standardized, everything electrified!" Ciara enthused behind her in the rear seat, speaking a little loudly to be heard over the hum of tires on wet pavement and the drum of the rain on the canvas roof above and the mechanical racket of the four-cylinder engine. "All factory-made and you just assemble the sections! Think of the possibilities for new low-cost housing after the war!"

"Lord, yes!" Henrietta agreed enthusiastically from beside her.

Luz caught a sideways glance from Julie Durán. She shrugged slightly; neither of them found that prospect at all appealing.

We aren't as Progressive as the youngsters! she thought ironically.

But then, both of them had spent most of their lives living in the sort of building that required architects and skilled craftsmen and monied parents. Ciara's roots were in a part of Boston that ranged from the Whelan family's painfully achieved lace-curtain respectability to outright slum tenements stinking of piss and garbage and cabbage, and in between the majority of cold-water walk-ups where even skilled workmen usually took in paying lodgers to help with the rent. Henrietta Colmer had been born to Savannah's tiny Negro petite bourgeois, who'd even more painfully pulled themselves out of even worse squalor than any in South Boston, out among the worn-out, mosquito-swarming Low Country cotton fields.

A weathertight prefab with enough rooms that there were three bedrooms—one each for the boys, girls, and parents of a family—could look very appealing from either standpoint.

Nobody paid them much attention at the base perimeter apart from checking their documents and using the usual mirror-on-a-stick to look underneath the Guvvie.

Inside it was a bit before evening mess call, and everyone they saw was hurrying along through the rain. The hangar they passed had a wavering brightness through it, the big *33-A* lettered above the half-open doors barely visible. They were probably left that way to help the fumes from solvents and cleaning fluids disperse; inside Luz glimpsed teams of men in overalls using overhead hoists to lift the engines free of a Falcon and lower them onto pallets. Others did maintenance in place, taking advantage of the weather that pinned the aeroplanes to the ground to play catch-up.

Which is probably my fault, Luz thought. *Since I was the one who suggested a stepped-up surveillance flight tempo in the first place, when the Director told me where we'd be going. Of course, having the base here was also probably one reason the high command picked this location for the Dakota Project in the beginning.*

Julie swung the Guvvie along the side of the big building, down a lane half-lit by the glow from the clerestory windows, and halted at the rear, where an overhead lamp cast a puddle of light before a door leading into the closed-off block of office space at the rear of the hangar. They all piled out to where a sentry with a Thompson slung under a rain poncho and drops pattering on his helmet as if on a tin roof gave them a surprised look and examined their *laissez-passer* before letting them through.

A clerk behind a metal desk greeted them inside, a young woman in WAC uniform with glasses on the end of her nose as she worked on some sort of account book at a stamped-metal desk. Bare bulbs lit a pine-board and plywood interior and concrete floor; the metallic-chemical smells and muffled grinding and clanking noises hinted at the work going on in the hangar.

"Can I help you ladies?" she said, obviously bursting with curiosity.

"Tell Lieutenant Nudelman that the party he's expecting at 1630 hours is here, please, Private," Julie said pleasantly.

The WAC clerk's eyes went a little wider. The four of them would have been unremarkable in New York or Chicago, down to the attaché case Henrietta carried, and the practical raincoats and plain hats and sensible low-heeled shoes they all wore. Henrietta might have gotten a second glance in those cosmopolitan surroundings, or not. Here they were a mystery. Her eyes darted toward them as she picked up a telephone and hit a switch, then away again as she spoke into it.

What's going through her mind is some sort of Secret Service thing *probably*, Luz thought. *And she's keeping that to herself, which is good.*

Lieutenant J. Nudelman (Intelligence Corps, with the key-sword-sphinx badge on his collar) was prompt; he was also tall, skinny, pale with a parchment look that was sallow at the same time, frizzy military-cropped black hair already retreating a little despite his being only about Luz's age, and self-evidently Jewish.

"Can I help you ladies?" he said politely, in a moderate New York accent.

"You were told to expect a J. Durán and party?" Julie said, and showed him her ID.

Nudelman's glance flickered over her, and the rest of them. Creditably, he showed nothing except a widening of his mournful brown eyes; even more creditably, he didn't ask anyone else's name before simply saying:

"This way, ma'am. I'll bring the men you requested immediately; they've been told to expect some visiting firemen and to cooperate fully."

The room set up for the interviews was as bleakly functional as the rest of the base, with chairs on either side of a long deal table, and corkboards on the walls stuck with cryptic notes. One wall had a poster of a Puma fighting scout doing a victory roll in a blue sky as a German Albatross plunged in flame and smoke.

The inevitable presidential poster was near it; this one showed Uncle Teddy operating a huge steam shovel while dressed in a white linen suit, done from a photograph of his famous visit to Panama in '06 to inspect the progress of the canal that was his brainchild, the first time a serving president had left the United States. Beneath in block letters was:

AND NOTHING GETS IN HIS WAY!

"Would you like coffee, ma'am?" Nudelman said to Julie.

"Thank you, Lieutenant. Send in the pot, in fact, and some extra cups for our interview subjects. I'll have my staff forward you a redacted transcript of the results."

Because the last thing we need is you looking over our shoulders, Luz thought. *Not if you were a fool and even less so since you aren't.*

The clever Lieutenant Nudelman took the hint and left.

The WAC clerk returned with a tray and poured for them all and set out cream and sugar. Luz sighed as she sipped; it was nostalgic, but not in a particularly good way. She'd long ago lost track of the number of bases, bivouacs, and in-the-field campfires where she'd drunk varieties of vile Army coffee during the Intervention; somehow soldiers managed to keep it uniformly bad even in Mexico, where they *grew* excellent coffee and usually brewed it well.

To be fair, this was the way Uncle Teddy liked his coffee too: cowboy-style, burnt and strong as the devil.

The room was warm after the coolish wet outside, kept that way by the hissing kerosene stove in one corner. They hung up their hats and overcoats to hooks on the wall; Julie also removed her jacket, and after a moment Luz imitated her, guessing the reason; Henrietta and Ciara followed suit. They sat at the table, Luz by Julie's left and Ciara by hers; Henrietta took the right. The two local Black Chamber operatives set out their files, and Henrietta put down a steno pad in addition and checked the lead in her mechanical pencil because she'd be taking shorthand notes.

Julie took a gauze-wrapped parcel from her secretary and opened it; within were the remaining *pan dulce*—campechanas, conchas, empanadas, and other Mexican pastries—from their meeting with Captain York in the *salle d'armes*. It was a small touch, but interrogation was a delicate art, a matter of fluctuating moods and tripping signals in people's minds they weren't aware of themselves.

"Send them in," Julie said, taking a cigarette from a gold case.

She lit it with a Ronson Wonderlite—a thing like a little whiskey flask, except that when you pulled on the knob at the top a metal perpetual match came out and lit as it made contact with the air.

New as the building was, it was obvious that she wasn't the first to smoke in it, and not just from the ashtrays. Luz sometimes thought that the military ran on coffee and tobacco as much as on rations and ammunition. To the Army, Uncle Teddy was a mystic seer sent from some military Asgard or Olympus, and General Wood sat at his right hand, Thor to his Odin or Apollo to his Zeus . . . but they certainly weren't paying any attention to the presidential view of cigarettes.

Four young men filed in from the door opposite them, in uniforms that were neat and clean but field-service drab and practical. Two were lieutenants, the others a sergeant and a corporal—the pilots and the observers of the selected Falcons from the flight that had engaged the guerillas in the Sierra. You couldn't talk effectively with a group of more than four.

One of the officers was tall and lanky, a blond with a bleached complexion and pale eyes in a lumpy, horsey immobile face; that would be Lieutenant Isaac Stoddard, the name and the old-stock Yankee look were unmistakable, and the file said a ROTC commission from Harvard. The other was nearly as tall, as olive-skinned as Luz with a heavy tan on top of that save for a slightly paler area around the eyes where his goggles would rest in flight. That contrasted with snapping black eyes, a heavy fleshy nose, and the blue-black stubble of a man who had to shave twice a day; his raven hair would have been curly if it weren't cut so short.

Lieutenant Nicolas Vlastos, she thought.

His parents had fled Turkish oppression in Smyrna and ended up running a diner in a Rhode Island mill town. Their son had gone through officer's training and flight school at the same time.

Sergeant Michael Rourke, brown hair and freckles and a snub nose, from Esplen, a sooty working-class neighborhood under the shadow of the blast furnaces and open hearths in Pittsburgh.

Corporal Jack Hayes, a stolid-looking fresh-faced farm boy with a dark russet crop and jug ears and green eyes, from Washington's rolling Palouse wheatlands.

The young airmen stopped and looked around for the males they'd assumed would be waiting for them, a little puzzled to see four women instead.

"Ah, ladies, is this some sort of Red Cross or YWCA thing?" Lieutenant Stoddard said, in purest *Ha'va'd Yaahd* tones. "Or an interview for a newspaper article about our bombing run on the bandits?"

Vlastos was a little quicker on the uptake; he blinked three times, and Luz thought she could follow his mental processes as he snapped his eyes to the identical shoulder holsters and .40 automatics all four women wore, added in that his orders had been to report for a further debriefing, ran through a roster of U.S. government organizations, and settled on one that best fitted all the facts in front of him.

Black Chamber was what rang up in his eyes, and definitely what he whispered to Stoddard, though she got that from lip reading rather than sound.

Four female operatives conducting an interview about an incident involving an attack on Mexican guerillas wouldn't be *likely* under any circumstances . . . very unlikely indeed . . . but unlikely things did happen, this one was happening right in front of him, and the Black Chamber was the only real *possibility*. The Chamber had a reputation for not following any conventional rules . . . for mad but effective eccentricity, in fact. Legend had it that anyone from a circus performer to your kid sister could be a member without your knowing it.

Then he nudged his observer and the process was duplicated. All four men came to ramrod braces and saluted.

Someone who can see the obvious when it bites his foot, Luz thought. *Good. So many would rather hug the mast of the Good Ship* Preconception *as it sinks into the shark-infested waters of reality below, muttering* Not happening! Not happening! *as the dorsal fins draw near.*

Julie smiled in a friendly manner. "At ease. No need for excessive formality; we're not in your chain of command. Do sit down, gentlemen," she added. "Coffee's in the pot there; help yourself to a pastry if you feel the need, we may be here a while and I know it's near mess call for you. Would any of you care for a cigarette?"

She produced her monogrammed gold cigarette case and opened it, offering the Moghuls. All four men murmured thanks and took one as she extended the case, and a light from her Ronson, with only Stoddard not giving the cigarettes a quick look of surprised pleasure at the mellow strength of the tobacco. Even Luz had to admit that the smell wasn't as unpleasant as she usually found the weed, particularly compared to what soldiers usually smoked, though she had personal reasons for that.

It was the perfumes of Araby compared to the chemical blowtorch smell of a French Gitaine.

"Now, let me make one thing clear. I'm not here to appraise your performance as war aeroplane crews. That's not my area of expertise," Julie said.

She placed a finger on the files.

"Your superiors' reports say that your behavior was exemplary and I'm not going to second-guess them. What I need is to pull information out of you that you may not know you have."

She took a pull on the cigarette and blew smoke meditatively. "You may have noticed that the fighting with Germany has died down since we withdrew from France a little while ago?"

They all nodded. "Yeah, and I don't like it for . . . beans, ma'am," Vlastov said. "Nobody here does."

His voice was half New England and half generic working-class Eastern big-city, with only a hint of his parents' speech in the way he rolled final *r*'s and separated the last syllable of a word.

"After what they did to Savannah, killing American citizens on American soil, they need a good kicking to teach 'em respect for Uncle Sam. The sort of kicking where you hear bones snap."

Beside Luz, Henrietta stiffened and vibrated in agreement at the remark, and her fingers tightened on her pencil, though none of it showed on her face.

"Well, those decisions are made above any of our pay grades," Julie said pleasantly.

She met their eyes one by one and continued: "That doesn't mean the war I and my colleagues fight has gone quiet. Quite the contrary. The enemy's malice never sleeps. Think of the plots against America that *have* been broken. *That* fight doesn't stop."

Their faces were absolutely serious now. Everyone in America knew about the foiled horror-gas attacks on the eastern cities; even with time to evacuate most of the people, the one on Savannah had been terrible enough. The official communiqué had simply said that *American Secret Service personnel* had foiled the Breath of Loki by giving the locations of the U-boats to the Navy for capture or destruction. The Department of Public Information saw that everyone with access to a printing press used that phrase and nothing else, but most people believed the whispers that said *Black Chamber.*

"Ma'am?" the horse-faced Yankee said. "I was in Boston on the 6th. I'd like to show you something, if you don't mind."

He reached into his jacket pocket; he didn't notice the very slight pistolward motion of Luz's right hand before it was checked by her conscious mind, and a fractional instant later of Julie's. The other lieutenant did, though, from the way his quick dark eyes flicked between them, and his thick black brow with the bridge of hair over his nose rose a bit.

I'm sure Stoddard's brave and a good pilot, Luz thought, noting the faint byplay. *But in any sort of fight, my money would be on the Greek. I like his instincts.*

What the New Englander brought out was a small leather folder, like a wallet but one that opened out in accordion pleats. Inside were photographs, small ones and slightly battered. They showed an older couple whose kinship to the pilot was plain as day, a moderately pretty girl in her best, sitting stiffly—her best obviously included an old-fashioned laced and boned corset under the frilly white dress—and smiling the same way and holding a bouquet, a couple who also looked like relatives with a pair of toddlers, and two younger editions of the pilot showing how much more unfortunate his looks would be if you were a girl in your teens.

"Ma'am, I was there because I had leave, and my older brother . . . he's in the Navy, detection officer on a destroyer . . . did too. Me, my brother, my two sisters, my sister-in-law and my niece and nephew, my fiancée . . . the whole family."

Ciara started to catch Luz's eye and give a slight smile: *We did that; the Chamber did; you and I did.* We *saved them, people we never knew.*

Luz shook her head, just the beginning of the motion, but it was enough. *From the shadows, steel. As we do our deeds in darkness, we win no public praise.*

Ciara went expressionless, but there was a message in her eyes: *But we did* do it, *and you and I know.*

And another when the younger operative glanced over at Henrietta's immobile face: *This must be very hard for her. This man's family lived and hers died that day.*

"You say what you need done, ma'am, and we'll do it," Stoddard said flatly.

The others all nodded. Luz thought one of the noncoms unconsciously mouthed something on the order of *Fuck, yeah.*

Julie nodded impassively and Henrietta's mechanical pencil poised over the pad.

"Here's what will happen. I will ask you questions. My colleagues *may* ask you questions. *You* do not ask us questions unless they're necessary to clarify your answers. It will take some time and it will be . . . strenuous, because we'll be asking the same things over and over in slightly different ways, which we know is as irritating on the receiving end as it is boring on ours. You're intelligent and spirited men and you'll want to know things yourselves. Suppress that urge; the information flows from you to us, not us to you. Once we're gone, you just had a meaningless interview with some bureaucrats about . . ."

"Carburetors," Ciara said. "They've been having problems on them with the Falcon V's engines since they increased the compression ratios so much, they need redesign work."

The sergeant from Pittsburgh looked at her. "Yeah, miss, you got dat right," he said. "Don' I know it. Gotta keep at 'em all the time, is what, and replace 'em all the fff . . . foolish time too. Everyone bitches about it . . . pardon my French."

"I understand a replacement will be out in a month or so, Sergeant," Ciara said.

"Or what was that idea you had, Lieutenant?" Julie went on. "The YWCA doing an article? That might be better, for us. *Don't* try to make up detailed lies about this afterward. You're not trained for it. Just be vague if you have to talk at all and don't talk about it if you don't absolutely have to, and don't be ostentatious about not talking either. Don't talk to each other, or to your best friends when you're drinking together, or to your sweethearts or fiancées."

She touched a crucifix she wore at her neck. "Not to your confessors, either, if you're Catholic. Nobody. Ever."

Stoddard nodded, and gave his companions a glance as he did. They all soberly repeated the gesture; that was about as good as they were going to get. Threats would be useless and worse than useless in this context. Right now they were all pulling together, and team spirit . . .

Or tribal spirit, Luz thought whimsically, remembering her conversation with Ciara on the train to Zacatecas a few days ago.

. . . could work wonders on the human mind. Even beating down the almost irresistible urge to talk about something that made you look important.

"Now," Julie said. "Your aircraft are . . ." She repeated their registration numbers. "And you've named them *Hellpig* and *Mr. McBeelzebuddy Flies?*"

Possibly a faint tinge of bemusement showed in her voice. Rourke from Pittsburgh answered again; he seemed to have an inbuilt cocky, scrappy approach to the world. Luz would have guessed his father and uncles had all been steelworkers and union men to boot, back when that was dangerous beyond the real and hideous dangers of the work itself amid fire and molten metal and gigantic unguarded machinery. Because it could mean pitched battles with the Pinkertons that Carnegie and then U.S. Steel had used as strikebreakers and goons, or with the Pennsylvania Coal and Iron Police. Nowadays everyone in the mills belonged to the Party-aligned United Steelworkers of America, and things were settled by arbitration boards, but memories lingered and attitudes would for longer still.

"Yeah, lady . . . uh, ma'am, we did. We drop bombs . . . fire and gas bombs, ma'am. Should we name the crates *Merciful Mother of God* or *St. Francis of Assisi*, or som'ptin' like dat?"

"A point," she said. "Now, what caught your eye first?"

Two hours later, the pilot of *Hellpig* was wearily going over his attack run with the firebombs one more time.

"Yeah, we were low. You gotta be low if you're gonna put 'em anywhere near where you want 'em, the firebombs. They don't have fins, they just tumble and fall. I was aiming for this bunch of bad guys, and I got 'em, neat as you please. It's sort of like you draw a thick line on the ground from the spot where the first one hits, so you do it in your head—you've got to *feel* where they're going to hit, then draw that line over the target. Two got away but they were way ahead of the others and moving like bats outta hell."

He smiled. "Well, three got away, if you count the one being carried."

A small swift bell rang in Luz's head. "Excuse me, Lieutenant," she said, feeling something like a cold breeze in the overheated room. "One being *carried*?"

He glanced over at her, since she'd been mostly silent until now.

"Yeah, there was this guy out in front—in front of all of them—and he had another guy over his shoulder. Well, it could have been a girl, I suppose, if she were in those sort of pajama things the campies—"

Which was Army slang for *campesino*, peasant.

"—wear."

"And he was running with someone over his shoulder?"

"Running like his . . . the seat of his pants . . . was on fire, flat-out. Running fast over broken country. He had one arm over the guy across his shoulder, sort of a fireman's carry, and a rifle in the other one. I'm not sure about that, but I think it was one of ours, an R-13, which isn't exactly a feather either."

In fact it weighed just a fraction under ten pounds with a twenty-round magazine loaded.

"I'd put him on any football team I was coaching, I'll tell you that, even if he was an old guy."

"Why did you think he was old?"

"Well, I'm not sure—"

"You don't have to be, Lieutenant Vlastos," Luz said, and smiled. "You can leave that to us. We're not always right, but we're usually sure."

He laughed, relaxing, which had been her intention.

"Well, yeah, I know how that works, ma'am. Reason is, his hat was off, no surprise there, and his hair was white, like an old man's, like my dad's these days. It really stood out."

He was obviously going to ask her something, something along the lines of *Does that help?* Then he smiled thinly and nodded: *No, I don't ask the questions.*

Then his eyes went to Julie Durán's locks, pale yellow where they weren't sun-streaked to the color of tow, and to Lieutenant Stoddard's close crop, like a cap of old gold.

"Oh," he said.

Luz said nothing at all, and he nodded again.

Blonds were rare in Mexico, but they weren't *outlandishly* rare, any more than they were in Andalusia or Sicily or around the lieutenant's parents' birthplace on the Turkish side of the Aegean. If you excluded people who were outright *indio*, perhaps three in a hundred and twice that in the northern tier of states, both depending on how light a shade of brown hair you put into the blond category.

When the airmen were thanked and gone, Julie looked at her over a cup of the now even-more-vile coffee. "You got something," she said.

There was no resentment in her voice; this type of interrogation was a fishing expedition *pur sang,* done on the off-chance something went click with something else. As often as not, being an operative was like walking around with a bag of puzzle pieces, trying them against the ones the world handed you. It meant a lot of tedious mental work that had to be done with painstaking attention to detail and a focus that never wavered no matter how bored you were.

Luz thought carefully. The foremost cause of failure in her line of work was saying too much. Unfortunately, saying too *little* ran a close second. It was a business that ran on trust and in which you could trust nobody, and its occupational disease was hoarding information.

"Last year," she said carefully, "I saw a man . . . a tall blond man . . . throw another man, an elderly one about my weight, over his shoulder and run with him. Run across a railway trackside, vault onto a four-board fence, then do high-speed broken field running across three hundred yards of ridge-and-furrow potato field covered in knee-high vines. His name was . . . is . . . Horst von Dückler. Freiherr Hauptmann Horst von Dückler, Abteilung IIIb. Code name at that time . . . *Reichsschwert.*"

Which meant *Imperial Sword,* literally. Though *Blade of the Realm* might be more accurate as a colloquial translation.

"Horst, here?" Ciara said, her eyes going wide in alarm. "Well, he did escape from the prisoner-of-war camp in El Paso . . . The Director told us that last New Year."

Luz stilled a flash of irritation; she would have said that herself, but not until she'd thought carefully about it. One reason she and Ciara made a good team was that they were on opposite ends of the insane-suspicion scale and so corrected each other.

Julie smiled. "What does he look like?"

"We've got pictures on file. Short form . . . did you ever see a picture of that German fighting-scout pilot, the one they call the Red Baron because he paints his aircraft red? Manfred von Richthofen?"

"Mmmmm!" Julie said appreciatively. "Impressive specimen, then!"

"Horst is a distant cousin of his and the resemblance is striking. It was even more so before I shot him in the face last October," Luz said. "I hoped I'd killed him, but I was firing from a moving automobile. Instead I just destroyed his left eye. He wears a patch on it now."

Henrietta started to say something, and Julie made an air-patting gesture: *Don't ask.* She'd undoubtedly put two and seventeen together— starting with the horror-gas attacks last October. And the rumors about the Telemobiloscope, and how a German intelligence officer had been captured when Theodore Jr.'s tanks overran the wreckage of an airship equipped with it.

"I gather he'll be . . . peeved with you?" Julie said cautiously.

"Very, because of that and some other things," Luz said. "He was peeved after I shot him, and then even more peeved when . . . our subsequent meeting ended with him being captured in France. He was unconscious at the time. Because he'd been shot . . . and pounded with a large rock . . . and penultimately because I'd kicked him in the head. With hindsight, I should have just killed him with malice aforethought in the heat of the moment, but I wanted him taken for interrogation. Alas, that ended up with him being interrogated by Military Intelligence, not us."

Military Intelligence were usually quite competent, but they operated by an entirely different set of rules, especially when dealing with POWs captured in uniform. If the Black Chamber had been in charge, von Dückler would have been interrogated by what was antiseptically known as the *third protocol* and then privately shot in the back of the head and anonymously, hygienically, and progressively cremated. He was entirely too competent and motivated to be allowed to live if there was an alternative.

Julie suddenly smiled like a cat; Luz could tell more things were going *click* in her friend's cynical and crafty brain. Things that her husband had heard from the Deuxième Bureau in Algiers, things Luz had said about the French thinking she was a German asset during a mission in Europe before the 6th . . .

"Ah, well, yes, he would be a bit annoyed," Julie said. "Being taken for a fool and shot in the face and then thinking you're going to get revenge for it and being beaten *again* will do that. And men . . . delightful creatures often enough, but . . . so emotional."

Luz looked around the bleak bare room, gathering her thoughts. The picture of Uncle Teddy was a minor inspiration; as he said, if you had to hit . . .

Hit hard, never soft, and don't stop until the enemy is down.

"Miss Colmer . . ." she said.

The secretary's mechanical pencil poised over a fresh page on her steno pad.

Luz went on: "Wire to HQ, requesting transmission of full . . ."

She stopped herself before using the name *Bildtelegraph* for the system of sending pictures over the wires, which would be tactless nowadays, though it *was* a German invention. With Henrietta here it would be a violation of her self-imposed rule of never causing someone she knew personally *unintentional* pain.

". . . photo-telegraphic record of subject Horst von Dückler, Abteilung IIIb agent, and print file updates from all sources sent soonest. Alert that subject has been detected in the vicinity of Zacatecas; photographic posters to be distributed by FBS to local police forces soonest repeat soonest. Advise general alert subject highest threat level: Kill on sight."

They packed up and were rising to go when Lieutenant Nudelman put his head discreetly through the door.

"Mrs. Durán?"

"Yes, Lieutenant?" she said.

"It's your office, ma'am. They say it's urgent and that you'll need to make a confidential call to a third location. You can use my office, ma'am, it's private and we can route it through the base telephone exchange."

Julie didn't glance aside, and her expression was still the polite social smile.

She'd have given her second-in-command notice of where she'd be, Luz thought. *But she'd also have ordered there be no calls except in an emergency.*

Emergencies were always bad news for a spy.

THIRTEEN

Lieutenant Thomas Selfridge Army Air Corps Base
Town of Jerez
State of Zacatecas
United States Protectorate of México
JUNE 21ST, 1917, 1917(B)

Lieutenant Nudelman's office had doubtless started as a bare cube painted in the usual institutional-bile color that had always struck her as being just the shade you'd expect from the vomitus of a bureaucrat's soul given physical form.

Now besides the usual office furniture there was a reprint of a rather impressionistic treatment of sunflowers by a very obscure European painter, and a few family pictures, including one of himself having his bars pinned on his shoulders with his parents in the background looking fit to burst with pride, and another of a pretty Jewish-looking girl who was probably his wife, with a baby in her arms. Julie Durán sat in his chair and raised the one-piece military handset, giving the number of the warehouse in Jerez to the base operator.

Luz waited through the nonconversation until the other operative replaced the handset in the cradle, keeping her mind occupied by looking at the bookshelf. Which, besides the usual items common to those in the trade, had the usual suspiciously crisp and unmarked-looking copy of *The Promise of American Life*; those who were really concerned with appearances often marked them up deliberately, and all the way through.

But the shelves *also* included a *Complete Works of Freidreich Nietzsche* in the original German (in the most recent edition, the one not edited by the unpleasant and very intrusive hand of the dead philosopher's sister) . . . and a slim volume of Emily Dickinson. Which was a useful reminder not to trust entirely to your initial summary of a human being.

The interval lasted about twenty seconds; Julie's mind was obviously working overtime.

"*¿Disculpé, lo iré a buscar de inmediato?*" she said.

The station chief was staring at the handset in her palm and obviously repeating the last thing said to *her*. Then she swore comprehensively . . . in ancient Greek, quoting from Aristophanes.

"And he *hung up* on me? Sandoval's been made!" she said. "Probably he's dead and that was whoever just killed him."

"Who was talking?" Luz asked sharply.

"A man, youngish . . . deep voice but not a bass, a bit choppy," Julie said alertly. "There was something about it . . . Can't put my finger on it . . . Are you going to do your party trick, Luz?"

They could both speak accent-free Spanish and French and German, to a level that let them pass easily as native speakers.

What I can *do that Julie* can't *is sound convincingly like a Mexican or a German or a Frenchwoman speaking one of the* other *languages with a typical accent, and vice versa.*

"Like this?" Luz said.

She repeated the phrase the station chief had quoted, but let just a little of a staccato accent into it, as little as she could and still identify it to her own ear.

"Yes, that's it, but I can't place it," Julie said.

"It's a fainter version of this," Luz said, and repeated it, this time letting the *r*-sounds go a little more flat and clipped and deepening and biting off the vowels. English was spoken farther back in the mouth than Spanish, and German farther still.

"German!" Julie said, as her suspicion was confirmed.

"I'm afraid you have an infestation, and it'll be as annoying as cockroaches, and probably as difficult to get rid of," Luz said.

"You don't get to play on my territory, Fritz," Julie snarled at the telephone.

Julie's fury turned white-hot; obviously surviving *revolucionarios* were just part of the day's work to her, but having Germans operating on her patch was another matter entirely.

"And if you try it I'll ἐγὼ δὲ κινήσω γέ σου τὸν πρωκτὸν ἀντὶ φύσκης!" she went on.

Luz didn't translate, despite Ciara's inquiring look and Henrietta's frustrated one: That was another quote from *The Knights*, an obscene threat specifying intent to commit an act that if taken literally would require that someone on the other end of the phone line have an anus and Julie to have male genitalia, and invoking a very graphic metaphor involving stuffing meat up into a sausage skin with a plunger and hammer.

The classics weren't necessarily very . . . genteel.

"What—" Henrietta and Ciara both began to speak, almost echoing each other, then stopped, waiting to be told what they needed to know.

"Whoever answered the call this time had a very faint German accent," Luz said grimly. "Since Julie's informant asked her to call back at that location—"

"It's Sandoval's warehouse," Julie amplified; her voice was absent now, obviously cataloging what she had to do, and in what order.

Then she reached out and picked up the phone again, giving the number of her hacienda.

"McNaughton?" she said, when the call had passed on through several hands, and looked at her wristwatch. "Sandoval's been made . . .

yes, *that* Sandoval, do we have another one on the source list? So get some muscle and evacuate Sandoval's household immediately—that's his mother, maiden aunt, wife, and four kids. There's a northbound train in a little while, that'll do, so put them on it with a couple of reliable guards."

A pause, and then: "Where? El Paso, obviously. Michaelis handles that at that station . . . she can feed them into the Protected Assets system; give her advance notice once you've gotten them on the train. Tell her a routine friendly-subject interrogation when they get there, don't take time for it here. Be as polite with them as you can, but quick is more important."

A moment of silence as she listened to his response, and then she barked:

"No, of course you *don't* tell them he's dead! For God's sake, man! Just say he's in danger and they're being moved for their own safety and we'll take care of them. Tell Lee to meet me in Jerez at the police station, fast, and bring his sharpshooter and someone to work as his spotter; you hold down the station HQ in Zacatecas after you've seen to the family and await further orders."

She clicked the cradle down and spoke: "God give me strength . . ."

Then she let it rise and spoke again into the instrument: "Operator, get me 2nd Philippine Rangers HQ."

Then looking over her shoulder and extending the telephone: "You handle Captain York, Luz, he seemed to like you. Whatever assets he can scramble, *fast*. We don't absolutely need more than a platoon's worth, though more is better, but I want him personally, he struck me as an asset. Oh, and I'd appreciate it if you'd notify the FBS in Hermosillo."

Luz raised a brow as she took the handset.

"Won't they know you better?"

"That's the problem," Julie said frankly. "I had to smack their CO repeatedly, metaphorically speaking, to get him to pay attention to me—anatomy, you know—"

All the women nodded, some without realizing they were doing so.

"—and the experience left him with a set of psychic bruises."

"Understood," Luz said. Then: "Captain York, please," when someone who identified himself as Lieutenant Larsson picked up on the other end. "Code—"

She rattled off one that meant *Black Chamber, and we need you really fast*, and waited through the clicks and murmurs on the other end while people hunted up Captain York, who by her judgment wasn't the type to sit around in his office if he could avoid it.

"Any hints on how to handle the FBS?" Luz said, once York had given her a short *Surely will, ma'am, we're on our way.*

Julie nodded: "Tell them to go away and mind their own business until we call them in to sweep the floor and tidy up, but politely, and with portentous formality. They'll like it better coming from someone sent in from HQ with the Big Dogs behind her, which will make them less likely to try to stick their oar in anyway, and you don't have a bad history with them locally, which will also help."

Julie rose and stuck her head out the door as Luz said: "Special Agent Denkins? Executive Field Operative O'Malley here . . . Yes, the one Washington warned you about, I'm afraid . . . It's an emergency—"

Nudelman was waiting at a discreet distance outside his office, talking to his secretary; he looked up alertly.

"Lieutenant, use your secretary's phone and get me a line to the Jerez police station—"

The drive to Jerez took less than ten minutes, through scattered rain lifting as twilight deepened; Henrietta drove, Luz and Julie sat in the backseat with a street map illuminated by Julie's flashlight between them, and Ciara knelt on the front passenger seat, facing backward to watch and listen as the station chief outlined the geography and her plans. Luz let her handle that, because she knew her friend's abilities, she was more familiar with the ground, and there was no time to waste.

They all also finished off the leftover empanadas as they went, though Henrietta had to choke hers down despite a pretense of non-chalance. It was usually a good idea to eat something sweet before going into an action involving stress and heavy effort, if you had the time.

Jerez was a big town or small city, twelve thousand people or a little more counting recent migrants from the countryside, lying on both sides of a north-south-flowing river that actually had water in it this time of year, and they were heading for the southern edge of the older, western part. The evening vehicle traffic was sparse with the late-ish hour and the recent rain. There were more autos than horse-drawn wagons or coaches, though now that the clouds had broken up there were plenty of people strolling and visiting and listening to bands. Much of the land along the river itself looked muddy and torn up and littered with tools and materials, since a big chunk was being turned into a park and two new bridges were under construction.

"Do you think they'll still be there?" Luz asked. "I don't, really."

"About even odds, I'd say," Julie replied. "Granted, most of my experience isn't with Germans."

"We'll have to *assume* they are still there, anyway, until proven otherwise," Luz said noncommittally. "I would really, really like to wind this up fast. That's worth some risk."

I could just take over here, but that would be counterproductive.

"Agreed," Julie said, as Henrietta pulled over by the police station. "It's about a thousand yards that way."

The Jerez police headquarters was a new building differing only in details from hundreds of others built over the last few years across the Protectorate to help nail the country down and maintain the new order and incidentally reduce the number of murders, assaults, rapes, and robberies; this had never been a very orderly country, even during the Porfiriato. It was a square a hundred feet on a side with a squat round three-story tower at one corner, and contained the local lockup and the lower-level courts as well. If Luz remembered correctly, this block had been scorched rubble in September 1913, the result of some holdouts encountering a battery of field guns and trying to reply with dynamite bombs. The replacement stood out by its newness, and because it was done in a style that was slightly out of place.

Ironically that was because it was an Andalusian-derived neo-Hispanic architectural fashion popularized in California as the latest successor to the Mission style, all roofs of red Roman tile and walls of pure white stucco, two things that weren't all that common in this particular district where *flat* roofs and bright varied color schemes were popular above the *jacal*-and-adobe-hut level. The main doors—which, like the walls, were discreetly stout and bulletproof under the veneer— were open.

They hopped out, and Julie pointed southward. "That roof there, see?"

Luz nodded, taking a deep breath as the sharp awareness that she might be about to die surfaced for an instant. Pushing it down—or aside—or acknowledging it without letting it *affect* her—was a practiced reflex by now. And the added fear for Ciara paradoxically made it easier to control; they had to wear the mask of unconcern *for* each other.

I value my life more now and have to show fear less, if anything, she thought wryly, and went on equally so aloud:

"Back in business at the same old stand."

Most of central Jerez was stone-built but single-story save for churches and the Cathedral of Our Lady of Solitude, the Hinojosa Theater, and the scattering of government buildings right downtown around the Plaza de Armas. A few town houses for wealthy landholders and some of the storage buildings (usually owned by the same families if not individuals) were substantial, and the warehouse was one of them, two tall stories and about ten feet higher than any of its surroundings.

The coping around the exterior of the flat roof was probably about a yard high, or a little more. She swung down the small baggage compartment at the rear of Julie's Guvvie, took out the Thompson gun racked inside and a drum of ammunition, and handed them to the station chief, who clicked it home and looked a question at her.

"No, I'll stick with this," she said, and pulled the shotgun out of its canvas-and-leather case.

It was a pump-action Remington weapon, with a seven-round tube magazine, a barrel only five inches longer, and in this case the stock cut down to a pistol grip ending in a steel-capped knob.

"You always did like that model," Julie said as Luz thumbed fat red cardboard-and-brass rounds of double-ought buck into the tube magazine. "Old friends meet again."

Then she gave a very false melancholy sigh as she racked the action of the Thompson and added:

"Ah, how the sight of that scattergun brings back memories of our innocent girlish pleasures of yesteryear."

Ciara grimaced slightly as she checked the magazine of her own pistol and reholstered it. Luz had used the same shotgun to clear out the gondola of the German Navy semirigid they'd stolen in Staaken near Berlin last December, in an assault that had lasted about four and a half very eventful minutes. Which for Ciara had meant wiping the crew's blood . . . and sopping bits of uniform, sticky bloody hair, and gelatinous shreds of skin . . . off the controls as she helped get them into the air immediately afterward. Being basically sensible she'd seen them as perfectly legitimate targets, uniformed men in the service of an enemy country, but she was still a little squeamish about things like that.

"I don't suppose I can persuade you to stay here, sweetie, since putting the knuckle on isn't your specialty?" Luz said quietly in her ear as she slipped a box of the shells into the pocket of her coat.

"When frogs grow hair," Ciara replied likewise, with a brave smile; she was a little pale, but controlling it well.

That Spanish saying about frogs was a phrase Luz was fond of for *not going to happen*, and she smiled wryly to have it turned back on her.

"Stay behind me, then," she said.

"We'll do backup together, Ciara honey, we non-knuckle-specialists," Henrietta said. "They didn't teach me about this at the Clerical-Vocational Institute in Baltimore, either!"

There was a very slight quaver underlying that. Ciara caught it—she'd been getting better at reading people—and patted her on the shoulder.

"I hadn't done anything . . . active . . . like this either until late last year," she said. "And I had to learn from Luz and on the spot too. Don't worry. Thinking about it is harder than doing it! Once things . . . start, if they do . . . you just forget about it and get through moment to moment."

Henrietta nodded with a smile of thanks. That slid away as she took a deep breath and said with quiet grimness:

"I hope we meet this German agent that Executive Field Operative O'Malley was talking about, Ciara. I purely, surely do, God's truth. For my momma and poppa and my sisters."

Luz nodded very slightly to herself; it was always good when your snap judgment about someone panned out, and having a sound record at that was an essential skill in her line of work. As a motivator, blood revenge was always a good bet. There was a slight but definite chance Pancho Villa might be alive today, for example, if his men had managed to kill *all* the O'Malleys back in 1911.

"I hope we take him alive, too," Henrietta said. "So I can sit there taking notes while he's squeezed dry."

Luz looked over sharply at that. "Don't try for a capture, Miss Colmer. Not with this man. Just . . . don't. Kill him if you get a chance, and count yourself very very lucky if you do."

"Understood," she said, and Julie and Ciara both nodded.

I was lucky the high command wanted so badly to take Villa alive. Though someone *would have killed him eventually.* ¡Por Dios, *but he was a profoundly annoying man! And since Horst was deeply involved in the Breath of Loki, he's a perfectly legitimate target for Henrietta on a personal as well as a national level. But the mission comes first. Always.*

"Ah, Captain Menendez," Julie said, greeting a man as he came down the stairs. "Good to see you. As I explained, we have a bit of a problem."

"Señora Durán," the municipal police officer said in a neutral, respectful tone that implied he'd met her fairly often, saluting and not apparently much surprised by the party of armed gringas on his doorstep either.

He was a hard-faced man of about thirty, whose close-clipped mustache and haircut—short on the sides and back, just long enough to comb on top—was notably on the modern American model for men and of the type favored by the military, by people in the secret services when not imitating something else, by Party activists, and by the rising generation in general. It made you look youthful, hard-driving and *efficient* and *Progressive*, like a smooth precision-engineered product of alloy steel and ball bearings.

His uniform was blue and brass-buttoned; the FBS had re-formed the Protectorate's town police forces along American lines, down to the way they looked, although the riding boots and the big-roweled silver spurs were local preferences.

They clinked on the cobbles. Some of the Jerez streets had been paved, but the Department of Public Works' insatiable appetite for pouring concrete on anything it could pin down long enough for the stuff to set hadn't gotten around to this bit of country-town road yet.

A pair of local civilians followed him, a young lower-middle-class couple in ordinary and slightly shabby dress including a standing collar and an ankle-length skirt of a cut Luz's mother's cook might have worn ten years ago. At a guess they were a clerk and his wife, or possibly small shopkeepers, and definitely looking distinctly apprehensive.

"This is Señor Luis Gutiérrez and his wife, Señora Juanita González. The señora saw something of importance."

"Thank you very much for your cooperation, Señor Gutiérrez, Señora González," Julie said in a tone at once polite and firm.

She handed the Thompson gun behind her to Henrietta for a moment—you were much less intimidating without an automatic weapon in your hands—and stepped a little closer. Mexicans started feeling comfortable talking to you at about the distance that most Americans felt slightly crowded and encroached upon.

"Please tell me what you saw, señora," she said briskly but with a slight smile. "I do not wish to detain you and your husband longer than necessary."

Which was a hint to get on with it, Luz thought.

"I was walking home," Mrs. González said, keeping her eyes down and her voice flat and quiet, though she might well have been reluctant to talk directly to a man at all. "It was just after the rain stopped. And I saw Señor Sandoval. He . . . he was out of the window of his warehouse, the one that looks out of his office. Hanging out, you see?"

Julie nodded encouragingly, which hereabouts meant *I hear what you say* rather than necessarily full agreement.

"He was hanging out . . . headfirst. He had pushed aside the bars on the window—I do not know how, they are iron, as such things are. And he was shouting: 'Call the police,' that first, and then a scream of pain, of fear."

She swallowed, her olive-brown face underlain by gray. "And . . . and then he went backward. *Quickly*, as if something very powerful had pulled him. Like . . . my uncle Juan once told me of seeing a man in the water, in Veracruz, pulled under by a shark. Like that. And I heard another scream, from inside the warehouse, and men's voices. So I ran home, quickly, quickly, and my Luis—"

She looked at her husband and he moved closer to her, putting an arm around her shoulders.

"—said we must report this."

"Thank you very much, Señora González, Señor Gutiérrez," Julie said. "You have undoubtedly done the right thing, and those who harmed your neighbor Señor Sandoval will be punished. Your commendable sense of civic duty will not be forgotten."

Her hand began a movement toward her pocket, then stopped before anyone who didn't know her could have detected it.

Good for you, Julie, Luz thought. *Having a Black Chamber agent publicly hand you money on the steps of the local* policia *HQ is not the way to reward someone, even now. For that matter this may blow* my *local cover for good even keeping in the background with the brim of my hat down, but it's worth it.*

The young couple were looking unhappier by the moment; getting involved with something political was much more than they had bargained for, as opposed to reporting a common crime against a respectable neighbor; everyone feared and detested robbers and burglars. Instead of bestowing a reward, Julie caught Captain Menendez's eye; he murmured to the couple and they went back inside. There he would drop them a modest but welcome amount from the contingencies fund privately, later, when this was settled. And they'd be owed a favor or two, which would make them happier when they remembered it. Successful administration ran on favors and obligations, whatever the rulebooks said.

"I have established a perimeter, Señora Durán," he said when the couple were back inside. "And evacuated the nearby buildings. Firefighters are standing by, and an ambulance and doctor from the air base should arrive very soon."

Julie nodded. The military helped with emergency services whenever it didn't directly affect missions they were tasked with, on general public relations grounds.

Menendez went on: "Unfortunately, that leaves me with only five of the *policia* here at headquarters including the switchboard operator and a guard for the cells and my secretary. That is after recalling the off-duty men."

By Protectorate policy there was roughly one urban policeman for every five hundred inhabitants within city limits, which would mean a force of about thirty-five or forty here.

"Excellent work, Captain, done quickly: I'll note your display of initiative in my report," Julie said. "We'll have troops arriving in a minute or two, which will free up your men for other tasks. Here's a list of suspects I'll want you to round up; just note *detention by administrative procedure on suspicion of activities prejudicial to the security of the State* on the paperwork."

He nodded; that was the general form for a political-security arrest here in the Protectorate. Or north of the border, for that matter, though those still had somewhat more in the way of formalities attached even with drastic wartime streamlining—habeas corpus had never been a factor here.

"And keep them separate, as much as you can, until we take them off your hands."

He saluted again and left to alert his men that they were about to be relieved.

"Dark in half an hour," Julie said grimly to Luz as she shifted back to English; it was around eight o'clock. "I want to get this done as quickly as possible."

"It's your territory and you're in charge, Julie—just a warning. I have a nasty feeling that Horst is *here*. And he's really dangerous, completely out of the ordinary."

Though that simply can't be as important to you as to me, Luz thought. *One of those* live-and-learn *things.*

She resisted an impulse to check her shotgun or her pistol once more and instead carefully surveyed the street and buildings again, adding it to the information already in her mind from the maps of Jerez and previous visits—though none of those had taken her to this part of town. And did *not* stick her head out to look down the intersection toward the warehouse that was . . . had been . . . the place of work of Julie's snitch Zacarías Sandoval.

From the description, that informant was probably dead and whoever had made him might well be waiting with a rifle. It was far too late for them to make deals, and they could expect nothing but death if taken, after an interval that would make death welcome while they were being wrung dry. Luz had been in places where she faced the same choices herself and knew it made you want to take someone with you.

Or it does me, and I think whoever's in there will be hard cases too. If it's Horst, definitely!

Field Operative Lee arrived in an unmarked and nondescriptly battered-looking Guvvie at about the same time as Captain York and his five truckloads of cheerful Philippine Rangers with their disquieting, red-stained, file-toothed grins. The Ranger officer took in the situation in a glance and two sentences, sent three truckloads under a lieutenant who looked like a younger version of himself to take over the perimeter duties, and reserved a squad for the actual strike.

"Brought along some doorknockers, since this affair's in a town, ma'am," the lanky hill-country soldier said.

That meant a haversack full of explosives with a variable fuse. He had the grip of a Thompson in his right hand, propped with the butt on his hip.

"Excellent," Julie replied crisply. "Mr. Lee here will be giving us some overwatch from the rooftops."

Field Operative Lee wasn't very formidable-*looking* despite the Springfield sharpshooter cradled in his arms—the sniper version of the old bolt-action battle rifle, with a cut-down forestock and free-floating heavy barrel and a cheek rest, as well as a telescopic x8 sight. In fact, despite his outdoorsman clothes—dark khaki with lots of pockets and a coil of rope ending in a spring-loaded grapnel slung from left shoulder to right hip—he looked like a very fit jug-eared clerk, and wore a pair of spectacles with big lenses.

Luz knew how deceptive appearances could be; apparently and unsurprisingly York did too, from the long considering look and nod he gave the Black Chamber man.

Lee's driver hopped out after him, an American woman of about Ciara's age, with brown hair done up in an efficient braid, a canvas campaign hat, boots and riding breeches and a knee-length cord jacket, with a large binocular case slung over one shoulder—it had an adjustable miniature tripod strapped to it—and a Thompson on the other. She stayed quietly behind him after a short nod to Julie; Luz suppressed a pang of envy at someone who'd had time to change into something more practical than her own streetwear.

Lee wore an Annapolis graduate's ring, Class of '08, Luz saw with surprise. The Navy hadn't grown as much as the Army—it had already been a considerable presence by global standards even back at the beginning of the decade, when the American land forces had been a joke comparable in size to those of Bulgaria or Serbia. Even so, the fleet *was* growing and by now a talented Annapolis graduate from '08 might well be exec of a major warship or commander of a minelayer or destroyer.

Julie answered Luz's unasked question.

"Mr. Lee is the best shot I've ever met," she said.

And Julie's met me, *among others*, Luz thought.

"He also decided to apply his talents with the Chamber when the Intervention was the only action around."

Lee smiled and inclined his head respectfully toward Luz.

"I heard at the Yaqui Valley camp how you took down Villa's galloping horse at eight hundred yards with one bullet, Executive Field Operative. It's legendary," he said.

His accent was Kentucky, the soft almost-Virginian one from the rich rolling greens of the bluegrass country and not much like York's hill-and-holler rasp.

His driver nodded enthusiastically behind him and looked at Luz with rapt admiration; it suddenly occurred to Luz that the young woman—her name was Dora Parkinson, and she was from Oregon—might have ended up in the Chamber because of the example *Luz* had set. Emulation was a powerful force. She was also probably *here*, specifically in Zacatecas state, because Julie was station chief and HQ tended to send women to the same places so they could work together, to put the most charitable interpretation on it. Or to the same places so the sort of troublemaking females who ended up as Black Chamber operatives could irritate the minimum number of men, if you were feeling *less* inclined to be charitable; or possibly both were true.

And Lee's remark made her charitably inclined; capturing Villa had been the most satisfactory day of her life.

Until the one when Ciara told me she loved me, she thought, and went on:

"Legends grow in the telling, Field Operative. It was *five* hundred yards, Mr. Lee, though the horse *was* at a gallop. Which means it was good shooting *and* good luck, but not supernatural, thank you. Cold still air, several thousand feet up, and excellent light—ideal conditions."

Behind him York took time from talking to his men to give her a brief marksman's nod.

"You take the high road, Lee," Julie said. "Any problems with that?"

Lee looked up. "No, I've got a good route mapped, did that on the way over, and I *should* know Jerez by now," he said, tracing a course with his eyes. "There's a spot with acceptable . . . not great but the best available . . . coverage about three hundred seventy-five yards out. But I'm not a cat, ma'am, even if I am a good shot."

Which was a polite *Get going* hint. Julie was a meticulous planner but could take too long at it sometimes.

"Come on, Dora, light's a-wastin'."

The two operatives, sniper and spotter here, trotted off to get a staircase; the flat roofs of this section of Jerez made it fairly easy to travel unobserved across them, if you were fit and had a strong head for heights when you jumped over a narrow alley.

"We'll give him five minutes," Julie said. "Then we go in. Captain York, we'll have your men blow the main doors. Your lieutenant will have teams watching all the potential exits and replacing the police perimeter by now?"

"Yes, ma'am. Sure you don't want to leave it to us?"

Luz grinned friendly-wise. "It's hard to interrogate decapitated subjects, Captain York," she said.

Julie shook her head with a matching expression. "No, I don't think we'll do it that way, Captain."

"Didn't rightly figure you would, ladies, but a gentleman should offer."

Julie looked at her watch.

"Lee's in place. Let's go."

FOURTEEN

Town of Jerez
State of Zacatecas
United States Protectorate of México
JUNE 21ST, 1917, 1917(B)

The approach to the warehouse was swift and very quiet—and without obvious spectators. Word spread quickly in a situation like this and *nobody* wanted to be involved when the Bugkalot were out to collect more household ornaments. Not many thought the Chamber was good company either, for that matter. Since when you thought about it, ending up anonymously cremated by people who then denied they'd ever heard of you—and questioning the claim really, really wasn't wise at all—didn't amount to all that much of an improvement over your skull hanging in a net.

Shutters were firmly closed and locked, though eyes were probably ... almost certainly ... watching through them as the Americans and their Filipino soldiers approached Sandoval's place of business ... and Luz wouldn't be surprised if most of the neighbors had already heard about *him*, too.

Gossip had always moved fast; it moved faster still with telephones, but fortunately most people hadn't yet realized how easy they were to *tap*. There was absolutely nothing like getting unfiltered conversations nobody knew you were listening in on. People on telephone lines often lied to each other, but they weren't trying to lie specifically to *you*.

They halted two buildings away and across the street.

"A little closer and you'll be covered by the raised section around the edge of the roof," Julie said, and York nodded.

That meant anyone on the roof would have to show himself to shoot downward, which would be dangerous with Field Operative Lee waiting in the background.

"And we're in shadow down here as the sun gets lower. Let's—"

PTANG! Crack! Chunk!

A white-red spark slammed off the cobbles not far from Luz's foot, and a fragment stung her ankle just above the line of her shoe. From behind them Lee's sharpshooter cracked, close enough to the round fired *at* her that the sounds and echoes of the two weapons blurred together.

Mierda! Luz thought as she dove for the ground, crawled on her elbows, and huddled into a doorway.

That was from the roof—good shooting in this light from that angle, too damned close. But he was probably hurrying because he suspected someone like Lee would be waiting for him to show himself . . . Hope Lee got him, but I doubt it.

Ciara was right behind her, she was glad to see, pistol in hand and face stark white but fixed in an iron calm.

"I *think* that was from the roof but I can't be sure," she said.

"*Shit!*" Julie said crisply as she hit the ground at about the same speed.

In the same moment she also snaked out a hand, grabbed Henrietta by an ankle, and yanked her foot out from under her.

The younger woman landed with a squawk, the last of their party to end up prone, but fortunately on a reasonably well-padded posterior. The sound was covered by an eruption of gunfire that blended into a continuous stuttering roar. All the Rangers had opened up with their R-13s and Thompsons, concentrating on one spot on the second-story roof right above the big vehicle-sized door gates in the front of the building. Brass tinkled and rang on the cobbles, muzzle flashes stabbed orange-white in the shadow thrown by the walls, and the sharp chemical scent of nitro powder overrode wet dirty cobbles and old donkey dung and piss.

The limestone blocks of the coping started to splinter under the impacts, sparks whipping off at sharp tangents to mark ricochets.

"Cease fire!" York shouted.

They did—which was unusually good fire discipline for men who'd just been shot at in an unfamiliar environment. Then he added something in their own language, of which she had not a word; if she'd had to guess Luz would have put down:

Don't shoot unless you've got a target! and *Watch the windows too!*

Luz felt her mind expand and narrow at the same time. She was aware of everything, every hair on her body and her ears and skin and eyes drinking in every morsel they could. And she was thinking . . . but thinking *only* about what happened next, because if you died in the next few moments the future became sort of pointless. The pain from the bruises—which going flat fast on cobbles inevitably caused—was there, but it wasn't *important* and she barely noticed it.

"When everyone else gets down, get *down*," Julie snarled at Henrietta without turning her head.

Which was good advice; it was infinitely better to hit the dirt when you didn't really need to than to take a chance on not doing it when you *did*. No amount of training could *really* get the habit in deep until you'd been shot at a time or two, she thought, or even better been shelled. And seen . . . and smelled and heard . . . the slow die.

A fact flashed into Luz's mind. Two of the bars covering the window next to the main doors were lying on the cobbles and a scatter of broken glass was lying across them. That would be where Salvador had tried to escape and been dragged back by something that had scared the witness profoundly, and the glass could well have been put there by a rifle butt even more recently . . .

"Watch the right-hand window!" Luz barked; her own scattergun couldn't reach that far to any effect.

In the same instant four of the Rangers rose to their feet and dashed forward, with York on their heels; Lee was firing steadily from behind and above, into the expanse of the flat roof and probably trying to keep the head of the shooter there down.

Two of the little Filipino Rangers carried canvas satchels stuffed with explosive, pulling the toggles that set the fuses going as they ran. The others had their weapons to their shoulders, and the remainder of the squad opened up again, this time at every opening in the façade as well as the coping around the roof. The shadow outline of a rifle's muzzle and the flash of a shot *did* show from the broken window; York and Julie both responded instantly with their Thompsons, and Luz thought both struck inside the window—which was good shooting for her and near-miraculous for him because he was doing it on the move and from the hip.

One of the Rangers went down, dropping his satchel charge and howling as he clutched at his leg. His comrade scooped up the satchel by a loop and kept running toward the warehouse doors. York bent as he ran by, grabbed the wounded man by the back of his webbing harness with his left hand, and hoisted him over that shoulder without breaking stride, jinking in the same direction like a broken-field runner—being that close to the target would have been certain death when the charges exploded. He stopped near the end of the building, laying the wounded man down and doing a quick field dressing; the window over his head started to open as he did, and he pulled a grenade from his webbing and pitched it neatly through the gap into the interior.

Thud!

A scream, loud even at this distance, sounded as the fragments bit someone inside, and York finished tying off the bandage.

Both satchels landed at the base of the big iron-strapped wooden doors and the Rangers dashed after their commander, racing to get far enough away and then diving flat. Luz ducked her face into the crook of her left arm and counted with her mouth held open to equalize the pressure on her eardrums:

One . . . two . . . three—

CRUMP!

The air battered at her, lifted her up and dropped her a few inches, and left her head ringing. She spat to clear blood from her mouth. Most of the energy from an open-air explosion followed the line of least resistance . . . which meant a fair amount went toward *her.* She took a quick glance backward and felt a moment's sharp alarm when she saw red running on Ciara's face; her partner shook her head and pressed a sleeve to her nose, showing that it was just a nosebleed.

The two satchels between them had more high explosive than a shell from a heavy cruiser's guns, so there was also plenty of force punching *into* the gateway they'd been tossed *against.* The heavy timber-and-iron doors were blown off their hinges, shattered and sent inward in a funnel of shards and splinters that would scythe like the blades of flying daggers through the interior of the building.

The Rangers all bounced to their feet and charged before the sound of the explosion had died to catch the enemy while they were still stunned, their inward-curved *Ginunting* knives in their hands and the Bugkalot war screech loud even to the others' battered eardrums. A rifle cracked and flashed from the darkened interior and one of the little men went down with a boneless, limp bounce-and-flop that spoke of instant death to an experienced eye. The rest poured through howling, and York followed them with three more at his heels.

"Go!" Julie called, and the four Black Chamber operatives followed close behind.

The interior was dark, but the Rangers had popped a few flares— York or one of his Bugkalot noncoms had been thinking ahead—and tossed them up into the room. York stopped in the doorway to throw his tomahawk in one draw-and-overarm-cast motion; another scream followed that, and he plunged into the darkness with his Thompson to his shoulder.

The flares smoldered and sputtered and threw up oily stinking smoke that clung to the inside of nose and mouth with a vile burnt-mutton taste, but they cast some light from the burning magnesium. That and the rancid greasy odor and the wisps from the burst bales and the look of most of the interior—as if stacks of giant soft gray-brown dice had been tossed around in heaps or remained tottering in skewed blocks—explained why everyone inside wasn't dead or unconscious.

Great bales of wool, Luz thought disgustedly, as she took cover behind what remained of one despite the wisps of smoke it was giving off, and Ciara thumped down behind her.

If you designed *something to absorb an explosion, this would be it! And it'll be full of holes and tunnels and pockets now where they're leaned against each other—we're going to need to stop until we have more troops!* ¡Ay! *No, there may be a* real *tunnel out of here that leads beyond our perimeter. We* can't *wait.*

A bullet went by her ear, close enough that she felt the hot wind and saw the burlap binding the wool bale six inches from her face pucker and tear. Luz pivoted toward the rifle's sound without being consciously aware of where it was. Almost at the same instant she heard Ciara's pistol snap; in the fractional second it took to complete the motion and bring up the Remington she saw the man with the rifle, and saw him trying to recover from a duck-induced stagger on footing of spilled wool and work the bolt at the same time.

Ciara's shot had missed by a bit, but it had probably saved her and killed the man at the same time.

Bam!

A hard thump, and the recoil brought the muzzle of the Remington up against her grip. The spread of double-ought caught the rifleman squarely in the chest. No need to worry about *him* anymore. At that range it would blast a patch the size of her palm through ribs and breastbone, like a blow from a serrated meat-tenderizing hammer swung by a giant.

Shick-*shack*, as she worked the pump action and the spent shell flicked away, looking everywhere in general for slivers of movement. One more, a man twelve feet up on a pile of bales, extending a hand with a revolver in it. Luz started to aim, but a Bugkalot was already on the move, bounding up the tumbled bales with an agility that made her eyes go a little wide—and Luz had trained with professional acrobats. The little man was screaming like a power-driven file driving through metal as he made his final leap and swung his blade.

No need to worry about that *bandit anymore, either.*

Luz leapt up and around the corner of what had been the laneway between two stacks of bales and was now a shadowed triangular-topped cavern. A man lunged at her, knife edge glittering in the jerky actinic light of the flares as it came up in a gutting stroke.

Bam!

This time the red spear of the muzzle flash from her cut-down shotgun touched the man's shirt and set it on fire. The heavy shot hit him in the gut like the kick of a mule; he collapsed without any histrionics, dead from the massive shock that hammered at his heart. Usually at this range knife beat gun . . . but it all depended on the person holding the knife. And the one holding the gun, in this case.

Shick-*shack*. There was another man behind the one who'd come for her with the knife; he prudently whirled in place and ran, then started to scramble up a low pile of bales. She held the shotgun in her left hand and pulled the .40 with her right; this was going to require precision, especially given the bad light.

Crack! Crack! Crack!

The first two shots went below the climber's feet. The third hit him, she thought in the ankle or the foot itself, which was what she'd wanted. Contrary to popular fiction, there was no safe spot to shoot someone in the legs or torso because there were so many big blood vessels. Not if you wanted to be sure they didn't die, and an arm wound wouldn't necessarily put down someone very determined.

The man she'd shot screamed and toppled backward, falling from bale to bale and screaming again when he thumped hard to the flagstones. Luz leapt while he was still in the air, landing with her skirts billowing as he fell back. He'd thumped his head on the stone but was awake enough to start moving his right hand toward something. Luz kicked him in that elbow, hard, and then stamped even harder on his hand with her heel and he shrieked once more as bone crackled—but he wasn't going to be needing the hand ever again, after all. She kicked him over onto his stomach and grabbed the collar of the jacket he was wearing, yanking it down so that his arms were pinned; by then he was limp and moaning.

"Luz!" Ciara said sharply.

Luz heard it easily as she reholstered her .40, even over the middle-distance mad-typewriter snarl of a Thompson gun and the quickly dying shrieks and screams and eerie triumphant wailing as the Bugkalot pack hunted through the darkness.

"Luz, here, quickly!"

Luz followed the voice, dragging her captive as she went. Not everything in here had been wool. There were a scattering of boards from packing crates, the sort used to move heavy goods with built-in pallets in their bases, and another almost-intact one that had spilled sideways as the bales were tossed; this was farther from the doors, anyway. It had splintered too as it fell, and through the gap Luz could see the dull gleam of a steel cylinder. An elemental jolt ran through her, half like a punch and half like gripping a bare electric wire, more frightening than armed men. She'd met plenty of those and come off best, or at least been able to escape and survive. But you couldn't shoot or cut primed explosives . . .

Can't run away screaming Bomb! Bomb! *either. There's no way everyone would hear me, not in time.*

Ciara was kneeling beside it, with a leather rectangle she normally carried rolled up and tied with a bowknot laid flat and open beside her on the flagstones. Tools glinted in rows from the loops inside it. Late last year they'd both nearly died—along with several hundred others—because it had taken precious seconds to persuade aircrewmen on the ANS dirigible *Manila Bay* to stand back and hand Ciara the equipment she needed to defuse a bomb that would have killed them all. Since then she'd taken to carrying this roll of pliers and whatnot when they were working in the field, just in case.

Bless her! Luz thought. *And I'm more certain than ever that Horst is . . . was . . . here. I left that little present behind for him at Rapsstrasse in Berlin when he was on our trail there . . . and from the Military Intelligence transcripts of his interrogation, it made quite an impression when it decapitated that secret policeman right next to him. That's his reply. Turnabout, I suppose . . .*

"What do you need, Ciara?" she asked.

"You can't help except by getting me more light. There's a fusing mechanism screwed into the end of this but it's awkwardly placed for me," Ciara said, her voice detached and her fingers feeling—gently, gently—through the gap. "It's not just a bomb, it was *designed* as a bomb, only part of this fuse is improvised, but the rest fits right into this socket . . . and it's a very *big* bomb too."

"*Julie!*" Luz called, careful to make her voice loud but not frantic. *"You're needed here, right now! Bring the flashlight!"*

They knelt to either side of Ciara, with Luz looking out until York and several of his Rangers came up and took guard duty over. Julie held the newfangled flashlight steadily, the tube at the rear braced on her shoulder and the puddle of light on Ciara's hands and the interior of the crate. The portable electric lights had only become common in the last decade, and a lot of people still didn't believe they were reliable enough to be worth the weight and trouble. Only last week back home in the Casa de los Amantes Ciara had spent twenty minutes at breakfast talking about the many virtues of tungsten-filament bulbs . . .

Bless Julie's Progressive instincts!

"Well, now we have some idea of what that U-boat north of Tampico was probably landing," Julie said softly to Luz, though they'd have had to be much louder to break Ciara's brown study of concentration as her hands moved like a surgeon's. "This, undoubtedly a good deal else, and at least one German agent and probably several more. Damn the German who invented the bloody sneaky things!"

"An Irishman named John Philip Holland invented them, or Seán Pilib Ó hUalacháin if you want to be picky, to use against the Royal Navy. Though the Germans have certainly run with the idea," Luz said. "And those agents met Horst; he probably passed some sort of message to Abteilung IIIb using surviving *revolucionario* networks—he was here in early 1916 and made contacts then. The message moved slowly since there aren't many of them left, or something would have happened earlier, but it got through. Anything more here?" Luz said.

"Still combing the place, but we did find the entrance to a tunnel and we're trying to trace it. Henrietta, get a note on that to Lee, he's just outside now. Give a full description, with my code and Executive Field Operative O'Malley's. Tell him to see that it's sent to HQ . . . just in case. There's something odd going on here; they didn't send explosives in a heavy steel cylinder just to send explosives—there are much less awkward and conspicuous ways to do that. Or buy them from mining supply companies, or buy them under the table from people working in construction, with a little effort and a lot of money."

The confidential secretary trotted out to hand the message to Julie's subordinate . . . *just in case* they were all blown to kingdom come in the next instant, so the information wouldn't die with them. There was a slight sheen of sweat on Julie's face, picked out by the odd light, and Luz could certainly feel more running down her own flanks, and not just because of the brief savage exertion of the assault. She nodded very slightly in approval when Henrietta trotted *back* not long later, without much joy at the prospect of standing next to the bomb but no hesitation either.

The station chief looked over at Luz's prisoner. "Oh, and Captain York, if you could have a couple of your men take the prisoner out? Without removing his head, please—I do so want to have a nice long chat with him. In fact, get the doctor to see to him as soon as he's seen to your men. An *untimely* death would be tragic."

York did, with simplified command English and gestures and bits of their own language; a Ranger with sergeant's stripes apparently had more command of English and amplified the translation. From hand motions it included *Don't kill him.*

"They wouldn't take the head, anyways, ma'am," York added. "Wouldn't be . . . sportin', since they warn't the ones as caught him."

"It's nice to know that sportsmanship lives," Luz said. "They'll be playing baseball next. Not with heads, hopefully, that would be very unsanitary."

He chuckled as he left to oversee the cleanup, without even bothering to glance at the bomb or Ciara's tiny, intent movements with her tools. Julie went on quietly to Luz:

"I wonder why my snitch didn't tell us about the tunnel."

"Probably holding it back to have something spectacular to hand you later," Luz said. "You really can't expect much altruism in those circumstances."

"You're ruining my faith in the essential goodness of human beings, Luz."

"Turnabout is fair play."

Ciara was stock-still for ten long seconds. Then she reached in with a pair of needle-nosed pliers, seized something Luz couldn't see, and bore down.

Then she waited *another* few seconds . . .

Waited for us to die if she guessed wrong, Luz thought. *That's my girl!*

Ciara shivered in reaction, and Luz put an arm around her shoulders. The younger woman seized her for a brief violent hug.

"Sorry," Ciara said into her neck. "Didn't mean to be a goose. I thought that dry cell connection was corroded . . . but I couldn't be sure."

"Goose? You're a *lioness*!"

Even then, Ciara frowned thoughtfully as she rose. "This bomb . . . it's odd. It's very odd. The casing is substantial, and the way it's shaped and the bolt attachments . . . I need to think about this."

Luz gave her a final squeeze. "Do! ¡Ay, you're so good at it! And what about getting this thing somewhere safe?"

"We'll need lifting tackle, and someone who really knows how to use it . . . a flatbed truck would do nicely, there are hooks for pulleys up on the overhead beams . . . though it would be better to stick to *good* roads and go *very slowly*. I really need to take a look at this somewhere with shelter and tools and good lighting, try to make sense of it . . ."

"There's plenty of workshop space at the ranch, some of it usefully far from anything damageable," Julie said helpfully. "And it's close to this location but out of the way. That's come in handy before."

Ciara gave her a brisk nod. Luz recognized the tone and the firming of her lips; this was Ciara with a job to do, running over the details in her mind. Henrietta had been even more quiet than usual after her quick hand gesture to Julie to show *Task done*, and Ciara looked at her, blinked, and spoke:

"Henrietta, could you get in touch with Major Dicot? He could get us some combat engineers and their transport from the 32nd. And be . . ."

"And Andre could be *not* noisy and conspicuous, he surely could," Henrietta said, grinning, and looked at Julie, who gave a brief *Do it* nod. "He's a right clever man."

"Is this thing safe now?" Luz asked. "Or as safe as a large bomb can be?"

Ciara frowned. "Well . . . I cut the electrical connection and blocked the mechanical plunger with some wire and crimped that securely," she said. "But the *detonator* is still there—that needs much better positioning and some wrenches to remove, since it's threaded solidly in. I wouldn't . . . well, darling, I wouldn't, you know, *kick* it or anything. Just in case."

"I will not kick the bomb," Luz promised solemnly, making a cross-the-heart gesture.

"I'd better go along with Henrietta too in case Major Dicot needs details on what to send," Ciara added. "If they could put lots of padding under it . . . or a rubber sling in a timber cradle, that would be just perfect."

"Use the line at the police station, but let Henrietta do the talking as much as possible," Luz specified. "You've got the code list we agreed on with them?"

"Memorized."

"Keep it all verbal, then."

Julie let a long breath out slowly and clicked off the flashlight as the two younger Black Chamber operatives left, touching one gingerly finger to the exposed casing of the bomb in a dimness lit only by burning wool somewhere near, throwing ruddy flickers and making the air thick with a greasy stink.

"I won't kick it either. That was a little too racking for *my* nerves!"

"You could have just handed me the flashlight and left," Luz pointed out.

"I suppose I could," Julie replied dryly, and they both snorted; nobody with those reflexes would have ended up as station chief.

Then she went on thoughtfully: "Sucking us forward like that when they discovered Sandoval had sold them out, with the bomb to finish us off if we rushed in . . . We've found his body, by the way."

"Don't tell me—neck broken with a twist?"

"That and a stab wound. And the bomb ready to reward us all for our boldness . . . It all rather reminds me of the sort of thing *you* used to do. Except the neck-breaking, but the stab wound was so *you*, and so was the bomb, very much. You fiery Latin charmer, you."

Luz nodded. "I know exactly why, too. I'm morally certain now that Horst is involved, and I . . . ah . . . arranged something like this for him in Berlin, planted in a safe house just before we departed with him and the *Preußische Geheimpolizei* and a bunch of *Stoßtruppen* and Uncle Tom Cobbleigh and all on our heels. Probably including representatives of the Lower Saxony Forestry and Game Service."

"Never change, Luz! It would destroy your charm!"

"*Gracias.* My little parting gift didn't kill him, unfortunately, he went flat too fast, but from the Military Intelligence records of his interrogation a colleague standing right next to him got spattered about the landscape and all over Horst."

"So this"—Julie touched a fingertip to the bomb again—"is him blowing a kiss back at you?"

"*Más o menos*; just my thought. That and it was too heavy to move at the last minute . . . but from the look of the place, there was a lot more until recently . . . including at least, what, a total of four of these bombs?"

"That would be my take. All those empty crates labeled *agricultural machinery.*"

"How *irritating* it is when the enemy learn from you instead of doing the same thing over and over!"

"The sincerest form of flattery!" Julie said, and glanced after Ciara. "Your partner saved our bacon well and truly. Quite a girl you've got there, old friend," she said.

"Oh, she's young, but I think she earned a promotion from *girl* some time ago, if *solo un poco*, and not just because she'll be able to vote in the next election," Luz said, realizing she had a fond smile on her face and showing in her tone.

"You've got it bad! Bob and I weren't that spoony on our honeymoon!"

A sly grin in the darkness, as much heard as seen: "You realize she's jealous?"

"No reason for it," Luz said a bit shortly.

The grin turned to a chuckle. "None at all, beyond my occasional malicious teasing, but did I just hear you put *reason* and *jealousy* in the same sentence? This from the star of Professor Ganz's philosophy class?"

"A point."

"She's remarkable, but . . . I wouldn't have thought her your type, frankly. Fresh-faced dewy innocence and all. I doubt you were that dewy when you were *Alice's* age."

"I was an intolerably bossy, obstinate, bad-tempered, and incipiently murderous little bitch," Luz said with a grin of her own. "Only my big-eyed, raven-curled adorability kept Mima and Papá from strangling me. And have I ever told you how hurt I was when you didn't name your firstborn after me?"

"I didn't think you were as influential as *el jefe's* firstborn, so I flattered her, not you."

"Princess Alice? Though that was one pair of frilly knickers you never did get off," Luz observed.

"Alas, but not for want of trying at one point, I assure you. Oh, my God, those eyes! The way she can flay people alive with three words and a raised brow . . . watching that always made me breathe faster and go faint! Why, if things had gone differently, *I* might be ambassador to Japan myself now instead of poor Nicholas Longworth."

They shared a laugh at the playful absurdity; Alice Roosevelt Longworth's husband had been shuffled off to honorific exile in Tokyo due to some rather lurid family dramas that straitlaced Uncle Teddy hadn't enjoyed *at all*. In fact he'd muttered something about Augustus

Caesar and his troubles with his daughter Julia, though to date it hadn't been Alice herself who was deposited on an island of no return.

"Or *el jefe* might have had you torn apart by mad longhorn bulls attached to each limb," Luz said. "Or Alice might have had you stuffed and mounted in a glass case like one of her father's hunting trophies; she's that dangerous."

"I know. We're much alike."

"Too much so. Ciara and I aren't at *all* similar, but that's a good thing sometimes. You and I are *quite* alike too, for example, *mi amiga*."

"Which is why it didn't work? On the other hand, Bob and I suit perfectly, and we have a great deal in common."

"With enough differences to be piquant. I'm coming to the conclusion that Ciara is my link to the human race, for starters . . . which is odd since in some ways she's one of the more unworldly people I've ever met . . . or otherworldly . . . rather like a very Progressive changeling from the Danaan Sidhe."

"The Girl Engineer from the Green Faerie-Mounds? *There's* a new Celtic deity for you! Lug of the Long Spear, Brigid of the Cauldron, and Ciara of the Electrical Circuits! It's obvious that you're both very happy, though, Luz. And in all seriousness that *is* good to see."

A pause, and then Julie went on: "Though loving someone in our line of work . . . Bob and I worry about each other a fair bit; and about the children, of course, if either of us were gone. Or both. Quite a few *are* gone, from those who crossed the border with us in '13."

There was a soft bleakness to Luz's reply: "I learned long ago that the Pale Horseman can come for anyone, untimely and without warning, whether everything seems safe or not. Anyone at all."

Julie shrugged in the darkness. "True enough," she sighed, and produced an enameled flask, raised it, and took a sip. "Absent friends, and confusion to the Kaiser!"

Luz accepted it when she offered, inhaled the aroma of ripe peaches and jasmine, and swallowed a little. It had an unmistakable smooth bite and taste with echoes of almond and toffee . . . Courvoisier XO, obviously. Nobody was going to be making this in the future, unless some lucky German colonist could emulate the formula, which she doubted even with the same land, vines, and machinery: There was reverence in her sip. Her father had laid down three crates of Courvoisier the year she was born . . .

"Amen," she said. "And here's to an early, painful death for Colonel Nicolai."

"Apropos of which, another late working supper, I think," Julie added as she took another nip to wish Nicolai the worst, returned the flask to her jacket, took out her cigarette case, and lit one.

"Yes," Luz said, glad to be back to the practical. "We've made some progress, but we're still in the dark about what they intend to *do*."

"Blow up the Dakota Project, I thought? This"—she pointed with one toe—"would seem to indicate that. With luck, our prisoner will know some details. Thank you for resisting the irresistible impulse to chop off his head and do a dance, by the way."

"And probably he'll have been kept in the dark doing the donkey work," Luz snorted. "Would you brief local dupes in their position?"

"Well, no," Julie said. "Still, they definitely brought these bombs—"
She flicked a fingernail against the casing.
"—with malice aforethought."

"But how? That's the question. I keep trying to imagine *how* and my mind keeps boggling. Fifty bandits carrying these big steel bombs—"

Luz mimed a kick at the broken crate; it would have relieved her feelings to do it, though probably it would have hurt her foot.

"—through the 32nd defensive perimeter on stretchers while pretending to be a troupe of folk dancers? Smuggling it in with an oxcart under a load of cornstalks? Building a very large catapult? Using a circus cannon? *What are we missing?*"

"Have I told you how much I do not appreciate your arriving to dispel the rural quietude of this district?" Julie asked ironically.

"De nada, mi amiga."

"Oh, and you're certain that this Horst fellow is here?" Julie said. At Luz's affirmative sound she went on: "Since we're alone, there *is* something I'd wanted to ask about the delicious, dashing baron . . ."

Luz sighed. "Beautiful in a very masculine way, rather like a blond Apollo or a Thoroughbred racehorse."

"Well, I'm all for beauty, but sheer looks only go so far. Unless you're a male yourself, and they have low standards above the eyebrows, bless them. Erotic arousal turns off the post-ape-man part of their brains . . . shortage of blood, I suppose."

Luz nodded: "He's also intelligent, well-read, even a good conversationalist, reasonable sense of humor even if a bit full of himself . . . like another of my inamoratas . . ."

"Oh, ouch!"

"If the shoe fits . . . The mutual stalking was great fun, even leaving aside my ulterior motives and that extra little thrill of risk. But once his clothes came off . . . all the stamina in the world, but no imagination at all. Rather boring, in fact. Well enough briefly, but it might have become a trial after more than a few days if it weren't under false pretenses, even if I hadn't fallen into something so much better."

FIFTEEN

City of Zacatecas
State of Zacatecas
United States Protectorate of México
JUNE 22ND, 1917, 1917(B)

The tables of Madame Teffeau's Café y Panadería Francesa weren't very busy at ten to eleven—this wasn't an hour when Mexicans usually ate—but even the open courtyard's fresh bright air was full of the scent of the morning baking, which Luz inhaled along with that of the—excellent—coffee, and the flowers that also flavored the mild warmth of the highland day. They'd avoided the breakfast rush and the Dakota Project workers stopping in on their way to the plant site east of town to pick something fancy up for lunch. So far all the customers had bought and left with their booty, or left orders to be sent around today or tomorrow, often via notes in the hands of servants who'd have the next day off in whole or part. The orders had Madame Teffeau beaming with their massiveness, since tomorrow would be a fiesta day, and kept her grandson busy on his motorized delivery tricycle . . .

The *tarte Normande* the two of them were sharing was a simple dish, at least by French standards: a porously tender pastry crust, some slivered almonds, a custard of eggs and sweetened heavy cream and creamed butter and a little Calvados, some subtle spices, a spiral of thin-cut apple slices, and an apricot glaze topping slightly caramelized in the oven as it baked.

But as with anything else, it's all in the execution.

Ciara made a muffled sound of appreciation, swallowed, and said:

"I see why you made us such a light breakfast, darling!"

"A little fruit and toast is the ideal prelude to this."

"Or Kellogg's Shredded Wheat."

"Yes, but chewing on dry grass is much cheaper."

"Snobbery!"

"Taste. It's nice to see a bit of France surviving, too, *querida*," Luz replied, wielding her fork and taking a bite herself. "Any more thoughts on you-know-what?"

"It's definitely structural, somehow," Ciara said.

She often came up with ideas early, but after the time when her morning stupor had worn off; by now the fruits of yesterday's long labors over the bomb at the hacienda would have had time to ferment. Luz smiled to herself. There were times when Ciara went to places completely beyond her, and that made her feel . . .

As if I'm mated to a very strange eagle, and have to watch her flying into the sun. But I know she'll always return.

"It's designed to be *incorporated* in something, not just carried in it—it was meant to act as part of a framework bolted together, with subassemblies attached to *that*. That engineering officer Major Dicot found us, Captain Jones, agreed, and he seems quite clever. Once he got over being so shy. I felt like an absolute ogre at first, pushing at him."

Luz nodded and sipped at coffee that was wonderful if you liked the European style, which she did. The engineering officer had looked desperate and tongue-tied, until one of Ciara's observations prodded his professional pride and they were off into technicalities she couldn't follow.

Though to be fair, being too chatty with a young white woman might well have gotten the man killed, back where he grew up, which from his voice was a long way from Boston, or California for that matter. I imagine it's a hard habit to break. Many are the marvels, but none more marvelous than man and his idiocies.

Luz thought and then spoke. "Let's break this down into steps from the enemy's point of view. Working backward from the explosion they want at the crucial point in the factory."

Ciara nodded enthusiastically, and Luz went on:

"They want to get explosives to a target. The target is heavily guarded. They probably can't get explosives through the perimeter ... but *over* it? Could it be designed to fit in an aeroplane?"

That was the modern, *Progressive* answer to obstacles: Go over if you couldn't go through, which was one reason why everyone was mad for airships and aeroplanes these days, not to mention using them constantly as metaphors ... and in Luz's opinion, losing sight of the essential distinction between the literal and metaphorical all too often.

Unfortunately, or sometimes not, Germans were just about as modern as Americans that way.

Ciara sighed. "I thought of an aircraft, but it's definitely not intended to be *dropped*, you see, it's meant to be built into a structure ... meant to be *part* of a structure, load-bearing. I think the Germans *could* get a disassembled aircraft into the country by the cargo U-boats. But what would be the point of an aeroplane that couldn't drop a bomb without falling apart in midair? It would have to crash to explode! And bombing from the air is so inaccurate unless the aircraft gets dangerously close anyway. Those pilots we talked to at the air base were only a few hundred feet up in the attack they told us about!"

Luz blinked and touched a forefinger to her lips as that image ran through her mind. Germans were just as patriotic as Americans or just as crazy or both, if there was a difference. For a really high-priority target, if you tried you could find ...

"You could get a volunteer to crash—" Luz began to say, working out the thought aloud.

Her eyes went wide at the thought; it made far too much sense, given what they'd found so far. Moro Juramentado fanatics in the Philippines had been a bad problem in Uncle Teddy's first administrations, even with only a yard of razor-sharp *kampilan* to take as many infidels with them as they could. Here in Mexico individuals had occasionally done something similar with dynamite under their coats, and you couldn't even deter them by burying them chopped up and stuffed into a gutted pig carcass.

They were infernally hard to stop, or at least to stop before they could inflict losses on your guards and security details; fortunately they were rare, even in a grudge match like the Intervention at its worst. Someone like that in an airplane and riding a giant bomb . . . which would be functionally the same as a bomb that could see and react on its own . . .

"Wait!" she said.

She walked quickly back into the shop room of the bakery, dropping into French:

"Madame Teffeau? Could I so greatly impose upon you as to request the use of your telephone?"

The *pâtissière* wasn't handing out any more free pastries—French shopkeepers were rarely *that* sentimental—but Luz's effortless Parisian still got her a smile:

"But of course! Mademoiselle may use the one in my office," the Frenchwoman said, as she hoisted baskets of crusty loaves onto shelves with easy flexes of her muscular arms, and smiled as Luz took an instant to enjoy the smell and the slight crackle of the crusts.

"Just for a moment, madame."

"Feel free, my dear mademoiselle."

The office was a room giving off the arched portal that surrounded the building's main courtyard . . . which in turn enabled any occupant to keep a close eye on what was going on in said courtyard with its tables, while being discreetly hidden if they chose to draw the curtains. Inside it was neatly organized, with shelves for ledgers, file cabinets of the latest variety—the type with hanging folders in drawers stacked one above the other, something that big American businesses had only started to adopt when she was a child, and small French ones much later—and a modern telephone on the desk. Everything had been bought second-hand, but it was neat as a pin and functional as a knife blade.

The personal touch was a dozen photo portraits; most showed a family resemblance, and all of them had a black mourning border except one of a much younger Madame and Monsieur Teffeau in wedding garb. The groom had a round, plump, cheerful face, but judging from his absence from dealing with the public, he'd probably suffered physical or mental damage in his family's escape from the destruction of Paris and the ongoing apocalypse that had followed for mainland France.

Luz made a mental note to advise Julie to cultivate Madame Teffeau; she could be very useful and was probably well-disposed to the regime since she'd ended up here rather than in the National Redoubt of Overseas France in North Africa. Probably chance had played a role in that, but there must have been an element of deliberate choice and very hard effort, too. And judging by the pictures, as long as the United States had Germany for an enemy, it would have the Teffeau family as friends.

Julie's very keen but she does tend to be a bit snobbish sometimes. Teffeau doesn't have the sort of direct pull and clout here the de Moncadas do, say, but . . . Más vale maña que fuerza. *Sometimes smart beats strong.*

The office at Universal Imports came through loud and clear once she'd dialed the number; the new rotary phones still weren't all that common yet even in the United States proper, but the local telephone network in Zacatecas was as good as any medium-sized American city these days. There were advantages to being late off the mark, and Bell-Western had been *strongly encouraged* to start fresh with the best in its extensions in the Protectorate. Being allowed the effective national monopoly meant you *listened* to encouragement of that sort, these days.

Zacatecas had special priority now with the Project, too, of course. "Durán here," Julie said. "Luz?"

"*Sí*. We need a standing air patrol over Zacatecas city and the Dakota Project plant, Julie," Luz said. "Soonest. And tell Dicot to tell

General Young that all those antiaircraft assets he was considering mothballing should be packed around the Dakota Project plant *right away* and told to keep their eyes peeled."

"An *air attack?*" she said wonderingly. "Here?"

"Probably not but possibly yes," Luz said, and explained. "In this war . . ."

"The bizarre is normal, yes," Julie said. "And frogs grow hair. And here I thought calling fighting-scout pilots *suicidal* was just a metaphor!"

"Sometimes a metaphor will bite you in a sensitive place . . . why not in the air, when we've seen it with people attacking us on land?"

"Hopefully not too often. We've been processing that prisoner you brought us—"

A type of processing that had something in common with the one that turned pigs into strings of sausages and tins of leaf lard in an Armour & Co. plant in Chicago.

"—and he seems to have been some sort of bandit muleteer. He met what sounds like your old flame Horst up in the Sierra the day of the air attack, still pining for you—"

Do not say that in front of Ciara, Julie, Luz thought. *Do not, do not, do not.*

"Together with *another* German, more recently arrived, a soldier with really spectacular facial scars, whom you've also met."

"I have?" Luz said, scanning back through her memories.

"Construing *shooting at you from some distance* as equivalent to a social introduction. In that little tiff of yours in France last December. His name's Ernst Röhm, Major, formerly of the Bavarian part of the Imperial army and more recently of the *Stoßtruppen* before he became one of Colonel Nicolai's prize hatchet men. Since you kicked the previous one in the head and . . . the real atrocity . . . sent him to live in El Paso."

"I thought it was *Stoßtruppen* in France in December, from the tactics. And the weapons. We had the dubious privilege of being on the receiving end of their first field use of the assault rifles, too."

"Lucky you; incidentally, Röhm had a couple of the assault rifles with him—that was where the spent cartridge cases came from; he was giving a demonstration when our Falcons crashed the party . . . or bombed, gassed, and machine-gunned the party. I had Henrietta make a call to HQ and they identified Röhm by a cross-check—a couple of European newspapers we monitor published pictures of him last summer, which was useful, and the word in the German Army was that he . . . and your beau Horst, by the way, they're actually *named* after him . . . were responsible for the assault rifles. But there were definitely *four* Germans in that warehouse shortly before we arrived, preparing a cozy *Gemütlichkeit* welcome for us."

"But not in a positive way," Luz said aloud. "No impromptu beer garden and chorus from *The Student Prince*."

"Too right, just a heaping helping of *bombe surprise*. And your boy Horst has his hair dyed black now, the Byronic image to go with the eye patch you gave him—everything but a dark cloak billowing in the wind as he stands on a precipice and contemplates roiling clouds below."

"Better—"

"Correct the *shoot on sight* posters, yes, that's being done. From what he's said, I think the other two Germans are technical specialists on transfer from the German army."

"Why?"

"Because your boyfriend and Major Röhm both scared him—absolute killer *chingones*, he says—but the other two . . . he keeps babbling about smart-ass sissies."

"Ah. And they wouldn't send men who needed protection unless . . ."

"Unless they had some other overriding usefulness. One of the Mexicans they're traveling with seems to be a rogue named Pablo, originally Pablo Escobar, a bandit leader of sorts who's been giving us problems for years. We have his prints on file locally and they match with ones from the warehouse. He's not one of the dead ones, either. Dammit. I'd really like to have caught *him*; we could learn a great deal from him when we put him on the disassembly line."

"Well, that's all nice to know, or at least things it's better to know than not," Luz said. "Nothing absolutely crucial, though."

"The technicians might be a very substantial clue. The surprise is going to be a *technical* surprise. They wouldn't need specialists just to blow something up; that's not a rare set of skills and there are plenty of fighting men who can double in demolitions."

"Possibly a point, and they do have a long list of cackling Herr Doktor Professor types with mad schemes for mass slaughter and world domination through applied science, as we've found out to our cost. And whatever they do, they're going to be doing it *soon*. They know we're on their tracks and we'll kill them or scoop them up within the next week or two if they linger. So . . . soon, Julie, soon."

There was motion through the window. "Got to go, it's a source," Luz said. "Hopefully. Potentially."

"I'll get on to getting us . . . air cover," Julie said, her tone conveying how she was shaking her head in wonderment. "German air attacks in Zacatecas!"

María Luisa Muñoz Herrera had been the one at the gathering of altar cloth repairers most disturbed and thoughtful about the V-gas attack on Paris. Now she was too distracted to enjoy the slice of *mille-feuille* she was toying with.

Though her much older, darker, and stouter maidservant—it was of course impossible for a young woman of her respectability to go out *alone*, and even just a maid was a little daring—was off in a corner happily and methodically stuffing her face with pieces torn off a loaf of bread and smeared with strawberry jam and knocking back hot cocoa. Both were much cheaper than pastries but still well above her usual pay grade, since normally she'd be eating corn tortillas in the kitchen, with the luxury of risen wheat bread reserved for her social superiors except on holidays.

Luz thought Luisa's preoccupation was a pity; the three alternating layers of puff pastry and vanilla-fragrant *crème pâtissière* topped with cracked hazelnuts and fresh raspberries in a matrix of thick whipped cream were really too good to be pushed around a plate by an indifferent fork.

All what you're used to, Luz thought, taking another forkful of her *tarte Normande* and giving it full attention. *I don't suppose she's had many occasions to discuss terrorist attacks with people she must at least slightly* suspect *are American spies themselves.*

She could sense Ciara about to speak and nudged her ankle gently under the table.

A little while ago Ciara had tried to explain the daring new theories of some Jewish physicist from Switzerland to Luz, one of which was that gravity was things like planets and stars making a downward dimple in space. Rather like a cannonball on a sheet of rubber, and everything rolled down the slope it made toward it. Silence could function that way in human affairs; it was something a lot of people found intolerable, and eventually they spoke compulsively to fill it up.

She judged that the young Mexican widow would best *come ripe*, as the term of the trade put it, if she was left to come to it mostly on her own, with an occasional gentle, subtle assist. You didn't want to interrupt someone who was about to decide to do what you wanted them to do, just as the most successful seductions culminated in someone trying to kiss *you* first, convinced that the whole thing was their idea.

"You . . ." Luisa said. "You ladies were in Jerez the day before yesterday, weren't you?"

They both nodded.

"Have . . . have you heard the rumor that there was a bomb there?"

"Yes, we heard an explosion yesterday," Ciara said, which was true if a bit misleading, and sighed. "Such a pity that stubborn men make so many others suffer for their folly."

Good craft, sweetie, Luz thought.

"I do not love the United States," Luisa blurted, then relaxed as neither of them looked angry. "I wish Mexico could be independent!"

Ciara patted her hand. Luz rested her elbows on the table, set her chin on her linked fingers, and nodded encouragingly, helped by the fact that it didn't necessarily mean *agreement* here.

"I would too, in your position," Ciara said.

Luz added silently to herself:

But I'd also expect it to actually happen *when frogs grow hair. Also, Uncle Teddy would never have invaded Mexico if Mexicans hadn't messed up so spectacularly right next door. I'll let Ciara carry this, though—Luisa seems to like her more, or at least fear her less, which is perceptive.*

The Mexican woman looked down at her plate, then stabbed her fork into her cake and ate a mouthful, obviously without tasting it.

"My husband fought for Madero," Luisa said, which Luz had looked up in the local Chamber files.

He'd also managed to die doing it, with what sounded like the blundering heroic idiocy of a brave clueless amateur, leaving his new bride alone in the world. That wasn't untypical: Madero had been intelligent but eccentric, a spiritualist, a theosophist . . . and an idealist naïve enough to actually *believe* Porfirio Díaz when the old tyrant said he wanted a free election and would be ready to step down if he lost.

A lot of Madero's better-educated followers had been about as gullible, their ideas of politics a matter of books and dreams. There had been plenty of politics in Mexico during Díaz's reign, but most of it had taken place in smallish cliques, secret camarillas operating behind closed doors, leaving a lot of the literate class below the level of great wealth without any direct experience. For that matter Madero's family *had* been of great wealth, and even they hadn't known how things were really managed, having been on the outs with the pro-Díaz clique that governed, or feasted on, their home state of Coahuila.

"He just wanted a free government! *Everyone* was sick of Don Porfirio staying on and on, and the ones around him taking everything and selling everything and spies behind every mesquite bush . . . I was happy too when Don Porfirio resigned and left for France, it was like a fiesta and everyone acting as if they were relatives . . . but then Huerta killed Madero . . . and . . . and men went mad! Killing each other . . . we could see the smoke of the burning haciendas on the horizon . . . robbing gri . . . *Americanos*, killing them . . . anyone should have known what a man like *Presidente Teodorito* would do then! He *said* so as he campaigned in the U.S. elections, said so for all to hear! And the stupid *revolucionarios*, and the crazy puffed-up northerners who followed Villa, they who thought they were such heroes, they did worse; after everyone knew he would be president in *el Norte*, they crossed the border and planted bombs and shot people there and shouted mad dreams about taking back Texas and California. We couldn't beat the *Americanos* in the time of our grandfathers—"

She meant what Americans called the Mexican War of 1846–1848 and Mexicans referred to as *La Primera Intervención Americana en México*. Which was when a million and a half square miles from the Gulf to the Pacific had abruptly gone from being northern Mexico to constituting the southern and western United States, including Luz's own birthplace. Though in fact at the time most of that had been Indian country, some of it inhabited by tribes who'd never even *heard* of Mexico, or the United States either.

Though the Apache had, Luz thought. *They used to raid nearly as far south as this in those days, looting and killing and burning.*

"—how did those idiots think we were going to beat them . . . you . . . today, now, when the Estados Unidos are ten times as strong, one of the great powers of the earth, and we are still poor and weak? *And while we were fighting each other, too?* Stupid, stupid, *stupid*!"

The table jerked and plates and cutlery rattled as Luisa thumped her fists down on it.

"I am no soldier, no general, but if *I* could see that, why couldn't they?" she added plaintively.

Ciara sighed and patted her hand again.

Because you're not a fool mesmerized by your own heroic reflection in the mirror of your mind, Luz thought. *Self-inflicted stupidity, thy name is Vanity.*

Ciara tapped a finger on her own temple: "Men don't always think with this, not when their blood is up," she said, and sighed again, possibly thinking of her own brother.

Women didn't always either, but their characteristic follies only partially overlapped with those of males. And their circumstances in most places made them a little less prone than men to delusions of omnipotence, always a mistake in a world where even the genuinely powerful were often puppets of forces beyond their control, their choices made for them by necessity and likely as not to be undone or twisted into something unforeseeable by the giggling idiot hand of chance.

Luisa Muñoz's life wouldn't have left her in any doubt she was someone history happened *to*, like anvils falling on her head, not someone who made it. A mouse that knew it was a mouse had a much better chance of scurrying through the walls unseen than one under the delusion it was an elephant and hence given to walking around in full view of God and the household cat.

And these days even elephants need game preserves and wardens to protect them from men with guns after their ivory or meat or just their heads as souvenirs—mice survive under our feet no matter how much effort and ingenuity we put into wiping them out, Luz thought.

She tapped Ciara's foot under the table and flicked her eyes at Luisa in a signal to go on.

"When men start daring each other and showing off for each other, waving their fists and baring their teeth . . ." Ciara said.

"And snorting and pawing the earth like a bull in the *corrida* . . ." Luz added, lest her silence seem ominous.

"Peacocks! Roosters!" Luisa said, hitting the table again. "They decide on war, and women and children weep and bleed for it, go hungry and cold, see their homes and the work of their hands burn! We are left to nurse the cripples and bury the dead!"

Luisa took a deep breath. "You *Americanos* here have not dropped that terrible gas on us, or murdered millions of the unarmed, or driven us out of our country, or taken our houses and lands and forbidden our language and customs or burned the records of our history or changed the names of everything, and the Germans have done all these things in Europe. I have spoken much with Madame Teffeau—she only escaped by a miracle. She is strong, she does not weep, but I have wept for her."

"And in the world as it is, the choice is not between us Americans and nobody, it is between America and Germany," Ciara said. "It's a hard world for small nations."

Unless you've got the British or Japanese on your doorstep, Luz thought. *They're better than the Germans, but only marginally. This isn't a time that's easy on the weak . . . but then, what time is? Kings and empires come and go, but Darwin rules forever.*

"Yes!" Luisa said. "The *Americanos* have not tampered with our religion—"

She crossed herself, and Luz and Ciara echoed the gesture.

"—and their soldiers have not treated our women with disrespect. There is work and food for the common people. All these things could be worse, much worse. They *have* been worse, and we did it to ourselves—I remember the civil war."

Bless you, Uncle Teddy and General Wood and Plenipotentiary Lodge, Luz thought. *Sometimes virtue* is *its own reward, and in a quite tangible sense. At the most surprising moments, sometimes, and that makes a hardworking spy's life easier.*

"And now . . . *los malditos alemanes,* the accursed Germans, bringing that awful stuff to Mexico! Bringing it *here.* With fools of our own to help!"

In point of fact they weren't using V-gas here, but when people heard the word *German* now, *horror-gas* popped up spontaneously . . . which was poetic justice of a sort, and something of which Luz intended to take full advantage just as unfairly as she could. Luisa breathed out through her nose and ate another forkful of her cake, giving it a surprised look, as if she'd just realized she wasn't eating clumps of sawdust. Luz waited again, and indicated Ciara should do the same with a flick of the eyes.

Let the information roll downhill . . .

This was someone talking themselves into talking . . . and about to go from the general to the particular.

"If . . ."

Luisa's dark eyes glanced aside.

"If someone who . . ." she began, then paused and began again: "If someone who knew something . . . not because they were part of it, not *really* part of it, but who had kept silent out of fear . . . were to . . . come forward . . . would such a one, such a man, be forgiven?"

Luz ate a piece of her *tarte*, feeling a hot flush of hunter's delight at finally scenting a break, a bit like opening presents at Christmastime and a bit like carnal congress. At this point the *safest* thing to do would be to say something noncommittal, then have Julie grab Luisa and sweat what she knew out of her, which wouldn't be hard. Ciara sent her a combination of an appealing look and an *Up to you* shrug, and Luz replied with a very slight nod: *Make the promise.*

Because on the other hand, I was never the safety-first *sort of person, and that's worked out fairly well.*

"Yes. Provided he did speak . . . or that someone did on his behalf . . . I think I can *promise* that such a one would be pardoned. And protected," Ciara said.

There goes the last shred of our cover, Luz thought, as she watched Luisa blinking and working through the implications. *No, she's no sort of fool. Good-bye, cover, you lasted a whole long week from one Friday to the next . . .*

"My brother-in-law . . . I live with him and my sister . . . is a book-keeper who works for Don Raul de Moncada. He travels between the de Moncada estates, and reviews the accounts kept by their *mayordomos*, you see? And checks that they are correct, and inspects things . . . live-stock, crops, granaries . . . to make sure they correspond to the numbers in the books."

Ciara nodded encouragingly to keep the flow coming. Luz wasn't surprised; that was the usual sort of precaution that wealthy land-owners took here, necessary in a country where stocks and banks were recent innovations and not fully trusted or for that matter very trust-*worthy*. The problem with delegating management here was that you were inviting your hired managers to cheat you; accounting was one way around that, as were patron-client relationships and using your network of extended kin by blood and marriage.

Family ties were deeply respected here, and to further degrees of kinship than most Americans kept track of, and so were the bonds of patronage and clienthood and *compadrazgo*; but *commercial* morals made people like Fred Foreman of Fred Foreman's Fords . . . or even merci-less predators like Carnegie and Frick and John D. Rockefeller of Stan-dard Oil . . . look like paragons of selfless scruple.

"He is a relation of theirs—a distant one, to be sure."

Which might mean something a century or more removed, in cen-tral Mexico. The women of the upper classes here had always married young and had big families—not even counting the innumerable by-blows and bastards, since rich men routinely kept one or more unoffi-cial households as well in the course of their lives—and the younger sons of younger sons at the fringes filtered downward generation after generation into less and less aristocratic layers. It was a major reason why Mexico was as Spanish in blood and custom as it was, despite the inflow from Spain being a long steady trickle rather than the obliterat-ing flood the English preferred.

"Efraín is not a *bad* man," Luisa said earnestly. "He is kind and cares for his family and cares for the sacraments. He took me in when my husband was killed for my sister's sake—our parents are dead too—and has never treated me as anything but his own sister by blood. He has helped many of his other relatives who became poor during the fighting, this is why he was so very short of money. But he . . . he . . . is not a *strong* man either. He talked about Madero but did nothing."

Coward and weakling governed by the last person to frighten him, Luz filled in to herself. *Which has its advantages. Once he realizes the Black Chamber has him he'll be very cooperative indeed.*

"And lately, something has frightened him very badly," Luisa said. "He weeps when he thinks nobody can hear. And he has been making plans to take us . . . the whole household . . . out of the city, to *visit* his aunt in Puebla, even though his work is here and he is not a rich man, he cannot afford such a thing and does not even like her, he never speaks to her save when he must for decency's sake. When my sister complained, he shouted at her to be silent and do as she was told—that is not like him at all. And . . ."

The two Black Chamber operatives waited.

". . . and," she said reluctantly. "And he has been looking at weather vanes and testing the wind with his finger—again, when he thinks people are not watching him, for the last few weeks, since he began acting strangely. When the wind is from the west, as it usually is, he sighs with relief. But when it is from the east . . ."

She mimed a man with clenched teeth and hunched, tightened shoulders holding his fists tightly. They all looked eastward.

Toward the stretch of barren rocky pastureland where the Dakota Project was being built . . . and which nearly everyone with any education had by now realized was to produce something chemical, something chemical and military, and something chemical and military that had to be guarded even more closely than a conventional poison-gas works. The implications were obvious, to anyone not blinded by wishful thinking.

On the other hand, if the brother-in-law has figured it out, he may just be jumping at shadows on that account. Best to let her continue. She'll come to it.

Luisa stared at her fork, then glanced eastward and back at the plate before she spoke:

"This is *my* city. I was born here, and my mother and father and my grandparents before me for many generations, they walked these streets and worshipped at these altars and bore their children and were buried here. It is watered with their blood and tears and it was built with their sweat and their dreams."

"Your *patria chica*," Luz said.

"Yes! Yes, that is it exactly."

Luz and Ciara both nodded in understanding. *Patria chica* translated directly as *little homeland*; its meaning was very similar to the German *Heimat*. It meant the earth that gave you birth, your home country in a more direct and visceral sense than a nation-state, the place where you were truly at home among your own kin and kind.

"Everyone I know and love and nearly all my relatives live here. I will not see it destroyed for the profit of wicked foreigners. I will save it, even if I am hated and killed or driven out for it."

"And very many could die if something . . . unfortunate . . . happened to the east of town," Ciara said soberly. "*Would* die."

Luisa nodded, her mouth firm.

"When did your brother-in-law plan his trip to Puebla?" Luz asked, carefully not staring, keeping her voice soft and gentle and monotonous, without any of the little triggers of challenge.

A long pause, and then: "Efraín has told us we leave the day before the fiesta of St. John the Baptist, early in the afternoon, the very first train. My sister said why not the evening train so that we would arrive in the morning rather than late . . . and he went gray and said, *No, any time but that.* That was also very strange."

"Tomorrow," Ciara said thoughtfully, and exchanged a glance with Luz.

But the fiesta is a perfect day for an attack. Maximum distraction, but it's not an American holiday so the plant will keep operating . . . it's high-priority and doesn't take Saturdays either . . . and it's already doing its first full-scale trial run.

"Wait a moment," Luz said; Ciara had missed a detail. "You said your brother-in-law *was* short of money? But he isn't now?"

"Yes," Luisa said, in a monotone herself and with her eyes closed for a long moment, but without hesitation. "He was able to buy us tickets without difficulty, for cash—and as I said, he has been helping many relatives, but now he complains less about that. And he has paid debts I knew he had."

Luz blinked in thought. "Did this start before, or after, he became so frightened?"

"After . . . Why do you ask that, *Señorita Graciela?*" Luisa asked sharply.

Luz smiled slightly. "Because you said he was a good man, a man with a kind heart, but . . . not strong. If bad men were trying to prevent him from revealing their evil plans, plans he had stumbled across, they might well first threaten him, and only then pay him money."

They didn't kill him because that would have drawn attention precisely where they didn't want it. They probably will *kill him later. Killing him* now *would be too likely to trip alarms, but later you couldn't leave a broken reed like that alive with important secrets in his sweating fear-filled head. They'll have someone waiting to do it in Puebla, if they have the assets. And kill his family because he might have told them something,* Luz thought clinically, before she went on aloud:

"First threats to put him in fear of them, you see, and then the money to put him in fear of the authorities, because he would think they would punish him harshly for taking a bribe from terrorists and German agents. To put him *between the devil and the deep blue sea,* as they say in English."

We'll pay him too, eventually. Partially because the information is worth it and partially for exactly the same reason . . .

Luisa thought, blanched a little as if she'd seen a dish cover lifted at dinner to reveal maggots, then nodded with a queasy expression.

"He will not be punished?" she said, her eyes pleading. "Even if he *has* taken such . . . such tainted German money?"

"No," Ciara said. "Not if he cooperates once he is taken into . . . protective custody."

"Oh, he will," Luisa said absently, obviously thinking hard; that off-hand judgment betrayed an exceedingly low opinion of her brother-in-law, even allowing for what she'd said explicitly. "What must *I* do?"

"Nothing," Luz said. "You have already done enough to save your family and your city. You must show no sign that you know anything and leave tomorrow with your brother-in-law. The train will be stopped out of sight of anyone and you will all be taken into protective custody until this . . . matter is over. Then you may return, or possibly go to live elsewhere, but that will be your choice. You understand that your brother-in-law cannot be allowed to speak to anyone until then?"

Luisa swallowed; *protective custody* could potentially cover a multitude of sins. Her eyes flicked to Ciara, who gave a reassuring smile and a slight nod; that relaxed her a little, but not completely . . . which confirmed her initial judgment that Señora Luisa Muñoz was nobody's fool.

"We keep our promises to those who help us," Ciara said firmly; that was in all the manuals she'd read, and it was generally quite true.

That relaxed Luisa a little more in one way, and increased her fears in another—that was one of the mottos of the Black Chamber, and the Chamber kept its promises for good or ill. And people knew both those things. Luz gave a very slight nod as Luisa's eyes went wide, judging that it would help her keep her family from suspecting anything until tomorrow morning.

When she'd been given a little more reassurance and sent on her way—every moment they were seen together now was one too many, since there was no way of being absolutely sure the *revolucionario* underground couldn't follow all of Efraín's family—Luz split the last piece of the *tarte*.

Ciara frowned. "It sounds to me as if this . . . aeroplane thing . . . is on one of the de Moncada properties. Do you think they're part of the plot?"

"Almost certainly not," Luz said thoughtfully, eating another forkful and raising her empty coffee cup; the Teffeau daughter hurried over with the pot, spruce in her white apron.

"Not Don Raul, at least, or anyone close to him," she said thoughtfully. "No, his political record makes that very unlikely indeed; not to mention that he's too conspicuous to get away with a conspiracy. But one of his *mayordomos* certainly is, and the family owns enough land around here that there are a lot of them. It's the perfect place to conceal a distance weapon, an aeroplane, precisely *because* the de Moncadas have close links to the Protectorate. And they'll probably be hoping . . . *they* as in the Mexicans involved with this . . . that we blame him afterward, which would be just peachy-keen from their point of view and stick a piece of pipe in the spokes of our political wheel in the region."

"We *won't* blame him, of course?"

"No. But having one of his employees being naughty like this will put him more in our debt—he's probably been getting a little above himself, what with being the governor's father-in-law."

"What do you think this brother-in-law of Luisa knows?"

"At the least, he knows *which one* of the de Moncada haciendas is being used to hide the aeroplane; probably it's east of town where most of the land is in grazing, and not too far from the target. He saw whatever it is, and he has some idea of when they're going to use it."

Ciara frowned. "You don't want to question Luisa's brother-in-law . . . Efraín . . . immediately?"

"Of course I want to, but the minute we do that . . . They're almost certainly watching *him* at least until he leaves town, if not his sister-in-law—he knows too much and he's not really one of them. That warehouse manager ratting them out in Jerez will have put them on edge, too. If we scoop him up, they'll know right away and run for it—and come up with another attack we *don't* know anything about later. Or worse, they'll launch the attack before we know the location it'll come from. Now that we know it's an air attack . . . or strongly suspect it . . . we can guard against it."

"But if we wait *too* long we risk them getting to their launch time. The air patrol will very probably intercept any aircraft they launch, but it's not certain."

"Calculated risk," Luz said with a sigh.

Deciding on those went with higher rank; you had to remember that more conservative decisions didn't necessarily mean better, or even just safer.

Ciara nodded. "I'm glad it's you, not me, that has to decide that! We should tell Julie to cultivate Madame Teffeau, I think, too . . . Look at the good she's already done us!"

Luz chuckled. "Great minds, sweetie—I just thought of that myself."

"And Luisa's brother-in-law, what do you make of him?" Ciara said.

"I'm not sure if he's as innocent as she paints him, but that doesn't matter—I'm quite sure he's as *weak* as she thinks, and that he'll fold like wet cardboard once we have our hands on him without needing any pressure beyond that. He'll tell us where it is . . . and once he does that, he's committed, so we can treat him *as if* he's nothing but the brainless, not to mention spineless, dupe she makes out and he will be glad we do . . . either way."

Ciara clapped her hands together, and then her happy smile died away.

"What's wrong, darling?" she said. "You're not as pleased as you should be."

"There's something we're *still* missing, somehow. How many of those bombs do you think there were?"

"From the looks of things at the warehouse . . . another two? Possibly three, not more than that."

Luz nodded. "Which means they brought four aircraft, engines and fuselage and all. Each one, even knocked down, is heavy and bulky and dangerous to transport with us watching things. They wouldn't send more than they absolutely must . . . and I think it's very likely that Germany could find *one* pilot willing to kill himself to improve his country's bargaining position at the peace talks eventually . . . but even in Germany, could you find *four*? Not for something like this, I'd say, not four competent and reliable ones."

"Someone with an incurable disease, as well as being patriotic? Hoping for rewards for his family?"

"Yes, but there just *aren't* that many pilots, and by definition they're young and healthy to start with—German medicine is very high-standard and their checks are meticulous. And our prisoner saw only two Germans beside Horst and this Ernst Röhm, and neither of them sounds like a pilot. More like a clerk and a technician."

"The pilots could have been stashed somewhere else," Ciara pointed out.

"True . . ." Luz sighed. "No matter how much you know, you never know enough . . . Let's get over to Universal Imports. We're going to have to manage this delicately if we want to scoop up the Germans and solve the problem they present, as well as stop the immediate plot."

They rose, nodding and smiling at young Monsieur Teffeau and his mother as they left.

What are we missing? Luz thought. *¿Qué diablos es ésto? ¡Ay, but I hate that nagging tickle!*

On the other hand, it was a *lot* better than false certainty.

SIXTEEN

City of Zacatecas
State of Zacatecas
United States Protectorate of México
June 23rd, 1917, 1917(b)

The Dakota Project had put up a lot of vehicle parks and associated structures in the western parts of Zacatecas City, some well outside the construction site proper. And some were disused but not yet torn down or repurposed now that the dirt-shifting and foundation-laying stages of the construction were well past.

This particular big sheet metal shed on a concrete pad had been very convenient for assembling the Black Chamber's strike team; besides their own operatives, there were two platoons of the 32nd Infantry's reconnaissance battalion and Captain York's company of the 2nd Filipino Rangers, and their vehicles and equipment. Including enough trucks to move them quickly and a six-vehicle squadron of the 32nd's Lynx battle cars, boxy vehicles of riveted armor plate, each with three large wheels on either side and a machine gun and one-pounder pom-pom gun in its rectangular turret. The assembled armed might occupied most of the space . . .

But firepower is not our problem, Luz thought. *It never is here on our own ground, not from the Chamber's point of view.* Finding *the targets to apply it on,* that's *the problem.*

The engines made the stuffy air acrid with their exhaust, and the noise echoed off the sheet metal, amid the sweat-gun-oil-tobacco-old-socks scents of soldiers. The Bugkalot smelled subtly different, their body odor less meaty and musky but sharper than that of the Americans'; they and the 32nd troopers were passing around baskets of *gorditas* and nontalking in a friendly way, since they had little in the way of common language.

"Well, *he* sang like a canary," Luz said.

She was quickly doing another scan through the transcript from the interrogation of Luisa's unfortunate brother-in-law Efraín; the main problem with it was that he seemed to want to vomit out his entire life story, starting with the first time he skinned his knee as a toddler in 1885, which was why they'd been using the redacted summary while they waited for the air attack. The Air Corps had assured them that no bombing aircraft could get through the cover, so they could wait and scoop up the Germans and their local helpers . . .

Efraín, his wife, his five children—three girls, two boys, ages ranging from twelve to two; his gimlet-eyed and silently disapproving mother; and Luisa, plus a brace of maidservants—were over in one corner of the big echoing shed, in a sort of room made by piles of crated equipment. With them was the Zacatecas station's junior operative Dora Parkinson, who was soothing them down and jollying them along, aided by boxes of Madame Teffeau's best, tea from Julie's private stock, and some brandy now and then for their father, and sleight-of-hand tricks from her training to distract the children. He'd have drunk himself insensible hours ago if they'd let him.

She'd been cheerful and uncomplaining about the assignment, which Luz liked, even when she had to take crying children to the improvised latrine behind more boxes. A field operative's business was dealing with people.

And while violence is always a solution to a problem with people . . . it's not always a good solution.

It was approaching sundown outside; the buzz of the Pumas and Falcons circling over the Dakota Project plant a few miles farther east and over Zacatecas itself had sunk into the background. Luz hated the thought that they'd alerted the enemy to what they knew, but there was no way to be inconspicuous about dozens of fighting aircraft circling. They'd put on acrobatics that had gathered admiring crowds below, and Julie had spread a rumor, soon taken as fact, that this was a contribution to the fiesta of St. John the Baptist, courtesy of Gobernador Don Carlos Seelmann. He'd been informed so he could deny everything with the right polite insincerity.

"The difficulty is getting him to shut up," Luz added, pushing the rest of the transcript across to Ciara and sipping vile Army coffee from a tin cup. "I hate it when they babble like that. It's mildly . . . disgusting. Though it was at least smart of him to tell everything without trying to filter it."

"Except that it wasn't, it was just the most complete case of immediate moral collapse I've ever seen—and I've been doing interrogations since June 1913!" Julie said, after a meditative draw on her Mogul cigarette. "His teeth were chattering but he was weeping with relief at the same time. What do you think we should do with that family?"

"Give them favored status, as things stand, pending the outcome. If the information is confirmed, we should cultivate them, but carefully. Start by telling de Moncada to keep him on in his present job."

"Efraín is putty to whoever squeezes him, and useful within those limits as long as we keep that in mind, but Louisa is another matter entirely on brief acquaintance."

"*Absolutamente*," Luz said. "I think she resents being dependent on him, and despises him."

"Agreed, especially after watching him vomit out everything he knew. Not because he was talking, but because he was so abject about it."

Luz nodded. "She came to us for her own good reasons; we would have had to break her to get anything if she hadn't made that decision. But I'm guessing she doesn't let herself fully realize how *much* she despises him and hates living off his charity, because it would make her miserable and her confessor wouldn't like it, and she's devout. And she genuinely hates the Germans. She was very interested in the Vocational Institute project, ostensibly for *unfortunate girls* but deep down she'd like a job and skills herself; charity and church work and helping with her nieces and nephews aren't enough to keep her from being bored. I think she also at least somewhat resents her former husband for running out and getting himself killed and leaving her to make the best of it, but she *really* doesn't want to admit that to herself."

"Ah, that might be useful. You think she's the type who'll feel obliged to you if you do them favors and *don't* ask for anything in return?"

"Exactly. But it would have to be done very, very carefully. Don't spread the honey too thickly on the bread."

"In other words, she's potentially an earnest middle-class idealist?"

"Aren't we all, in the Party?" Luz said lightly.

Julie smiled, a remarkably evil expression in the lantern light.

"Speak for yourself. *You're* upper-upper-middle-class, if you squint the right way, from a self-improving, strive-and-succeed family with an engineer in it and a lot of higher education—you were *made* to be a Progressive. I'm upper-class and from a family who made just scads of money by their careful choice of ancestors, and a class traitor like *el jefe*... Either that, or we're *saving* our class despite their own entrenched stupidity. While having fun and avoiding dying of boredom."

Luz blinked. "Sometimes your cynicism makes me feel . . . inadequate, *mi amiga*."

"That's because you had to work at yours. I was born with a brimming silver spoonful of the blackest, bitterest variety in my mouth."

She looked fretfully at her watch. "Pretty soon it's going to be too dark for the aeroplanes and the fiesta fireworks will start. Has your old . . ."

She paused with malice aforethought, didn't say *boyfriend*, and then went on:

"—sparring partner Horst decided to call it off because the fighting scout aeroplanes overhead say we're onto them?"

Suddenly Ciara spoke, slamming her finger down on the page of the transcript she was reading.

"This man Efraín is an *idiot*!"

"No, he's just utterly terrified of several things at once and as *el jefe* says is the type who has all the backbone of a chocolate éclair," Luz said. "That numbs the brain and makes you look, speak, and act like an idiot whatever your IQ is."

"I've been terrified, and it never made me *stupid*! I was terrified when I defused that bomb on Thursday—I cried and shook afterward— and it never made me *stupid*! We'd all be dead if it had."

"That's because you're brave," Luz pointed out. "Courage is dealing with fear so it *doesn't* paralyze you. Why? What's he done that's *particularly* stupid?"

"What he's describing here isn't an aeroplane at all—but he doesn't know how to describe it, so he keeps calling it that!"

Luz leaned over to read upside-down, absently turning up the lamp, feeling a hunter's tickle at the back of her mind.

"Wings, engine, propeller at the rear . . . that's not so common these days but it's still done with some models . . . sounds like an aeroplane to me."

"No. He says it's on a *ramp*, not on a takeoff field. He doesn't mention wheels or a cockpit. And he says there's a *cross* at the front, with *long metal thorns*. What does that *mean*? And he says they had an electrical cord to it, and when they turned on a switch it *whined*."

Then Ciara's face lost its frown; instead it went white as milk, despite the sun flush she'd gotten in the last few days. She held up a hand to stop Luz's question and instead scrabbled for paper and pencil of her own. She began to draw, and despite the rough surface and poor light and tools, it was as precise as any draftsman's working diagrams.

Luz reached out her own hand and put a finger on Julie's lips; this was precisely the state when Ciara must not be interrupted. When the drawing was finished she sprang up with it and ran for the enclosure where Efraín sat with his head in his hands while Dora did card tricks and his children squealed and his wife, mother, and sister-in-law sipped tea and tried to pretend none of this was happening.

You can still tell she's not used to wearing pants when she runs, Luz thought as she and Julie exchanged a glance and followed her with their eyes.

They'd all had time to change into breeches for this operation, except Dora, who this time was in a conventional shirtwaist to keep Efraín's family from being too scandalized and distracted by the horror of a woman's legs in close company. The junior operative swept up the cards and put a finger to her lips to the children; their mother and aunt moved in to sit on the bench amid them and put arms around shoulders.

"Look at this!" Ciara said, from the sound remembering to say it in Spanish just in time. "Look!"

She shoved the paper in front of his face, and he blinked blearily. With a sound like an overheated teakettle she grabbed him by the back of the head and moved his gaze to the paper.

"*Look!* Is that—"

Luz saw the change in his face before Ciara noticed it. She did when he tore himself loose and backed up, pointing as the chair fell over with a crack on the stained concrete, gibbering wordlessly and then squealing:

"How . . . how . . . how do you know *everything*!"

Even so, Ciara was back at the table completing the drawing before Julie and Luz arrived to look over her shoulders. What Luz saw was like an aeroplane with a single high wing supported by struts bolted to its midsection, and a pusher propeller at the rear, mounted on some-thing like an upward-curved ramp, and with no wheels or pilot or cockpit for one, just . . .

"It's like wings on a torpedo," Luz said in wonderment.

"That's exactly what it must be!" Ciara said, her voice high with a mixture of technical interest and horror. "An . . . *aerial* torpedo! A *sky* torpedo! See—"

She sketched in a power cord. "This is why he heard it *whining*! A Sperry automatic control system with an electromechanical gyroscopic feedback system, they must have been spinning it up to test it—"

"You've lost me," Julie said sharply.

"A man named Sperry invented the system in 1911 and made one for aeroplanes in 1912—it uses gyroscopes to maintain a constant head-ing in an aircraft or ship automatically through hydraulic control mechanisms . . . it's still experimental . . . and if you know the range to the target, the engine could cut out, you'd use a revolutions counter for that, and it would dive down. *Just* like a torpedo! But it wouldn't be very accurate at a long distance."

The torpedo had something on its nose; a thin metal cross in the shape of an X, with a long spike pointing forward from the end of each arm.

"But this, this is different," Ciara said, stabbing her pencil at it. "This is a receiver for wireless transmissions—radio. It would be . . . you could . . . it would sort of, of *home in* on the transmitter, if you—"

She looked at them, obviously unendurably frustrated by their not seeing the implications:

"*But you wouldn't need daylight for any of this.* You could just set it up and start a timer—like they did on the U-boats for the Breath of Loki—and leave!"

"*¡Ay!*" Luz said in alarm.

The standing air patrol they'd been counting on had just been ren-dered completely useless.

"If you could hide the transmitter just where you wanted the air torpedo to land . . ."

"Then it would be quite accurate, yes. We could . . . you could jam the transmission, perhaps—"

And we sat here all day with our thumbs up our . . .

"No time!" Luz barked aloud.

Julie was already diving for the Army field telephone set up on one end of the table and spinning the crank.

"Now!" she shouted into it.

Outside a man applied a match to touchpaper. Rockets shot skyward, and a pattern of silver and crimson stars appeared high in the sky. Through the half-open doors they could hear, faintly, the cheering from the crowded streets of Zacatecas to the west over the ridge of ground, where it was taken as a signal for the start of the fiesta's fireworks.

Several miles northeastward, Field Operative Lee would see it, where he was lying up with several assistants, ready to start interdicting—killing—anyone trying to get in or out of the de Moncada grazing property Efraín had revealed to be the place the conspirators had picked. It was a good choice from their point of view, a stretch of thin grassland used as summer grazing for stock from other properties rather than a real hacienda, no *casa grande* and not much in the way of a village, just pens and quarters for the shepherds, shearing sheds and wool sheds . . . and the *mayordomo*'s quarters, nothing much for the very junior man in charge of a minor operation . . .

Julie turned and her finger shot out like a spear. "Henrietta! You go with Luz—she'll need to deal with Major Dicot. Call Dicot now on this phone. Captain York! Captain Julius! We're going now, *now!*"

They won't find much, Luz thought, as the station chief ran for her Guvvie and the engines blatted and the troops scrambled for their transport.

"Like the U-boats for the Breath of Loki," Ciara said again, as their eyes met, echoing the thought with words. "The crews put them on the bottom and evacuated them and those electromechanical instruction machines were set to launch the rocket-mortars."

"My family weren't even killed by people," Henrietta said with quiet bitterness as she lifted the phone. "They sent a *machine* to do it."

"And I'll give you any odds they did the same thing here," Luz said. "But the radio homing transmitter . . . they'll have to have set that by hand at the target. And just before the attack, because the whole plant's inspected regularly. Ciara, where will they put it, on the storage tanks? They're doing the first production run right now."

Ciara had the plans of the Dakota Project plant open before her.

"No," she said. "Not from these and what I saw on the tour. They're underground and the construction is really heavy and the bomb will have lots of explosive but not much velocity—the explosion will . . . will sort of bounce its blast force off something like that, you see? No, the maximum damage would be here, just where the pipelines run. Damage here will spill the largest possible amount—it's liquid, remember, not all that volatile—and then vaporize as much of it as possible and scatter it, depending on the direction of the wind."

Which is from the east, right now!

Luz looked where Ciara's finger was resting. In the background, Henrietta's voice was talking on the field telephone and she heard Major Dicot's name.

"*Goddammit to hell!*" the young woman from Savannah swore, the first time Luz had heard her use blasphemy.

She looked up. "An American major with one eye and papers that are *perfect* except that they don't check on the expected-arrivals list got into the plant an hour ago! Andre just got the report! Nobody's seen this *major* since!"

"Tell him to meet us at block C-17 of the plant," Luz called over to her; she checked her pistol, snapped the magazine back in, and holstered it. Then she touched the hooked hilt of her *navaja* with one finger.

"Let's go."

I t's sort of ironic how many people involved with horror-gas end up dying of it themselves—like Herr Doktor von Bülow," Ciara said, sounding commendably calm as they drove toward possible death. "And he *invented* it."

"He did?" Henrietta said, coming out of her brown study in the passenger seat as the Guvvie sped through the night behind the light spears of its headlamps.

The road was good, and ahead the bright floodlights and perimeter searchlights of the Dakota Project works loomed.

"Yes," Luz said from the backseat. "Not our doing—not Ciara's and mine personally—but we were in Staaken when it happened. He was killed when the Chamber sabotaged the German works last December. And we'd met him before that, in the course of . . . work."

Henrietta knew better than to ask for the details, though she obviously burned to do so.

"Good!" was all she said, but there was a savage satisfaction in it.

Fair enough, though he wasn't a bad old abuelo, *for someone behind the greatest single massacre in human history. He just thought it was necessary for the Greater Good, or at least for Greater Germany, which was pretty much the same thing to him.*

"Horst von Dückler worked closely with him, developing the strike plans for the American part of the Breath of Loki," Luz said. "I can tell you that much."

Major Andre Dicot met them at the nearest main gate instead of block C-17, and he was cursing quietly to himself in South Louisiana French, crossed with the standard Parisian variety, just a hint of the Creole accent in the almost-*w* sound of the *r*'s. Luz's mind absently noted the confirmation of her initial guess. She stood as Ciara brought them to a halt, swaying with her hand on the overhead bar that supported the canvas roof when it was up, and jumped down with a lithe hop, walking over to him and shaking his hand.

The entranceway was flanked by two octagonal concrete pillboxes, with the muzzles of twin Brownings just visible within in the sharp blue-white light of the floods; there was a squad of infantry on hand, gaping a little at the woman in breeches with a pistol on her hip in a high-set cutaway holster exchanging greetings with an officer of the 32nd.

The gates were double frames of stout wood and steel pipe, laced with barbed wire, one rolling to the left and the other to the right to let the roadway be used. The perimeter stretched off to either side in the darkness, coils of barbed wire clamped at intervals to angle-iron posts that hadn't even had time to get rusty yet, then a good graveled perimeter roadway constantly patrolled, then a wire fence fifteen feet high with more pillboxes just behind it. Guard towers with searchlights and yet more machine-guns stood at intervals, and behind it the tangle of tanks and piping and blocky buildings that made up the factory of death.

"C-17's blacked out, Field Operative," he said as the gates opened; he and Henrietta exchanged a glance, shy and quick, but nothing more. "It happened after I got your message and sent a reaction squad toward the location you indicated—someone must have been watching. I've put troops on the perimeter around C-17, but I pulled the men out. A firefight in there . . ."

Luz bared her teeth; part of that was the scorched-metal-and-ozone scent of the chemical plant that stretched away behind the fencing, and partly . . .

Dicot probably didn't really think that she was laughing, but his look was freighted with the anxiety that had struck him so suddenly.

"Something amuses?" he said, harassed enough that his birth tongue bled over into his usually faultless English diction.

Luz suspected that Dicot's roots were in an old family of *gens de couleur libres* in New Orleans, free and well-educated even before the Civil War; that tradition of schooling and a home familiar with the world of culture and books would have eased his rise through the ranks after the General Staff decided several years ago that men of color should be commissioned in larger numbers for the Negro divisions.

"It's just that everything here reminds me strongly of the German V-gas plant in Staaken last year . . . including the abundance of guards and wire, and how little it helps sometimes, but now from the other side. So that I feel as if I'm stamping *elle ne sait rien faire de ses dix doigts, celui-là* on my own identity card."

That meant feeling completely useless; not entirely accurate, but enough so that it wasn't a lie, and it helped Dicot override his own sense of startled inadequacy. And it reminded him that the Black Chamber were experts in sabotage from both angles.

She showed him Ciara's sketch of the German weapon and he swore again, his head whipping up. The sky was quiet now with the fighting scouts back at base—though there were still fireworks exploding from the direction of Zacatecas—but she supposed they might hear the air torpedoes coming.

"So if we find this transmitter, they won't hit?" he asked.

Ciara spoke up: "They'll still hit *somewhere*, Major. In the general area, with the gyro-guidance system. But with the transmitter . . ."

Dicot winced; there weren't many *good* places for a heavy load of explosives to come down in a chemical plant dedicated to making poisons, though some were much worse than others.

"What we need to do is find the transmitter, and then take it somewhere else . . . quickly!" Ciara said. "While it's still working. If we can do that we can make things safe, not just safer."

"I hope the strike force keeps them from launching, but it's not the way to bet," Luz said. "A sniper probably isn't going to be able to interdict them in the dark, either. We're going in now. There's no time to waste and this is our specialty. Keep the gate open," she added. "And keep working on getting the lights back on—darkness is the saboteur's friend."

"At least they didn't smuggle explosives past us," he said.

"They weren't stupid enough to try; that would be obvious," she replied grimly.

I wish I could have brought some of the Rangers, she thought as she swung back to her seat and they drove through; the Bugkalot were just the people for night work. *Better them than me! But there wasn't time to alter plans . . . air torpedoes! And I thought Burroughs was fanciful!*

Three long breaths, and she touched Ciara briefly on the shoulder. *And I* really *wish* mi amor *weren't here . . .*

The breaths pushed the thought out of her head, all thought, leaving only readiness and wariness as they drove through the gate, turned left toward big concrete tanks set low in the ground, and then into the darkened area. It wasn't pitch-black; enough glow came from the arc lights elsewhere to produce a twilight full of shadows.

"Slow down," she said.

Ciara did; the Guvvie came down to walking pace, its headlights piercing the gloom. The road ran beside a long line of twin pipes supported at about head-height on widely spaced concrete supports, welded steel that looked odd without the rivets you usually saw in this type of construction. Not far away the pipes ran through a set of bulbous valves and control wheels before continuing on the other side, and those did have rivets. Everything was pale, painted with some aluminum-based coating, nothing to hint at the death of millions that the pipe contained except a faint high-pitched hissing.

Hissing like the Midgard serpent, Luz thought. *The Devourer of Worlds.*

She hopped lithely out of the Guvvie and walked alongside it crouched, invisible in her dark clothing to anyone beyond arm's reach.

Henrietta did the same, but stumbled; Luz grabbed the back of her jacket for a moment and the younger operative steadied, using the same instinctive crouch, her pistol in her hand.

"You are *definitely* getting a transfer to Field Operations, Miss Colmer," Luz said quietly, and Henrietta broke off a startled giggle and walked more smoothly.

"Close," Ciara said tightly.

She could read this wilderness of pipes and retorts and pumps with its sounds of rushing and hissing and muted distant *clanks* and *whirrs* as easily as Luz could a forest or a crowded street.

"The next set of control valves would be the optimum target."

"Be ready," Luz warned.

A box rested just beyond the valves; it showed clearly because there were glowing spots on its surface illuminating dials and switches, and stiff wires stretched out to either side, four of them, turning upward through spring-mounted elbow joints and stirring in the darkness with the slight wind, a near-invisible crown of thorns.

That's it! Luz thought, restraining an impulse to shoot it.

Electronic equipment, something easy—relatively easy—to get past guards if you had a plausible cover story because so few people knew them as anything but powerful mysteries, unlike the dynamite or blocks of gelignite everyone looked for . . .

"Stop now!"

Ciara did, and killed the lights. Almost in the same instant there was a *CRACK*, the distinctive snapping boom of a .45 automatic, and a crash and tinkle of glass as the round punched through the windscreen.

Fred Foreman's military-surplus Guvvie is back at its old trade, some distant part of her mind jibed. *Just like me.*

Ciara rolled out of the other side of the Guvvie, landing with a muffled *ooof!*

"Cover me when I stop firing," Luz said quietly, and came to one knee with the pistol flowing into her hand.

Crack! Crack! Crack . . .

She emptied the twelve-round magazine in the direction of the muzzle flash, not expecting to hit anything, just covering fire. As the brass from the last round spun out and the receiver locked back she was already dropping flat and rolling for the other side of the road, the magazine dropping out and another slapping into the well and the *click* of the slide moving forward as she rolled into the ditch—the stagnant smell and the cold of dampness soaking through her clothes telling her as much as anything.

Henrietta came to a knee as Luz began to move, and Ciara braced her pistol hand on the hood of the Guvvie.

Crack! Crack! Crack!

The muzzle flashes showed Henrietta and Ciara in silhouette as Luz crawled forward. Then there was another *CRACK!* from ahead, and Ciara spun to the ground with a cry of pain.

"*¡Mierda!*" Luz snarled under her breath and came up again, bracing a knee against the neatly cambered side of the ditch and emptying another magazine at the area of the flash and where she thought the shooter would displace.

Silence fell, with only the hissing of the death pipe and the muted ticking of hot metal in the Guvvie's engine to break the almost-quiet of the night. You didn't hear by straining in a place and time like this, you heard by paying attention. Not to the rapid panting of Ciara's breath— that was a good sign. For the thing that broke the pattern of noises, the thing that didn't fit . . .

Horst would be stalking her through the darkness, a tiger with the mind of a man, with weapons and hands that could pluck her apart once they closed on her. Horst and a confederate, and Horst wouldn't have picked just anyone to come along on a job like this. She was in a darkness full of hungry animals and teeth, and she bared her own in an instinctive snarl of defiance. The rest of her floated on a calm that was balanced, not relaxed, forces in equipoise and ready to move. Ciara would be bleeding . . . but they were all going to die unless she settled this.

Her own muzzle flash and the battering of the gunshots covered the presence behind her almost to the last instant. Something in the night alerted her just as the slide locked back again, a sound like the whisper of air, a smell of old sweat and mules. A hand grabbed at her head to immobilize her, burying its fingers in her hair. Alarm and terror flashed through her, through her and past her to a place where she could let it return later, in some night when it was safe.

Luz dropped the gun and spun as the wig came loose in the man's hand, ignoring the painful pull at the short strands of her own hair drawn through the lace. The curved extension at the back of the *nava-ja*'s hilt snagged on her forefinger and the brass and mother-of-pearl slapped into her palm as the other's knife whirred through the air where her neck *would* have been.

Snick, the blade said as it opened, and Pedro El Andaluz's coldly impersonal teacher-voice spoke too in her mind:

Now you are ojo a ojo, *eye to eye, and someone will die very soon.*

"*¡Estás muerta, puta!*" the man snarled—what he'd planned to say, but he was starting to stare at the wig bunched in his left fist with the incredulous look of a man who'd seen a fish fly.

"No, *you're* dead," Luz replied, the scarred tip of his nose only inches from hers and the stink of his breath in hers.

The six-inch blade of Toledo steel slid into him below the ribs in the same instant, angled upward, twisted free, came up for the slicing backhand stroke under the angle of the jaw, and his eyes rolled up in his head as the blood dropped out of him and the brain failed.

She continued the motion in a blur, using the torque to bring her up on the roadway in a crouch with the blade flickering back and forth before her, ready to lunge like a striking snake.

Then Horst von Dückler was there, the big Colt automatic looking rather small in his massive, capable fist. His grin showed dimly through the darkness, and Luz prepared for a lunge that could end only one way.

"So, Winnetou is dead, but Shatterhand lives on," he said mysteriously.

Sin duda, el que las hace las paga, Luz found herself thinking. Things *did* tend to come around.

"I'll finish off your technician bitch afterward, if the first shot didn't get her—"

I must get to him before I die. For her *sake!* she thought, and knew it was impossible.

Crack! Crack! Crack!

Horst staggered, looked down at the three black dots in his midriff, and folded to his knees.

"*Mutti*," he whispered. "*Heim*—" then fell on his face and died.

"For my momma!" Henrietta Colmer half screamed, as she stood and slapped in another magazine and emptied it into the body and the dirt around it. "For Poppa! For Anne and Mary-Lou! And Elisabeth and Pearl and little Beulah!"

Luz blinked again. "You shouldn't have stopped to say anything, Horst," she said. "Gloat afterward. Before is unprofessional."

Then she paused just long enough to wipe and close her knife, not even bothering to scoop up the pistol as she trotted back and lifted the radio transmitter with a grunt and slung it into the backseat of the Guvvie. Henrietta was frantically finishing a rough tying-off of a bandage across Ciara's arm; she got the other woman onto her feet and into the back of the little vehicle, then dove into the passenger seat as Luz turned the car.

"I can hear engines!" Ciara said through gritted teeth, pointing upward with the bloodied fingers of her right hand.

Luz couldn't, her ears knocked into temporary dullness by the two dozen rounds she'd fired. She didn't reply, or acknowledge Dicot as the

Guvvie sped past him into the night; Henrietta pointed frantically back in the direction they'd come from and made gestures, and the intelligence officer ran that way with a dozen soldiers at his heels. There was no way of being absolutely sure that more of the conspirators weren't there.

She *did* hear the rasping stutter in the air nearly three minutes later; heard it swell, and then a banging *chunk!* in the sky as the engine of the air torpedo cut off.

THUD!

She wrestled with the wheel as the explosion tried to flip the little auto and compressed air punched at her eardrums, and it banged down again after the left wheels raced crazily in the air for a moment; then *that* tried to flip them too.

"The wings fell off! The wings fell off! It's designed that way— more accurate—no, Henrietta!"

The young woman from Savannah was leaning back and twisting in her seat, about to throw the transmitter over the side.

"There are two more, we have to keep them following us away from the gas!" Ciara shouted. "I love you, Luz!"

"I love me too!" Luz shouted with a wild laugh, as the Guvvie accelerated to its not-very-impressive thirty-miles-per-hour maximum. "And you even more!"

"*You* bookra *are both crazy!*" Henrietta shrieked, but she waited for the signal.

I'm driving through the night being pursued by air torpedoes following us by wireless signals . . . Burroughs has nothing on this . . .

A ratcheting snarl in the air, and even more nerve-racking the sudden clanking and then silence and her mind filled in the torpedo arching toward them—

THUD!

The rear wheels came off the ground like the hooves of a kicking mule in a blast of hot air and gravel. Her face knocked painfully into the wheel, and then the Guvvie smashed back and the front bucked into the air for an instant. Luz's teeth clicked together painfully and she tasted blood. Something parted with an unmusical twang in the suspension, and the wheel fought back against her.

"Now, Henrietta, now! Next—" That was Ciara, but the voice was interrupted by a shriek as their passage jarred her wound and she clutched at the sopping bandage.

Henrietta's hand pushed the transmitter over the side of the Guvvie.

"Now is the last one!" Ciara said, as the bang and *chunk!* sounded in the air behind them, far too close. *"Here it com—"*

Pain. Blackness.

EPILOGUE

Casa de los Amantes

Santa Barbara, California

July 1st, 1917, 1917(b)

Theodore Roosevelt waved the bodyguards aside, suppressing a flash of irritation when they looked at Director Wilkie instead of obeying instantly. They were brave men doing their duty, which might involve throwing themselves between him and a bullet, and he wasn't in their immediate chain of command. He was their responsibility, and he could give the Secret Service orders through its hierarchy, but their obligation was to their task, not his whims.

"John, I'm not having dinner at an old friend's house with two men standing behind my chair with Thompson guns, any more than I did when we were here for New Year's. I've been visiting and coming to parties here most years since I got back from Cuba in 1899!"

John Wilkie, who was head of the Secret Service in his public hat as well as the Black Chamber more privately, looked slightly pained, but nodded confirmation.

"It's a new world now; you can't expect to party as if it were 1899. But if you insist, Mr. President," he said, and then to the agents:

"Agent Crowfeather, your unit will watch the entrances. See to it."

"Mr. Director! Liebgott, Russo, you'll take the front door," Crowfeather said, his hawk-nosed brown face impassive. "Smith, Duquesne, you're on the vehicles. The rest of you follow me and I'll assign you your posts."

The first two men turned outward, their conservative suits and homburgs clashing a little with the Thompson guns they carried, and the chief of their detail moved off to set the others in position.

"You still think you're my mother, John," Roosevelt chuckled. "After all these years."

"Someone has to be, Mr. President. The country can't spare you just now."

"Nonsense . . . the Negro girl will recover? Henrietta Colmer?"

"Two broken legs are no joke even with modern medicine, but yes, Mr. President. Apparently she was the one who shot this Horst fellow—a very dangerous man, then killed by a slip of a girl from Savannah."

Roosevelt smiled grimly. "Bullets are no respecters of persons, John. And they don't care who shoots them. I agree that she should be transferred from Clerical Support Section and ranked as Junior Field Operative as Luz and the station chief recommended . . . but assign her to the Zacatecas station, it'll cause less disruption. One mild concussion, one arm broken by a pistol bullet, and two broken legs . . . your people got off fairly lightly this time."

Luz O'Malley was waiting at the head of the four broad semicircular stone stairs that led up to the solid rectangular stuccoed bulk of the big house's frontage, the long light of a summer sunset throwing the comely high-cheeked face into silhouette and giving a hint of how it would look when age had taken youth's beauty and left a handsome strength. She was in a striking but simple long dress of striped wool that he recognized as a North African djellaba, perfectly suited to this area's mild summer warmth and occasional cool nights.

Then she smiled and was a young woman again, though one with fading bruises and healing scrapes on the left side of her face.

May she live long enough to grow into what I saw for a moment, he thought. *She came too close to dying again this time!*

The stab of guilt was more personal than the burden of sending men into combat generally; he'd first seen her here, when she'd still been a girl of nine, not long after the return of the Rough Riders. Her father had gravely introduced her to Colonel Roosevelt, and he'd said as he looked down into the solemn pigtailed face . . .

But you must call me Uncle Teddy, *since your father was my brother-in-arms in Cuba.*

Her smile was wide and white now against the sun-darkened olive of her face, and she opened her arms.

"Uncle Teddy!"

They embraced and she kissed his cheek; then he put his hands on her shoulders for a moment, met her eyes, and nodded a brief, silent *Well done.*

"And John," she added, turning to Wilkie and shaking hands briskly. "Good to see you."

"Good to see you again too, Luz," Wilkie said. "And for once, after a mission and yet *not* convalescing from wounds!"

She and the Director were on social terms outside business hours, and this was theoretically a social occasion, dinner with the daughter of an old comrade of Theodore Roosevelt's and the friend and colleague staying with her.

It *was* that, but he knew it was not *only* that.

"Miss Whelan?" Roosevelt asked.

"Recovering well. The arm will heal—there's no nerve damage—but it'll take a while. The doctors were afraid there was some internal abdominal bleeding from when she was thrown out of the car, but if there was it's stopped since."

"Thank God!"

She crossed herself. "Amen! Do come on through to the patio," she added more cheerfully, linking arms with both of them once they'd handed their hats to—slightly to his surprise—a maid, who took them with wide-eyed awe. Luz added to her:

"*Gracias, Jimena. ¡El presidente tiene dientes muy grandes pero no muerde!*"

Roosevelt snapped slightly—Luz had just said he had very big teeth but didn't bite—and the girl bobbed and fled giggling.

They strolled through the tile-floored entrance hallway between the curling twin staircases and toward the open wrought-iron doors that led to the central courtyard of the Hispanic-style house. They framed a fountain of stone shells around a central pillar, water dancing white beneath the azure California coastal sky dotted with clouds tinted pink by sunset.

Luz's father had built the *casa* to remind her mother of the Cuban homeland she'd eloped from with the dashing young American engineer whom her family considered far, far beneath her. It was just the sort of building Luz's hacendado sugar-planter maternal ancestors might have built anytime in the last four centuries, at least as far as layout and general appearance went.

"Belén will have dinner on the table in a little while, bless her, but there's no reason we can't have an aperitif while we wait," Luz said.

"You finally broke down and got a cook?" he said, a little surprised again.

Luz had relied on a cleaning service and kept no permanent staff here since she went into the Black Chamber not long after her parents were killed. Operatives spent a lot of time on assignment in the field.

"A housekeeper and a couple of maids, at least," she said. "Cooking I intend to keep in my own fair hands as much as I can—and just because I enjoy it as a hobby, frankly. We're having Baracoa-style shrimp in coconut milk tonight, *Costillitas* . . ."

Roosevelt groaned with pleasure, exaggerating it for comic effect, but only a little.

Costillitas were Cuban-style baby back ribs, marinated in a mix of sour orange juice, lime juice, oregano, garlic, and olive oil, and grilled over charcoal while being basted with more of the same sauce. The dish was sweet and tangy and richly meaty at the same time, and he'd enjoyed it in Cuba during his spell there with the Rough Riders and at the O'Malley household since, but the last time had been years ago. The White House kitchens under Edith's supervision set a wonderful table, even a far-famed one these days, and he didn't interfere in her bailiwick. But his wife was a traditionalist of a deep-dyed Knickerbocker style, and the chefs concentrated on French-inspired menus with some East Coast American specialties like terrapin and shad and canvasback thrown in, very much like Delmonico's.

People were more eclectic here on the Pacific.

"And a few other things Mima taught me," Luz added. "And some I learned elsewhere. The bread should be still just a little warm from the oven, but nicely firmed up. It's German style, *Bauernbrot*. Unconventional, but I think it will go well with hearty dishes like those. And *pastel de mango* and *tarta de crema de plátano con ron* for dessert."

"My God, you're an even better cook than dear Luciana was," he said, rubbing his hands; he wasn't sure whether he preferred frosted mango cake or liked rum-and-banana custard tarts better, so he'd have to have some of both. "John, you're in for a treat. And whatever favor you want to ask, Luz, it's yours. Unless you want to be empress of North America."

"Ah, Uncle Teddy, you're talking to your honorary niece, not your firstborn," Luz said, with a sly sideways glance.

"*Touché!*" he said, while Wilkie bit down hard on a startled bark of laughter.

Roosevelt also felt a slight inward wince at the thought of Alice Longworth, née Roosevelt, who'd make a ruthlessly capable absolute monarch if she ever got the chance . . . and who'd enjoy every minute of it, now that he came to think of it. Especially signing the death warrants. When the Roosevelt family left the White House in '08—briefly, as it turned out—she'd buried voodoo dolls of the Tafts on the grounds, with pins struck through head and chest. He wasn't a superstitious man . . . but poor Taft's overly ambitious wife had had a crippling stroke not long after she moved in; the man himself had dropped dead of heart failure in the summer of '12, at what hindsight said was the perfect time for Roosevelt to seize the nomination before the Old Guard could rally; and then the widow passed on not much later.

Alice had silently smiled like a cat at both pieces of news.

They walked past the open wrought-iron gates into the patio, and past the tinkling fountain and into the more-than-tropical Californian blaze of the plantings and vines, amid a scent of roses and frangipani and lilac. Ciara Whelan made as if to rise from her chair, despite the sling and bandage on her left arm.

"No!" the president said. "You don't stand for *us*—even if we'd never been raised as gentlemen, Miss Whelan!"

She smiled a little shyly as he and Wilkie both bowed, and held it just a little longer than needful to show that it was in recognition of her deeds for the country and the honorable wounds she had taken to do them.

She was in the same style of striped robe as Luz, and it flattered her more rounded form—modern fashion favored an athletic slimness for women, which made Luz even more eye-catching in 1917 than nature required anyway, but *his* tastes had been set in the 1880s, when *ample* was a term of praise and Luz would have been thought too boyish for perfection. Ciara's milk-pale complexion was even paler than usual, another disadvantage when an outdoors-style tan was coming to be favored.

Roosevelt and Wilkie were dressed casually themselves, in ordinary sack suits of the type that a gentleman wore during the daytime, to emphasize that this was no type of formal occasion but instead a family meal with very old friends in the casual Western style. He recognized the importance of ceremony and ritual, but they could be very wearisome, and he'd come to appreciate the looser frontier manner as a young man ranching and cowboying in the Dakotas. And on hunting trips all his life, from the Rockies to Uganda and the Sudan, and to an extent on the family estate at Sagamore Hill on Long Island—what the wits were calling the Summer White House now.

At that moment an all-black kitten with bright blue eyes poked its head out of her robe's big hood and claw-walked its way onto her shoulder, regarding the strangers with the hardened self-regard that a well-treated cat six weeks old had, and the utter confidence in its own armor of adorability.

"*Safira!*" Whelan began in a chiding, scandalized tone.

Roosevelt broke into a broad grin, gave a glance that asked for permission, and then scooped it into an experienced hold, tickling expertly under the chin until he got a slit-eyed purr of bliss with paws that were too big for the rest of the little beast kneading at his thumb. Then he set it down to run around their feet and pounce on shoelaces and make astonishing twisting leaps at passing butterflies as they sat at the stone-topped table under its pergola of crimson-blossomed coral vine.

"Permanent staff and a cat of your own. You must be thinking of settling down!" he said to Luz.

Luz shot him a glance, and her smile had a certain wryness to it.

"It's a good thing our enemies can't read me as well as you, Uncle Teddy!" she said. "Lemonade? Wine?"

"Lemonade would be pleasant, thank you," he said.

Ciara poured, careful of her left arm in its sling; the fruit was fresh-squeezed from the trees in the gardens, in a jug of frosted glass beaded with condensation, coolly tart-sweet and perfect for a summer's evening.

Wilkie and the two women all took glasses of chilled white wine instead. A few minutes passed chatting and discussing how little Safira's name matched her sapphire eyes, and nibbling at *chicharrónes*—crisp pork rinds—little balls of fried sweet plantain, and various *bocaditos*.

"In point of fact, Uncle Teddy," Luz said with the directness he'd always admired, "Ciara and I *do* have a favor we'd like to ask. And ask of John, too, of course, since it's related to our duties."

"Ask," he said. "And it shall be granted!"

John nodded. "After what you two have done on your last three missions—all in the past twelve months!—there isn't much you're *not* due," he said, and Roosevelt signaled assent.

One of the benefits of knowing someone really well was that you could anticipate them. He knew that he could make the promise without qualifiers because he wasn't going to be asked for anything he couldn't give. Luz was too sensible. And Wilkie was entirely right— they had both earned anything he *could* in good conscience deliver. One of the many reasons he enjoyed power was that he could reward those he considered deserving.

I might even swing a Cabinet post for her, he thought whimsically. *If it weren't for the fact that Luz would rather be sentenced to a lifetime breaking rocks!*

"Well, first, I don't anticipate that . . . the war will be doing anything very dramatic in the next little while," Luz said delicately. "Am I right?"

Wilkie nodded, but reluctantly. Roosevelt did the same, and kept his teeth from grinding with a sudden flush of frustration and rage by an effort of will; one of the *disadvantages* of power was that it taught you just how powerless even those in the highest places could be.

In fact, they were probably going to be announcing an armistice before the end of the year, and then would come the negotiations . . . not for a real peace, but at least for the absence of open war, on the basis of *uti possidetis.* He detested the thought of letting everyone get up from the table with what they held, and the country would be bitterly disappointed that Germany wasn't beaten into dust no matter how Croly's propagandists labored to put a favorable gloss on it, but the current grinding stalemate was killing men and sinking ships and taking food from the mouths of hungry children all over the world to no great purpose.

Avoiding political embarrassment or the facing of hard truths was just not worth that.

"It's a stalemate," Roosevelt growled. "Time to admit the truth, though I'm not looking forward to the reaction."

He snapped his fingers. "I know! When we make the announcement, we'll abolish rationing on the same day and move ex–Food Director Hoover over to . . . oh, some foreign famine relief agency we'll create for him. He'd like that, and be good at it. God knows the world has enough places that need it."

"That'll be popular," Wilkie observed. "And Hoover isn't. Everyone hates those meatless days—there wouldn't be so much black marketeering if they didn't. Thank God you quashed that idiotic proposal to prohibit alcohol; enforcing *that* . . ."

He shuddered. Roosevelt looked at Luz as a sudden thought occurred to him. He knew she wasn't overly scrupulous about legalities—she was a spy and secret operative, after all—but he had to be more careful.

She laughed. "Personal-use exemption, not the black market," she said, reading his unspoken question. "All the rationed materials in dinner tonight are from the gardens here, except that the meat's from the people who lease the ranch we own over in the Santa Ynez Valley. Even Hoover knows better than to try controlling what farmers put on their own table from their own fields."

"Ah, thank you," Roosevelt said. "And incidentally, Hoover *knew better* than to try that . . . after I told him so."

"So we may not be urgently needed in the field again for a while?" she continued.

Wilkie nodded again—and again, reluctantly. Roosevelt sympathized, since the head of the Black Chamber didn't want to deprive himself of valuable assets, but they *had* earned anything within reason. Knowledge that you were considered valuable—and wouldn't be asked for sacrifices unless they were actually necessary—helped preserve morale. Besides being the right thing to do in return for brave and self-less service to the country. Loyalty had to work both ways or eventually it didn't work at all.

"We'd like to be put on the home-service list for a while, then," Luz said. "Not permanently, but for a while. Several years, preferably."

"I'd like to do a degree program at Stanford," Whelan said earnestly. "I don't think it would take me more than two years, but there are things I need formal classroom tuition for, and I need more hands-on experience under experts in experimental work. I'll be more valuable to the country and the Chamber then, Mr. President."

Wilkie chuckled dryly. "It may interest you that the head of the Technical Section recommended just that to me for you, Miss Whelan," John said.

Whelan blushed to the roots of her hair—not all that hard for a redhead like her with skin pale as a cloud—and her eyes went wide.

"Really?" she squeaked, and put her right hand to her throat in a display of hero worship that made Roosevelt smile.

Brilliant was an accurate description of Tesla, but *eccentric* was a kindly euphemism.

"Really?"

"N said"—and they all knew the Director meant Nicolai Tesla—"that *even the remarkable Miss Whelan* could go only so far with self-education, and that it would be a *crime* to waste any potential part of such a talent. He was impressed yet again that you deduced the guidance system of the Alberich device so quickly and improvised a solution."

Roosevelt nodded. "Those air torpedo things are going to be a bad problem . . . and we're working on making our own, too, of course. As of Thursday, the Germans are launching dozens at British targets every night . . . with conventional warheads, but a reminder of what they *could* do with horror-gas . . . and they're building ships to carry them. You gained us some time and useful information there too."

The blush turned crimson, and Whelan looked down and swallowed.

"And while Ciara's studying, I can too," Luz said. At his raised brows: "No, not the sciences—the cobbler should stick to her last. I speak fair Japanese, but it's a Hiroshima Prefecture peasant version from a generation ago I picked up from family friends as a child."

She smiled impishly before she went on:

"In English the equivalent would be . . . *Suh, mah lill' ca-yt heah ain' nohow no respektah o' pussons, a-clawin' an' a-carryin' own laak tha-yt 'roun yo' faahn presahdenshul feets.*"

Soberly, though they were all smiling in turn at the perfect Mississippi gumbo dialect:

"I think having native-quality *standard* Japanese might be an asset a few years down the line, for a field operative. And I need to fully master the script and pick up a good deal else. Besides, I want to read the *Tale of Genji* in the original. Plus it might be useful to look into Chinese. Everyone says it's very difficult, but that *is* my area of expertise and here in California it's easy to find people to practice with."

"You always were sharp, Luz," Roosevelt said. "Yes, everyone's going to be dipping their spoons in the Asian stewpot, probing and subverting, and we certainly can't leave our side's share of that completely to the British, even if the Imperial Secret Service do have more experience there. The Japanese are stretched thin . . . though agents who can *pass* as Japanese are going to be a problem."

"There are a couple of people here named Taguchi I could recommend who might be interested; you met them and their brother and parents briefly when you were here at New Year's. They're very bright, and their loyalty is beyond question. I've known Fumiko and Midori since I was a child. And Station Chief Reiter in San Francisco is always on at me to help with the training program; I could do that too."

"Make a note about the Taguchis, John; it could be important," Roosevelt said, and then gave her a keen look. "That's what you'd like? Leave to attend university so you can both extend your talents? Working on the training program? Not really what I'd call much of a *favor*, Luz!"

Luz cleared her throat and raised her eyes a little. "Ah, *mas o menos,*

Uncle Teddy. But you know there are many types of obligations, and ... well, you also know we're not ... the marrying kind."

Whelan looked as if she'd like to melt and ooze through the cracks in the tile floor. Silence fell for a long moment, and he cleared his throat in turn to fill it.

"Yes," he said shortly. "I'm aware of that."

He knew, and he disapproved ... but found there wasn't much heat in it, under the circumstances. His strongest regret there was that it meant that their germ plasm would be lost to the nation ... the American people ... since they were both individuals of extraordinary fitness in their different ways. Not to mention that his old friend and comrade Patrick O'Malley and the woman the comrade loved more than life wouldn't have *their* bloodline preserved, to go down through the future of the nation.

If there was one thing that gave him the most joy in his personal life, then after Edith and the fact that all his sons had survived the war it was the growing passel of grandchildren his six offspring had furnished him. Even young Quentin was engaged—he was barely twenty, but being a fighting scout pilot wasn't an occupation for men who hesitated—to a young lady named Flora Whitney whom Roosevelt liked a good deal. Even if she was a granddaughter of that old pirate Cornelius Vanderbilt and her parents were reactionaries of the first water who gargled with throttled rage at the mention of the Roosevelt name.

Luz spoke into the loaded pause: "Well, there's no reason why we shouldn't ... adopt, though. Study and training here in California *is* compatible with caring for very young children in a way field service isn't."

"Oh," he said; there were certainly enough orphans in the world, and that was better than nothing, but ...

And then he said: "Oh!"

In a completely different tone as the nature of the euphemism sank in, helped along by the significant hesitation, a raised raven-black brow and inclined head. And by Whelan's agony of embarrassment as she nodded while visibly willing her vital functions to shut down.

Wilkie blinked a moment later as he realized they meant a more ... Roosevelt supposed *natural* was the most appropriate word ... form of reproduction than raising orphans. And one that would require prolonged holidays before returning with infants who would then go through the solemn legal formalities of adoption to give them names and official status as heirs. He dredged his memory for the statutes: California was one of the states that had legal adoption—not all did quite yet, and when he'd been born in 1858 only one or two had—and the paperwork wouldn't be very difficult.

"Yes, I see that could be ... time-consuming," he said. "But there is a eugenic duty to the nation, as well, and to one's own bloodline."

Logically, I can't object to someone solving what I myself considered a problem.

"Yes. John, in your official capacity, make whatever arrangements these operatives need. And put it under *most secret*."

Luz leaned forward and put her hand over his, gripping firmly with slim callused fingers whose strength always surprised him. He returned it.

"Thank you, Uncle Teddy, for both our sakes. And for my *mima* and *papá*."

"Thank you, Mr. President," the younger woman whispered. "For my father as well ... My brother died so young, there's only me ..."

Silence stretched, this time not uncomfortable but not without awkwardness either. It was broken in laughter as he started and swore at the feel of tiny needle-sharp claws in his leg as Safira started to climb to his lap. They passed the little creature around, and she played with ferocious enthusiasm and devoured offered bits of pork rind as nothing less than her royal-princess due before collapsing into rag-doll limpness with sudden sleepiness, yawning, blinking, smacking her lips, and curling up as Roosevelt laid her on the cushion of his chair.

"I warn you, *human* infants are a lot more work than that!" he said, to general laughter. "And Miss Whelan, *Mr. President* is a little formal—why not Colonel, if you must use a title? You've fought under my command, after all, in a sense—and fought well."

A bell rang, and they formed up to go into dinner, each of the men extending an arm; there was a tantalizing scent of garlic and hot tomato sauce in the air.

"And Uncle Teddy," Luz said. "Think of it this way: another set of children for you to visit, and play Bear with in front of the fire, the way you did with me."

He mock-groaned. "I'll be too stiff for that by then!" he said. "Have mercy on an old man only fit to sit in the sun and dream of the past!"

In fact, he was grinning at the prospect, a show of teeth nobody here found very alarming, though Ciara Whelan blinked and was probably surprised at how closely it resembled the caricatures that had followed him since his days as police commissioner in New York City nearly . . . he blinked himself in startlement at the thought . . . twenty-five years ago.

And in a way, he was smiling at the thought of doing one last favor for Patrick O'Malley's memory, as well as for his daughter.

"Too old to play Bear and tell your stories? Never!" Luz said. "Not while you're breathing, at least!"

Photo by Anton Brkic

S. M. Stirling is the author of many science fiction and fantasy novels. A former lawyer and an amateur historian, he lives with his wife, Jan.

Ready to find
your next great read?

Let us help.

Visit prh.com/nextread

Penguin
Random
House